i live in Saffron Walden also

Carol Ann Frazer has lived in the Saffron Walden area for nineteen years. Before that she lived in Loughton and Buckhurst Hill in Essex. She has always written stories, and remembers being sent by the nuns in her convent junior school to read her own stories to the other classes. After grammar school she took a secretarial course in London and worked as a P.A. She married young and had two children in her early twenties.

Can a Pen Guin

She then worked as the school secretary in the preparatory school which her own children attended, and it was not until they were in their teens that she felt the need to take up the pen again and write. Quite soon she had a short story accepted on Radio 4, and became a regular contributor to the "Morning Story", which later took the afternoon slot it now occupies. She also sent stories off to various women's magazines, but often had to amend the ambiguous endings she enjoys to give the "happy ending" required by their editors. She has written plays for junior school children which have been performed in several schools and drama clubs, and has had articles published in The Daily Telegraph, Yours Magazine and Essex Homes & Gardens.

BIRDS FLYING HOME

Carol Ann Frazer

Birds Flying Home

Vanguard Press

VANGUARD PAPERBACK

© Copyright 2006
Carol Ann Frazer

The right of Carol Ann Frazer to be identified as author of this work has been asserted by her in accordance with the Copyright, Designs and Patents Act 1988

All Rights Reserved

No reproduction, copy or transmission of this publication may be made without written permission.
No paragraph of this publication may be reproduced, copied or transmitted save with the written permission of the publisher, or in accordance with the provisions of the Copyright Act 1956 (as amended).

Any person who does any unauthorised act in relation to this publication may be liable to criminal prosecution and civil claims for damage.

A CIP catalogue record for this title is available from the British Library

ISBN-13: 978 184386 2970
ISBN-10: 1 84386 297 2

*Vanguard Press is an imprint of
Pegasus Elliot MacKenzie Publishers Ltd.*
www.pegasuspublishers.com

First Published in 2006

**Vanguard Press
Sheraton House Castle Park
Cambridge England**

Printed & Bound in Great Britain

DEDICATION

To my children

Prologue

They used to trap birds in La Avenida San Juan. Small birds like thrushes and finches, who struggled frantically in the nets until they gave up. Caca a coll, they called it; caca a coll. I'm glad it's been stopped; I know how they felt, trapped and helpless and in despair. But now, nearly twenty years on, tourism is more important to both of us. Money screamed so much louder than mercy and money prevailed. It usually does. No more nettings, and I too escaped.

The mountain road through Deya is steep and winding, with sudden terracotta vistas threaded between cypress and lemon trees. The village climbs in tiers like a wedding cake up the sturdy slopes of the Tramontana Mountains. High on a hill overlooking the entire south western coastline is my favourite place; a tiny, ancient church surveying the scene with an air of quiet detachment. The poet Robert Graves' heart is buried here; and I want mine to be too. It belongs here after all. Deya has been my parent, my healer and therapist; patching up a broken heart and giving me back a good life worth enjoying.

The wind is getting up now and a delicious breeze blows my hair across my eyes. I brush it away and find tears on my hand. I'm too high up for salt sea spray, it must be tears. That surprises me for there's nothing to cry about. Life is good and the hotel's doing well. I turn and scuff my sandals back down the stony path from my favourite haunt near the chapel and jump down onto the road. The tarmac is sticky-hot like toffee. I glance at the white watch on my brown arm – twenty to twelve. The bar will be filling up. I need to get back. New guests are due in from Palma Airport at four, and I must check the number of lunches. Antonio Alfabia is bringing a party of businessmen up from Soller – they are important to me; after the season's over, local people are my only clients.

Sparrows fly up in the dust ahead and I turn into the lane. The black gates are open as they always are. Open wide and welcoming. I am home.

Chapter One

When did it all start? Maybe on that fierce September day as she had scrambled down from that tiny chapel and noticed a sandy-haired boy crossing from the café and cycling down the lane towards the hotel on a borrowed bike. He was scarlet with the effort; sweat breaking out on his pleasant freckled face, and as he abandoned the ancient bike at the gate he pushed back a blue and white bandeau from his sticky hairline, a sheaf of fine pencils sticking up like feathers on a squaw. He looked up at the square stone building and blew air out of his lips with a mixture of boredom and irritation. God, it was hot. He might as well stop and have a drink here; he had nothing else to do now that Emma had gone. He had tired of painting peppers and Mediterranean views. With only four weeks left before he flew home to his final year at the Slade he knew he must get down to some serious work. He'd thought he could cycle to the next village up here to do some sketching; obviously he was mistaken. It was a dead-end. "Like the rest of my life," he thought as he pushed open the heavy Spanish oak door.

The cool stone flagging was a balm. Huge fans were turning above him and there was a tranquil air of light and calm. A corner reception desk was occupied by a dark haired young Spanish woman who looked up and smiled. "Buenos dias, Senor," she said.

He responded and asked for a beer. She led him into a cool green bar overlooking a side garden and poured him a long drink.

"Cerveza," she said, handing him the glass.

"Gracias."

"De nada."

She returned to the hall, leaving him alone with his thoughts. No one else was around. It was a small, family-run hotel, he guessed, and too early for lunchtime trade. He dismissed the ever-present thoughts of Emma and her hasty departure. There was no point going over it all again – she'd packed up and gone back to England and that was it. He wasn't running after her and if that was how she felt so be it. If only it didn't bloody hurt so much. He'd thought she'd felt the same as he did. He'd never understand women. He downed the beer and heard a laugh and a fast flowing torrent of Spanish, followed by a quiet reply from the receptionist. Another laugh, and he saw a blonde woman in white jeans and a long navy shirt cross in front of the doorway, the gold bracelets on her arm jangling as she continued talking and gesticulating to the receptionist. A minute later she returned, holding some papers and glancing in his direction. She hesitated, and turned into the bar.

"Hi! Have you got everything you want? Has Conchita been looking after you?"

"Yes, I'm fine. You're quick to guess I'm English."

"With your colouring you'd hardly be Spanish!" She smiled, showing even white teeth in a relaxed, tanned face. Her eyes had fans of laughter lines and were an extraordinary deep sea green. She held out her hand to shake his, transferring the papers to her left hand. "I'm Angie Roberts; I own La Casa d'Or. Are you booked in?"

"Hell no. I just cycled up here and thought I'd have a beer. I can't afford hotels – I'm a student – Andy Carter."

"Oh well. Have another beer, Andy – you look pretty warm – I guess you're not used to the heat; how long have you been out here?"

"Nearly five weeks. I came out for the summer to paint. I'm an art student at the Slade."

"Right. Plenty of artists around here – hardly surprising – just look out at this view."

He followed her into the dining room and they stood at the window where the blue Mediterranean glinted through pine trees far below.

"Isn't it stunning? I still can't quite believe I actually live here, you know! Every morning I pinch myself when I look out of my window and see that. I'm so lucky – but then you make your own luck, don't you? It took me long enough – twenty years – to drag myself up this particular mountain. Here –" She passed him another bottle of beer and he drank it straight down. She smiled. "Stay for lunch. We haven't many booked in today. It's getting quieter. Last week was pandemonium but most of them have gone. Schools are back in England, I guess."

"I don't eat lunch usually – well – just bread and cheese and olives maybe."

"Have Chef's Special on me. He always cooks too much – one main hot dish at lunchtime – it's terrific. I'm not that busy – tell you what – I'll join you; I've just got to check some guys from Soller and then I'm free. You look as if you could do with some feeding up. I know what students are like!"

He grinned. He was beginning to feel better and he had to admit he hadn't been eating properly for weeks. And this woman was nice; a curious mixture of maternal fussing and sexual charge – he could do with a little ego massaging just now. And no student ever turned down a free meal.

"OK. Sounds great."

"Make yourself at home. I won't be long."

She disappeared through a small door and he wandered back into the bar, where a German couple were now sitting, watching Conchita pour Sangria from a rather stylish glass jug. His eye caught the light on her hair and the shape of the jug as she poured the red liquid into tumblers. He sat in the corner as the room gradually filled up. A party of Majorcan businessmen entered, their local guttural dialect completely incomprehensible. The German couple were joined by a friend in large khaki shorts and thick knee-length socks. He watched, trying to bring an artist's eye to the scene, and to commit it to memory. He drew out his sketch pad and did a surreptitious pencil drawing. He was concentrating on Conchita's hand on the jug when Angie returned. It was tricky; the thumb was all wrong. She stopped to joke with the businessmen at the bar – her Spanish adopting their guttural tones as she spoke. He noticed the look of sweet amusement which passed between her and Conchita; way beyond that of employer and employee. She placed a hand briefly on the German woman's arm and then stood looking straight at him with a teasing smile.

"Gambas!" she said. "Gambas con huevos y merluza. It'll be good; it always is and the prawns and fish are all caught locally."

"Wicked. Thanks a lot."

"Salud. Have an olive; they're local too – from the market in Pollensa."

She raised her wineglass to him and passed him a dish of

olives. He took a couple and said, "Funny way to run a hotel, giving away the lunches."

She smiled and looked into her glass. "I don't usually. But you happened out of nowhere and kind of reminded me..." She stopped and took a gulp of wine. "I don't know what I'm talking about really! Complete nonsense – but I don't like eating alone and you're on your own so it seems to make sense. I'm like that – impetuous – always have been. I also know immediately when I meet someone I'm really going to take to – and I've taken to you!"

He took another couple of olives to cover his embarrassment. She pointed the three Germans in the direction of the dining room.

"How long have you run it?" he asked, for want of something to say.

"Ten years – almost eleven. It was a shambles when I first found it. I painted all the rooms myself – all eleven of them. I modernised the kitchen and I tamed the garden; I never stopped working for the first four years, honestly. A fourteen hour day was normal. But it's easier now – I've a lovely staff."

Her gaze left his face and she stared out into the hibiscus filled garden. Now Arthuro Garcias tended it, but for two years she had planted bougainvillaea and hibiscus and plumbago. The almond and olive trees had been here before her, delighting her with almond blossom in February and olives and nuts in the summer. Paradise in her opinion. She loved this place so much; it nourished her spirit in a way that England never had. The heat suited her and she felt relaxed and happy most of the time.

"Do you miss home?" asked Andy suddenly, wanting her attention to revert to him.

"This *is* home, sweetheart! Do I miss England? No. Hardly ever. Not the cold and the greyness and the dirt, I suppose there were things I missed that first summer. It was hot and airless in Palma and that was where I fetched up eleven years ago. I wasn't used to pacing myself like the locals do. But by Christmas – when I found I could still eat lunch outside most days – Majorca had won me over. My sister had been out to visit me and it began to feel right. Now I can't imagine ever living anywhere else. I simply adore it."

She looked down at the sketch on his knees and put a hand out to turn the paper around. "Umm," she said. "You've caught Conchita's sweetness in just that outline sketch. Amazing. Did you say you're at the Slade?"

"Yeah. For another year."

"Well, you must be good then. I'm impressed. Come on – let's eat!"

She led him to a little corner table set back from the other diners. A short, good-looking Spaniard rushed up to her and placed an opened bottle of red wine on the table immediately.

"Gracias Jose," she beamed, and he poured it out slowly. "You taste it," she said. "Marvellous flavour – see if you think so."

He took a sip and raised his eyebrows. "Wow! Knock out! What is it?"

"My favourite. Rioja."

Jose poured two glasses and turned away.

"They're my family now," she said, smiling at Jose's white coated back. "They've all worked for me for years. Local people – salt of the earth. I couldn't manage without them. Especially Conchita."

"Salud!" he said, and drank noisily. "Why did you come here in the first place?"

"Oh God – how long have you got? That's a *very* long tale, Andy. I was a cook in London and I had this thing with an actor who came to Palma doing a film; that's what brought me first of all. But I guess I was always running away – my whole life was running away till I fetched up here and stopped running."

She sat back in her chair as Jose brought steaming plates of prawns in garlic, hard boiled eggs and strips of local fish, perched on saffron coloured rice. It smelt amazing.

"I thought you drank white wine with fish," he began, "but I'm only just getting into wine stuff and that."

"Depends. This is such a full flavoured dish that the red will stand up to it. You can get white Rioja too, of course. See what you think."

He dipped his fork into the fish and rice and chewed thoughtfully. His eyes met hers and he smiled, an easy relaxed sort of smile as if he'd been having lunch with her like this for

17

years. He had another gulp of wine and heard himself saying, "I'd really like to paint you, what d'you reckon? Why don't I give you a portrait in exchange for lunch? I've done complete crap the whole time I've been out here. You know? Still life like you do in school and saccharine seaside views like a bloody birthday card. I've nothing to take back with me – nothing. It's all complete shit." He drank another mouthful and looked suddenly morose.

"What's gone wrong?" she asked, stabbing a gamba and concentrating on her plate.

He fiddled with the rice before he spoke.

"Oh – girl I met here – met her on my first day. At the café. It was fantastic, you know? Well, I thought it was. Four bloody marvellous weeks spending every hour of every day and night with her, and then – wham, bang, thank you man – she's off. Packs her bags and says she has to get back to London. Won't say why. She'd told me she was here until the end of September but suddenly – she's gotta go."

The quiet grew between them and for the first time they became aware of the German and Majorcan voices around them. Jose hovered and was sent away by a glance from Angie. She stretched a soft brown arm across the white cloth and gently touched his thin freckled hand. She said nothing.

He picked up his fork and began eating again.

"So that's why I need to paint your portrait. A real person – a project with some life in it and maybe then I'll be able to go back to college and not feel I've wasted the whole fucking summer. Sorry."

She sipped her Rioja and wrinkled her nose.

"Depends how much time that would take. I've got a hotel to run. Don't know whether I can be a 'project' just at the moment."

He looked up and their eyes met again. He fleetingly recognised an unspoken understanding and dared to push her further.

"I really need to do this. The preliminary drawing would probably only take a few hours, and then I could paint without you. Any time that suits you, obviously. I just feel it would be good – I don't know why."

She smiled and the mood changed.

"Oh well, if it's only a couple of hours of course we can. Though why you'd want to paint *me*, I can't imagine. Forty-six, with a line for every single year! Still – I'm not exactly Rembrandt's Mother but I don't suppose you're Rembrandt! Not yet, anyhow. OK kiddo – what about tomorrow morning? Where are you staying? We can't do it here."

"I'm at Julio's – he's got a little studio place round the back of the café. I sleep there too."

"Oh I know Julio – I think he's Jose's cousin as a matter of fact. About ten tomorrow?"

"That's brilliant. Thanks. A couple of hours with you and then I can work all afternoon. Maybe you could spare an hour another day?"

"Sure. We're not that busy. You can tell me all about your – what's her name?"

"Emma. No. I don't want to talk about her. We can talk about you. I want to hear more about how you started up here. I get the feeling there's a lot more to it."

She leaned over and removed his plate, piling it on top of her own as if they were a mother and son at home.

"You can say that again. But you don't want to hear the rambling nostalgia of a middle-aged woman – you'd be bored out of your skull."

"It helps actually – you talking. It helps us both to relax while I'm drawing and it gives me a sense of who I'm painting – you know – the real person and not just the outward appearance."

"God! Sounds more like going into therapy! I thought you just wanted someone to sketch. Still, if that's how you work. Did you paint the lovely Emma?"

"No. I started sketching a couple of times but we always had sex on our minds so nothing ever got finished. I guess she wasn't very good for my career. I just forgot everything when I was with her."

"She was pretty special then."

"Yeah."

He drained his glass although it was empty and Jose leapt forward to pour the last two inches from the bottle into his glass.

19

"Queso?" she asked, "or fruit?"

"Queso would be great."

Jose removed their plates and then pushed a strong smelling trolley of cheeses towards them.

"That's the local mountain goat's cheese; that one's made from ewe's milk, and that's my favourite. Brought over from Barcelona on the ferry. Try some."

She handed him a generous sliver on the end of her knife and he raised his eyebrows.

"Yup. That's good. I don't know much about cheese – we only ever had two or three types at home and since I've lived in London I just go for the cheapest. That's great though."

He looked at her more carefully as she turned to speak to Jose. Forty-six she'd said. He was surprised; his mother was forty-nine and this woman looked almost a different generation – so vital and brimful of enthusiasm. Her blonde hair was cut well, at just above shoulder length and her skin soft and tanned. But it was the sea-green eyes that captivated – deep and speckled with arching, enquiring dark brows. Her hands were small with short, rounded nails painted in a pale pearl polish. She looked happy in her own skin. He envied her that. He had never hated his own sandy hair and freckled pallor more than he did now. Would Emma have left him if he'd been dark and mysterious looking? Probably not.

"Coffee?"

"Con leche, por favor."

"How good is your Spanish?"

"Not bad. I did a GCSE and I've had quite a few holidays here and on the Costa Brava. I can get by."

"I arrived with no Spanish at all – not a word! But then I didn't have much of an education because I ran away from home at fifteen so my schooling effectively ended then. Apart from the cookery course later."

"Ran away? Why?"

"Oh – dos café con leche Jose. Gracias. Salimos."

She stood up and walked towards a side door leading to the garden.

"Let's have our coffee under the trees. I need to chat to Alfonso Diges before he goes so I'd better not be more than ten minutes. You stay as long as you like."

"Can I get down to Valdemosa from here?"

"No. You need to get back to the main road and go down to the fork. It's not far. Do you want me to call a taxi?"

"No thanks; I borrowed a bike."

They sat on two canvas directors' chairs under a huge pine tree and he repeated his question.

"Why did you run away?"

"Oh, I was just a kid. I told you I'm impetuous. My dad had died and mum had taken up with this vile bloke – Len the Louse my sister called him – he'd moved in with us. He drove me crazy – wouldn't leave me alone – pretending all this heavy parental involvement thing when I knew all he really wanted was to leer at me in the bathroom. He was always barging into my room, sitting on my bed, and mum never seemed to notice. That particular day he'd caught me in a private moment, sitting on my bed in my slip and writing my diary. He'd pushed his tombstone teeth so close that I had to pull away. 'Oh Angie's diary – let dad see!' and I'd snapped it shut while he tried to take it and knocked me over the bed. That's when I knew I had to get out. He'd pawed at me and said 'Oh go on – let your dad see what you've written! Am I in it?' And I kicked him hard and shouted, 'You're NOT my dad and never will be – now get out of my room!' I remember him narrowing his eyes. Like a pig's eyes, they were, very small and watchful. So later, when they'd gone out, I just pushed off. Dead easy. Took some money from the kitchen drawer and packed my bag and took a train from Harlow Town to Liverpool Street. You hear about homeless kids a lot now but it always happened. Nothing new in it. It was summer time and the weather was lovely. I stayed in a hostel near Tottenham Court Road and worked in a café washing up for the first few weeks. I told them I was sixteen. I missed Rita a lot; that was my sister. I sent her a postcard from Trafalgar Square once. They found me, of course, but not for ages and by then I'd met Roy. Roy Cavalieri – did you ever hear such a romantic name? Italian, he said his dad was, and he certainly looked Mediterranean. That dark hair and sallow skin and brown eyes – marvellous, I thought he looked, but I was only fifteen. He said I was his angel – can you imagine? But with long blonde hair and green eyes maybe that was an angel in his book!"

Jose brought the coffee on a wooden tray and placed it beside her, but Angie didn't notice. She was turning a red hibiscus flower in her fingers; round and round, round and round. There was a silence, and Andy wondered if he should pour the coffee.

Then she said, "He'd come into the café looking for somebody, just as I was putting out the clean plates. I was staring at him; well, I fancied him straight away of course, so I tripped down a stupid step and dropped the lot. Most of them broke and the crazy Greek who ran the café went berserk, swearing and shouting, all over ten or twelve rotten plates. Terrible cheap thick things they were anyway. So Roy came over and took my side; he argued and when he saw that wasn't any use he paid the old fool – far too much of course but it certainly impressed me. He said he could get me a much better job than the café, so I just picked up my jacket and left. I never went back. Roy took me to a nightclub; at first I thought he must own it by the way he talked to everyone, but he didn't. He just worked there behind the bar, but he knew everybody and they all loved him; I could tell. He got me a job there and the money was much better than at the café. All I had to do was dress up in this gorgeous costume – it was like a silver sequinned bikini, really, with fishnet tights and a powder-puff on my bottom and a pair of pink rabbit's ears on my head! Daft, but I looked good in it – believe me, I looked terrific! All I had to do was sit on a high stool at the bar and talk to customers and get them to order drinks. That was all. Of course if you wanted to go off with them afterwards, that was your affair, but the job was just getting them to buy drinks – and *the price*. Incredible. It was a rip-off of course because if they offered me a drink I had to ask for gin and orange, and the barman would put just a tiny drop of gin in the glass and charge for a double. But there, that was how it worked. So when mum and Len finally tracked me down I was working there, earning good money, and had left the hostel and moved in with Roy. I wouldn't go home, and I was sixteen by then. Roy was much older of course – I think he was twenty-seven when I first met him. There never was anyone better than Roy. Believe me, I tried them. He was kind in his own funny way; yes he was

– kind. It took me twenty years to work out that that's the most important characteristic a man can have – and the rarest. Roy taught me such a lot about life. Sex, of course, but lots of other things – cooking, making the best of myself, fashion, driving a car. He even taught me a bit of Italian; he was *crazy* about Italy – Italian food, Italian clothes, music, cars, everything. He was always buying me Italian shoes – beautiful soft Italian leather shoes; I've still got a pair somewhere."

"Did you marry Roy?" he asked eventually, leaning forward a little.

She screwed the flower into the palm of her hand and stretched her eyes wide, then she sat up straight and poured the coffee.

"No. I didn't marry Roy. I should have, of course. But it was that whim thing again I suppose. I was nineteen – we had a row – something stupid."

She handed him his coffee and he took a long slug. It was strong and a little acrid. He glanced up at her but she was staring at the crumpled flower looking suddenly tired.

"I must go and speak to Alfonso Diges," she said, taking a quick sip and returning the cup to the tray. "I can't imagine what made me tell you all that stuff. I'm sorry. I'll see you at Julio's about ten tomorrow, OK?"

He half stood up as she began to walk away, aware that he had shared an unusual and unexpected intimacy. He walked round the side of the building to the front drive and retrieved his bike from the bushes. As he swung his leg over the saddle he heard her laughing and joining in the jigsaw of Spanish voices that faded away as he cycled down the dirt road to Valdemosa.

Tomorrow he would start to paint. Tomorrow he would begin his career as a serious artist, and maybe learn a bit more about women from Angie. He pushed the pedals faster and faster in the afternoon heat. He was really looking forward to tomorrow.

Chapter Two

He slept a little better that night. The stifling stuffy room was no cooler at first, but at about two in the morning a light mountain breeze had crept in the open window and moved the heavy air enough to lull him to sleep. He awoke at nine to the sound of church bells and swung his legs off the narrow bed as he remembered.

Why had he arranged to paint a woman he hardly knew? He scratched his damp chest and yawned. Well, he had nothing else to do so he might as well give it his best shot. He drank some water and pulled on black boxer shorts and walked to the doorway to stare out into the relentless sunshine. Julio's mother was sitting across the courtyard at her own back door, shelling peas. She gave him a toothless smile and a guttural "Dias!" as he nodded in her direction and walked past her to the WC in the corner. She had disappeared when he returned to his room, leaving a rather fine upright wooden chair. He wondered if he could borrow it for the portrait. Mahogany, he thought, or maybe old Spanish oak. There was the clatter of plates and pans from Julio's cottage so he assumed they were eating breakfast. He'd ask later. He rummaged in the cupboard by his bed and came up with a stale croissant and an apple. He stood at the doorway munching, and wondering about composition and light. Julio's mother reappeared holding a huge cup of coffee and sat herself back on the chair – clearly he could not borrow it at the moment. He withdrew to pull on an ancient pair of denim shorts and a grubby black T-shirt ringed with sweat. He glanced around the room – pretty disgusting actually, but how did she think artists lived? He was fairly certain there wasn't much of the bourgeois housewife about Angie anyhow. He brushed the crumbs of croissant off his hands and opened the cupboard again, this time to retrieve brushes and a pot of pencils which he placed on the bare pine table beside his bed. He pulled the only chair over to the window where a dust filled shaft of sunshine illuminated the greasy cotton fabric. He moved it about an inch to the left and then cleaned his teeth at the basin in the corner of the room, ending this ritual with handfuls of cold water all over his perspiring face.

He was kneeling on the floor, sorting out sketching paper, when Angie arrived, a quick tap on the doorframe preceding her laugh as she inspected his backside and said, "Are you facing Mecca, or what?"

He stood up awkwardly, and flapped A3 sheets of paper onto the table. "Hi. It's a bit of a mess I'm afraid, but…"

He stepped forward to shake her hand, but she threw back her head and laughed a great roar of unaffected amusement.

"Bloody heck, we're formal this morning, aren't we? You're worse than a Spaniard! Give us a kiss and don't be so daft, darling, or I'll turn straight round and go home. Here – put this down for me – I thought you might like some."

She handed him a pot of steaming coffee and then enveloped him in a sweet-smelling hug, kissing his cheek noisily as he lunged downwards with the coffee pot.

"Easy tiger!" he said, to conceal his embarrassment.

"Now – to business. Where d'you want me? Or shall we have a cup of coffee first?"

"Over there – by the window please – but yes, I'll get a couple of mugs."

He went over to the sink and rinsed out a cracked cup and a pottery mug and poured the coffee. It smelt wonderful.

"Grief! Have I got to sit on that bloody thing for two hours? Haven't you got anything more comfortable? What about the bed? It would be more relaxed – something like this?"

She sprawled languorously on his dishevelled bed with one arm behind her head and a self-mocking expression in her smile.

He sipped his coffee and merely said, "No. The light's wrong. It's got to be the chair by the window."

"Sorry, Picasso! Not funny. I know. I will be serious. I will. I like art – I do really. I'm not as ignorant as you might think. We had a wonderful watercolourist here last year and she painted the view from by bedroom – I paid her £300 for it too, so I appreciate good painting. I'm serious now – really."

She sat up and drank her coffee, the brown mug dark against the cream of her shirt and knee length trousers. Her tan was deep and silk-smooth. She walked easily toward the window and sat down, her head half turned towards the open doorway.

"This OK?"

"Better. Your chin a little higher. That's fine. Try to hold that position for my preliminary sketching. Great."

"I'll come up to the hotel after lunch and show you how it's going, if you like, around 2.30?"

"Well, have a late lunch with me then."

"You sure?"

"Of course I'm sure."

The quiet grew between them and the room became hotter. Her thoughts wandered as she gazed dreamily out to the familiar street scene – the dusty Peugeot parked by the gateway, the skinny cats asleep on the wall, the grey dog sniffing the gutter in the heat. Julio's mother, parked opposite like a pram by her door, was now at her lace making, the white tablecloth trailing across her black skirt as her fingers moved expertly across it.

"You were going to tell me more about how you came to be here – you know – after Roy?"

"You don't really want me to go over all that stuff – it's a hell of a long time ago."

"Honestly, it does help. It'll make me concentrate better and you relax. Otherwise you'll be thinking about how you're looking, and stiffen up and everything."

"OK. If you're sure. You just tell me if I'm doing it wrong. I've never been an artist's model before; there's always a first time for everything, I guess."

"What happened with Roy? You were nineteen, did you say – and you had the big row?"

"Yes. I told you I was impetuous. He wanted to go out bowling with a crowd from the club on our night off, and I didn't. So he went anyway, because he was far too macho-Italian male to be told what to do by his girlfriend, and I'd made the mistake of issuing ultimatums! After he'd gone out I went to the nightclub for something to do – you could always get a cheap drink on your night off and there were people to talk to – and that's when I met the bastard."

"Who?"

He was sketching faster now, his pencil skimming across the page like a pebble on a frozen pond.

"Saul Richmond. It still sends a shiver down my back to say

his name. I wasn't dressed up or anything – just ski pants and a sweater and my hair loose but he spotted me straight away. 'You should work here, honey', he said. 'You'd look fantastic in that bunny get up!' So I went round the back into the changing room and got into the costume. I stood in the doorway and saw his face. I think that was when I fell for him. I'd never seen so much admiration on anybody's face before – and all for little me – it was fabulous. He was old – nearly forty – with a thin sort of face and skinny hands. I noticed his hands straight away.

'Did you play the piano?' I said. 'Look at your hands. They're pianist's fingers.' And he laughed; I got the impression he hadn't laughed much for a long time. He stroked my face with his pianist's fingers and made me want to make him happy, I suppose. Something like that. I've asked myself over and over what I saw in him – anyway – we had a few drinks at the bar and then he asked me to dance with him. I'd never danced with anyone like that before. He had the most fantastic rhythm. He just glided taking me with him and we melted. We were still dancing at three in the morning when the club closed.

'I'll drive you home,' he said, but we drove to Clapham Common and we stayed in the car and made love until the sun came up. Next day I packed by bags and moved out of Roy's place. Madness. Complete madness. Do you know Roy *cried* when I left? He did – darling Roy. It was the second most awful mistake of my life – and I've made some. Maybe I'll look him up one day. There can't be that many Cavalieris in the London phone book, can there? Saul was married, of course, you've guessed that. He told me the usual rubbish about his wife not understanding his needs and how they were going to get divorced but now wasn't quite the right time. He got me a job in his office answering the phone and filing – he said I couldn't stay at the nightclub if I was going to be his wife, and somehow that made me believe him. Got me a poky little room somewhere and was forever buying me presents. When I look back I realise he reminded me of my dad at first – my real dad. He'd been thin with pianist's hands and he'd always spoiled me rotten buying me presents, and he was about the same age as Saul when he died. I needed to find my dad again, I guess, or I'd have stayed with Roy."

"Then?" said Andy. "Keep that expression. Try not to change it – right. Then?"

"Yes. *Then*. I told you I was young and naïve. He kept on saying he had to work late and had 'a friend' in town who needed to be shown the sights, and would I mind looking after him? They seemed to assume the rest. I tried saying no – of course I did – but some of them got nasty, and I was pretty scared most of the time. It was easier to let them get on with it. Then there was the one who said 'Look darlin, I paid fifteen quid – don't mess me about' and I finally twigged. He'd paid Saul. They all had. I was trapped. I didn't have any money of my own. Saul had said he'd open a bank account for me, but he'd never got round to it. He just handed me small amounts of cash from time to time and paid the bills. I was like a caged bird, wasn't I? They used to trap birds here in Deya – did I tell you that? Great big nets stretched across the road between the cottages – filled with terrified, tiny, fluttering birds. It was horrible. But tourism put paid to all that, thank God."

She blinked, and touched one eye with her finger. A lorry chuntered past the window behind her head. It had 'Agua Potable' painted in blue on its side, travelling the few miles from the water processing plant at Lluc, further down the mountain road.

"You can relax for a few minutes, Angie. Stretch your muscles – move around. Thanks. It's going really well."

He opened a small box fridge on the floor and pulled out two cans of Coke.

"Salud," she said, slipping off the chair and taking the can from him and walking across to the doorway. "Here's to our painting!"

He pulled a face and drank noisily

"Saul was a sort of part-time pimp, I guess," she said, with her back to him. "By the time I realised what was going on I was too ashamed to go back to Roy, although I wanted to so much. Then someone told me he was getting engaged so I stayed away. I was too proud to admit to him of all people what a blind idiot I'd been, and what a mess I'd made of everything."

"Why didn't you just walk out?" He put his can down and inspected the tips of his pencils.

"Sound so simple now, doesn't it? But I had nowhere to go. No money. I didn't want to go back home to mum and Len the Louse. I was pretty desperate, but it wasn't until the doctor told me I was pregnant and Saul fixed up for me to have an abortion that I somehow found the strength to go. I telephoned my sister and she came to fetch me."

"Can you sit down again? Same angle? Just for about twenty minutes more. Great. That's it – keep you head at that angle. Shoulders relaxed more – down a bit. That's perfect. Go on."

"Well, Rita was married by then and so we planned I was going to live with them and keep the baby, but her doctor in Harlow arranged for me to give birth in this Mother and Baby's Home run by Catholic nuns. Don't ask me why. That changed everything. They convinced me I was being dreadfully selfish trying to keep him. 'Think of the baby,' they said. 'Not yourself. You have already sinned by bringing him into this world and now you must do your very best for him. Don't think of yourself. Let him go. We can find him a lovely Catholic family who will love him and give him everything you can't. Believe me, Angelica, it's Almighty God's will you give him up. You've nothing to offer the child, have you? No job, no husband, no home of your own, have you?

'Give him up, now, there's a good girl'. So I signed the bloody papers, Andy.

I was twenty years old and I'd just given birth. Two weeks – that's all it was. Two bloody weeks. My milk was pouring out, my hormones were all over the place, and I was expected to make this life-shattering decision. Rita said maybe they knew what was best Until they actually took him away I don't think I believed it would happen. I think I'd just signed the papers to stop them going on at me. But when they took him – they took everything from me. He was such a perfect, beautiful baby boy. Dark eyes, dark, soft, downy hair, pink skin. Perfect little eyebrows. He was asleep when they wheeled him away but I heard him crying as they went down the corridor and that was the beginning of the darkest time of all – my black tunnel, I call it now. I went mad – completely and utterly crazy with grief – when they took my baby away from me. I didn't know what was happening…"

"You've dropped your chin – sorry, Angie – turn towards the door again – up – yes, that's it – go on."

"I can – I can talk about it now. I couldn't for years. Never mentioned it. Not even to Rita. I was so ashamed. Mental illness is so frightening, isn't it – such an unknown territory. We'd call it a breakdown or hypermania or something now, but quite honestly I think I just went plain crazy with grief for six months."

She fell silent, gazing with unseeing eyes onto the dusty street, where two small boys were kicking a football in the heat, their brown skins sugared with dust on sweat.

She stared beyond them, at the line of dark cupressus trees against the amazing azure sky, and remembered another sky, and another row of trees.

Chapter Three

Back in the hotel Angie went straight to her room and lay down feeling drained and exhausted. Why had she told him all that stuff? Now she couldn't get it out of her head. It would haunt her for days. She closed her eyes and allowed herself to remember.

I'd been behaving oddly for weeks. I'd stayed in my room in Rita's little house in Harlow all day sometimes, just lying on the bed, unable to summon up the necessary effort to step off it. Rita and Patrick were both at work and I was supposed to be job hunting.

"What can I *do*, Rita?" I'd groaned when they'd brought the local paper and we'd looked at all the jobs available in town.

"I can't type and I haven't got a single piece of paper that says I can do anything. All I could do here is wash up or pub work or a shop – I don't want any of that."

"Well you're going to have to find something soon," Patrick had said. "We haven't got enough money to feed an extra mouth for long. You need to get yourself a job, Angie. Anything."

When they'd gone to work I'd intended going down to the agency in the High and trying anything which didn't sound too bad, but when I opened the glass front door and looked down the short cement path edged with tired crêpey daffodils, I'd closed it again in alarm. I couldn't do it. It was just too terrifying. So I went back to bed instead. It was a bitterly cold March and the house was freezing after nine o'clock, so I'd huddled under an old pink Paisley eiderdown and waited. What I was waiting for God only knew, but I lay there, sometimes shivering, from nine in the morning until six at night, when Patrick and Rita came in together, heaving great carrier bags from Sainsbury's onto the hall floor.

"You back, Angie?" Rita called, and I'd swung my legs over the side of the bed and walked tipsily to the bathroom. The room tilted a little.

"Any luck, Ange?"

"Luck?"

"With a *job*? How did you get on?"

"Oh. I didn't get anything."

"Oh no! What happened then? Did you get an interview?"

"Yes. Well, no, not exactly. There wasn't anything really. They said come back tomorrow."

"Oh. Well – maybe they know there will be something for you tomorrow – what d'you reckon?"

"I don't know. Don't keep on at me. I don't feel well. I think I've got flu coming or something."

"Did you peel any spuds?"

"Spuds?"

"Yes. Did you do any for tea? I asked you to peel three or four big ones so I could make mash. We've brought sausages and a cabbage."

"Oh. No. Sorry, I forgot."

"Angie! What on earth have you been doing all day? No job, no potatoes, and you obviously haven't done the hoovering."

I looked down at the fuzzy carpet and frowned.

"I didn't get round to it that's all, I'm not well. I feel so tired."

I turned and stomped back into the bedroom where I re-cocooned myself in the eiderdown and tried to sleep.

For days I lived like that. Sometimes I lied and said I'd been to the Labour Exchange or the Agency but there was nothing suitable, until one morning Rita announced she was coming with me.

"Get your hair washed; we are going to fix you up. Have a bath – you look terrible – no one would ever guess you were a Bunny Girl – you look more like an old dog! Come on. Sweetheart – shake a leg! We are going to sort you out."

It was then I found I couldn't go up the road without shaking. My heart thumped fit to explode and my palms were sweaty and I had an inexplicable sense of dread.

"It's no good, Rita. I can't go. I think I've still got flu."

"You really do feel rough, don't you? You're all sweaty. Well, I'd better get you down to Doctor Rose's. You can't go on like this. Come on – we'll catch the bus down to the centre."

"I can't. I can't get on the bus. I know I can't."

"What d'you mean, you can't get on the bus? Of course you can. What's the matter?"

I was rooted to the tarmac. Rita watched me as I raised a

shaking hand to my damp forehead.

"I feel sick – and sort of frightened, I think I'm scared to get on the bus."

"Don't be so daft, Angie. How could you be scared of getting on a bus?"

"I'm sort of scared of everything at the moment, Rita. I don't know what's the matter with me. I haven't been out for days."

Rita looked at me.

"Haven't you? What – not down to the Labour Exchange or the shops or anything? No job interviews?"

"No. Nothing. I haven't been anywhere. I can't."

I turned around and without another word I ran back up the road to the safety of Rita's house off Fourth Avenue. Rita ran after me, biting her lip, no doubt praying that Patrick would be understanding.

They called out Doctor Rose that evening, when they found me kneeling on the landing reciting Hail Mary's at ten o'clock.

"We're not even Catholics, Doctor. Our dad was, of course, but she looked so peculiar. And today – this morning – she said she was too scared to get on a bus – I tried to bring her down to the surgery but she was shaking and too frightened of something. What's the matter with her?"

"I suspect she's been having panic attacks for some time, and is now agoraphobic. She's afraid to leave the security of the house. Probably brought about by a hormone imbalance and the stress of giving up the baby – is your mother nearby?"

"Oh she won't want mum. She ran away from mum and her man years ago. They live on the other side of town but we don't see them. We don't really get on."

"I see. Well, Angelica is going to need some help – I'm going to refer her to an excellent colleague of mine who runs a psychiatric unit for young people in Epsom. I think he's the best person for her to see. I'll give her a sleeping tablet for tonight and arrange things in the morning."

"Epsom? That's Surrey isn't it? That's *miles* away. How're we going to get her there?"

"Don't worry about that. I can arrange transport. Just leave everything to me."

"Can't she go back to somebody in Harlow? Patrick and me can't visit her in Epsom can we? It's too far – we haven't got a car, you know."

"Often in cases like this they do rather better without too much family contact at the beginning. He really is the best man. I wouldn't want to send her to our local psychiatric hospital; she'd end up in a ward with deranged old people and alcoholics – all sorts. This will be much better. Trust me, Rita."

"I'm going to have to, aren't I?"

"It will be for the best, you'll see. I'm giving her this to ensure a good night's sleep for all of you, and I'll be back in the morning."

"How long's she going to have to be there?"

"It's impossible to say. It could be three weeks or three months. Or longer. These cases vary enormously. But it's a marvellous place – you'll see."

And so began the months at St Ebba's. Another sky, and another line of trees.

It was April 1st – All Fools' Day – when the doctor's wife drove me through the guarded gates into the impressive parklands of St Ebba's Hospital. Each unit was self-contained, and housed young nut-cases like me. I was to celebrate my twenty-first birthday a month after leaving this place, but I didn't know that as we swept up the drive and into the reception wing where all new patients were assessed and spent their first night.

Dr Rose's freckled wife hugged me before she handed over my suitcase and returned to her car. I don't think I said a word. I was too stunned.

Through the day room window I could see lost souls pacing up and down, up and down, and vacant faces turned towards me like radar scans. A woman shrieked and was silenced. My hands began to shake and I handed my belongings to a red-haired nurse with a hard, professional manner.

"Cup of tea?" she asked, and I nodded dumbly.

She bustled through double doors, unlocking them from a huge bunch on her waist, and locking them again as we passed through.

"It seems strange at first," she said, noticing my expression. "But you'll find it's not so bad. Sister Malpatt is in charge here;

she's more than fair."

It seemed an odd comment to make, but I had no time to wonder, as I was guided into a huge room with hideous red plastic armchairs, a TV the size of the Gaumont, and vomit-coloured linoleum.

"Angelica Roberts, Sister. Referred to Doctor Bott – he's seeing her tomorrow."

"Oh yes. We were expecting you, dearie. We're going to have tea in twenty minutes so I'll show you where you'll be sleeping just for tonight. Tomorrow you'll be in Walnut. Walnut's very nice. They're all young in there."

She could have been speaking in Arabic. I gazed past her at the troubled souls shuffling round the room, or sitting laughing for no obvious reason, or crying desperately in a corner.

"It's just for the first night," said Sister, opening a door. I stopped dead, like a horse refusing a fence. The door was padded, the walls were padded, there was no furniture except a small divan fixed to the floor, and the only window was high and barred.

"Am I in prison?" I asked quietly. "What did I do?"

"No, no. It's just like this because patients can be very troublesome on their first night here. But you won't be —I can see that. You'll be quite safe here. Now the bathrooms are along here – make sure you go before we lock up for the night at 9.30 – because you won't be able to go again until 6.30 when you're unlocked."

"You're going to lock me in? In there?"

"Yes, yes. Everybody's locked in here, dearie. You'll get used to it. It's for your own safety think of it that way. Come and have your tea in ten minutes. Have a wash and brush up and put your case in there. All right?"

Nothing will ever be so bad again – nothing anyone can do to me – not after the sight of that padded room with the barred window and the locked door.

"I must be really mad," I said to myself as I obediently washed my hands. They didn't feel quite clean so I washed them again. A nurse came looking for me when tea was almost over and I was still washing them.

"Washing obsession, is it?" she said, rather cheerfully.

"That'll do now – come and have some tea. They've almost cleared up."

There were all ages at the long table, with plates of bread and butter and pots of blood red jam. She pulled out a chair for me next to a chalk-faced girl with bandaged wrists. I couldn't eat a thing; a dull nausea rose as I lifted the white bread to my dry lips. But I drank the tea. Strong, sweet tea in thick, cream cups. A television blared in one corner with Blue Peter. I could never watch that programme for years afterwards without a sickening dread in the pit of my stomach.

"Here's one I made earlier!" joked John Noakes, and I longed for the old lounge in Harlow where only six years earlier Rita and I would have been sitting after school, nibbling biscuits, half watching TV and talking. Suddenly I saw my mum, standing in the lounge doorway in the pink frilly nylon apron she always wore when she was cooking, and saying, "Come on, you two! Do some homework before I set the table for tea!"

I longed to see her; to smell the cheap Coty scent she wore, to put my head on her shoulder and cry and cry, but I knew I would never ask for her, and I couldn't cry. I didn't know how to. The girl who couldn't cry. I hadn't cried since the day they took my baby.

"Any more tea, darlin'?"

I looked up as an enormous West Indian woman in a green overall bent over me with a large brown enamel tea pot. "More tea, dear? More tea?"

I nodded. This was not happening to me. Yesterday I'd been in Harlow with Rita and Patrick, unloading cornflakes and Nice biscuits out of supermarket carriers, and putting Typhoo tea into their blue kitchen cupboards – and today – today this nightmare freak show. It must be a dream. Must be. I would wake up soon. I couldn't possibly be going to be locked up in that room with padded walls and a bar across the window. It had to be a nightmare.

Someone wailed at the far end of the table; a strange sound full of pain and fear, like a rabbit caught by a fox, and I spilt my tea. I watched the brown pool spreading outwards on the blue gingham cloth.

"Oh dearie me! No problem! No problem!" The maid laughed in a good-natured fashion as she mopped up with a brown dishcloth and the meal seemed to be over. Some people remained seated while others shuffled to plastic armchairs grouped around the TV. I was unsure what to do, hoping a sudden loud noise might wake me up and I would find myself back in my bedroom in Harlow. Even my old room with mum and Len the Louse would be heaps better than this.

"Mummy…" I wanted to call out, but no words came. I found myself standing with my back to the wall, pressing myself against it, feeling safer while I felt its solidity behind me.

"Come and sit down, Angelica. Such a pretty, unusual name!" Sister Malpatt breezed up to me, her white starched apron arriving ahead of her like a sail on a yacht, and holding out a commanding arm to guide me to a chair. "Sit here, next to Jennifer."

Jennifer was the chalk-faced girl who did not speak. I didn't want to sit there, I didn't want to watch the Six o'clock News bringing further mayhem and misery into my nightmare. As soon as she had bustled off to boss someone else I moved uncertainly to the safety of the corner and stood there, leaning onto the wall.

I looked out through the window and saw them again – the line of cupressus trees against a now darkening sky.

At seven we were all given pills. I don't know what they were; an assortment of bright yellow, red and green – like Smarties.

At eight I was told to bath and get into my pyjamas and we were given cocoa, made with water, and two biscuits.

At nine there was a queue for the toilets and at nine-twenty I was taken to the room.

"No! No – I won't sleep in there!" I yelled, as a small wiry nurse pushed me in. But she was quick and had done it many times before. The door slammed shut and I heard a key turn. What if there was a fire? I grabbed for the handle but there was nothing. The door had heavy squares of padding and a spy-hole, but no handle on my side. I looked around the room, my heart somersaulting. Nothing, No chair. No table. No cupboard. A plain divan – I tried pushing it nearer the window but it was bolted to the floor. The window was high and small. A silver crescent moon shone above the bars and was strangely comforting. That same moon was shining over Harlow and Rita, and London and Roy. One day I would be back out there with them. I knew that. My head was feeling heavy and strange. As if someone were pressing down very hard upon it. The pills, I supposed. The yellow and green pills. I was a bird trapped in a cage. I climbed slowly onto the bed, my hands clenched like claws on the hard stiff sheets and my eyes wide open. But not for long. The pills were efficient and obliterated the room and the window with the bars and the moonshine. Dark night enveloped me with heavy hands, and I slept.

"Wake up, Angelica! Doctor will see you in three quarters of an hour. Come on dearie – quick wash and breakfast. You're the last to wake up!"

Was the nightmare over? My head throbbed and I felt queasy, but I opened my eyes to see another nurse's retreating back and the padded door wide open. I sat dizzily looking through the doorway.

There was a bedraggled queue for the toilets again and I pushed my feet into pink towelling mules and joined in behind a woman bobbing her head like a demented Noddy.

After three mouthfuls of cornflakes I was ready for Doctor Bott. He had a small office just off the day room, and the new nurse pushed me slightly as we entered.

"Angelica Roberts, Doctor," she said, and closed the door.

It was then that I noticed the elegant grey chalk-striped suit and his neat, middle-class bottom. He was standing with his back to me, one hand in one pocket, lifting the tail of the suit jacket, and holding a patient's notes in the other hand, reading them by the light of the window. He turned, and I felt the long forgotten surge of sexual excitement.

He was the handsomest man I'd seen since Roy Cavalieri.

Chapter Four

"Sit down Angela – no – it's Angelica, isn't it? Pretty Name. Make yourself comfortable. Have you settled in all right? I expect it feels very strange but everyone here is kind and we're all working together to get you well again. That's right, isn't it?"

He crinkled his blue eyes at me in an endearing manner and I felt myself wanting to tell this man everything.

"It's *terrible* here. It's like some awful dream. I want to go home. I'm not stopping here. You can't make me. It's like prison."

"Oh not that bad, surely? This unit is only the reception centre of course. It is a bit of a shock to the system, but you'll find it much more homely when you've settled in to Walnut. It's one of our houses for young people like yourself."

"Will they lock me in?"

"All the dormitories are locked at night – for your own safety – but not the day-rooms. You'll be free to walk in the grounds and visit the shop and the recreation hall at certain times."

"So I won't have to sleep on my own in that padded place any more?"

"Not unless it seems advisable for your own safety. I wouldn't anticipate that. Now, Angelica, tell me what has brought you here. Your GP thinks you've been experiencing panic attacks and other problems. Do you want to tell me about it?"

"I don't know really. I'm so tired, and I got sort of scared, and didn't want to go out or anything. I feel tired all the time – I thought I had the flu. A bit depressed – you know?"

"Yes. And how long do you think you've been feeling like this?"

"I don't know. A few weeks. A couple of months. Well – since – a few weeks."

"Since? The baby? Since you gave up your baby?"

I couldn't answer him. No one had called him that before. All anyone had said was 'the baby'. In my mind he had been Paul – I'd named him secretly as soon as I knew I was pregnant – but after I'd lost him even Rita had only called him 'the baby'. In fact she hardly ever mentioned him at all. Thought it best, I suppose. 'Just put it all behind you, Angie', she'd said. And I'd tried. I thought I was succeeding too.

But now – here – he had said what mattered. I'd lost *my* baby forever. Somebody else had taken him home and he was theirs now. Forever. I'd thought for a moment I might cry – how I longed to cry – but it didn't happen. I didn't seem to be able to dissolve the huge lump of glue in my chest – solidified pain. So I drew on his desk with my finger instead and spoke very quietly.

"Yes. I lost my baby. I gave him up for adoption."

There was a long silence in the room. I listened to the clock ticking on the wall beside the rows of books with names like 'The Psychology of Fear', 'Overcoming Guilt', and 'The Clinical Roots of Schizophrenia Concept'. I read along the rows for something to do in the silence. Somebody screamed.

"That must have been very painful. Do you want to talk about it?" He asked very gently but I shook my head and stared at my shoes. I realised for the first time that they were Rita's sensible flat shoes on my feet. My own pointed stilettos had obviously been left in Harlow as unsuitable here.

"Do you cry for your baby, Angelica?"

"No. Not really. I don't cry at all."

"Do you feel it was a wrong decision to have him adopted?"

"I didn't have a choice, did I? It was all my fault, wasn't it? I'd been living this awful life with Saul Richmond – it was my punishment, just like the nuns used to say. 'God is not mocked', they used to say – and I didn't believe them! I do now."

"The nuns? You're a Catholic?"

"No. But my dad was. And when I was little I went to the Ignatius Loyola Convent School – went there until I was ten. But after dad died mum took me away and sent me to the local state school. She wasn't Catholic. But the nuns always told us that God could see us wherever we were and whatever we were doing."

"What if I tell you, Angelica, that it is fairly common for decent young girls to make mistakes and get pregnant, when they're in no position to keep the baby? We all make mistakes, don't we?"

I stared at his cheap hospital desk with its green table lamp and pile of beige manila folders and said, "I expect so, sometimes. But this was all my own fault. If I'd stayed with Roy it would never have happened."

"Roy?"

"Roy was my – first, you know. So lovely and kind – but I was stupid enough to leave him for Saul Richmond. I must have been mad – or I am now, aren't I?"

I looked straight at him for the first time. He was tapping the fingers of both hands together and gazing at me from his elegant face, slightly tanned despite it being early April, against a startling white shirt and crimson tie. His brown hair had soft auburn streaks in the sideburns and his blue eyes were warm and sympathetic.

"No. You're not mad, Angelica. Just experiencing a few temporary difficulties. It's not uncommon given the hormone imbalance your body had gone through plus the grief of losing your baby and the problems of your present situation. No job, I gather?"

"No. I didn't feel up to it. And what can I do? I was a waitress and a bunny-girl before working with Saul – and then I was answering a telephone and being some sort of call girl I suppose."

"What were you good at school?"

"Nothing much. I ran away at fifteen. I like PE and English best really, but I've got no exams, or anything."

"You must get a training. We can help you with that. We have an excellent OT department and a career guidance officer. But that's all in the future. When you're well again. We have two lines of approach to your illness, Angelica, drugs and ECT. We shall put you on sodium amytal, and if that doesn't help then we'll consider ECT – it often works quite dramatically – but we'll see how you get on. You'll have a chat with me twice a week and Sister Malpatt will monitor your progress with Sister Clare on Walnut. Do you have any questions?"

"What's ECT then?"

"Well, it's electroconvulsive therapy – an electric current is used in difficult cases of depression and can have quite startlingly good results. But we shall try the drugs first. I'll also prescribe a light sleeping tablet for a few nights while you settle in; then we'll drop them and see how you are managing. Try to take a short walk around the grounds each day; I know you'll find that difficult, but give yourself goals – a very short walk – say to those trees and back today – and then a little further tomorrow, and maybe down to the shop by Friday. You'll find that forcing yourself to reach your goal will help you much more than giving in to your feelings of panic."

"And what if I can't?"

"You *can*, Angelica. You're only afraid of feeling afraid. Of the sensation. You won't come to any harm by making yourself go out. Ignore the shaking and just *do* it. I think that's probably enough for today. We'll talk again on Friday and you can tell me how you got on. Sister will take you over to Walnut shortly. Goodbye."

He stood up and so did I, mesmerised by his crinkling blue eyes smiling at me and the attractive laughter lines around them. I was such a sucker for the older man.

Angie opened her eyes and looked around her room, startled to find herself there in such calm and tranquil surroundings. She lay breathing slowly as she adjusted to the present. She had agreed to meet Andy for a late lunch; she lifted her arm and inspected her watch; 2.10 – she swung her legs wearily over the bed, and washed her face in cold water. She was beginning to wish she'd never agreed to all this. It had seemed a bit of harmless fun yesterday, but now memories were swamping her and she didn't want them to. She changed her shirt and applied some pale lipstick and walked slowly down to the bar, where Conchita was serving two new visitors.

Andy was coming in the front door as she sipped a gin and tonic. He was looking very pleased with himself and waved as he saw her.

"It's going really well," he said, after he'd ordered a lager. "I'm dead chuffed with it. Best thing I've done all year. I'm not going to show it to you yet though."

"O.K. I'm so glad it's going well. How old are you, Andy?" she asked.

"Almost twenty-one."

There was a brief pause while she ordered tapas and he

added, "My mother wants me to go home for this big birthday bash. You know – all the relations – the big do – soap on a rope and all that unbelievable stuff with your aunties!"

Angie laughed.

"Ungrateful little bugger! Your mother will love it. What does your dad say?"

There was a pause as he drank noisily.

"He won't care much either way," he said at last, wiping the back of his hand across his mouth.

"How d'you mean?"

"Well, they split two years ago and now he's got this new woman. My birthday will just cause problems. He'd come, of course, but then so would she, and my mum hates her, so it's very much easier to just forget the whole thing really."

"Have you painted her?"

He recoiled, as from a flying object.

"What – dad's bit?"

"Yes. What's her name?"

"Carolyn. Very posh. Thinks she's God's gift and all that."

"So she's young and attractive then?"

"Well, not *that* young – but too young for dad. She's thirty-nine or something and he's fifty."

"You must paint her, Andy! Concentrate all your anger and pain – *that* would be some picture! Why are you wasting your time out here when you could be doing that back home?"

He inspected the bottom of his glass thoughtfully.

"I don't think I could do that. She wouldn't want me to either. She knows how I feel about her. So does dad."

Angie put her glass onto the bar with a bang.

"Hell, are you going to be an artist, or will you apply to your local bank for a job straight away? You need some *passion* in your painting, Andy. You said yourself there's no life in it. Get your pain down – confront it – it won't go away – I learned that at St Ebba's if nothing else. Come on – let's take this plate of tapas into the garden. It's quiet out there."

He followed her, carrying a tray of prawns and delicious looking nibbles through the side door and out into the sunshine. They walked into the olive orchard at the side of the hotel.

"Go on with your story, then, after you'd given up your

43

baby, you had a breakdown, did you?"

"Something like that. I was sent to a psychiatric youth unit with an amazing psychiatrist, Graham Bott – 'Gabby' as everyone called him, I soon discovered – even the nurses. His initials – GAB – and the fact that he was a wonderful talker. They all worshipped the ground he walked on – if the nurse in charge could have clasped his head to her starched bosom there and then she would have, but instead she just kept bringing him coffee and chocolate biscuits, I seem to remember. He was like a film star – I remember thinking 'Damn the ECT – just plug me into this man – that should do it'. Every time he left the room we all gazed after him like a flock of lovelorn sheep!"

Andy grinned and flopped down onto the brown grass on one elbow, as Angie spread out their picnic underneath a gnarled olive tree. He began to pick at the prawns in garlic as she continued.

"Goodness knows why Rita had packed so much! How long did she think I was going to be there? Forever? She must have packed almost all the clothes I possessed into that Revelation suitcase. Roy had bought that too, the first summer we'd lived together, and he'd taken me down to Brighton for a long weekend. The only real holiday we ever had together. 'You must always have a good leather handbag and a smart suitcase, darling,' he had said. 'Italian women always have at least one really classic handbag – it will last for years. English women have all these nasty cheap plastic things in all colours for all their outfits – and they look terrible. Better to have one classic bag – and maybe a small cream linen one for summer.'

"Roy was a man with style. He had pictures of his mother everywhere; she had been so beautiful; a tiny bit plump, but such a lovely face – creamy skin and big brown eyes and hair like the young Elizabeth Taylor. I remember one full-length photograph of her taken in Rome by a fountain – she had a cream linen dress on with a straight skirt and boat necklace and she was tanned and laughing – such a beautiful woman. He used to press that picture to his lips sometimes – and then there were tears in his eyes – but he was half Italian.

"So I had a smart red Revelation suitcase and a classic black patent leather handbag. He was quite right – they did last for years. I've still got the suitcase somewhere."

"Can I carry on sketching?" interrupted Andy, sitting up suddenly and pulling his sketchpad towards him.

"Sure. I don't mind. God, its extraordinary how much I remember... We went into this long room with black wrought iron bedsteads and blue counterpanes. Between each bed was a narrow chest, and at both ends were walls of numbered wardrobes. There were twenty beds and had I ever seen a dormitory in a girls' boarding school (which I hadn't) I would have had difficulty in telling the difference. I was taken to my bed and cupboard and shown the bathrooms and showers beyond. It didn't seem too bad. It seemed quite normal and hopeful. I'd sat on the bed and looked around. I can see it now; a big sunny room with windows on two sides overlooking gardens of daffodils and narcissus. I remember thinking that my hands had stopped shaking and that I wasn't so scared. But that didn't last long. This mad girl shot in and screamed at me 'Who sent you?' or something like that. She was absolutely terrifying. Hair in yellow greasy spikes. Bare feet, purple and scarred. Wearing some sort of knitted mini-dress above mauve mottled legs. Then I felt panicky again. Oh yes – heart banging, head thumping. She began chucking my clothes – which I'd only just put in the wardrobe – out onto the floor and commenting on them and clutching at my arm. I tried to call out, but I think I was just too frightened to make a sound. Then just as suddenly she let go of me and ran off screaming. It wasn't a posh girls' school after all, was it? We were all bloody mad. I sat on the floor for ages, sobbing and shaking, until a young nurse, about my own age, who said her name was Ginger, came and took my hand and led me back into the day room. No-one had held my hand since Roy. It felt nice.

I remembered my promise to Gabby to try to walk a little each day, and I asked one of the less crazy looking girls, who said her name was Heather, to come with me. She thought I wanted to walk to the shop for cigarettes or chocolate, and when I said I just wanted to walk to the line of trees she really thought I was off my trolley.

"Well, my goal for that day was those trees and back and no further, so I left Heather pulling on her jacket and marched purposefully towards the fir trees, a biting wind whipping up my hair. I felt sick and afraid, but I made myself put one foot in front of another until I reached the grass in front of the trees and then I touched a tree and turned and ran back as fast as I could.

I'd done it. I'd gone out alone, so I had done it really. My first goal was reached. I guess I've been giving myself goals ever since."

She blinked and looked at Andy in surprise. He honestly thought she had forgotten him completely and was now wondering who the hell he was.

"You really went through it, didn't you?" was all he could think to say, and he knew it was trite.

She stretched out a hand to the tapas and began to take small bites in silence.

"Well," he said awkwardly, "I guess I've taken up enough of your time today. I'll see you at Julio's in the morning then. Can you spare another hour?"

She did not reply as he stood up, clutching his sketches to his chest and standing stiffly, looking down on her. She chewed absent-mindedly.

"See ya then," he said, and backed round the corner and out of the orchard and onto the path.

I was dreaming. It was disturbing, leaving me with a vague sense of menace and unease. All I could remember was that my teeth had been crumbling, shattering, falling out of my mouth. I sat up in bed, trembling and wanting to cry but unable to do so. I was a small child again, needing the warmth of my mother's body, but she was not there. I was alone. I was surrounded by crazy people. I looked around the dormitory in the silver light of an early April morning. It was freezing cold and I guessed it was between six-thirty and seven. The ear-splitting electric bell would jolt everyone awake at 7.15 so Heather had told me, so I waited, heart pounding, and looking to see if anyone else was awake. I slept between Heather and a strange dark girl whose name I had forgotten. She was unbelievably ugly and looked heavily drugged; she slept with her mouth open, with hideous missing teeth and a stink of cigarettes. I could smell her now,

46

and her breathing was snuffling and difficult. Heather was still asleep too; a mildly twitching sleep where she muttered and moaned, her eyebrows zigzagging up and down and her lips moving. I propped myself up on one elbow and yawned quietly.

The violent girl who had attacked me was sitting bolt upright in her bed across the room. She seemed to be staring into space with sightless eyes. Certainly they were not focused on me. I slithered down the bed under the covers before she could spot me. Dear God – what a place. How long would I be here? Had Rita forgotten me completely? I decided to telephone her today. That would be my goal – I would walk to the phone box wherever it was and telephone Rita. I would need to go straight after a quick breakfast though or she would have left home for work. I needed to hear her voice; to talk of ordinary things like shopping and clothes, and to leave this madhouse behind me. When would she be able to come and see me? Or more importantly, when would I be able to return to Harlow for a weekend?

Although I'd been told to expect the loud electric bell I still jumped. It was deafening. The crazy girl jumped out of bed with both hands clasped over her ears and ran past my bed down towards the showers in the shortest nightdress I had ever seen. She had no pants on, I noticed in dismay. She looked utterly haunted. My heart had begun the fearful pounding which was becoming normal, and I felt a little dizzy. Heather spoke first.

"Hello! You OK?"

She sounded so ordinary I turned to her in relief.

"Well, they gave me some pills so I slept really heavily. I've only just woken up. I feel pretty awful actually."

"Don't think about it. It gets better – it does honestly. Gabby will make you feel better. Isn't he gorgeous? He's just like that film star – Omar Sharrif or something – you know? I see him tomorrow – I wish it was today – I could talk to him about *anything* – anything at all."

"Yes. I felt like that. He's very – well – warm, and sort of accepting, isn't he? You couldn't shock him, could you? Mind you, I expect he's a randy old bloke like the rest of them really, don't you? They're all the same."

Heather looked shocked.

"Oh no! Not Gabby! He does get people better and he's lovely. I wish I could take him home with me I can tell you! Ginger says he's got a really beautiful wife and three kids though – she's a psychologist or something too – must be clever – got it all, hasn't she? Ginger says she looks just like Grace Kelly."

I swung my legs off the bed and sighed. Would I ever have it all? I'd thought so once. Been so sure. Now it seemed completely unattainable. But I would concentrate on *today*!

"Take a day at a time, Angie, and *don't worry*."

That had been my doctor's wife's advice when she'd driven me down here. Such a kind lady and such sensible advice – I must try to take it. A day at a time.

I washed and stared back at my white, dripping face. I looked like a frightened white rabbit. The green eyes Roy had found so alluring were listless, and the once shining golden hair was lank and lifeless. There was a greasy patch down my forehead and my limbs felt like concrete.

"I'm only twenty," I thought, "and my looks have gone."

"Good morning, everybody! How are we all today?"

It was Sister Murphy, doing her rounds and checking the lavatories for drugs, razor blades or other forbidden commodities. This I learned much later. At the time I thought she was checking if we were cleaning our teeth or using a deodorant.

"Breakfast in fifteen minutes!" She bustled past, the starch in her apron sending it before her. I hoped Ginger would be on duty this morning – she'd seemed so approachable and warm – more of a hot water bottle, and I felt in need of some childish comfort right now.

The lavatory doors banged as Sister checked them all and returned along the lines of the basins.

"Good morning, Angela," she said as she noticed me.

"Did you sleep well?"

"Yes thank you," I muttered as I thrust my toothbrush into my mouth and began scrubbing my teeth vigorously.

"Good, good."

She was gone, her hard black shoes tapping her message on the grey stone floor.

I noticed that the girls made little conversation, apart from

Heather. Sad, withdrawn faces contemplated their reflections without interest or with varying degrees of disgust, before they emptied water from basins or dragged cheap combs through matted hair. Heather was like a drink in the desert.

"I'm dying for a bacon sandwich," she said, as we dragged jerseys over our heads and stuffed our pyjamas into our cupboards. "I'd better have a boiled egg though as that's all there'll be! My boyfriend says I must put on weight – I lost nearly two stone when I was ill, and he's stuck by me all through so I'd better try, hadn't I?"

I told her she didn't look too bad to me, and I hoped he wouldn't let her down.

"What's he like then?" I asked.

"His name's Alan and he's a mechanic and he's lovely. We've been going steady since school. I'm eighteen now so maybe we'll get engaged when I'm out of here. He wants us to, and he's twenty and earning good money in the big Ford garage in Guildford."

"Did you have a nice job?"

"Yes, it was all right. I worked in a shoe shop but I lost it 'cos I kept nicking things. I kept on taking shoes home – without paying for them! I couldn't stop it. I had twenty-seven pairs when they caught up with me! 'Compensatory', Gabby calls it. My mum died nearly two years ago – cancer – and I never cried. Never once. I left school and thought I was managing all right, but I wasn't eating and I kept on having to pinch stuff. You know – sweets from the corner shop – that was dead easy – then a blouse from Marks, and some make-up from Boots, and then when I got the job in the shoe shop I was away! Silly really I took some I didn't even like! But Gabby explained to me I was sort of buying love or something – presents my mum would have brought me – sort of comfort, you know? Well, it made sense when Gabby explained it all to me anyhow. I don't think I want to work in a shop again. I can do a training at Guildford Tech so I might do Beauty Therapy – how about you?"

We were sitting at the long table by the window, eating cornflakes, the first occupants of the morning, and I looked out at the line of fir trees in the steady drizzle which was washing the garden grey.

"Oh, you'll never believe it, but I was a Bunny Girl in a club! Ears, powder puff, the lot! I was really pretty before… well… a year or two back, anyway…"

"I think you're pretty now. You've got lovely hair and your eyes are ever so unusual. They're sort of greenish one minute and not the next! I bet you've got a boyfriend!"

"No. I haven't."

I stirred my tea and stared into its swirling depths.

"I don't know what I'll do when I get out of this place."

"Do you live at home?"

"Not with my mum and dad – no. My dad's dead and my mum lives with this awful bloke, Len. I ran away years ago. He wanted to grope me, I could tell. I've been living with my sister but I can't keep on doing that. She's married and got her own life to lead. I've just got to pull myself together."

"Gabby will help you – honestly – he will. I *am* going to have an egg. Do you want one?"

"Ugh – no thanks."

"He'll send you down the OT place when you're up to it."

"OT?"

"Yeah – you learn to type and do bits of cooking and stuff, and see what you're good at, and then they fix up for you to do a proper college course or something when you leave here. They give you lots of help. What are you going to do this morning?"

"Ring my sister. I'm going to do it now actually or I won't catch her before she leaves for work – where's the phone?"

"There's a public phone in the lobby by the front door – you can use that. Got any money?"

"Yes, thanks."

I grabbed my purse and ran, feeling as excited at the prospect of hearing Rita's voice as a small child queuing up to see Father Christmas on December 24th.

It rang and rang. And rang. No one answered. I was sick with disappointment. A terrible loneliness overwhelmed me and for the first time in months a tear splashed onto my hand and I sat on the window seat gazing out at the rain. Where was Rita? Had she abandoned me to my fate and gone to work without a thought? It was only five past eight. She normally left the house at quarter past at the earliest. How I longed to hear her voice, talk of ordinary things, see her bright face, even if she grumbled at me. I stared at the front path as a bedraggled Ginger in a navy gabardine raincoat trundled her bicycle towards the front door. She shook off a plastic rain hat as she pushed open the door, cascading drips everywhere.

"Hello, Angie!" she said, beaming at me like a welcome ship steaming into port.

"What's the matter, Lovey? You look as if it's the end of the world!"

She walked towards me with her arms outstretched and a sympathetic smile on her freckled face, and I suddenly howled like an abandoned dog. She sat down beside me on the window seat, her arms encircling me and saying nothing but a comforting "Sssh, sshh, it's all right, it's all right."

And I cried the tears that had been walled up since they'd taken my baby. The rain beat against the window pane and the wind lashed the trees and I sobbed for my vanished youth, my lost love and most of all for my precious son, who now looked at another woman and thought she was his mother.

Angie awoke with a start, to find herself sprawled on the grass under the old olive tree alone. She sat up, brushing tapas crumbs from her shirt and looking around the deserted garden in relief. When had Andy left? She had no idea. She had not had that nightmare for years. And she must not indulge in lunchtime dreaming again. She had a hotel to run.

She stood up and picked up the two trays and carried them towards the kitchen. Conchita's anxious face told her she had seen her asleep in the garden and needed reassurance. She put an arm around her shoulder and smiled.

"Que tal?" asked Conchita.
"Muy bien," she responded.
"Muy bien."

Chapter Five

Andy realised he hadn't been painting for some moments. So engrossed had he been in Angie's story that he'd been frozen with the brush in his hand, mesmerised by the emotion on her face. She was quiet now; still and quiet; her face in repose.

He forced his gaze away and onto the paper in front of him – had he captured that suffering in paint? Had he ever experienced such anguish himself? Probably not; although the deep sadness he had felt when his parents split up had been buried deep and had perhaps hampered his relationship with Emma.

He'd been trying not to think about Emma; perhaps he should.

"Tell me about yourself, now Andy. I need a break. I'll go on later if you really want me to, but I must be back in the hotel earlier than yesterday. I haven't talked about all that St Ebba's stuff for years. It's taken it out of me. I hardly slept last night. I don't know why I told you – you're a brilliant listener, of course, but I think it must be something to do with discovering you're the age I was then. Coincidence, isn't it?"

"Do you want to break for another drink? You're looking very hot and exhausted."

"Yes, yes, it's getting hotter. Must be thirty-five degrees; they said it would be. Got any ice?"

He fumbled in the fridge and found a tray of ice cubes and poured two Cokes into greasy glasses.

"A su sulud!"

"Maybe I should talk to you about Emma. Perhaps you'd see what went wrong, because I certainly don't know. It was terrific at first and then suddenly – no, not suddenly – *gradually* – gradually it all went wrong. She went back home saying she had no intention of ever setting eyes on me again."

"Is Emma at the Slade too?"

"No. She had just graduated – Maths – so she's really clever you know – and she was in Deya for a month staying at her uncle's place in the mountains for a holiday before she starts a fantastic job in the City. We met at the café and we were crazy about one another from the start. She's a real firecracker – tiny and dark and funny and beautiful – just about perfect really."

He drank in two long gulps and stared into his empty glass.

"And what went wrong? You still sound pretty keen to me."

He put his glass on the floor and folded his hands behind his head.

"Yes. I still feel the same. Trouble is – she doesn't – she said I'm cold and not in touch with my own emotions – that's brilliant for a bloody artist, isn't it? Fucking terrific."

"And is she right?"

Angie spoke gently and didn't look at him, but stared at her gold sandals intently.

"Maybe. She must be. She knew me so well. I've never felt like that about anybody before. I thought we'd live together when we got back. I'm not sure how, but that's what I wanted and I thought she did too. She had a flat, and we were both based in London, so it was perfectly possible. But I fouled it up somewhere along the line."

Angie stretched her legs straight in front of her and frowned.

"I don't claim to understand young women today, Andy. They're another species to me. I was brought up to fancy strong, independent, macho sort of guys and I freely admit that's what I still find sexy – but young, educated women *say* they want men to share everything – do the housework, the cooking, practically have the baby for them – and then, when they've got all that – they get very angry and dissatisfied and say that's not what they really wanted at all. Makes it bloody difficult for you blokes, doesn't it?"

"Not really. I suppose I grew up used to it. Girls have always seemed in charge all my life, from my mother and sister who are both unbelievably bossy to my old man's bit who tells him what to do all the time, to every girlfriend I've ever had. Even Emma – although she was subtler about it – but I guess she expected to get her own way and lay down the ground rules most of the time."

"And you accepted that? What happened to male pride? The leader of the pack? The male animal?"

Andy laughed.

"It's not like that anymore – if you start throwing your weight around, girls accuse you of harassment, rape, anything you can think of. You of all people to say that – you're an independent woman – hotel owner – successful without a man. How can you say all that?"

"Independent and lonely. We are higher animals, after all, Andy. The female's deadlier when she has young, of course, but she respects the male's power and strength. She has to."

"But that's the point – girls *don't* have to! They earn their own living, own their own houses and cars; we can't throw our weight around any more or we're out on our ears. If I lived with Emma it would be in *her* apartment. I can't afford one, she can."

"Maybe. But girls can't be so biologically different in one or two generations, Andy. They *say* that's how they want things to be, but it goes deeper than that. Maybe your Emma wanted you to throw your weight around; insist she stayed here – or follow her home – or whatever caveman-like demonstration of your love for her and claim on her she was wanting you to make. I don't know her, of course, and I'm just guessing based on my own instincts as a woman. I bet what she *didn't* want was for you to meekly take it and let her go without a fight. When did she go back?"

"Eight days – no, nine days ago. And I haven't heard a word since."

"Have you done anything about it?"

"Course I have. I rang. Twice. But she wasn't there. Or her flatmate said she wasn't. Her mobile was switched off. Then later I texted. But she hasn't replied."

"Andy! Andy! You sent her a text message! Surely she wants some huge gesture of unending passion, not a bloody one-liner! First flight home after her – you know the sort of thing. Fight!"

He flushed angrily and looked up.

"I can't afford to jet around like that. I'm a student. If I fly back to London that's it. I'm back then for the summer. I can't afford to come back here and I've hardly painted a thing. I told you – I'm meant to take back a portfolio of serious work. It wasn't a one-liner – there was masses of stuff – telling her how I feel about her. But she hasn't bothered to answer it. Well not yet anyway."

Angie smiled tenderly.

"Maybe she didn't want to just text-message you. The post is unreliable up here in the mountains. Maybe she has written and her letter is sitting in some mailbag in Palma. Maybe you'll get it tomorrow. Cheer up – you can go and see her – you know her address, don't you, so everything's still up for grabs!"

"It's not as simple as that. You were on about male pride – well, I see it more as personal artistic integrity – I can't go back with no work done that I'm proud of. I've got nothing to offer her if I'm not a working artist. She fell in love with Andy Carter – artist. That's who I am. I'm not crawling back to her with nothing – I've got to succeed first on my own terms."

She pulled a wry face and turned away, putting her empty glass on the table.

"I can understand that. I've felt that for years – satisfaction in my own work is the only fulfilment I've had. You can hold your head up if your work is going well. That's how I feel about my hotel. But hang on – you're taking a hell of a risk if you're not intending getting back to her until you're a successful artist. She could be married to some other guy with four kids before that happens!"

He flushed again and hung his head. Angie watched his hurt face and sprang towards him.

"Oh, don't look like that – I'm sorry – I'm a tactless idiot! But artists take *years* to become established, you know that. She'll know too, and if she loves you it won't matter. But you've got to stake your claim or she'll simply assume you don't really care at all. Whatever you say. Believe me, Andy!"

"What's the point? I'm not going to go and live off her. She's going to earn mega-bucks in the City – how can I go and say 'Let's live together' while I'm an impoverished art student with possibly no talent or future at all."

"Stop feeling sorry for yourself. Of course you've got talent. You wouldn't be at the Slade if you hadn't, would you? You've got to believe in yourself – no one else will unless you do first. She said you were cold – she wants some hot-blooded action by the sound of it. You can paint anywhere – get back on a plane and paint in London. Paint your father's lover who you hate, and Emma who you love! They'll be paintings worth looking at.

How's this masterpiece coming on?"

Her peel of laughter jolted him from his mood of depression and he grinned sheepishly.

"Not bad. You can't see it yet. I'm quite pleased so far. How much longer can you spare?"

"I need to be back in the hotel by one. You could come over with me and I'll treat you to lunch. Tortilla de los prelados. Marvellous. How about that?"

"Sounds great. What sort of omelette is that?"

"Crabs' tails. I think Chef has made 'postre con pera' today."

"OK. Thanks. I'll work for another hour then. You're bloody marvellous you know, Angie. You've got more life in you than I'll ever have."

"Nonsense. You're just inhibited. English public school? Boarder? You should try a convent school for guilt trips – unbelievable! Gabbie and I had several enlightening chats about the convent's unfortunate effects on me – it was very helpful and I certainly got to understand myself better afterwards. Tell me more about Emma."

She got up and moved across the room to stretch like a cat.

"I'll do that over lunch. I can't talk and paint at the same time. You go on with your story. Back on the chair, Angie – and I'll concentrate. This painting is going to be the best thing I've done all year. I just know it."

"Life settled into a pattern at St Ebba's. I'd see Gabbie twice a week and the medication helped up to a point. I think Ginger and Gabbie were the real saviours, though. Without them I'd never have made it. Ginger and I became real friends; we're still in touch. In fact she came out for a short holiday last year with her husband. A nice man – he's a chemist. And Gabbie made me understand myself as well as giving me back my sense of being an attractive woman, because he really turned me on. As I began to feel and look better I felt a stronger and stronger attraction for him, and I knew he was aware of it. Of course, he was well used to female patients falling in love with him; a regular occurrence with vulnerable people needing affection from a father figure – and he was an exceptionally handsome man. But it was more than that. I found I was regaining my looks and sex appeal. There was a hairdresser in the shop twice a week and she got my hair in much better condition.

'You're looking lovely today, Angie,' Gabbie said to me one morning at the beginning of May.

'I'm very pleased with your progress. Sleeping tablets dropped, anti-depressants halved –excellent.' He said he had some news for me.

"I looked at him in anticipation. God, he was gorgeous! He had a brown tweed jacket on with a cream shirt and suede tie – every inch the country gentleman. I liked that jacket – I wanted to touch it; in fact I wanted to touch him. To lay my head on his shoulder and run my fingers around his neck. But I just said 'Oh!'

He smiled into my eyes.

'You're looking very pleased with yourself about something.' I dared to say. We both laughed. He had a very attractive laugh; deep and free.

'Who would you most like to see this afternoon?' he asked. My heart beat fast. – 'Who?'

He smiled and closed the folder on his desk.

'Your sister is coming to see you, and I've said I think you're well enough to go back with her until Sunday evening.'

"I sat rooted to the chair in shock. Rita – here? Me – home? I experienced the now less familiar feeling of panic and anxiety once more. Could I cope with 'out there'? With Harlow and normal living?"

"Hold on," interrupted Andy. "Can you move your face a fraction round – nearer the window? That's better. Thanks. Sorry – go on."

"I was feeling jumpy and really mixed up. Of course in one way I did want to go home, but in another I felt so frightened it would be easier to stay in hospital. Gabbie told me to relax and enjoy the weekend and keep taking the medication. He said he'd see me on the following Wednesday and check how I'd managed. I told him how much I'd enjoyed the cookery classes he'd organised and how I thought I might do cooking as a job when I got out. He shook my hand when I got up to go. I remember that I clasped it like a life-line and there was this fantastic surge between us. He stepped back a bit and looked embarrassed. It was good to ruffle his feathers a little. I felt in charge again. That was good. Being the one in charge was very good. I walked out of that room with my head held high. I wanted to see Rita, of course I did, but I wanted to see him again the following week even more.

Lunch was rushed. Heather had now gone home for good, and I sat between Bridget, who rarely spoke, and Charlotte, the demented, attacker. After treatment she was a completely changed person and was quite nice to talk to. She'd had a drug problem and was now getting to grips with normal life. She was even hoping to do a university course and was gabbling on about all the forms she had to fill in.

'My sister's coming later on,' I told her, 'and I can go home till Sunday.'

She said she'd miss me and I asked her if she felt worried each time she went home. She said 'always' but she was sure Gabbie had worked his magic this time and soon she'd be going home for good.

I wondered how Rita would fetch me. They hadn't got a car, and eventually a blue Ford pulled up outside and I shouted, 'That's Dr Rose's wife! She brought me here! She's brought Rita!'

I rushed to the front door and flung it open before Rita had taken two steps down the gravel path. She was looking apprehensive but smiled bravely when she saw me. She was wearing a new coat, and it was frumpy and far too old for her, but I flung myself into her arms and buried my face in her skinny shoulder. Mrs Rose laughed and patted my back.

Rita said I looked wonderful and asked me if I felt as good as I looked. I told her I did and that I wished she could see Gabbie. She'd drool over him; he was like a film star.

Mrs Rose sat down beside me and held my hand.

'He is gorgeous, isn't he,' she said. 'He was at medical school with my husband you know. We've known them for years. He's so good with young people; he's the reason why my husband desperately wanted to send you here rather than anywhere else.'

I couldn't believe she actually knew them. She told me Mrs Bott was a psychiatrist too, specialising in drug rehab and that she had children – beautiful blonde children like her.

Rita was overwhelmed with the horror of the place. I told her I'd got used to it, and that if she thought this was bad, she should see Admissions. That would really freak her out. She cried a bit and said she hadn't realised. Mrs Rose pasted a 'Let's Think Positive' expression onto her face and smiled determinedly.

'Can I get us some tea do you think? It was a long drive.'

I leapt into the kitchen, glad of something to do. I still wasn't sure how Rita and I would resume our old relationship and whether Patrick would want me back in their home at all. I stared out of the kitchen window while I waited for the kettle to boil, at the brick wall and the washing line of green striped tea towels, and shuddered. How quickly I'd got used to the horrors of this place. Rita's reaction had reminded me of how I'd felt about it only four weeks ago and now it seemed acceptable; almost normal.

I poured tea into the cream enamel tea pot and rummaged in a wall cupboard for sugar. It felt good to be doing these small domestic tasks once again.

Dear Mrs Rose had thought of everything. She produced Penguin biscuits from her handbag like a magician pulling rabbits from his top hat, and we nibbled happily, feeling ordinary and homely.

I asked after Patrick and Rita looked awkward.

'He's working today. But he finished at five, so he said he'd cook something for tonight so we don't need to worry.'

I asked if he'd mind me being there again.

She flushed indignantly and said, 'Of course not. It's your home, Angie, for as long as you want.'

But her eyes wouldn't meet mine. Something was up. I knew my sister. Something she didn't want to tell me.

It was strange driving out of the gates and through the town of Epsom. It was like another planet. All those ordinary people's ordinary lives going on outside the fence, never knowing about the pain inside the walls of St Ebba's. Never imagining. Never wanting to know. Determined not to know.

We drove for miles with dear Mrs Rose keeping up a constant chatter which didn't require an answer. Rita talked a little, but was obviously preoccupied about something. Just the responsibility of having a crazy sister home for a few days perhaps.

London looked dirtier than ever. There seemed to be rubbish everywhere – in sacks and outside them. It was so crowded and noisy that I began to shake a bit, but I remembered Gabbie's words, 'You're only afraid of feeling afraid'. I tried to talk myself out of it and relax. Easier said than done, but I was more or less in control by the time we drove into the green and grey uniformity of Harlow New Town. I had forgotten how regimented it appears. Perhaps I had never known.

All the streets look exactly the same, I thought for the very first time. No rush of nostalgia; no sense of coming home.

Rita asked if I wanted to see Mum, because she'd been asking after me. I was shocked when she said she'd seen her I knew I didn't want to.

Rita was lifting my case out of the car and Mrs Rose said she'd be off and would pick me up on Sunday.

She leaned out of the car window and I bent down to kiss her warm cheek. She smelt of scones and Nivea cream. A strange combination but nice.

We stood, waving, as the Ford drove away, and then turned up the concrete path to the glass front door. Nothing had changed. A paper bag scuttled round the front garden and the gate clanged shut.

Patrick was in the kitchen peeling potatoes and he welcomed me with a bear hug. There were carnations in my bedroom and the sheets were new.

'The room looks lovely!' I said, dumping my case.

Patrick made tea and Rita and I hugged naturally. I thought it was going to be O.K. although I sensed Rita was hiding something.

'What is it, Rita?' I asked, wanting to get it over with before it made me really anxious and spoilt the weekend.

'Whatever you're hiding or trying not to tell me.'

'Don't be silly.'

She sat down suddenly on the bed, patting the eiderdown beside her. I stared at the newly hoovered stripes on the carpet.

'You could never keep secrets from me, could you?' I said.

She was blushing and turning away from me; fiddling with

the buttons on her raincoat. She said Patrick had told her not to tell me. Had thought it best. But she didn't want to leave me out.

'Of what? What are you leaving me out from?' I yelled.

She told me she was pregnant.

The room rocked. I closed my eyes on the pain. A fist churned in my stomach.

'In October. I'm having a baby in October,' she said

I didn't want to cry. It would seem so selfish.

I put my arms over my head and curled into a ball and rocked. A strange moaning sound came from somewhere. It must have been me.

Rita shouted down to Patrick and he came running.

I felt arms going round me and Patrick's face against my own.

'Be happy for Rita, Angie,' he said. 'For both of us – we're so glad about it – it wasn't planned, but now it's happened we're over the moon.'

Over the moon – I thought of the padded cell and the crescent moon and my lost Paul, and rocked and sobbed and rocked and sobbed until Rita ran out of the room.

I curled up on my pink eiderdown, drawing my chin up to my chest and closed my eyes on both of them. Eventually I slept. A long time later – when it was dark – I woke to find Rita sitting beside the bed holding a cup of tea.

She said she was sorry and she wouldn't have hurt me for the world, and that I must take a yellow tablet. She'd rung Doctor Rose.

She told me Mum was downstairs and wanted to see me.

'Not so much that she bothered to come to Epsom,' I said. 'And I don't want to see her. I'm too tired. I'm going to sleep.' I screwed up my eyes, tight shut against them all. I could do it. I could make them all go away."

Angie blinked and looked at Andy, who was pushing a rivulet of sweat from his brow. He avoided her gaze.

"I could always do that, Andy. I could always make them go away."

Chapter Six

Andy and Angelica came out into the sunlight, screwing up their eyes and putting on sunglasses at the same moment.

"It's even hotter than yesterday," said Andy. "I'll never sleep tonight."

"You need to buy a fan. I have mine going all night from July to October. It's unbearable otherwise. I'll get you one in Soller."

They walked along the dusty lane in quiet companionship.

"I suppose going through all that has made you – sort of accepting," Andy said. "I sensed it when I first met you. There's nothing judgmental about you. You accept people as they are."

"Do I? Good. I hope so. There's no point in expecting otherwise. People are as they are. Can you tell me about your Emma now you're not painting?"

"I don't know what there is to tell. We had four fantastic weeks – I thought we both felt the same, and then she started getting irritated with me and nine days ago she packed her bags and flew home. Something went wrong somewhere, but search me…"

"Sex?"

"No, The sex was fantastic up to the night before she went home. It was me basically, I guess. She said I was cold – I told you. But I didn't feel cold – anything but. I don't know what she wanted."

"Tarzan, sweetheart. That's what she wants… Tarzan to sweep her off her feet – *not* to send her text messages and give sensible economic reasons why he hasn't flown home after her."

"I can't buy that. You don't know Emma. She's not some dim bird – she's got an Upper II in Applied Mathematics – she's about to earn mega-bucks in the City and she owns a flat in Islington. Maybe I was just a holiday lay and she didn't feel what I felt at all. Maybe she suddenly got bored and wanted to get shot of me. Maybe there's some other bloke waiting back home in London."

"You'll never know if you stay here, will you?"

They turned up the dusty drive to the small hotel, Angie

pushing a cascading purple bougainvillaea into place as she passed. The blue sea glinted down below, a small white sail bobbing past timelessly.

"You really think I should just leap onto a plane tomorrow and turn up on her doorstep?"

"With a complete armful of red roses! Not just a bunch, now, Andy! But every rose you can get from the market that morning. This is the time for the Big Gesture!"

"Sounds a bit corny to me. I'm not sure she'd go for it. Anyway, I've told you – I'm a penniless art student. I can't afford air fares and armfuls of roses. Sorry, you're just a hopeless romantic – you should be writing novels."

"Bet Emma is too, underneath the maths books. I'll buy my painting – at whatever stage it's at. You've got to buy an air ticket home some time – this is not the time for penny-pinching, Andy. Believe me. The Big Gesture! It's a sure winner – unless of course you're right about the guy back home."

They entered the dining room which was cool and pale green, with an enormous ceiling fan bringing blissful relief from the midday heat.

"Buenos tardes, Jose!" she smiled, as the short, plump waiter approached.

"Una botella de Rioja blanca, por favor."

"Si Senora."

They sat together in the corner of the room after Angie had greeted the guests at all six tables. "Le gusta el paisaje?" she asked, as he gazed across the bay window to the garden beyond.

"Si. Muy bonito."

She smiled,

"Your accent is good."

"Do you think so? I've got a good ear and I have been here five weeks – Julio doesn't speak English, don't forget!"

The waiter brought the wine in an ice bucket and Angie checked the label.

"Dos tortillas de los prelados, Jose, por favor."

"Si Senora."

"Do you do any of the cooking yourself?" Andy said.

"I used to. For three years I did *everything*. But now I have Julio – no! A different Julio – he is a wonderful cook.

Sometimes I make one or two dishes, but I can take things a bit easier these days. It's going so well."

"Is cooking what you finished up doing at St Ebba's?"

"Will you never drop the subject and get onto your own story? Yes, I did a little cooking and enjoyed it enough to get enrolled at Harlow College to do a year's Cookery and Hotel Management. But get back to Emma – can she cook?"

"I've no idea! I suppose I don't really know her as well as I thought I did. We ate in the café or bought bread and cheese and pâté and ate on the beach or in her uncle's garden. He wasn't there much – he works in Soller as an estate agent, so he's out all day. I never heard her mention cooking!"

"Who does she live with in London?"

"A girl called Susie. They were at uni together. This is good – I usually drink the really rough red plonk in the bar. Did you say Rioja? I thought that was red."

"It's the region. They do make delicious reds but also some superb whites. This is a favourite of mine. Salud!"

"Salud. So you think I should fly back and surprise her? Risk getting sent packing even though I can't afford to fly back here if it's definitely over?"

"Yes. I do. You seem fixated with the idea of painting here. You'll paint much better in London, I'm convinced of it. The summer's over for you here. It's finished. You'll learn nothing more."

"Maybe you're right. I do feel kind of 'end of the seasonish' about things, I guess. Except about you. I'm so glad I met you."

"So am I! I just hope it works out for you and your Emma. Oh good, here come our Tortillas! Mmm – don't they smell marvellous?"

"Terrific. I'm starving – I haven't eaten anything since last night."

An easy camaraderie fell over them and he wished she were twenty years younger. Or he twenty years older. She was so easy to get along with.

"Is there a man in your life over here?" he asked suddenly, drinking his second glass appreciatively.

"Not at the moment – no. There was – until last December. But this year has been a kind of – how shall I put it? A quiet, retiring-to-lick-my-wounds sort of year. I have a dream now – which will sound silly to someone of your age…"

"Why will it? Try me."

She twiddled the stem of her wine glass and it was a while before she spoke.

"For years I hardly thought of him. But since my relationship with a local travel agent ended rather unpleasantly last Christmas, I've been dreaming of someone – someone from way back. Of Roy Cavalieri. I dream I shall meet him again…"

"Your first love? How long since you saw him?"

"Over twenty years. When I left Harlow College, I got a job in London through Gabbie, bless him. We kept in touch, and he knew someone who knew someone – you know how it is in London. I was cooking chic dinner parties with this smart woman in Fulham for rich brats who liked to entertain but didn't want the hard work, or didn't know how to cook. And then I met Roy again. But he was married."

She tossed back her drink and placed the glass carefully on the tablecloth.

"He seemed very happy and settled, with twin baby daughters. Italian men *adore* their children."

"How did you meet him?"

"I was cooking a dinner party for eight in a small but smart terraced house in Clapham. This was before Clapham became fashionable and it was the first time I had been there. The hosts were two journalists who worked long hours and wanted someone to do the cooking. It was only the second dinner party I'd done on my own so I was a bit keyed up. I'd made moules mariniére, beef Wellington, a Dutch apple tart and lemon syllabub. They had a very pretty house, and I was fiddling with some freesias when the first guests arrived. I thought my heart would stop forever when I looked up and there was Roy! He was staring at me with the same look of disbelief I was giving him. He looked as gorgeous as ever.

'Angel? Is that really you?'

"We fell into one another's arms in an entirely natural way, to the consternation of the two hosts! Roy's wife, I noticed, when I finally made myself look at her, was smiling in a pretty relaxed fashion. We were then introduced, and Roy said to her, 'You remember I told you about my lovely Angel, well, here she is, as beautiful as ever! Angel, meet Heather – the most wonderful wife and mother in the world. We have two perfect daughters – twins – you would adore them!'

How could I have forgotten his transparent honesty? He had never lied to me and obviously never lied to her. She came over and hugged me and stunned me by saying, 'Roy loved you very much you know – he told me. I'm so happy to meet you at last!'

What more was there to say? Thank heaven I'd already cooked the dinner – so I served it and went home and cried myself to sleep. I was so devastated and happy for him, all together. He had a lovely wife; that I could see. And he had babies. She had Roy's babies."

The fan punctuated the silence and Andy ate his tortilla deliberately.

"Then what?" he said at last, as Angie didn't seem to be intending to say any more.

"Then what, indeed. I worked like crazy, and made a real success of the dinner party circuit. I started living with a Canadian – that lasted almost three years, but I never really lost my heart to him. Which was a pity, cos he was a real sweetheart, but human nature is strange. I can hardly remember what he looked like. Whereas Roy – I can see Roy's face in every detail."

She picked up her fork and began toying with the crab omelette in a half-hearted way.

"Will you do something for me, Andy?"

"Course I will. What?"

"Will you accept £300 for your painting and second – when you're back in London – will you try to trace Roy for me and let me know where he is? Please?"

His young, bony hand covered hers on the crisp white tablecloth. He squeezed her fingers hard.

"Is that yes to both requests?"

"Of course it is. And thanks for the money. But I don't want you to be hurt."

"Don't worry about me. I may have a great investment in that portrait. Imagine – when you're famous and winning Turner prizes and whatever – I shall be able to say 'I bought Andy Carter's first portrait – of me'!"

They both laughed but she had tears in her eyes.

"Don't let Roy know it's me enquiring about him though, for God's sake. I don't want him disturbed in any way. He'd be – what – fifty-eight by now. God – it doesn't seem possible, but he would. If his marriage is still fine, then so be it."

"You are going to get hurt, aren't you? You're bound to be disappointed and then what?"

"I'm a tough cookie – don't worry about me! I can manage. I have so far. Tell me, do you need me to sit anymore to finish the painting? I don't actually mind if it's incomplete; might be a metaphor for my life – interesting!"

"There's nothing incomplete about you, Angie. You seem to me to be the most well adjusted human being I've met for ages. I can paint all afternoon, I don't need you to sit any longer. How can I find out about air tickets?"

"The agent in Soller. His office is highly efficient. There's a brochure at Reception. The telephone number's on it."

"Do you mind if I go and ring now?"

"Course not. I think you should. I'll fetch us iced coffees."

Andy scraped back his chair on the white tiled floor and rushed to the reception desk. Angie smiled. "Ain't love grand?" she thought to herself, as she finished the rest of the bottle of wine and left the table to find some coffee.

It was now half past two. A lazy heat had settled over the hotel and nothing stirred. The air hung heavy with eucalyptus and pine and the guests had all retired to the garden or gone down to the tiny beach to swim off the rocks. Julio and Jose were sitting at the table in the kitchen having a glass of wine and a joint. Smoking cannabis in Deya was no more unusual than drinking Sangria, and she rather liked its sickly scent with its happy association with her years in Majorca. They were reliable workers and did not often smoke until their work was done. All six hotel rooms were booked until the end of September and two well into October, so she was content in her little world. Well, almost. This place plus Roy would be perfection. But could anyone ask for that? It seemed unreasonable even to want it. And other longings? They must be kept at bay. As she had always done, for years. Kept hidden and buried, where no one could touch them.

Andy flew out of Palma Airport on the following afternoon, his portrait of Angie finished to his own satisfaction and £250 in his wallet. No portfolio of stunning paintings to impress the Slade admittedly, but maybe Angie was right – maybe he'd paint something truly impressive back in London. He couldn't see Carolyn agreeing to sit for a painting, but maybe Emma would. If only he didn't feel so unsure of himself where Emma was concerned. He rang her flat from Gatwick and heard an answer machine. He slammed the receiver down, undecided as to his strategy. According to Angie, it should be first stop the florists and armfuls of flowers, but his own instinct told him Emma would regard this as crazy and a silly waste. He hesitated, considering the options, as he waited for his suitcase to appear on the carousel. Maybe just one perfect white rose? Or nothing at all? Just himself on the doorstep? After all – he had nothing to offer her but himself, so she may as well get used to it. Yes. That seemed right. Just himself – declaring undying love and devotion, and offering a candlelit dinner at some sexy Italian restaurant tonight. That sounded fine.

He caught the coach to London feeling more hopeful. Angie couldn't know how Emma would feel – there were twenty-four years between them after all. It was a completely different world. She just had no idea how different everything was now. She hadn't got a daughter, and she hadn't lived in England for years. She couldn't possibly know.

The coach whined to a stop. It was now eight-fifty. The air in London was foul and he hated it. He longed to be back up in the mountains of Majorca breathing the pure air and feeling the sun on his face. He found Emma's flat quite easily. It was a Victorian conversion and not as grand as he had anticipated. He rang the bell while his heart pounded like a laundry press. Footsteps tapped across a wooden floor. The door opened and a short blonde with owl-like glasses stared at him.

"Yes?"

"Uum. Is this Emma Pearce's flat?"

"Yes. She's out right now."

"Oh. What time will she be back?"

She shrugged.

"No idea. She's gone clubbing. Can I give her a message?"

"No. No message. Don't say anyone called."

He almost ran down the steps. "Gone clubbing." Thank God he hadn't stood there like a prat with a truckload of fucking flowers. Why had he listened to her? Why had he allowed a blousy fat woman in Majorca to tell him how to run his life?

He caught the first bus that stopped and left Islington through the blur of his tears or the light drizzle falling on the grimy glass of the number 52. He would not go back. He would not go on a wild goose chase after Roy Bloody Cavalieri. Let them all rot in hell.

Chapter Seven

"Café, Senora?"

"Con leche, gracias Jose."

Angie sighed, closing the petty cash book. She'd probably added it up all wrong; her mind certainly wasn't on balancing figures this morning. She had been remembering too clearly. Had it been a mistake pouring out her past to that boy? It had been instinctive. She was missing him in a funny sort of way.

She stared out of the window and got up, taking her coffee out into the small area of garden by the washing lines, where guests could not come. The morning was sweet and warm, with a light breeze flapping the tablecloths like sails leaving harbour.

Poor Rita. How guilty she'd felt when she'd let slip about her baby. And now, this morning, a letter from Rita asking if that same child, Clare, could have her honeymoon in Deya! A wedding she would have to fly home for, she supposed, and then arrange the best suite for her niece and new husband in her hotel. She was flattered they wanted to come; she had always kept Clare at a distance.

Sitting on the grass hugging her knees, she remembered that first weekend out from St Ebba's. By the Saturday morning she had calmed down and had even managed to congratulate Patrick on the baby and they'd had an almost normal day; shopping in the High, watching TV and going out for a Chinese meal.

"You frightened us silly last night, Ange," Patrick had said, munching a crispy pancake. "But I can see now how much better you are. That doctor knows a thing or two, doesn't he?"

"Gabbie? Oh, Gabbie's lovely. And there's Ginger — I talk to her a lot too."

How distant they'd all seemed from a Chinese Take-away in Harlow.

Angie had toyed with her chopsticks, turning over the sweet and sour pork and wondering what they were doing in Walnut. She could hardly admit to Rita that she was missing the mad world of St Ebba's, could she? Longing for the security of the fixed routine and sense of community, however bizarre. She felt an interloper in their lives; they needed to be together on their own now, and she needed to be back where she belonged – in St Ebba's – talking to Gabbie about her feelings and asking him how she would be able to cope with Rita's baby.

When she returned she waited impatiently for her Wednesday meeting. She sat outside his office, heart thumping; did she imagine it, or did he seem excited to see her too? He was, as always, entirely professional and proper but there was an undercurrent.

"How did the home visit go?" he'd asked, tapping his fingers together in the now wonderfully familiar way.

"Disaster," she admitted. "Well – on Friday it was. I suppose it sort of got better. My sister's pregnant – she's going to have a baby."

"I see."

They talked about Angie's feelings of envy and guilt and loss, and how she was going to cope.

"You'll have other children in the future," he'd said. "You're so young. There's plenty of time."

But she did not believe him. She knew she never would. It was her punishment. She had thrown away that precious gift – discarded it.

"In a few weeks we shall try to enrol you at Harlow College. Are you quite happy to stay living with your sister?"

"No. Not now. I want a place of my own by the time... by the time she has the baby."

"Are you sure? It could be a healing process, helping your sister with her first baby. I can help you through it."

"No. I want to be independent. When I'm well enough to leave here I want to find a room of my own. Not too far from Rita – but separate."

Angie picked at the grass at her feet and remembered those early days in the bedsit in Harlow. She'd enjoyed the course, and had a room with a motherly woman called Cazzie Gilbert, who'd cooked her evening meal, which was just what she needed after a day's cooking. When she'd qualified, Gabbie had helped her by introducing her to the smart woman who ran private dinner parties, and she soon became popular, partly due to her culinary skills, but mainly to her looks, which improved through her late twenties. She made a success of her career and bought a large, airy flat in Snaresbrook, which was convenient for central London, and not too near Rita and her family. It was a smart, clinically white apartment; even the sofa was white, with permanently plumped cushions, which were rarely sat upon. She tended to work all hours and return home and go straight to bed with a whisky. Or a man. There were plenty to deaden her painful thoughts of her lost baby and Roy.

Charlie was the last – a Canadian actor she picked up at the cheese counter in Sainsbury's. They'd got talking about goats' cheese and before she knew it, she'd asked him back for a coffee and Danish pastry. He was 'resting' at the time, and living in a grotty bedsit in Leyton in East London. When he saw Angie's apartment he raved about it so much that she had suggested he move into the spare bedroom as her tenant, when she had only known him for an hour! Madness – but her instincts had been OK – there wasn't much wrong with Charlie. He was tall and blond with an open, smiling face. 'A six foot hunk' was how a girlfriend described him, but although they became lovers for almost three years, Angie really felt more sisterly love towards him than desire. He was such a thoroughly nice guy to have around. When he wasn't working (and that was more often than when he was) he would prepare supper and clean the flat and arrange flowers, so that for the first time in her adult life she felt she had a home to return to.

When Charlie announced he'd got a bit part in a film being shot in Majorca, Angie had said, "Great! I've never been there. Let's go! I'll take three weeks' holiday and join you. Spring on the Med – what could be better?"

She had a small wedding reception to cook for on May 7th, but the following day she joined him in Palma. There were a few production hitches but it was all going to be sorted out in the next week.

The film crew were great. It was like one continuous party. Palma was a beautiful city in May. Holiday makers had not yet arrived in their droves, so they had a fantastic time eating in harbour restaurants, swimming and water-skiing in the mornings and dancing half the night. After two weeks, Angie realised she had picked up one restaurant tab too many, and was heavily overdrawn.

"I'm going to have to go home and earn some money, sweetheart," she told Charlie. "I'm running out of cash. I thought you were here to work?"

"The filming will start next week," he'd promised. "There's a production hitch, that's all. Why don't you chuck it all and stay here? You could cook for all those stinking-rich folks living in Palma – retired Brits – Germans – you'd make a pile of money! You know you would."

"And what about the winter?"

"I could get bar work. We could do it together, honey."

"I thought you wanted to be an actor, Charlie."

A silence had fallen between them. He was never going to make it as an actor. He was a nice guy who enjoyed living off other people and not working too hard. It was why he was such good company – considerate, amusing, unstressed – of course he was unstressed – he hardly ever did anything.

So she had flown home. After Palma, Snaresbrook in the wettest June on record seemed dismal. The next few jobs were boring and the people difficult. Charlie telephoned ecstatically from Spain; the weather was perfect, the film crew missed her, he missed her, finances were sorted. His small part in the film was great. He was terrific in it. When was she coming back?

Angie looked around her empty flat and stared at the wall behind the car park and thought of the twinkling Mediterranean. She went shopping in Sainsbury's and scraped her car on a concrete bollard and thought of the street markets near the harbour. She climbed into bed on her thirty-fourth birthday alone, without even a cat for company and thought of Charlie's neat brown body and cried. She cried not because she missed him, but because he was all there was, or ever had been. No little boy had ever run around this flat, and now he would be fourteen. He had been fourteen days old when she had last gazed on him, and now – fourteen years. It was unbelievable. So grown up – was he tall and lanky like her dad had been? Should she look for him? She believed that would be unfair. Where was he now? Where in the whole world was he now?

The next day she cooked lunch in a Directors' dining room in the city and was sworn at for spilling a spot of minestrone onto the sleeve of the Chairman's jacket. She apologised, sponged his jacket, walked out into the rain and put her flat on the market. She booked a flight to Palma the following week, and left her keys with the estate agent. In three months her flat was sold, all her possessions given to Rita or shipped to Majorca, and she and Charlie were finished. She knew as soon as she saw him at the airport that she hadn't done it for him; she had done it for herself. For Majorca. For sunshine and olive groves and pine trees in place of rain and sliced bread and dirty pavements. For pink bougainvillaea cascading over white walls instead of grubby privet hedges. For the aquamarine of the shallow sea over rocks and the deep purple of the distant waters at Puerto Andraitx where she sailed to Dragon Island. For the winding mountain road she took to Deya one winter's morning, when a light sprinkling of snow capped Puig Mayor like an iced bun. She was alone on the bus; just a gnarled old guttural Majorcan driver and herself.

She'd got on the bus intending to stop at the town of Soller and browse around. But Deya was waiting, beckoning her like a lover around a doorway, and she was enchanted.

"Aqui mismo por favor!" she shouted to the driver as she saw the terracotta roofs of Deya below.

"Si Senora – enfrente de la cafeteria. A dos minutos."

"Gracias. Adios Senor."

She'd jumped off, unaware that there would not be a bus back that afternoon because the driver would have a heart attack as he pulled out of Soller. How other people's lives affect our own unawares! She sat in the café drinking coffee and savouring the delight of falling in love again – but this time with a place. As near Paradise as she was ever likely to find, and her heart sang with the beauty of it. She had come home.

When the bus driver hadn't turned up, she had stayed the night in a tiny room over the café. The next morning she had explored every inch of the village; watching the women gossiping over their washing in the communal trough where they still banged sheets and hung them like flags across the street. She had climbed up to stand by the stone church of Saint John the Baptist, looking down on the shimmering Mediterranean so far below. In December the breeze in the mountains was cold, but the sun still gave enough warmth by midday to allow her to sit bare armed outside on a terrace to eat squid and drink a glass of white house wine. Afterwards, relaxed and off-guard, she had watched the quiet hum of the village winter life buzzing around her. Old women in black dresses carrying baskets of eggs, long crusty sticks of white bread, apples, lemons and oranges – the ubiquitous 'naranjas' – on carts, in baskets by the roadside, on market stalls, a few shrivelled and dried hanging like Christmas decorations on trees, quite forgotten.

She watched a young girl scuffing her way in raffia mules down the dusty track opposite, a plump dark baby on one hip.

"I need a walk," she thought, and calling the old woman in the café, paid the bill and left a 'propina' on the table. She had turned hesitantly outside and looked up the track the girl had left. It seemed to beckon irresistibly.

She had walked for some minutes, past scratching hens and a one-eyed cat who watched her malevolently, passing a rusting Seat and a small terracotta-topped cottage, and then stood still, looking at the wrought-iron gates ahead. They were grand gates, dusty black with good quality iron work, allowing a glimpse into the green garden beyond.

She had stood completely still for a moment, aware in the bright sunlight that this was a special place and a special time she must not ignore. The gnarled olives within were like friendly old retainers working slowly in the quiet of the afternoon sun. She had closed her eyes and smelt the pines and the eucalyptus trees and the salt in the air from the sea. She put a hand out to touch the gate; it swung open at her touch with a quiet creak. The dusty path to the house was scattered with last summer's almond husks, and the almond trees lined the path with their promise of delicate blossom to come.

The house, a square villa made of local stone, seemed fortified, with dark green blistering shutters closed against the midday sun like slumbering eyelids. A black kite circled overhead; the whole place seemed asleep – at siesta – waiting for someone – waiting for her to arrive that day. Her feet crunched on the stones as she walked around the back of the neglected building. No one seemed to be living there. The heavy studded wooden door had a bell-pull, so on impulse she gave a tug and waited. She had no idea what she was going to say, but no one answered. Rooks wheeled overhead, calling suddenly, and then screeched away down the mountainside like a motor cycle cavalcade.

She continued walking all around the house until she found a small side window without shutters. She cupped her hands around her eyes and peered inside. At first she could make out nothing, and then, gradually, as her eyes became accustomed to the gloom, she saw a dark narrow corridor, peeling paint, an air of abandonment. And yet a magical pull; a sense of recognition. She walked round to the front of the house again and stared at the shutters. Nothing. There was no one there. She would have to ask in the café, though she was uncertain whether her Spanish was adequate. After seven months, it was becoming quite serviceable in Palma, but the guttural Majorcan dialect in the mountains was difficult to decipher, and like country people everywhere, the Majorcans did not try too hard to be understood.

The old woman who owned the café was wiping tables with a rag.

"La casa..." she began uncertainly. "La casa grande – al final de la calle a mano izqueirda – esta cerrado?"

She did not look up but continued wiping the table and sniffing, a drip on the end of her long nose.

"Si. Cerrado. La famillia viaja. Cuanto tiempo se quedaron usted?"

So it was shut up and the family away. Angie explained she had to return to Palma on the next bus, and the old woman lost interest in her, shuffling off into a back room without another word. As the bus rumbled slowly along the mountain road, she leapt up, but there was plenty of time. The driver sat outside the café, explaining to an old farmer what had happened to his predecessor, and gossiping; he was in no hurry to return to the city. The timetable was flexible here. She found a seat in the back and waited impatiently for the bus to start. Even in winter she had some work to do. Tomorrow she would cook lunch for a German family living in Palma – fourteen people. Charlie had been right – her name was being passed around the well-heeled circles in Palma.

He had gone; once the film had finished and their romance over, he'd disappeared with a crowd of hippies to winter in Ibiza.

76

She wasn't sorry, and was ready for a new start. The money from the sale of her flat was now sitting in the bank, and although it wasn't a huge sum it would be a nice deposit should she choose to buy a house in Majorca. But wasn't it complicated? Should she risk sinking all her money into a foreign property? She gazed out of the dusty bus window as it started up, and sighed at the spectacular beauty all the way down the mountain road. Steep swathes of pine swept down to the rocks and the turquoise sea. Not until the flat road out of Puerto Andraitx and beyond Paguera did the beauty fade and the monstrous towers begin to blot out the sky-line.

She had not seriously considered buying a house here until now; until she had felt captivated and ensnared by Deya, and had experienced the strange and unexpected sense of homecoming in a village she had never seen before. It was not as if the villa were even for sale, as far as she knew, but she had a growing conviction it would one day be hers. Her own place; in a way that the flat in Snaresbrook had never been. A sanctuary. That was how it had felt. A fortress against an unkind world. She had settled back in the seat with her eyes closed as the bus trundled slowly through the dirty suburbs of Palma, and dreamed of Deya.

A series of surprising events had followed. The next week she had cooked dinner for a Spanish lawyer and his English wife, Liz. While clearing up, Liz had been helping her, glad of a new English person to befriend in winter, and the conversation had turned to property owned by foreigners. Liz had emphasised the importance of using a Spanish lawyer, and asked if Angie had anywhere special in mind.

"Only a silly dream," she'd replied, polishing a glass carefully.

"It's not even for sale. It's a house up in the mountains – would make a wonderful guest house – but I don't even know who owns it. It's empty – in quite a bad state – I think the family travels a lot."

"My husband has an office in Soller – I'll ask him to check it out with the real estate office there. What's it called?"

"Casa d'Or," she said. "It's this lovely honey-coloured stone. It's up a dirt track opposite the café in Deya and it has a wonderful garden full of olives and almond trees. I'm quite mad

– I don't suppose I could afford it even if it was for sale."

But it had been. The agent in Soller said it had been empty for two years and for sale most of that time. No one wanted it. It was too big for most people as a family home and it was a mess and too inaccessible for a business man to live in. The elderly couple who had owned it as their holiday villa had spent years in Barcelona and had died within six months of one another. Their heirs wanted it sold. Angie's excitement was contagious and Liz went to look at it with her.

"You're *crazy*!" she said, standing in front of it on the coldest, greyest morning in January anyone could remember. The mountain road had snow and was impassable further up, and the village children were throwing snowballs for the first time in their young lives. Everyone was a target! Even the elderly priest who remembered snow for a week in 1964.

The agent turned the key and opened the heavy door and they stepped inside. A musty smell made them cough, and Liz threw open shutters and windows muttering, "You are mad, Angie – utterly mad! It's horrible! How can you say it's wonderful? It's dark and shabby and lonely. You couldn't want to live here – not on your own!"

"You're seeing it at its absolute worst," Angie had retorted, hurt and angry to discover no one shared her enthusiasm.

"It's a wonderful house. And look at the view! Come over here."

She was clinging on to the window sill and gazing from a side window in one of the three reception rooms. Through a gap in the snow covered trees was a streak of steel blue.

"You can see the sea from here! Imagine the view from upstairs! Oh Liz! I shall have the room above here for my bedroom! Oh – it's heaven!"

"But Angie – think! How would you fund repairs? It's in a dreadful state. You may have a deposit and perhaps you could earn enough to pay off a mortgage, but how would you get it into any sort of order? You can't have guests in this place – no one would want to come!"

"I've got six months, Liz! Six months until the season starts, haven't I? I don't need to use all my cash in a deposit, do I? I can keep – say – oh, six thousand for the most urgent repairs. I can do the decorating myself. I'm a very strong woman, Liz. Really! There must be local plumbers and electricians and carpenters up here in the village – they'd be cheap, wouldn't they? And glad of the work."

Liz had laughed.

"You wouldn't be able to talk to them up here! You wouldn't make yourself understood! And what about an income while you're doing all this decorating? How will you cook to earn the money to pay the mortgage?"

"I'll work here half the day and cook in the evenings. I just need some introductions to people who want dinner parties in Soller. Palma's too far."

"You won't get enough. It's a small place. Soller's not sophisticated enough, like Palma. Maybe you could work in a restaurant, or a hotel, but…"

"Nothing's going to stop me. I *know* I'm going to buy it. I just feel it. This is going to be my home, Liz. My first real home ever."

And then the letter came from Rita. Their mother had died. Quite sudden – quite unexpected. A thrombosis. Only sixty-one – no age. Such a shock. Angie had flown home immediately and found that the house in Harlow had been left in its entirety to Rita and Angie. Len the Louse had been playing around once too often and had apparently never been a husband – only a live-in-lover. He had always been referred to as 'my husband' and she had told her girls that they had married, but apparently they had not. The house had belonged to their mother and now it was theirs. Len was out – where they'd always wanted him to be.

"It's so strange," Rita had said. "That horrid house we both hated so much is now worth £45,000. We're rich! Beyond our wildest dreams! And fancy mum having lived in sin all these years! What a hoot! Do you remember when they went on holiday to Bournemouth and came back and told us they'd got married? Why d'you think she said that?"

"For the neighbours' benefit, I imagine," Angie had replied, looking round her old room and experiencing the forgotten churning stomach.

"Patrick's going to buy us a caravan in West Runton in Norfolk – and we're going to have a new kitchen. Dear old mum

– fancy her seeing the light about Len and *doing something about it*! I never thought she had it in her."

"Neither did I. Don't you want to move, love? Leave Harlow? Go somewhere nicer?"

Bur Rita had been emphatic.

"No. Harlow's our home. The kids are at school now and happy. We all like it here. There's loads to do and we've got friends. No, we shan't move."

Angie did not shed a tear over her mother's death. She had never forgiven her for replacing her father so quickly, but she now felt she had redeemed herself. Her share would certainly make Casa d'Or a real possibility. She'd hugged Rita tight at the airport, knowing it would be many months before they'd meet again.

"Come out and stay as soon as my hotel is up and running, Rita. Promise?" she said, laughing as she pushed her suitcase onto a trolley.

"Blimey! Your *hotel*! I thought it was a little guest house last time you mentioned it – it's the bloody Hilton now is it?"

"You know me – think big! Come out in September! Before the kids go back to school. Have a week – you won't believe your eyes. It's so gorgeous!"

"I'll find out when they go back. We'll come out at the end of August p'raps. Take care, I'll write!"

They'd waved until Angie disappeared through Passport Control, and she sat on the plane knowing her future lay in Deya, and at the Casa d'Or.

Chapter Eight

"No way. I told you I didn't want a bloody birthday party – so don't start blaming me. It's my frigging birthday, mother, and if I don't want a party, who the hell would it be for? Think about that."

He had never hung up on his mother before and it felt deeply unpleasant. He downed a can of lager from the tiny fridge and hoped it would wash the bad taste away, but it did not. He could picture his mother's hurt expression; the slight frown, the chewed lower lip. She would be trying to reorganise her own features at this very moment; to compose herself and 'put a brave face on it' as she always did.

Andy sat back down and lobbed the can into a waste paper basket, throwing his head back on the greasy sofa and sighing.

"Oh God, why did I do that?" he said aloud.

"But why does she *always* take over? I should never have come back before term started. I should have stayed in Deya until the day before and then I would have avoided all this shit."

The next drama would be dad of course. He'd be round wanting to see his paintings, and when there weren't any he'd go off again about him wasting his money, and why wasn't he doing a proper job instead of farting about trying to paint. Hell, what a mess.

The phone rang and he closed his eyes. Probably his mother again – he'd have to apologise.

He got up and said "I'm sorry" at the same second he recognised Emma's voice saying, "Andy! When did you get back?"

"How did you know it was me? I asked your flat-mate not to say anything."

"Well she ignored you, fortunately. She described you very well – how've you been?"

"Oh, all right I guess. How about you?"

"Pretty miserable actually. I've missed you."

His heart began to pound and he struggled for the right words. "Have you? I thought you wanted to get shot of me."

"Idiot! Of course not. I just – I just needed to get back

home. Anyway – I start my new job in ten days – when can I see you?"

"Now?" He felt ridiculously happy. "What's wrong with about forty minutes? As soon as I can get to you?"

She laughed. He'd almost forgotten what a fabulous sound her laugh was. "Brilliant. See you soon then. Bye."

He punched the air and leapt up shouting, "YES!" as he threw his clothes onto the floor and ran into the shower. She had felt the same way. He hadn't got it all completely wrong. He needed to buy armfuls of flowers and tell her he loved her. Forget all the nonsense and blow her over. That was the trick. The strains of Eric Clapton singing 'You look wonderful tonight' floated up from the flat below and he sang along with it as he soaped his thin brown body all over.

The woman at the flower stall said, "What, *all* of them, love? You sure? Be thirty-five, forty-five, fifty quid. OK? They're luverly roses, mate – you won't get fresher than that nowhere – not even in Arrods."

Weeks in Deya had their effect.

"Call it forty for cash," he said chirpily.

"Can't do it, lovely. Gotta make a livin', ain I? Forty-eight's rock bottom. Honest. You try buying that lot in the West End and see what it cost yer. Hundred nicker more like."

He handed over the money grimly. It was not in his nature to spend so extravagantly, but he wasn't prepared to throw out Angie's advice at this point.

He reddened as he tried to jump on a bus holding this ridiculous armful of horticulture and was relieved that no one commented during the thirty minute ride to Islington. The scent invaded his head as he walked quickly along the street to her flat once again. Would Susie be there or could they be alone? His heart lurched as he ran up the concrete steps and pressed the bell. Feet ran along the corridor and she was in front of him; her pretty tanned face beneath her dark elfin haircut, a white T-shirt appearing to be all she was wearing above her long brown legs. Everything stirred and he stumbled over the doorstep saying, "Oh Emma, it's fantastic seeing you again." The flowers were dropped on the floor and his arms crushed her body to his.

"Darling," was all she said, as their mouths met and the

twelve miserable days and nights apart melted away.

She said, "It's OK, there's no one here. Susie's gone to work." And led him by the hand into the bedroom where they fell onto the blue duvet in an explosion of desire.

Afterwards, as he stroked the damp tendrils of her hair back from her forehead, he said, "If only you knew how terrible I've felt. I thought you had really finished with me. Didn't want me. That my life was over, you know."

She locked her leg across his hairy thigh and kissed his chest.

"Idiot," she said at last. "I just needed to get away – it was all so quick. I need to know if it was just a holiday thing, or if you really meant it. You can seem so – well – detached sometimes. I needed to know what you would do next. If you really cared about me."

"I cared enough to cut short my time in Majorca and bring you great armfuls of roses – you ungrateful woman – which are now withering on the floor while you take advantage of my body!"

She laughed and sat upright.

"So you did! An amazing bouquet – I'd better put them in water."

Her naked body, brown from Majorcan sunshine, ran into the corridor and he lay back listening to her delighted cries as she rediscovered the roses.

"Andy – they're *beautiful*! And the scent is fantastic. The whole flat will smell like a country garden. They are just perfect. Of course I haven't got a vase anything like big enough. What shall I put them in? I've only got this jug-thingy."

"Plonk them in the sink and we'll go and buy a huge earthenware pot. Then when we go to the country at weekends you can bring back armfuls of cow parsley and poppies and I'll paint them."

"Brilliant. I'll have a quick shower and then we'll do that. Oh, Andy, it's so fabulous having you here. It's a bit dream-like actually. Why did it take you so long?"

He considered a stain on the ceiling for a moment. He had his male pride, after all.

"I was painting. I was commissioned to do a portrait in

Deya, so I had to finish it. I got the first plane out of Palma when I'd finished."

That much was true.

"A commission? How did that happen?"

"The woman who runs that little hotel up the long drive past the café. Do you know?"

"No. We never went there, did we?"

"No. That's why I biked up there after you'd walked out on me. I was so down I didn't want to go anywhere we'd been together. When I found the hotel I went in for a beer. She was in the bar."

"Oh was she? What's she like?"

She stood in the shower-room doorway, with her head on one side.

"Fat and fifty! No – that's really unfair. She's forty-six – a little bit overweight, blonde, very friendly. Nice – I got on really well with her. A great character – and while I was drawing, she told me her life story for some reason. Come here, temptress, I don't want to go shopping in the least!"

She laughed, and came back into the room with one perfect white rose in her hand. She placed it on his flat stomach, laughing, and he pulled her on to him, putting the rose in her hair.

He held her by her shoulders and gazed into her deep brown eyes like a drowning man.

"Who were you out with when I called?"

"Nobody. No one in the least important."

She leaned down onto him, the scent of her hair and the roses filling his whole existence and the rhythm of their love making rocking the room.

Afterwards they slept for a while, their quiet breathing overlaid by traffic sounds from the street and voices from the flat upstairs. Somewhere a baby cried. They slept on, exhausted and fulfilled, until the telephone woke them.

"Hello?" Emma's voice was sleepy.

"Em. You OK? It's me."

"Hi. Yup, I'm fine. I was asleep."

"Oh right. Is everything OK? Only I was going to a film but I'll come home if you want me to."

"No. Everything is fine. Andy's here."

"Oh right. See you later then. Bye."

She put the phone down and smiled at his sleepy face.

"That was Susie. She's going to a film."

"Great."

She snuggled against him and pulled the duvet up to their necks. The room was becoming chilly.

"I shall cook us some pasta," she said. "With peppers and mushrooms and prawns – if I've got any mushrooms."

"Con setas y gambas!" he laughed. "And a bottle of white Rioja."

"You'll be lucky. There might be a bottle of Frascati somewhere."

"I never asked if you could cook. I suppose you can – you do everything bloody perfectly, don't you?"

"No. I don't cook much actually – mostly pasta – you know, chuck it all in. My mum is a wonderful cook and she spoils me, so I never do any at home. And Susie's quite keen, so I'm lazy. I got loads of cookery books for my twenty-first but I don't actually use them."

She hopped into the shower and he followed. It was a large power shower and very impressive. He sang as he soaped her but she slipped past him, grabbing a white fluffy towel from the radiator and encasing herself like a parcel.

She fried onions and mushrooms while he dried and dressed. Her kitchen was a small, narrow galley with everything neatly to hand. A bit of a contrast to his curtained-off unit in his bedsit. There cans of beans vied for shelf space with underpants and socks, but here utensils hung from cup hooks and a large fridge-freezer was well stocked and sparklingly clean. Everything about Emma was neat and methodical; a mathematician to her bra straps, he guessed. He'd have to have a bit of a blitz on his room before he could ask her round. She slit open the packet of frozen prawns and a large ginger cat appeared, miaowing piteously.

"That's Susie's cat, Jasper," she said. "We'll have to feed him or he'll be an awful nuisance. Could you give him one of those rabbit thingummies from the cupboard behind you? No – little square tins. Thanks."

Andy peeled off the lid and poked at it with a fork as the cat wound his way first around one leg and then the other. He left a trail of fine hairs on Andy's black jeans as he buffetted his head against Andy's shin bone.

"Persistent little bugger, isn't he?" he said, as he placed the dish on the floor beside a metal waste-bin.

"He's lovely – he came with Susie about eight months ago. It works very well. I've known her all my life."

They sat side by side on the sofa, watching an old war movie on the TV. They drank the Frascati and ate the prawns and kissed and Andy thought he couldn't possibly be happier.

"I need to paint you, Em," he said, as she pulled the heavy curtains shut against the outside world. "Will you sit for me? I'd love to paint you nude – will you let me?"

"How long would it take?"

"Depends how it goes. Maybe three days. I wouldn't need you to sit the whole time. I need one long stretch for the preliminary drawing – say four hours?"

"OK. Maybe at the weekend. Tomorrow I'm going to see someone at the office where I'm going to be working. I start on Monday week."

"Right. I have to go and see my mum tomorrow and make certain she's not going ahead with plans for some poxy party she thinks she's running for my twenty-first."

"Why? Don't you want one?"

"Absolutely not. I hate the idea. I loathe big family get-togethers anyway – let alone this one with me in the centre of it."

"When is it?"

"Three weeks. I need to see mum anyway. I was pretty foul to her on the phone this morning."

"I had a great big bash for mine. It was terrific – I really enjoyed it."

"You didn't have the complication of warring parents, did you?"

"No. I didn't. Shame for your mother though – I bet she was really looking forward to it."

"I know, I know, but she hates dad's new bird and he'll insist on bringing her and grandma will get upset – it's much easier to just forget the whole thing."

"So you'll go and see your mother tomorrow and suggest

something else – like a small dinner party or something?"

"I hadn't thought. Also – Angie – the woman I painted at the hotel – did ask me to do a bit of detective work for her – she wants me to track down her old lover!"

"Wow! How exciting. Does she know where he is?"

"No, that's the point. He was in London twenty years ago and married, with twin daughters. He's got an unusual name – Italian – Cavalieri. Roy Cavalieri."

"Let's look in the phone book then and see how many Cavalieris there are in London. I've got one somewhere."

She rummaged in a cupboard and emerged triumphantly, holding a new dark blue phone book.

"Cav – cava – how do you spell it?"

"Give it me – Cavalieri."

He ran his fingers down the page.

"Here we are! Cavalieri. God – there's only three – one in WC2 and one in Tottenham and one in Fulham – it can't be that easy can it – not after twenty years."

She passed him the telephone and sat, hugging her knees, tense with expectation. He jabbed the numbers twice, making a mistake and swearing impatiently.

"What's the time?" he asked, as it rang. "Is it a bit late to be ringing?"

"Quarter to ten."

"493824. Hello?"

A male voice answered, deep and well-spoken.

"Er – is that Roy Cavalieri by any chance?"

"No. This is Richard Cavalieri."

"Oh sorry. I must have the wrong number."

"Hang on a minute – Roy is my father. He doesn't live here though. Who is that?"

Andy paused for a second, stunned at the ease with which he had been able to trace Roy. Of course, it might not be the right Roy.

"He won't know me actually. Could you give me his number?"

"He lives in Italy. D'you want it?"

"Please. Hang on – Emma – pen!"

Pen found, he wrote in the margin of the directory and said,

"Thanks. Has he lived there long?"

"Two years. He retired there. Can you tell me who you are?"

"My name's Andy Carter but it won't mean a thing to him. I met somebody who knew him a long time ago and they asked me to look him up for them. Thanks for your help. Cheers."

He blipped the phone off and turned to stare at Emma.

"Bloody hell, I think I've found him!"

"It may not be the same Roy Cavalieri, of course. I mean – they'd all be of Italian parentage with a name like that, wouldn't they? So it doesn't prove it's him, does it?"

"No. And Angie never mentioned a son. She said he had twin daughters. I should have asked him about that. D'you think I should ring back and ask if he's got twin sisters? I mean, that would be pretty conclusive, wouldn't it?"

She unfolded her arms and touched his cheek sympathetically.

"You really care about this, don't you? You only painted her picture, after all – and they're so old now, what difference can it make?"

"I dunno. She's quite special. I really liked her. She's had one hell of a tough life and all through the bad times she kept dreaming about her first love – this Roy – I mean it could all be rubbish. He may have been a complete shit – but she thinks of him as this perfect bloke she let slip away and then he married someone else."

"What was so bad about it?"

"She had a kid and was made to give him up – have him adopted. They did that a lot in the sixties and seventies. These old nuns told her she was being selfish wanting to keep her own baby."

"Oh God, that's so terrible. Was it Roy's baby? Did he know?"

"No, it wasn't his. She'd left him and gone to live with some pimp and was having an awful time. I'm not sure who the father was – she never said. She was only nineteen."

"God. So who had the baby?"

"He was adopted by some Catholic family. That's all she was allowed to know. No contact of any sort. She finished up in a nut house with a complete breakdown."

"I'm not surprised. But now she could find out! By law you can make enquiries and trace your child – surely."

"I don't know. She never mentioned that. Perhaps she doesn't know the law's been changed, or perhaps she thinks leave well alone. After all she's lived on Majorca for eleven years."

"Oh Andy – what if we traced her son? Do you know the year and where she was living at the time?"

"You crazy? We can't do that! She only asked me to look up Roy, not delve into some guy's private life. He'd be – let me work it out – he'd be twenty-five or twenty-six by now. He might not even know he's adopted. Anyway it's none of our business."

"Well you might be able to get a name for her – you know – the family – a starting point for her if she wanted to find out?"

"It's not our business, Emma. I think I'll just ring this Italian number tomorrow morning and see if it is the same one. His wife's name was Heather."

"You do that. Imagine finding her son, though! You can't tell me she doesn't want to know where he is and how he's doing. Surely she'd love to know, even if she doesn't want to disturb his life."

"I'll think about it. I'd better get going soon. Where's the nearest tube?"

"You don't have to go. Stay here with me, Andy, please."

Her arms entwined his neck and she kissed his lips gently.

"I give in!" he laughed, rolling her back onto the sofa.

Emma could not leave thoughts of Angie's lost child. It seemed to her such an untidy, unfinished business. She worried at it like a nun with a rosary. She awoke early the next morning, her left leg numb with the weight of Andy's upon it, and slid quietly into the shower-room. She tried to imagine herself giving birth and then handing that baby over to strangers. It was impossible. What vile cruelty to bring such pressure on a kid of nineteen, only days after giving birth. How dare a *nun* of all people decide what was best for a mother and child. Her sense of outrage grew as she considered it. "The poor, poor woman," she thought, her eyes filling with tears. "No wonder Andy felt sorry for her. She has a right to know what happened to that baby. It's much more important than what happened to Roy Cavalieri."

Andy put his key in the lock and opened the door. He could

smell bacon frying and hear The World at One on Radio 4.

"Hi Mum," he said sheepishly, as he saw her shaking the frying pan in her immaculate kitchen.

"Andrew! Why didn't you say you were coming?"

She put the pan down, her face lighting up with joy. His guilt deepened.

"I just thought – well – I'm sorry about yesterday morning – I was pretty pissed off about something and I'm afraid I took it out on you. Sorry."

He kissed her in an embarrassed fashion but all was forgiven.

"Oh, I knew you were upset about something! Auntie Stella said, 'He'll come round. He'll see sense – everyone celebrates their twenty-first, after all!"

He sat down on a high white stool behind him.

"Mum. Listen to me. I do not want a party. OK? You've got that? Absolutely no party."

She looked away and turned to the pan of bacon.

"Bacon and egg sandwich?"

"Yes please. That'd be great. With loads of ketchup."

She opened the fridge to remove two eggs and sniffed.

"When Chris was twenty-one, he said his friends talked about the party for weeks afterwards."

"Well I'm not Chris, am I? I thought at the time what a waste of money such a big bash was. I'm a student, and I could do with the money. Honestly – I'd rather have the money, actually."

His mother cracked an egg on the side of the pan and watched it spit and bubble for a minute.

"Why? I thought you could manage."

"I know. I thought I could. But I met this girl in Deya, and I want to move into a flat with her quite soon. I've gotta be able to pay my way – not sponge off her – she's got this fantastic job in the City she's just about to start. I can't live like a leech, can I?"

She pushed a fading strand of hair back from her brow.

"No. But you don't have to move in with her, Andrew. I thought you liked your flat and you've only known her five minutes."

"I met her the first week I was in Deya and she's the one for me, Mum. I just know it. It's completely irrelevant how long I've known her."

"Well, it isn't really, is it? I mean – you're a student – it'll be years before you can think of settling down and buying a place and committing yourself to a mortgage. Do be sensible. You know how relationships can go wrong anyway – look at your father and me, for heaven's sake."

He looked down at the black and white tiled floor in desperation. He couldn't talk to her. He just couldn't. Everything led to The Failed Marriage. He was sick of it.

"Some people meet young and stay together. And nowadays they live together before 'settling down' as you call it. I'm an art student, for God's sake, how can I settle down? But I love Emma and we're going to be together and I need all the cash I can lay my hands on at the moment. I really would appreciate your seeing that and not wasting hundreds of quid on a fucking party I don't want."

He turned and stared miserably out of the kitchen window. He had failed again. He had come to make it up and had already lost his temper. Why did his mother have this effect on him?

"Your egg's done," was all she said, but her face had a crumpled look.

"Thanks, mum – that's great," was all he said, his heart sinking. He munched awkwardly, the silence hanging heavily between them.

"Aren't you having one? You were cooking bacon when I came in."

"I'm not hungry now."

She wore her martyr's crown like a saucepan – tough and resilient.

"Emma suggested a small dinner party – you know, just you and grandma and Paul and Sophie and Chris. What do you think? Then you could meet Emma."

"I think that perhaps this Emma should wait until I've at least met her a couple of times before she takes over the social diary of this family."

"Oh, mum – don't be silly. We're just trying to find a compromise, that's all. I'm more than happy to do nothing – you know I am. I don't care if the day goes by completely unmarked. Honestly."

He continued chewing as his mother ran the hot tap onto the

frying pan and shot a jet of Fairy Liquid onto it forcefully.

"Maybe you don't. It's quite important to me though. I haven't got much else to look forward to, have I? Sophie and Chris have had theirs and we've had Sophie's wedding, so I was really looking forward to your twenty-first. I'd gone to such a lot of trouble – it's only three weeks. I booked The Royal Oak months ago."

"But *why* did you? You knew all along I didn't want a big bash. I'm sorry if you're disappointed but let's do a small dinner – ask Sophie what she thinks. And grandma. Maybe we could still have it at The Royal Oak."

"I'd booked the functions room. I'll lose my deposit."

"Oh, mum. Why do you always make things so complicated?"

She wiped a piece of kitchen towel around the pan and placed it in a cupboard, straightening her back wearily.

"All right. I'll ring them and cancel it. But I think you're very selfish. I'll have to tell your father to cancel the champagne he was providing."

"Oh, was he now? Well maybe he'll just send a couple of bottles and let me have a cheque instead. It would be great it he did."

She looked older, he realised with a pang. Fifty next birthday. Unbelievable that she was only three years older than Angie. He put an arm round her drooping shoulders awkwardly.

"Oh, mum – you're your own worst enemy – d'you know that? Just relax and forget the Big Do. Ring dad and have an intelligent conversation about it. Or shall I? Do you want me to talk to him?"

"You ought to go over and see him. He was saying he hasn't seen you since Easter. I think he feels you never bother."

"Well – I can't stand Carolyn. He knows that. It's awkward. If he'd meet me on his own it would be OK, but she's always there. Silly tart."

A shadow of a smile flitted across her tired face and she turned away.

"Tea or coffee?"

"Coffee please. You have some."

It could have been worse. She hadn't cried and he hadn't

given in. A faint smile was victory indeed.

Emma had spent the morning at her new office and by lunch time was sipping Chardonnay in a City wine bar, nibbling an egg mayonnaise sandwich thoughtfully. She had already rung Richard Cavalieri's number again and checked that he did indeed have a mother called Heather and twin sisters. His parents were still together and lived near Florence. Roy had retired from running a chain of successful nightclubs, which Richard now ran with an older partner. This much she knew would close a book for Angie. The disappointment would be terrible, so she must be offered some good news and alternative hope.

Emma was determined to trace her son, however long it took.

She was becoming obsessed with the idea, and was not accustomed to failure. She had been told that Angie's sister still lived in Harlow in Essex; she would start with her. It was odd how passionately she was beginning to care about these people she had never met. Maybe they would go back to Deya in the spring. She would not stay at her uncle's place again. She hadn't yet told Andy that one factor in leaving so abruptly was her uncle's changing attitude. He'd realised she had a lover in Deya and had changed from being a distant but friendly relation to becoming unpleasantly familiar and leeringly attentive. She had begun to feel uncomfortable. Had he made a definite move she could have dealt with it; she was a strong, confident young woman – but the general atmosphere was unpleasant, so she had left. It had begun to affect even her feelings for Andy. She'd not mentioned it to him in case he had confronted her uncle – the last thing she would have wanted. There'd been no proof anyway and he was her mother's cousin. Now she had a week before starting her new job; she would dedicate a few hours a day to detective work.

She put her glass down on the bar and unflicked her mobile.

"How'd it go?" Andy asked.

"Not bad. Neil Dyson – the guy I'll be working with – is really nice, but his number two seems a complete shit. He was trying to put me down the whole morning. So I'm not exactly thrilled at working with him. Great offices though – on the fourteenth floor!"

"Shall we meet up somewhere? Can I do some preliminary sketches?"

"No. Not today, Andy. I want to make a start on our detection. That was your Roy Cavalieri. I rang Richard again. His mother's name is Heather and they're still happily married."

"Right. Oh well. What d'you mean then – detection?"

"I want to go to the home for mother and babies in Harlow where Angie had her baby, and maybe see her sister too."

"Oh no! I thought we'd agreed…"

"Not really. We don't need to tell anyone if we do find out where he went, but imagine how Angie is going to feel when she knows Roy is a no-no. You can't tell me she doesn't wonder about where her child went on a pretty regular basis."

"I've no idea – and neither have you. It's none of our business. God – I'm really sorry about Roy. She had this romantic idea he was sitting waiting for her somewhere – maybe divorced or widowed – and they'd go off together into the sunset. Daft, wasn't it?"

Well there you go. We can offer her something much more exciting than her disappointment, can't we? Meet me at Liverpool Street Station and we'll go to Harlow. Two o'clock?"

"Hell's bells. I'll meet you at whatever gate the Harlow train goes from. Two o'clock."

She clicked off the phone with a small smile of satisfaction and finished her drink.

They caught the 2.25 from Liverpool Street. Andy was holding a piece of paper with Rita's address on it and Emma had looked up the Catholic churches in the area.

"There doesn't seem to be a home for mothers and babies now," she said, staring out of the grimy window as the train pulled grindingly slowly out of the station towards Tottenham Hale. "I mean – these days – even Catholic girls who made a mistake would either have a termination or keep the baby, wouldn't they?"

"I've no idea. I've certainly never heard of anyone giving up a baby for adoption in our age group – but then I hardly know anyone who's had a baby. Rare creatures, babies, almost extinct in our circle!"

He laughed ruefully, watching the dingy terraced houses with strips of dusty rubbish-strewn earth rattling past. Occasionally one would startle with a riot of flowers and be left behind in the dirt and greyness again.

"We could ring up the Harlow Catholic priest!" Emma said suddenly.

"We could have done that from home," he retorted, stretching his arms above his head in boredom.

They looked at one another with a mixture of disappointment and failure.

"That's too passive for me," said Emma. "I needed to get up and *do* something. This is supposed to be detective work, Andy. You've got Rita's address. It won't be a wasted journey – you'll see."

The train lurched into Harlow New Town station and Emma flung open the door, almost beheading a small boy standing on the platform.

"Sorry!" she called, as she rushed off into the sunshine to the taxi rank. "Let's take a cab – he'll know where Almonds Avenue is. Can't be far."

"Sounds like an expensive day," muttered Andy as he beckoned a mini cab over and followed Emma onto the back seat.

"103 Almonds Avenue, please," she said, her tanned cheeks now flushed with excited anticipation. She clutched his arm. "Oh, this is really exciting. *I know* we're going to find out something. You'll see."

Andy smiled at her and slid his arm along her shoulder, stroking her neck and kissing her temple quickly.

"If you say so," he said. "Though why Rita stayed here when she came into all that money beats me."

He looked out at the uniform outlines of identical brick houses. They went round identical roundabouts down identical straight avenues for ages. Emma leaned forward and said to the driver.

"Was there a home for mother and babies' round here, do you know?"

He was a middle-aged man with greying curly hair and a red face. He half turned.

"A what?"

"A home for unmarried mums – you know?"

"Nah. Not round here. I bin ere for seven yer an I never eard of it. I fought you wanted Almonds Avenue?"

"Yes. We do. Just wondered if you knew where the home used to be, that's all."

She sat back in her seat, biting her lip.

"Of course if Rita's in there's no problem, but…"

"She probably won't tell us a thing, We're complete strangers. How does she know what we want to know for?"

Emma pulled away, looking petulant. He withdrew his arm and watched as the driver took a left and then slowed down.

"What number d'you say?"

"103 – please."

"Ere yar. 103. That'll be eight quid."

"Right. Thanks."

He fumbled in his jeans' pocket and produced the money as Emma leapt out and went bounding up the concrete path to the square brick house. He made a mental note to speak to her about his finances, but not now.

It was a small house, but detached, so maybe she had moved, but not very far. It was a tree-lined street, not unpleasant, but lost in a maze of similar streets – so similar that Andy wondered how the occupants ever found their way home at night.

Emma was ringing the bell and almost jumping up and down. There was an old Ford Escort in the drive. No one came. She rang again, and they waited, glancing round expectantly. Just as they were turning to go a spotty boy of about seventeen peered through a side gate, in tattered shorts and a vest.

"What d'you want?"

Emma almost pounced.

"Hello! Are you Rita's son?"

"Yeah. Who are you?"

"You won't know us. Is your mum in? We're friends of Angie's – you know – in Spain?"

"No. She's at work."

Emma's face fell and Andy stifled the words, 'I told you so'. He changed them into, "Does she work near here?"

"Just up the road – she works at the Centre."

"The Centre? Where is that?"

"The Medical Centre on the High. Up the road and turn right and then left. OK?"

"Brilliant. Thanks. Bye."

Emma was now bounding, hardly able to contain her excitement, and Andy almost ran to keep up with her.

"Are we just going to barge in where she's working?"

"We certainly are – now we've come all this way!"

"We can't Emma. She'll be busy and it's not an appropriate way of dealing with this."

"I know. We can see what time she finishes, can't we? It's twenty to four, so she may be starting a shift or she may be about to come off. Let's at least find out, Andy. Please."

He held her hand and was surprised at how warm and moist it was.

"You're really into this, Em, aren't you?"

"Yes. It's funny. I never even met Angie and yet I really mind about her. I mind about her being made to give up her baby and I mind about her knowing that Roy's still happily married. It would have been so neat if he'd been on his own too, wouldn't it?"

"I know. I'd hoped he would be too. She said he'd be nearly sixty. At least he's still alive. They could still meet up."

"Yes! After all, at their age they'd only be looking for companionship, wouldn't they?"

"Not Angie! She's quite sexy in a way. I even felt it. She's got a physical charisma – I bet she was absolutely stunning ten years ago. He's a lot older, of course."

They found the concrete medical centre with its smell of disinfectant and summer bodies. The waiting room was packed. At a semi-circular work station sat two middle-aged women, staring at computer screens, and Emma bounced up to the more attractive of the two – a redhead in a white T-shirt.

"Rita?" she said, and the women looked up simultaneously. The other woman, thin, with greying mousy hair said, "Yes. How'd you know my name?"

Emma gnashed a perfect set of small white teeth and said.

"We know Angie. When do you finish work? Could we

possibly talk?"

The woman looked flustered and anxious.

"Angie? Is she all right? I mean – she's not been taken ill or anything?"

Andy stepped forward and put his hand on the desk, trying to reassure her. "No. Angie's in great form. I saw her just a few days back in Deya. The hotel's going really well and she's looking terrific. In fact, I painted her portrait."

Both women looked at him with greater interest.

"Oh! What you mean you painted a picture of Angie?"

"Yes. That's right. I'm an art student at The Slade, and she bought it. She was really pleased with it. But what we're here about is a private matter. Could we meet up when you've finished work?"

The woman looked doubtful and stared at Andrew and then Emma.

"Well. I don't finish until six and then I like to get home. I've a meal to get ready."

Emma leaned forward.

"It is really important. And we've come all the way from Islington specially. Just ten minutes – *please*."

"What about your coffee break, Rita?"

The other receptionist smiled at them in an encouraging way and then noticed a red light on.

"Mrs Russell for Dr Khan please in Room two," she called.

"Your break's in ten minutes, I can manage."

Rita looked doubtful.

"It's very busy. But if you're sure, Paula. Just a few minutes. Sit over there and I'll come over in ten minutes then."

"Is she like Angie?" whispered Emma, as they sat down.

"Nothing at all. I would never have guessed they were sisters and this one looks about ten years older. This one looks so dull and Angie is so full of life. Blonde – probably dyed but it looks good. Glamorous and tanned. Big boobs – lots of nice jewellery. Fun, she's great fun."

"Well this one doesn't look a lot of laughs, does she? But I dare say the sulky lump at home doesn't help and she hasn't quite the same view from her bedroom window, has she?"

She was walking towards them in a navy pleated skirt and

pink nylon blouse. Her flat shoes were scuffed and her expression worried.

"We can sit outside," she said, and led them through a side door onto a dusty garden bench.

"Now, what's this all about then?"

Emma sat beside her and looked into her pale face. The eyes were grey and anxious looking.

We're trying to trace Angie's son," she said. "We feel she has a right to know. What do you think?"

Chapter Nine

Angie was watching the rain lashing the almond trees and wondering how soon she could hang out the sheets to dry. Rain was rare in August, but when it came it was often torrential for a short time, and then everything would look fresh and clean. She turned away from her bedroom window and smiled at the portrait on the wall. It was really very like her. It was unfinished, of course, but she approved of that. It seemed symbolic of her life – without Roy, without her son. Always unfinished and incomplete. That was what it amounted to.

She sighed; and she decided to join her new guests in the little bar. A nice German couple called Heistermann and two young girls from Sidcup; she'd go and be sociable – tell them all about the coastal train to Soller and the monastery in Lluch. She was a good hotelier and she knew it. She could always talk to anyone at the right level; she knew instinctively. 'You're a great communicator, kid!' That's what an American staying there had told her. She liked people, that was what really mattered.

She looked at her reflection in the long mirror on the back of the door – everything was a bit too heavy, she admitted, but not bad on the whole. Not bad for forty-seven. She'd told Andy she was forty-six; what a ridiculous piece of vanity – as if it mattered to a lad of twenty-one! She was as ancient as a Pict to him, and taking a year off was a stupid habit she'd got into lately. She shrugged and applied more lipstick. Her hair was thick and wavy, her teeth brilliant, why worry? She looked approvingly at the cream linen dress and gold sandals, and closed the door with a soft click. Senora Vila was coming out of her room at the same time; an elderly widow from Barcelona who visited the Case d'Or every August for three weeks; a treasured guest.

"Buenos tardes, Senora!" she called. "Me tomo un refresco!"

"Tardes! No tiene ganas de beber alcohol?" her guest laughed, knowing Angie quite well. They chattered as they approached the lounge where Senora Vila sat down with a newspaper and Angie patted her shoulder and passed on into the little bar.

The two young girls from Sidcup were perched like parrots on the bar stool, sipping Cokes.

"Hola!" she said, and they giggled.

"Hi!" said the more adventurous one, who had booked the holiday.

"How come it's raining? It's not meant to rain in Majorca!"

"Ah well, up in the mountains the weather's a bit different from Palma, but it doesn't often do this in August. It won't last; and everything will look fabulous when it stops. Brilliant colours – marvellous. Would you like another drink? Try my Sangria."

"No thanks. We don't drink. We thought we'd do that train – you know – the one on the poster?"

"Soller. You won't be able to get down there now. The last bus went at 3 o'clock – unless you want me to ring Alfonso Valeria – he's the taxi driver around here. He'll take you down but it will cost a lot more than the bus. I could take you tomorrow – if you'd like to wait until the morning."

"What d'you think, Steph? Shall we go tomorrow?"

Stephanie was blonde with an elfin haircut and freckles. She shrugged her shoulders as she sucked the last dregs of cola from the bottle through a straw.

"I don't mind really. We could go tomorrow. What are we going to do now then? It's still raining."

Angie could remember feeling cheated by rain in Majorca. Now, of course, it was a delight. Although there were many underground springs on the island, every gardener was glad of rain and this year April had been drier than usual.

"It will stop soon," she promised. "Have you climbed down to our little beach? It's lovely – very secluded, and you can swim off the rocks. By the time you've got your things together I bet the rain will have stopped. It's quite a climb back up though. Still – you're young and energetic – shouldn't be any problem for you two."

She passed on into the kitchen to have a word with Julio about this evening's menus.

"En primer plato..." Julio began, scratching his ear with a fork – a distressing habit she would dearly like to abolish but didn't know how.

"Gazpacho, sopa de pescado, melon con jamon Serrano.

Segundo – calamares, merluza al Horno, chuletas de Cordero, Pollo al Ajillo."

"Muy bien. Y para postre?"

"Tenemos pestinos, flan, alaju, queso…"

"Un poco detodo para me!"

She looked around the spotless kitchen – the stainless steel table, the huge electric stove. But she could still see it as it had been that first day – a dark hole of a room with a chipped china sink and a greasy wooden draining board, a grimy Spanish stove run on camping Gaz and ripped floor boards. She glanced through the tiny side window and saw that it had stopped raining as suddenly as it had started; as if someone had turned off a great tap in the sky. The pines dripped and shone; she was so lucky to be in this wonderful place. She touched Julio's arm with a squeeze of appreciation, and left. She would hang out the sheets herself; Maria had gone home early today as her mother was poorly. She knew all the intimate details of their lives; they lived as one big extended family. Jose's women problems, Maria's mother's gall stones, Julio's wife's pregnancies, Conchita's sore feet. They were her family now; they'd been with her for years and she loved them all. She knew they would never leave her, and hoped that Julio's eldest son would come and learn a trade in a year or so. He was fourteen – that awkward age; but a lovely kid.

She hoisted the big laundry basket onto one hip and stepped out onto the wet pine needles. Her sandals squelched and the cool rainwater felt good between her toes. She heaved damp sheets across the line, enjoying the fresh smell of laundry in the mountain air. She breathed in deeply and stretched. He had unsettled her; of that there was no doubt. The three days of pouring out all those memories to Andy had been both a release and an enslavement; she couldn't keep the memories at bay now. Whenever she was alone they came flooding back. Maybe it was her age; at forty-seven there would be no more babies. That was final. Not that she had ever expected it. Or maybe it was that now she didn't have to work so hard, she had the mental freedom to wander. In the early days here she had worked a fourteen hour day, and when she finally fell into bed had slept the exhausted sleep of the labourer. There had been no space to think. Now she had the liberty to remember; and she didn't know whether she wanted to. Maybe she should drive the girls down to Soller now – there was shopping she could do and their chatter would keep thoughts of her son at bay. And that other time – those bitter days only Gabbie had known about. Never shared with Rita, never told to Roy. Hideous days and nights of loss and pain – almost forgotten. Another life. He was another life. He'd almost be twenty-seven now – twenty-seven in December – two days before the end of the year. She still couldn't look on a tiny newborn baby. It was manageable once they were a few months old; then they held no memories; but newborn infants were quite unbearable, and she had never visited Rita in hospital with any of her three. No – that tiny, red-faced, shrivelled scrap with dark hair could not be looked upon without such pain.

"You're so young – you'll have another child," Gabbie had assured her, but even at twenty she had known she never would. The guilt would never go away. She didn't deserve one. She had given hers away.

She leaned her head against a white linen pillow case, its damp coolness a balm as the heat of the afternoon sun reached its normal August intensity. She turned and pegged the last sheet onto the line, hearing the scrunch of gravel and the sound of young voices as Stephie and Nicola set out for the beach.

"I will take them to Soller in the morning," she muttered. "The car'll be like a furnace now, anyway."

Herr Heistermann was standing in the side garden gazing approvingly at the wet bougainvillaea, washed clean by the rain.

"Now I shall swim!" he announced. "And after – a coffee!"

She smiled, and watched his thin, stiff legs setting off along the lane. Nicola and Stephie were already out of sight, and his panama bobbed past the old olive trees until she turned, making a mental note to check that all the bedroom shutters were fixed against the afternoon sun.

Would Andy bother? Would he really try to trace Roy? And what on earth was she digging all that up for anyway? It was ridiculous; it could only be a dreadful disappointment. Why look for more when life here was so good? She was a fool to herself – why not be satisfied with what she had? Maybe she'd call Rita tonight and have a long chat – there was Clare's wedding to discuss and the honeymoon here at the Casa d'Or. She needed to hear Rita's voice and talk. She looked at her gold watch – a present from the agent she'd parted from at Christmas – it was four-forty. She always reckoned on an hour to herself between 4.30 and 5.30 – before she changed and checked the tables and worked behind the bar herself for an hour. It was a good opportunity to talk to her guests in a relaxed fashion, and she enjoyed it. What would Rita be doing at this time in England? Three-forty? She might be at home or she might be at work. She could try.

She closed her bedroom door and picked up the white telephone and dialled England. As usual – all lines busy. She hung up and had a shower. Wrapped in a blue silk kimono, she tried again. This time she was connected and it rang and rang.

"Hello?"

Damn! It was Stuart. She could never talk to Stuart; he was such an inarticulate lump.

"Hello darling! It's Angie! Is Rita around?"

"Oh hello, Angie! No – she's at work."

"Oh right. What time will she be back d'you think?"

"I dunno. About seven, I think."

"OK, I'll ring late tonight, darling. Tell her to expect a call around eleven – that's twelve here. I'm not usually back in my room until then. How are you? What are you doing at home in the afternoon then?"

"I've jacked me job in. But I'm looking around..."

"Right. Well good luck with that, darling. Hope you find something soon. Must go – tell mum I'll speak to her tonight. Bye now!"

"Right. Cheers."

She replaced the phone and looked out of the window.

Well, quite communicative for Stuart – growing up, she supposed. She smiled as she remembered him here one Christmas Eve – rolling on the stone floor in excitement at the thought of Father Christmas arriving in a Spanish mountain village. What fun they had had.

There was a late afternoon post in the mountains. Sometimes. If Alfonso Escalas bothered. Sometimes he didn't. But she saw his bicycle turning back down the drive as she opened the front door. She bent down and picked up three letters from the mat. The handwriting on a blue air letter caught her eye. She recognised it but could not quite place it for the moment. She walked slowly into her office, turning it over in her hand. The sender's name and address had only two lines 'Graham Bott, Ascot'.

She sat down quickly and tore it open, a mixture of excitement and anxiety struggling to dominate. She hadn't heard from Gabbie for a couple of years, apart from the annual Christmas card, and she read the letter with a sickness in the pit of her stomach.

Dear Angie,

I should have written to you months ago, but I was too sunk in depression with my own troubles to bother with anything other than utter necessities.

Izzie died in January. She had flu with complications which our GP didn't pick up on quickly enough, and pneumonia set in. I lost her on January 24th. You will know how tremendous that loss has been for me – we'd been married for almost thirty-seven years. I wasn't always the best husband in the world, and that makes it worse. I had retired from the NHS and so we had been spending a little more time together – although my private practice was and is still flourishing. My children have been marvellously supportive and I don't think I could have got through it without them – especially Jane, who lives in Ascot too and has called in almost every day, bless her.

I wanted you to know. She so enjoyed our holiday in Deya with you and we had often talked of coming out again but somehow just hadn't got round to it. Golf had rather taken over our lives and we spent the last three years taking golfing holidays in Portugal.

Dear Angie – enough of my troubles. How are you? Is that travel agent still giving you the run around? I imagine the hotel is doing tremendously well – it is so delightful it couldn't possibly fail. I gather Richard Branson has a rival concern up the road now? He won't have your personal touch! You are so good at making people feel at home and totally relaxed.

Something I could do with just now – maybe I should come out and see you sometime in the autumn – when the holiday season's quietening down. What d'you think?

I'm trying to get on with my life and not be negative. She was a wonderful woman and is terribly missed – not only by us but by the Rehab Unit where she still did a day a week. I find it hard to believe that something as ordinary as flu could have killed her.

Write back, Angie, I'd love to hear from you.

Fondest love,
Gabbie

"Oh no," she said aloud, reading the letter again, hardly believing its contents. How could Izzie be dead? That wonderful, vivacious woman – how could she be dead?

She would write straight away. No – she wanted to hear his voice. She would telephone him; she had his number somewhere.

She fumbled with papers in a drawer and found what she was looking for. She entered the numbers with tears welling up and listened to the phone ringing. No reply. An answer phone clicked in and she replaced the receiver. This was no time to leave messages on answer phones. She would try again tonight. She would suggest he came out as soon as possible. She would fit him in somehow – even if she slept in her office.

She left the room full of plans. Dear Gabbie; they had formed such a close relationship after she'd left St Ebba's. He had helped her with her first job, and she had often cooked dinner parties for him and his wife and for their children. For a brief time they had had a short, passionate affair, but it had ended in a warm and friendly way and they had never lost touch. Since living in Majorca the contact had been spasmodic, but he and Izzie had come out one Easter for a few days and they had enjoyed a marvellous time together. It was the kind of friendship which could be put down and picked up with ease; a gentle, caring sort of bond between them which meant a great deal to her. And now this – this awful tragedy. She must help him. She must let Deya do its magic for him, as it had for her.

"God!" Rita held a pale hand to her forehead. "What is all this? I thought nobody knew about that baby. I mean – we're talking about twenty-six years ago, for God's sake. Who are you anyway?"

Andy got up from the bench and walked round in front of Rita, who was by now looking quite contorted with anxiety. He crouched down in front of her and tried to look reassuring.

"I'm sorry, Rita. We've done this all wrong. I said we shouldn't have come here when you were at work. I'm really sorry. The thing is I met Angie in Deya a few days before I came back to London – I'm an art student – and we got on really well, and I painted her portrait. Well, when you're painting someone for hours on end you talk – you know – you're in quite an intimate position, sort of stuck there together with no one else around – and – well – she confided in me. Practically told her life story in fact."

"Had she had too much to drink? She knocks it back a bit sometimes, does Angie."

"No, not at all. We just got on really well and we talked. She's a terrific character, your sister. I think she's marvellous."

"Yes. Yes, she is."

Rita pulled out a crumpled tissue and wiped her nose thoughtfully. "Does Angie know you've come to see me? Did she ask you to? I mean, as far as I know she's never tried to trace that baby. Never. She put it all behind her and got on with her life. She's like that. And she's got a very nice life. You've seen it."

Emma was having none of this.

"Oh come on now, Rita! I mean – you've got children – could you have given one up and then not wondered how he was – every day of your life? You couldn't, could you?"

Rita frowned, as if this feat of imagination was beyond her.

"I don't know. She only saw the baby for two weeks. They took him away then – that was what they used to do."

"But it was obviously a dreadful trauma because she told Andy she had a breakdown afterwards. Didn't she?"

Andy put his brown hand on top of her workaday pair, now twisting the tissue into tiny pieces.

"She doesn't know we're here. We wondered if you knew

anything about the home where she gave birth."

"Oh, that's not here anymore. It's been an old people's home for years. You won't find anything out there."

Emma stood up impatiently.

"Who would know then? Presumably you never had details of where he went?"

"Oh no. No one was allowed to know anything. It was all very hush-hush. We were just told he had gone to a good Catholic family who could give him everything Angie couldn't – you know – family life, money, all that…"

"Who was the parish priest at the time?" Emma was hanging on to hope like a terrier with a rat.

"How the hell should I know? I'm not a Catholic. I don't really know why Angie went in there – although dad was one, and for a while I thought she might be going back to it. We went to a Convent school when we were kids."

"Maybe it was just because it was here in Harlow. Or maybe your doctor had some connection?"

"Could have. Dr Rose was our GP and he and his wife were Catholics – I'd forgotten that. They were ever so good to Angie when she was ill – driving me to see her in Surrey and bringing her home for weekends. They were marvellous, really."

"Then *he'd* know! Where will we find this Dr Rose?"

"In the churchyard probably. He died a couple of years back – heart attack. Mrs Rose is still around I think. They'd moved out to a village near Sawbridgeworth when he retired – only a few months before he died. Sad it was. I worked for him here – at the Centre."

Andy's heart sank. More tearing across the countryside, more train fares. This was getting out of hand.

"So you can't tell us anything at all about the family who adopted the baby?"

"No, I can't, and I still don't know why you're doing this. If Angie had wanted to trace him she'd have done so herself, long ago. She's a very determined person, is Angie. She doesn't need other people to do her work for her. Not Angie."

Andy stood up and brushed his jeans.

"Just what I felt. What she actually asked me to do was to contact Roy Cavalieri – or at least find out if he was still married and where he lives. But maybe I shouldn't be telling you that."

"Roy Cavalieri? Wasn't that the bloke she lived with when she first ran away from home? What the hell does she want to trace him for?"

"Who knows? I think she feels he was the only man she ever really loved. She asked me – that's all."

"God, that's weird. She hasn't mentioned any of this stuff to me for years and years. Not the whole time she's lived in Majorca. I thought she had forgotten all about it. There have been plenty of others since Roy Cavalieri, I can tell you."

"But no one special quite like him, apparently. She wanted to know if he was still happily married, and we traced him fantastically easily. He lives in Italy with his wife and is a devoted family man by all accounts."

"So you see..." burst in Emma, "the poor thing is going to be heartbroken by that – we've got to follow our hunch that she still needs to know about her son – who he is and where he is. He's in his twenties by now, after all."

"He'll be twenty-seven in December," Rita said quietly, brushing the tissue pieces from her skirt. "My eldest is twenty-six and he was born the year before. I'm not likely to forget that, am I?"

"Well, we'll try to contact Mrs Rose. You haven't got her address anywhere, have you?"

"It'll be in the Practice Address Book. The Centre still sends her stuff from time to time – like Christmas cards and that. But I still don't think you should meddle. It's not your business. Leave it be."

"I tell you what," said Andy, touching her arm. "We'll just speak to Mrs Rose and if she agrees with you we'll go no further, and whatever we decide we'll keep you informed all the way. OK?"

"And you won't speak to Angie about it until you've told me?"

"No. We promise."

"OK. I'll go and see if I can find her address; you stay here."

Andy and Emma were silent for a minute after she left them. Andy sat down beside her on the bench, his head in his hands.

"You think she's right, don't you?" said Emma after a bit. "You think we should leave it."

"Well of course she's right. Angie would have delved into it all herself if she'd wanted to know. It's probably too painful to stir up now – after she's made such a good life for herself out there. And what about him? He's older than us – imagine – he may not even know he's adopted. Can you imagine the shock?"

"Surely they would have had to tell him – you have to these days, don't you?"

"I've absolutely no idea and neither have you, but twenty-seven years ago they may have decided not to. He doesn't want some strange woman turning up and calling herself his mother, for God's sake, does he? Would you? I know I wouldn't."

"You could be wrong. He may have always known he was adopted and may have tried to find her and failed. After all – since he was an adult, she's lived abroad. Not easy to trace."

"Well we've got so far pretty easily. Look – Rita's got something."

"Sheering," she said, handing him a yellow post-it note with an address on it.

"Where's that?" he asked. "Is it far?"

"Not far. It's a village near Sawbridgeworth – you could take a train to Sawbridgeworth and probably get a taxi. It's quite rural – there might be a bus, I suppose."

"Thanks, Rita. We'll let you know how we get on. Could we have her telephone number too? Just to check she's in, you know. We wouldn't want to go all that way and find she's on holiday or something."

"Hang on a minute."

She disappeared again and returned almost immediately. Emma got out her purple mobile phone and stabbed the numbers impatiently. It rang for some time and was then answered by a soft, elderly voice. "312454. Hello?"

"Mrs Rose? This is a friend of Angie and Rita's – you remember? Angie Roberts? Rita works in the Medical Centre in Harlow – she's a receptionist."

"Oh yes, of course. I know Rita. She worked for my husband. What can I do for you?"

"Well, we wondered if it would be convenient for my friend

and me to come over this evening to talk to you about Angie. It's a confidential matter actually."

"Oh. This evening? Oh dear, let me think. This is rather short notice, isn't it?"

"Yes, I know. I'm sorry not to give you longer but we both live in London and we're in Harlow now, so obviously it makes sense to come straight to you, rather than from London on another day – if you possibly could. Rita is here if you'd like a word."

Emma handed her phone to Rita, who looked flustered again. "Oh hello, Mrs Rose. Sorry about all this – it's not my idea at all, I can tell you, but these young people met Angie in Majorca – you know that's where she lives now – she runs a hotel – well they want to talk to you about her. It's a bit of a cheek asking, I know. Yes. You don't have to say yes if you'd rather not. Especially as you're on your own."

"Well, I'm not on my own actually. My friend from Australia is staying, so it's not terribly convenient, but I do see that if they're in Harlow with you right now... let me see... what's the time now? Hold on a minute... Moira! What's the time, dear? Is it? Already? Good heavens. We must have some tea. I'd no idea. Well, dear, maybe if they came over straight away it wouldn't interrupt our evening too much. We could have poached eggs straight away, so that would be finished with by the time they arrived – what d'you think?"

Rita smiled and handed the phone back to Emma.

"I think she's saying yes if you're quick about it."

"Thank you *very* much, Mrs Rose. We'll get to you by train to Sawbridgeworth. Is there a bus from there to Sheering?"

"Not many. But there are always mini cabs at the station. I should take one of them if I were you."

"Fine. We'll see you in about an hour then. Thanks. Bye."

Andy looked at Rita and held out his hand.

"I will phone you this evening and let you know what she says. If she can remember – presumably she's quite an old lady."

"Not that old. She was a bit older than Dr Rose, and I believe he was about sixty-seven when he died. He was a lovely man; we were all really choked when we heard he'd died so soon after retiring. It often happens though."

"Thanks for your help Rita. We'll be in touch."

They turned out of the garden through a side gate, almost colliding with a buggie as they both rushed through together.

"This is costing a hell of a lot!" grumbled Andy, feeling aware that he had less than £20 left in his pocket. "I can't keep careering around the countryside in taxis —I'm a student."

"Don't worry about it. I'm going to have more money than I know what to do with by the end of the next month – all expenses for our detection work will be met by me, OK?"

She kissed his neck and hung on his arm as they turned down the street towards the station.

"Ok. It is your madness, after all. I'm not at all sure we should be doing it."

"Oh look – there's a bus – it's got 'STATION' on it – quick – let's get on that!"

They waved their arms frantically in the middle of the road and to their amazement, the driver stopped.

"D'you wanna get yourselves killed?" he moaned, as they boarded the bus.

"Sorry. It was an emergency. We must catch the train very quickly," said Emma, throwing a handful of coins into his bowl. "Thanks for stopping, anyway."

"I'd 'ave bloody run yer dahn if I 'and't!"

The bus swayed and whined into the station yard and they bought yet another ticket and stood on the windy platform.

"We've been incredibly lucky so far," said Emma, pinching his cheeks.

"Yes, but why are we doing it? I agree with Rita – if Angie had wanted to find him, she'd have done it. You don't know her – she's strong, determined, single-minded. She didn't need to wait twenty odd years for me to come along and sort out her life – believe me."

"Then why did she ask you to find Roy? Why didn't she just pick up a phone and do that for herself? She didn't though – did she?"

"Well, I guess she didn't feel she could ring only to have Heather answer the phone – I mean – what could she say then?"

"Exactly. Too delicate. The same applies to her son. We can do the background digging and then it's up to her. I'm not suggesting we kidnap him and present him to her in Majorca!"

"I wish I knew what you were suggesting, exactly. Oh good – here comes the train. Let's get it over with."

"We'll just have to see how things pan out. Go with the flow, darling – go with the flow."

Chapter Ten

"Hi Dad! How's you doing? How's Mama?"

"She's missing you all as usual. As soon as the girls left she was pretty down, but we're spending the weekend in Firenze – you know how she loves shopping – so that should buck her up. How's business?"

"Burton Street pretty good – Soho Place fantastic – but the other two a bit slow. We'll pick up though. Robert's in Brighton now. He'll sort it."

"Do you want me to come over?"

"No, no. We can manage. I mean – we'd love to see you, but when you're ready. It's OK. There's no panic. By the way, I had a strange call about you yesterday."

"How strange?"

"A guy rang asking if I was Roy Cavalieri and when I said my father was, he asked where you lived. He said you wouldn't know him. I gave him your number – I hope that was OK? He said something about knowing you way back – or somebody knowing you."

"Yes, he rang here. A guy called Andy Carter. Said he was a TV research assistant working for a programme about nightclubs in the seventies or something. Goodness knows where he got my name from. He did mention someone knowing me way back. I answered a few questions and that was it. How's Caroline?"

"Great. She loves her new job. And we just got *another* cat. Well, a kitten really. You know what Caro's like. What have you been doing with yourself?"

"The usual. Playing golf. Eating and drinking too much! Lying in the sun – swimming in Ricardo's pool – it's a tough life!"

"Lucky beggar. Did I leave you my Michael Crighton novel?"

"Disclosure? Yes – it's great. I'm half way through it. Don't give anything away – it's a real page turner."

"I'll send you another one. Must go – the other line's ringing. Give mama a big kiss for me."

"I will. Love to Caroline. Ciao!"

Roy Cavalieri hung up and walked across the tiled floor to stand in the open doorway looking across the terrace to the garden beyond. His wife, her dark hair now streaked with silver, was carrying a trug of roses up the steps towards him.

"Look at these, Roy! They could be English – I've never seen roses like this so late in the summer. They are quite perfect. And the scent! Smell this one – it's Louise Odier!"

He walked towards her smiling indulgently. He knew she still missed her old garden in Surrey, and was glad to see her growing delight in this Italian version at last. It was quite different, of course, but the view beyond was spectacular; green wooded hills as far as the eye could see. He adored being back in Italy; he had spent his childhood in Tuscany and returned when his mother had insisted he must have an English grammar school education. Not that he'd benefited much from it, he supposed, but his mother had probably been homesick for Britain anyway. He knew Heather was, and she missed her children being just a short car ride away.

"I just rang Richard," he said, straightening. "I think I should go over soon. Maybe next week."

Her face lit up.

"And stay with Richard and Caro?"

"Probably. Or with Carla. Shall we have a coffee?"

"How are they both? Is Caro back at work?"

"Yes. They're fine. They have *another* kitten apparently. I'll have a large black please. I'll sit out here for ten minutes before I change."

He could hear her humming quietly as she made the coffee. It wasn't difficult to keep her happy; she was such a sweet-natured woman. He sat gazing at his terraced garden with intense pleasure. He had earned this; all those years of working twelve-hour days and more. Throwing out drunks and dealing with crooks and double-dealers. He hoped Richard and Robert would have it easier, but he doubted it. Human nature didn't change. He'd go and check out 'The Cat's Whiskers' just the same. Sometimes they needed his gut reaction – Richard was only twenty-four after all, and Robert wasn't family. Brighton was a great place to have a club; should be an absolute gold mine, but it was competing with so many other nightclubs and gay bars and discos that he had to make sure they were targeting the right clients. He believed in his gut reactions – and for that you needed to be there. Richard hadn't the experience yet. He flexed his hands impatiently; maybe he'd retired too soon. There were days when he longed to be back in the thick of it.

"Here you are, darling." Heather placed the fine bone china cup in his hand and sat beside him. She placed a plate of apple and honey cakes in front of them and sipped her coffee tentatively.

"You know, I've been thinking…"

"When haven't you? That brain of yours never stops! What are you hatching now, sweetheart?"

"Well, your sixtieth birthday, of course."

"My God – that's a *year* away! I've only just had my fifty-ninth!"

"I know, but you have to plan these things well ahead. If you want decent caterers and a super place. Remember my fiftieth? Wasn't it wonderful? I shouldn't think anyone will ever forget it! And the food…"

"That was when I was making a great deal of money! We're retired now. Can't we just have the kids over and a meal at Luigi's? We'll have that pink champagne I've got in the cellar."

"No – that's not marking a special like your sixtieth. I was thinking of a big party in London – maybe the Café Royale again? Everyone we can think of – you know – after all, we've got more friends in London than we have here."

She put her coffee cup to her lips and sipped thoughtfully.

"God, darling, do you want to bankrupt us? It's not like the days when I could move money around a bit from the clubs. Not any more! I don't think we can do that sort of thing – really."

"Well I think we should. And I'd love it. London's the place for a really big party, isn't it?"

"You miss it a lot still, don't you?"

"Naturally. It's my home town! And the children are there. But this is *your* home, or you feel it is, and it's beautiful, so I mustn't be selfish. It's beginning to get better – I don't wake up every morning thinking 'I want to go home' now!"

"Did you do that?"

"Oh yes, of course I did. For months. I felt physically sick for at least six months."

He put down his cup and stroked her bare arm.

"Honey – why didn't you *tell* me you felt like that? I'm a selfish bastard – you should have *said*. And I should have *known* without your saying, shouldn't I? I knew you missed the kids, of course, but then they do have their own lives to lead, and you see them almost every month – that's more than plenty of mothers in England get to see their grown up children!"

"I know. I'm stupid. But anyway, it's getting better all the time. And I'm so lucky to be able to fly home so often. My whole life has been lucky – I feel that, Roy. I do honestly. Once I met you it was like a season ticket for a wonderful life!"

She leant across and kissed his cheek and then picked up a honey cake.

"I'm never going to lose eight pounds if I keep buying these, but they are so delicious!"

"The bit of extra weight suits you. Mama got plump and she never looked old – always had wonderful skin. If you lose weight it goes in your face first. Terrible."

"In that case I shall eat these every morning! I had dried apricots for breakfast – nothing else – they're so gorgeous here. More coffee?"

"No. I'm going over to the golf club to see Leo. Do you want to come with me and have some lunch there?"

"No, I must do things here if we're away at the weekend. You didn't really answer me, Roy, about your party. What do you think, darling?"

"I don't think we need to decide now. But ring Carla – her house is big enough. See if she'd have it there with caterers. We're definitely not spending Café Royale sort of money."

"OK. I'll call her this afternoon – I wanted an excuse – she thinks I'm crazy when I only saw her last week! If we had caterers it wouldn't be too much hard work, would it? I don't want to give her any extra work – she gets quite tired with those two imps"

"She has an au pair, for God's sake! You had three children under three at one time, with no help at all, I seem to remember!"

"I know darling, and it *was* exhausting! Men have no idea. I'll call her anyway. Ciao!"

They kissed absently and Roy changed his shoes, grabbed a panama hat from a chair, and strolled back through the house.

Heather heard the Alfa Romeo purr down the drive and sighed. How could she ever complain when she lived in luxury in this beautiful place? With a loving and attentive husband and three happy, healthy children who loved her? She just felt so alien here; it was hard to explain it to Roy, who had slotted back into Italian village life as if he'd lived here always. Of course his Italian was fluent; hers not much better than a good holiday standard. She was no linguist and she felt shut out when he chattered animatedly with neighbours and his Italian friends. They felt like *his* friends, not hers. How could you have a real friendship with someone you didn't understand properly?

She ran the coffee cups under the tap and placed them in the dishwasher. Her kitchen was dark oak, with terracotta tiles on the floor and worktops. The view from the cream ceramic sink was breathtaking; heavily wooded slopes gently meandering into the distance with a few pan-tiled roofs dotted about in the valley. The sky was perfect azure and in the distance you could hear the squeal of tyres and brakes as local Italian drivers negotiated the hairpin bends on the main road to Florence. They were the craziest drivers in the world she thought; loving their cars even more than their women, and feats of macho daring were enacted daily on the road below, often with disastrous results.

She knew she was becoming neurotic about Roy on the road here. Every time he drove off without her she was worried sick until he returned. Morbid. Probably just her age.

She walked into the sitting room to telephone her daughter. She was a little afraid of Carla, she realised. Strong, independent, wilful – so different from Rachel, the younger twin, who'd been dominated by Carla from their earliest days. Rachel had married a musician and they had a small daughter who was the image of Rachel as a baby. Carla had two small boys of two and four who ran riot and ruled the household. Heather felt unable to offer advice as Carla made it very plain that she intended to bring up her family according to her own ideas; not Heather's.

"It's a different world, mama!" she'd laugh, as they ran round her beautiful cream sitting room, scattering crisps and spilling their Orangina.

"We don't all sit down to a family meal at seven o'clock like we did with Papa. I can remember being *starving* and having to wait until he got back from the club – and then one hour for supper and off he went again! Kids now eat when they're hungry – they know where the fridge is and what's in it. It's easy!"

"But what about their manners, Carla?" she'd protested.

"Oh, they'll pick them up as they go along – at school probably. Or when they watch us. We do have Sunday lunch together you know."

Heather dialled, biting her lip. It rang and rang. She was about to replace it when a voice said, "Hello?" And she realised the new au pair had answered.

"Hello, Marta!" she said. "Is Carla there? It's her mother."

There was no point in pleasantries; Marta was from Chile and spoke little English.

There was a pause while Marta digested this.

"No. Carla shopping. She shopping."

"OK, Marta. I'll call her later. Thank you, dear. Bye bye."

She replaced the handset and sat for a while, staring out of the window with unseeing eyes. She felt so much closer to Rachel, and when the two families visited her together there was no problem. The twins acted differently towards her when they were together; they reverted to childish roles, she guessed, but Carla and Heather alone – that was a different scene altogether. Heather felt reduced, somehow, stupid and incompetent. She knew Carla loved her, but she wasn't sure how much she liked her. But neither Richard nor Rachel had a large enough house for the kind of party she had in mind, whereas Carla's stockbroker husband had provided every possible material comfort. It was just a pity he was such a difficult person. 'Hard as stone' had flashed into her mind when she'd first met him, and knowing him better had done nothing to dispel that feeling. He was cold and arrogant; even in his dealings with his small boys. If they looked sweet and obeyed him, all well and good, but if they were wilful – which was most of the time – the balloon went up. Carla was strong enough to cope with it she supposed, but she wished she had found someone as tender and sweet as Roy. But then there weren't many Roy Cavalieris. She knew how lucky she was.

With so many hours alone in this beautiful but isolated place and with little to occupy her mentally she knew she was becoming neurotic. She must take herself in hand. She decided to clear out her wardrobes today. She would take into Florence anything she no longer wore and give them to the Sisters of Charity there. They distributed to the homeless. It was ridiculous having so many clothes. She would not buy anything new either – well, apart from perhaps a handbag. She was addicted to handbags and she knew a little shop near the Mercato Nuovo where she could always find something wonderfully stylish and not too expensive. They were staying at the Plaza Luccesi, on the Arno, and she knew Roy delighted in spoiling her, but if she was to go ahead with plans for an extravagant party she must rein in this year and not waste money on things she did not need. Of course she would buy clothes for her grandchildren; Italian clothes for children were so chic and it was such a pleasure to be able to give. She sighed again, and walked slowly upstairs, determined to spend the day profitably.

An hour later, when half her wardrobe was spread out on two beds, she telephoned Carla again. She was restless and needed the reassurance of one of her children's voices.

"Hello?"

"Hello, Marta. It's Mrs Cavalieri again. Is Carla back yet?"

"Wait please."

A short pause and then she heard Carla's voice in the background.

"Rupert? Put that down – no, take it into the garden. You *cannot* take that into your bedroom."

A longer pause and a thud as the telephone was knocked off the table.

"Hello?" It was Rupert. Heather melted.

"Hello sweetheart! It's Nona. What are you up to?"

"I found a little snake. It's not very big."

"Mama? Oh God, it's unbelievable here! It's a nightmare! Rupert's nursery has closed for August and he's just brought this ginormous worm into the bedroom, all covered in muck! Boys! AARGH!"

"He told me it was a snake! So think yourself lucky!"

"Well it probably will be next time. Much more exciting! God, were we like this?"

"*You* were! Rachel and Richard weren't really. I remember you breaking six eggs all over my satin eiderdown when you were about two! How are you, apart from small-boys-at-home-itis?"

"Oh fine, I suppose. Dominic's so busy I never see him, but I had lunch with Rach a couple of days ago so that was nice. How's Papa?"

"He's at the golf club. That's why I'm ringing. I want to organise a big party for his sixtieth and we wondered if we could hold it at your house? Caterers, of course, but would that be an awful nuisance?"

"No, of course not. We'd love it. It's not for a year, though, is it? You're getting frightfully organised."

"I know. You have to if you want tip-top caterers. Would Dominic mind? You'd better ask him before I go any further."

"Of course he wouldn't. You know he loves entertaining, and he won't have to *do* anything, will he?"

"Well if you're sure – thank you, darling. It's just too expensive in a hotel. Who did your New Year's Eve party?"

"'Hungry for Love'." They're three girls in Covent Garden – super. Shall I ring them?"

"No, no. You're not to get involved in the organisation – that's not fair – you have far too much to do with those two pickles. Just give me the number and I'll ring them."

"From Pratolino? Don't be daft, mama. I'll ring them. I can make a phone call without dropping dead with exhaustion for heaven's sake!"

"All right. Just a phone call. We must hold it on the day – on the 3rd."

"Right. Roughly how many?"

"Could you manage eighty?"

"Easily. We had ninety-six on New Year's Eve, but that was too many. Eighty would be perfect. Is this what Papa wants to do?"

"I think so. He loves a party. He thought it was extravagant now we've retired, but sixty is special… and well… I just feel I want to…"

121

She tailed off lamely, not wanting to say anymore.

"Right. Leave it to me. Marta! Will you take them *downstairs – now*? Thank you. It's hopeless trying to talk on the phone when they're in the same room – they vie for my attention the whole time. Rupert was swinging the worm over Charlie who's been hanging onto my legs the whole conversation! I should only speak to people when they're in bed!"

"Is Marta much use to you with so little English? Why didn't you get a girl who could speak more than that?"

"Huh. It's the stupid agency. They said she had done three years' English in school. Precious little to show for it if she did! I guess she'll soon improve now she's here. Look mama – I'll have to go – there's a horrendous noise going on downstairs – I don't think Charlie wanted to be unwound from my legs, or Rupert's stuffed the worm down his neck or something – I'll have to go. Take care – I'll ring you when I've booked the caterers. Bye now."

"Bye darling. Try not to work too hard."

Heather replaced the phone and pulled on a tissue. Ridiculous. Why should she cry? Carla was fine – her boys were fit and full of life and she had help. Why did she feel so close to tears all the time?

She returned to her clothes, wiping her nose with a flourish. She must watch herself; she was becoming tiresome. That would never do.

Chapter Eleven

"Bless me Father, for I have sinned, and it is four weeks since my last confession."

Father Davey slid back the door in the confessional and listened. A soft, well-spoken, elderly female voice – it was familiar, but he couldn't quite place it.

"I have lied about something important, and I am not able to trust in God's goodness; I seem to be anxious all the time and not able to give up my problems to Him like I used to."

"Can you pinpoint how long you have been feeling like this, and were you lying for your own benefit – or someone else's?"

The words were coming out of him on auto-pilot. He checked himself. This was a soul in crisis; he could hear her voice cracking with emotion; whatever it was, it mattered terribly to her. He brought his straggling thoughts under control.

"Would you like to talk to me privately – after confession?"

"Oh, I would. Yes please, Father."

"Wait in the back of the church until I've finished. Be reading through St John's Gospel as your penance while you're waiting."

He made the sign of the cross and absolved her, banishing thoughts of his supper and whether Mrs O'Rourke had remembered to leave a casserole in. She was getting very forgetful – last Saturday's lunch had been in the fridge instead of the oven – but then she was seventy-six.

He heard feet tapping slowly across the stone floor and waited. No one came. Maybe she was the last. He gave it five minutes while he checked his Racing Post to see if he'd missed the favourite running at York. Still no one. Father Davey gave up and opened the confessional. He looked around the empty church until he saw a small dumpy figure, bent over her Bible, in a navy raincoat, on the far side. It was Mrs Rose. He should have recognised her voice; she was a regular communicant after all. She never missed hearing Mass on a Sunday.

He walked over and sat beside her on the pew.

"Well now, Mrs Rose, what's on your mind? It's not like

you to sound so troubled."

Her usually serene face looked exhausted and her eyes puffy. She was crumpling a handkerchief in her hand behind the Bible which she held in her lap.

"It's a very long story, Father, and I don't know where to begin."

"How about the beginning? That's usually the simplest."

"Oh dear. This is very difficult for me. The beginning... well, that's a very long time ago indeed. Yesterday – no – Moira went home two days ago – it must have been a week the day before yesterday – I'm getting confused – my sister rang me from Devon and is worried sick about her boy. Well, he's not really a boy now because he's twenty-six, but I still think of him as a boy and he seems very immature to me. Since then I've not been able to get it all out of my mind – I've been unable to get to sleep for worrying about it – and then some people came asking about him and I lied. I lied about a very important part of it."

"Hang on a minute! This isn't the beginning, is it? Now – take a deep breath and start again. When was the beginning?"

His voice was like a drug – fascinating and addictive.

"I suppose the beginning was really when Meg – that's my youngest sister – there's four of us – well there were till Helen died – anyway, Meg married a lovely man – a Catholic too, Father, and we all liked him, and the years went by and there were no babies, and we could see Meg getting unhappier and unhappier. My husband was a GP as you know, and he arranged for her to see a very good man who eventually decided she was infertile. It was a terrible blow to both of them, and we all had children by then, so we really felt for them. The marriage was under a lot of strain, of course, and eventually my Philip persuaded them to consider adoption. He had a practice in Harlow and there was a Catholic home for mothers and babies nearby, and we knew a young girl – not much more than a child herself – was about to give birth – a girl Philip knew from the practice. She wasn't at all reliable, and had no job and no boyfriend and no home to give the baby, so when she finally agreed to have her baby adopted, Meg and Derek applied to adopt him. They didn't live around here, they lived in Devon, so they could offer the little one a lovely life by the sea, and virtually no chance of the girl ever crossing their path at all. Derek had a very successful ship's chandler's business in Dartmouth and a beautiful home. It was a wonderful place for a child – and a couple of years later they adopted another boy – half Chinese – but he's been no trouble. No trouble at all. Which is more than you could say about Jude. That's the first one. He's nearly broken my sister's heart. In fact, I believe he *did* break Derek's. Derek had a heart attack at forty-eight and died. Terrible it was. I thought Meg would never get over it. And after that Jude got worse and worse. You'd think he'd want to take on the responsibility of being man of the house after that, wouldn't you? He was eleven when it happened. But no. He was more trouble than ever – shoplifting, drinking, useless at school – you name it, he tried it. He's twenty-six now and I don't think he's ever held down a job for more than a couple of months. He spends most of his time on the beach – surfing. That's what he does. A 'beach bum' – that's what Meg calls him. And now – well this summer – she has reason to believe he's dealing in drugs."

Father Davey took the Bible gently from her shaking hands and placed it between them on the pew.

"And these problems that are worrying your sister – are they very recent? How does she know about the drugs?"

"Fairly recent. I think somebody local must have told her. Because that's the main worry – he doesn't keep in touch any more. She doesn't even know where he's living right now. And it's causing her such agony – I just don't know what to do to help."

"I see. Tell me, has Jude ever tried to contact his natural mother at all?"

"Not as far as I know. Never seemed interested. I'm not sure when Meg told him he was adopted. I do remember she said at first she wasn't going to, because she had him at two weeks so she felt he was completely hers and that she was the only mother he'd ever need. But after she'd adopted Jeremy – he looks a bit Chinese – I think she decided she'd have to tell them something, so she told them both together. I think Jeremy was about two or three and Jude five. Something like that. It seemed all right for a time, and then as I say, Jude became quite a problem child.

Jeremy's lovely – never given her a moment's anxiety. He's an accountant."

"Mrs Rose – you mustn't distress yourself. This isn't really your problem – your sister needs your support – of course she does – but this chap needs professional help and counselling by the sound of it. Can her parish priest not help?"

"I imagine she's told him all about it over the years. Nothing seems to help, but then these people called in enquiring about – about the birth mother. I said I never knew who it was – when of course, I did."

"That was a confidential matter, Mrs Rose. You did quite right not to divulge anything about it at all. And don't lose heart about your nephew – he may reform yet. Meet some nice girl and have a couple of kids – I see it happen all the time! Young tearaways on motorbikes one minute, and pushing the buggy round Tesco's the next – wonderful things, young women, for sorting out wild young men! Try not to worry so much."

She smiled in a weary sort of way and stood up, holding out her hand formally to shake his.

"Well thank you anyway, Father, for listening to all this. You've made me feel a lot better just getting it off my chest, though I'm none the wiser as to how to help Meg. I hope I haven't taken up too much of your time."

"Not at all, my dear. That's what I'm here for. We can talk again. Now go home and say your prayers and ring your sister. Just be there for her – that's all you can do. The power of prayer is a wonderful thing."

He watched her walking slowly out of the heavy church door and ran a hand round the back of his collar. He felt so inadequate sometimes. Maybe he would ask her the name of her sister's parish priest next time he saw her, and give him a call. He locked the church, his stomach rumbling, and mounted his bicycle to pedal the hundred yards round the corner to the presbytery. The smell of chicken greeted him; she had not forgotten.

Andy and Emma had finally got back on a train for London at 8.05. They were tired and bad-tempered and hungry. Mrs Rose had offered them nothing but weak tea, and in their enthusiasm they had missed lunch altogether.

"She knew a hell of a lot more than she was saying," muttered Emma, throwing herself into the corner seat and hugging her bag to her chest.

Andy's heart sank as he realised this wasn't the end.

"Not necessarily. She's quite an old woman, Em. She probably just doesn't remember. It's no big deal for her, after all."

"Well, you would think so. But didn't you notice how flustered she got when we mentioned the baby first of all? Her neck went all red and her hands shook. That's not the reaction of somebody who isn't particularly interested or doesn't remember much about it, is it?"

"Did she? I didn't notice that. I thought she seemed a bit shaky anyway. Maybe she's got some sort of illness. Old people are often shaky, aren't they?"

"She wasn't *that* old. No, she definitely knew more than she was letting on. I'm certain she knew where that baby went and was covering up."

"What do you suggest then – torture?"

"What if we leave it for a day or two, and then ring up and suggest we've found something out? Let her think we know? Maybe then she'd give something away – worth a try."

The thought of a mere phone call solution appealed.

"Brilliant!" he said, throwing his hands behind his head. "Your Machiavellian tendencies are paying off. I can't think of a better plan. Just at the moment all I care about is eating vast quantities of food – whatever's in my fridge."

"Shall I come back with you and see your place?"

The thought of the squalor of his bedsit made him lean forward. "Um. No. Not tonight. I've got… I've got to go to the launderette and things – and ring my mum."

"And wash your hair? I get the drift. See you tomorrow?"

He grinned and leaned forward to kiss her lips.

"You bet. Just try and stop me. Can we do the preliminary sketching tomorrow? *Please.*"

"OK. Come round about twelve."

The train trundled through the suburbs and the air took on the grimy smell of outer London. Andy perched on the edge of his seat and took both her hands in his. He inspected the perfect little nails resting on her tanned knees and smiled. He was a lucky bastard. Dear old Angie – thank God he'd taken her advice or he might still be sitting up a mountain thinking he'd paint the perfect picture, while all the time back in London was the girl of his dreams. Their eyes met and they both smiled. They rocked in companionable silence while the train gathered pace and clattered into town.

"There's always the parish priest, of course."

Andy grimaced. Did she never let go?

"Parish priest?"

"Yes. We could check with the present one in Harlow who was there twenty-seven years ago."

"You reckon he'd know where the baby went?"

"Bound to. It would be part of his job to go into the Catholic home for unmarried mums, wouldn't it? Course he might be dead too – like Dr Rose."

"There you are, then, Agent Parker – you have your goal for tonight – track down Father O'Flaherty from twenty-six years ago and give him the third degree! Go for it Scully!"

"It's not a joke, Andy. I thought you really cared about Angie. This is the most important thing in her life and we can help her."

"That's the thing, Em, I'm not sure. I really think you've got yourself hooked into this idea of poor little Angie – but she's not like that. It was Roy she wanted to check up on – not some poor sod who's a complete stranger – brought up a strict Roman Catholic – I mean – he could even be a priest himself for all we know – did you ever think of that?"

She did not answer, but gazed silently out of the train window as dull terraces of grey houses sped past. She would not give up that easily. She never did.

Jude Kennedy was packing. Hurling his few possessions into various bin liners and cardboard boxes; it was a regular event he was well used to. Since leaving home five years ago he had dossed down in friends' bedsits, tried three squats and even lived with a girl who had paid rent for a short time, but moving on was the norm – was what he was comfortable with. A few months in one place made him restless and by then he had usually irritated whoever was sharing his space beyond reasonable endurance.

"You're just so bloody selfish, Jude," the last girlfriend had complained, tears streaking her brown cheeks and touching his heart briefly. She had never noticed that, as he'd turned away and reached for his rucksack.

"I'm moving on," was all he'd said, and had been hitching to Plymouth within the hour. Now it was Polzeath – the surfing was great there and he'd heard of a good squat in a derelict Victorian house on the outskirts – friends from way back. He had only been in this room for six weeks and he was glad to leave it. Occasionally he thought of his childhood home in Nethway, but not often. The grey slate roof, the whitewashed walls, the cream Rayburn stove in the kitchen. That had been the heart of the house – his mother cooking as he came in from school, a ready smile on her oven-hot face, the old spaniel in his basket. Jeremy had always beaten him home – he had cycled while his brother took the school bus, but that was light years away.

He stuffed a toothbrush and grey underpants on top of his CDs and books and lifted the box into the hallway. Alex should be here soon with the van – he'd agreed to shift his gear to Polzeath for a tenner. Not that he had any money at all right now – totally skint until his giro came through – but Alex wouldn't know that, would he? He threw more books into another box and a letter floated down to the floor. He knew what it was immediately. He bent down to retrieve it and saw his mother's spidery writing – 'All my love, Mum XXXXX'.

He turned it over and glanced at the date: February 2nd. Hell – it was September. He hadn't contacted her in all that time and he'd moved two or three times since her letter. She'd be going spare. He could imagine. He threw the letter onto a chair. He hadn't meant to leave it so long. Maybe it was for the best. Hell – when he saw her all he could see was the worry etched on her face – anxiety scoring grooves like a record, and surfacing beneath guarded questions like, 'Are you eating properly, Lovey? You are bothering to cook, aren't you, Jude?' and 'Have you got a GP dear? P'raps you should have a check-up sometime as you do look dreadfully thin to me. You had such chubby cheeks as a boy and they're all hollow now. It doesn't suit you, you know.'

Well the tarts thought it did. They threw themselves at him and told him how great he looked in a wet suit. His mother had Jeremy after all. He wasn't a disappointment, was he? He'd done all the right fucking things, and was now a fucking accountant, and *married* at twenty-four! Whoever got married at twenty-four? It did his head in just thinking about it. And to that silly tart, too. He'd seen them once in Plymouth a few weeks ago, and dived into Dingle's to avoid them, but that had just been coincidence. Jeremy wouldn't be coming looking for him, not for a moment.

He heard a van door slam and looked out of the window. Alex's peroxide stubble was passing beneath and he leant out and shouted, "Hi man! We're outa here!" and heaved the last box through the open doorway. Alex's boots thundered up the uncarpeted stairs and came to a halt at the top.

"This it?" he said, a Marlboro hanging from the corner of his lower lip.

"Yeah. Just about. Couple of black sacks in there. About it."

"Right."

They lifted bags and boxes effortlessly and ran up and down stairs without speaking. The room now only contained a stained mattress and a broken-down armchair.

"What about them?" Alex asked.

"Nah; leave 'em."

He turned and banged the door shut behind him. The draught blew a piece of paper off the chair and it scuttered across the floorboards like a white mouse.

'All my love, Mum XXXXX' laid face upwards in the dirt.

The van revved and pulled away in a cloud of dust.

The dust settled. Jude Kennedy had moved on.

Chapter Twelve

"Rita? It's me. You OK? Did Stu tell you I rang?

"I know it's late. It's ten past twelve here; my dear guests have only just decided to leave the bar and go to bed! You weren't in bed, were you?

"Oh, sorry, Rita. I just needed to talk, that's all.

"Nothing in particular. Just – oh, I don't know, I'm a bit funny at the moment – I keep going over old times, you know. Must be my age.

"What?

"Sandy haired? About twenty – with a girl in tow? Oh that was Andy Carter – he was out here last week – he painted my portrait – it's quite good actually. I look quite sexy! What on earth was he doing in Harlow?

"I certainly didn't ask him to get in touch with you. What the bloody hell is this all about? He rushed back from here to sort out his love life.

"Well, presumably that was Emma. What did he want?"

There was complete silence in the softly lit bedroom. Angie's heart began pounding so frantically that she had to sit on the bed. She swallowed and tried to create saliva in her parched mouth.

"Yes, I'm still here. It's – it's such a shock. Why would they want to do that? Why?

"No, I never delved into all that. It's so long ago it wouldn't be fair. He's an adult for God's sake, and whatever he was told about me, he will feel he's got his own family, and doesn't need me barging into his life after all this time. Years ago I used to fantasise about seeing him, but now – he's twenty-six, Rita. I never felt it would be right to open that Pandora's box. What did you tell them?

"Bloody cheek, bothering you with all this stuff from the past. How dare he – I really wouldn't have thought he would do that – not Andy.

"Actually I had asked him to look up Roy Cavalieri in the London phone book. That's all. But he hasn't contacted me about it, so I thought he just didn't bother. You know what twenty year olds are like.

131

"Mrs Rose? Why Mrs Rose? As if she'd know anything!"

Angie stood up, changing the phone into her left hand, hoping it would shake less than the right.

"And that was the last you heard? They disappeared off to Sheering to talk to Mrs Rose to ask her about *my* baby? Oh God, it's ridiculous, Rita. You don't suppose she knows where – where he went, do you? I mean... why on earth should she? And after all this time...

"No. You're right. She wouldn't. After all, even if Dr Rose had something to do with the adoption it would have been a matter of professional confidence, wouldn't it, and he wouldn't have discussed it with his wife, surely? And even if he had mentioned it – she wouldn't remember after twenty-six years, would she? It's *nothing to do* with Andy, Rita. What does he think he's bloody playing at – I can't believe he's doing this to me.

"I talked to him a bit while he was painting my picture – I told you, I've been thinking about it recently, and I guess I found him sympathetic and he was there – I wish I'd kept my mouth shut now, I can tell you. You'll ring me as soon as they get in touch, won't you, sweetheart? Promise you'll let me know what they say. I'm going to bed now, not that I shall be able to sleep. He did promise to let you know what she said, didn't he? Well, that's something. I think he will if he said he would. I reckon his bloody girlfriend put him up to all this nonsense – it just doesn't sound like Andy to nose around in other people's business.

"Yes, OK. I'll speak to you very soon, sweetheart. Love to Patrick and Stu. Bye now."

She stood for a while with her hand resting on the telephone, gazing out of the dark window but seeing nothing. A slight breeze was getting up and the muslin curtain fluttered against her bare arm. A sickness was gnawing at her stomach.

"Dear God," she said aloud, "what if they find him?"

Inside the terror, she knew the long buried desire lay waiting.

To see the face of her son.

To experience the shock of recognition; her own darling son.

Did he look like her? He might even resemble her beloved

father – looks often skipped a generation. But this was crazy. She must not go down that forbidden path. She unzipped her dress, her heart pounding in her throat. She hung the dress in the oak closet and unhooked her bra. The room was stifling even with the breeze and she turned on the fan and lay on her bed, too exhausted to clean her teeth.

Down the mountain road, tyres squealed and then all was quiet. Somewhere in England her son slept, not knowing his mother lay in her mountain home remembering him. Not knowing that one day a stupid youth with a stubborn mission might shatter his peace of mind by knocking on his door and saying, 'I know your mother'.

Her head was beginning to reel. She sat up and swung her legs off the bed. This was hopeless. She'd never sleep. Perhaps she should walk in the garden, but Jose might think she was an intruder. He was the only member of staff to sleep in the hotel and had a tiny room at the back of the kitchen. He wouldn't be in bed yet; maybe she should join him for a drink. But she had no heart for gossip with Jose tonight; no interest in hearing of his conquests. She had noticed him turning his extensive charms onto Stephanie before dinner, and hoped her friend had fended him off.

She stood by the window, the fan cooling her hot breasts as she breathed in the wonderful night air.

"He can't spoil anything unless I let him," she told herself. "No one will give Andy confidential information – he has no authority."

But the lid was prised open, and underneath the long-preserved memory was waiting. Where was he? How did he live? What sort of person was her son?

She had thought it was all in the past, unable to hurt her anymore. But with the sudden shock of a lightning strike she was jolted into the sense of loss and loneliness she had thought had gone forever.

"I'd got so self-sufficient," she thought. "I didn't think anyone could ever hurt me again. Not ever. I liked that; it was comfortable. I don't want to feel like this again. Not now; I've earned this peace and quiet. I bloody have."

She turned away and walked into her bathroom and turned

on the shower. She let the cold water cascade onto her face and onto her breasts while she tried to compose her thoughts. Why had Andy been diverted from Roy to *this?* Presumably he had failed. Yes, that was it. He had failed to trace Roy, but in the process, somehow, he had got into all this – or his girlfriend had – and had started following the scent to Rita and to Mrs Rose. Why Mrs Rose?

She turned and water cascaded into her shoulders and down her back. She was feeling calmer now. She pictured the small, neat woman who had been so kind to her when she was in St Ebba's. A warm, motherly type, never without a small gift of chocolate or flowers or a home-made cake. Quick to hug or hold your hand – she'd been a lifeline at the time, and yet, so soon after – after Angie had left the hospital and moved into the bedsit near Harlow College – she'd dropped her completely. No more contact. She had obviously decided that Angie was fine on her own. It had never struck her at the time – she'd been far too busy rebuilding her life – but the contact had been completely severed.

"Well, she had other lame ducks, I guess," Angie muttered, as she stepped out of the shower and wrapped herself in a fluffy pink towel. "She knew I was getting on OK from Dr Rose, and I had Rita and Patrick, so I suppose she found other people to help. That's what she did all the time, I imagine."

She blotted her now cool body and lay down once more. Yes, her mind was calmer. No one would tell them anything. They would soon tire of her story – Andy had his own life to lead – he'd be back in college now. What had he said? 'I don't seem to be able to have a life, Angie'.

Well, let him bloody well start to, and get out of hers. She could organise her own life, thank you very much Andy Carter, and didn't need any help from him or from anyone else.

She closed her eyes, seeing again that tiny wrinkled red face, with its shock of dark, downy hair on the little pointed head. She turned her face into the pillow, pulling her knees up to her breasts, and wept.

What sort of person was her son?

Chapter Thirteen

"Is that Father Beamish?"

"It is – what can I do for you?"

"Oh, you won't know me at all. My name is Emma Parker. I'm making enquiries for someone else actually – who's abroad at the moment. I wondered if you could tell me who was the parish priest there twenty-six years ago?"

"Here in this parish?"

"Yes."

"I can do that. Am I allowed to know more than that?"

"Well I'm trying to find someone who was adopted from the Catholic home for mother and babies in Harlow twenty-six years ago. We thought the priest who was around at the time might be able to help."

"He would, to be sure. I'm pretty certain that would be Father Andrew Sinclair – hold a minute while I look up some dates – I won't keep you a minute."

Emma gave the thumbs up sign to Susie, who was sitting on the floor, cross-legged, eating Ravioli.

"Hello? Are you there? Right – I have it here – Father Andrew Sinclair – Priest-in-Charge 1961 to 1979. That's your man. But he'll not be a lot of use to you."

"Oh. Why not? He's not dead, is he?"

"No, he's not dead, but the poor fella might as well be, God rest him. He's in the Clergy Retirement Home in Brentwood with severe Alzheimer's. He doesn't know what day it is by all accounts. Had a wonderful brain too."

"Oh, God, no! Is there anyone else who could help us? What about the nuns? I think there were nuns running the home – what about them?"

"I've only been here ten years myself and the home was closed long since. But from my knowledge of the diocese, I would think it likely that at least some of them may be at the Sisters of Mercy Convent in Basildon. It's the only remaining one in Essex, I believe."

"Oh thank you! You haven't got their number by any chance, have you? I'm sorry to be such a nuisance."

135

"No, no, you're not a nuisance, not at all. Hold on again – I have it somewhere – it'll only take a minute – this desk's a tip."

She smiled at the Dublin accent and watched Jasper winding his way round Susie, miaowing piteously.

"He's lying," she said, "I fed him earlier. Honestly."

"Hello! I have it here. Have you a pen?"

She wrote the number down triumphantly.

"Thank you *very* much. You've been a great help."

"My pleasure. God bless you."

He hung up and she banged the receiver down with a whoop.

"Yes!" she yelled, and Susie grinned, licking her fork.

"Got it?"

"Yup – got the number where the old nuns live – apparently the priest is gaga so he's out, but *the nuns*! They'll *know everything*. We'll go there tomorrow. Basildon!"

"I thought you said Andy was sketching you in the nude?"

She popped the last square of Ravioli into her small mouth and pushed the cat away from the plate.

"He was – well – it will have to wait. We've so little time to crack this one – once I've started my new job it will be hopeless so I've got to do it this week. You know me – once I've started something I have to finish!"

"Bloody too right. Don't I know it! Poor old Andy doesn't know what he's in for, does he? Where is Basildon anyway?"

"No idea. There's an A-Z somewhere. Not too far I shouldn't think. I'm really enjoying this. Sleuthing suits me."

"Perhaps you should give up the day job and become Scully of Islington – London's answer to the X Files!"

"You just need a terrier mentality, that's all. Andy's *hopeless*. He gives up at the first problem. And there's this poor woman – never knowing what happened to that baby – and we're going to be able to tell her!"

"You don't know you are, Em. I don't think anyone will tell you anything. It's all confidential stuff. All you'll get is a polite brush off."

"No. I don't think so. I feel sure we're nearly there – I can persuade some old nun to talk to me – she'll love it. Going back over all that drama from years back. If she's old and retired it will be great for her; you'll see. Is there any more of that Ravioli?"

"It's in the saucepan. Salad's in the fridge."

Emma clattered around in the kitchen and called out, "What did you honestly think of Andy?"

"Nice. A bit soft for you, maybe – you'll get all your own way and then get bored. But quite dishy. Umm. Very tasty."

Emma was scraping Ravioli onto a brown pottery plate full of salad.

"He's got quite a stubborn streak underneath. Think how he flew back here with all those fabulous flowers – wasn't that amazing?"

"Umm. They certainly smell wonderful. He's mad about you; there's no question. But you know what you're like – short interest span – that's your trouble."

"I know, but this time I do feel kind of different, you know. I think this might be It."

Oh yeah?"

Susie lay back on the floor with Jasper walking across her stomach. His tail twitched.

"So – you're just going to turn up at this – this nunnery – or whatever – and say I want to know who adopted this baby boy twenty-six years ago belonging to Angie what's-her-name, are you?"

Emma sat on the arm of the sofa, spearing chunks of cucumber and chewing thoughtfully.

"I think I shall say that Angie is my aunt. Yes – that's it – Angie is my aunt in Majorca, and I've just left her, and I'm worried about her. I think she's depressed and brooding on her past – the menopause probably – and she needs to know what happened to him. I could be Rita's daughter, couldn't I? I'm the right age."

"You can't do that!"

"Why ever not? As you say, they're not going to pour out all the details to just *anybody*, are they? You've got to be two steps ahead of them, otherwise it's hopeless."

"I bet Andy won't buy that. Maybe you should go on your own."

"No way. We're doing this together. And he's the one who

knows her – yes – maybe we should say *he's* her nephew – yes – that's better. He'll be more convincing because he actually knows her – if they ask questions."

"He'll never agree."

"He will. He will if I say so."

"Angie's *my aunt*? Are you mad?"

Andy put down his materials on the floor and glared at Emma.

"You promised I could do my preliminary sketches today, Emma," he reminded her.

"I know, I know, but this opportunity has to be taken! We can't just let it drift. You don't seem a bit committed to finding him, Andy. I'm determined we shall. And soon. I'll always be here for you to sketch, darling. You can draw me anytime."

She wound her arms around his neck and kissed his mouth, her tongue exciting him. He reacted, pulling her shirt away from her breast, and stroking it tenderly.

"Please, Em," he said.

"We have to catch the 11.50," she said firmly, leading him into her bedroom. "I'm absolutely determined we're going today."

They fell onto the bed, bouncing Jasper off onto the floor, from where he regarded their passion with disdain and stalked out of the room. He gave a single miaow of irritation before disappearing through an open window. He was not amused.

The train trundled into Basildon three minutes late and Emma flung open the door as she commented on the rain.

"Did you say you'd telephoned?" asked Andy, feeling in his jeans pocket for their tickets.

"Yes, yes, we've got an appointment with Mother Ignatius at 1.15. Apparently it's really near the station."

"Oh good – we can walk."

"But it's raining."

"Not that much. Come on."

He was deliberating whether to mention the train fares now or later. He had no intention of blowing his birthday cheque entirely on Network South East.

They found the red brick building easily and rang the bell.

A short, rosy faced woman in the grey cardigan of a modern nun opened the door and Emma asked for Mother Ignatius.

"Come in! Come in!" she said, leading the way along a pale green corridor to a closed mahogany door. She knocked deferentially.

"Yes!"

The door was opened, and behind a green-topped desk and beneath a picture of The Sacred Heart sat the Mother Superior, her hair entirely hidden by an old-fashioned wimple, and only the lines between her brows indicating her great age. Her skin was paper thin, but her voice strong and authoritative. She was not the meek pushover of Emma's imaginings.

"Please sit down."

She indicated two upright beech chairs and they sat obediently. Her thin professional half-smile did not encourage them.

Andy cleared his throat and Emma began.

"We're trying to trace Andy's aunt's child. He was adopted from the Catholic home for mothers & babies in Harlow twenty-six years ago, and the priest in Harlow told us you were here. So we are hoping you will be able to help us."

Mother Ignatius withdrew a notepad from her desk drawer and fingered a fountain pen thoughtfully.

"Yes. Several of the sisters from St Ann's came here when it closed almost twenty years ago. There are few such homes left nowadays. A different culture and a different attitude to these matters entirely. Do you have a written request for information from the birth mother?"

Andy looked startled.

"The birth mother? Oh – Angie – er – no."

Emma leaned forward.

"Andy's aunt is suffering from depression and lives abroad. He's just come back from staying with her and feels she really needs to know what happened to her son – to know he's well and happy – and where he is – that she did the right thing – you know?"

Reverend Mother inspected the nib of her pen without replying.

"She's not going to turn up and interfere with this bloke's

life or anything," said Andy. "It's just that – well, we think she has a right to know about her son and how he is and everything – and because she's in Spain we're checking it out for her."

"She lives in Spain?"

"Yes. Majorca. Has done for eleven years."

"And she had made no attempts herself to contact her son at all?"

Emma looked at her shrewd expression and blurted out, "We don't know that – we just know she's never managed to find out anything. And now she's depressed and so far from home we want to help. She's a lovely woman who's made a great success of her life since that time – but she needs to know. It is her right nowadays, isn't it?"

The nun wrote on a piece of paper and then looked up.

"Your names?"

Andy looked embarrassed.

"Andrew Carter and Emma Parker."

"You are related?"

"To one another? No – just friends."

She wrote again.

"Your addresses?"

They told her, and Emma said. "You will be able to help us, won't you? Do you remember Angelica Roberts?"

The nun placed her pen exactly parallel to her notepad and folded her hands in her lap. She looked from one to the other.

"There were many girls in your aunt's predicament in the sixties and seventies. I do not remember them all. It would be possible to check central records for the adopting family's name but I would not be authorised to give that information to anyone other than the birth mother or the adopted person himself. Since neither person is requesting the information that is all I am able to tell you. You can, of course, tell you aunt how she would be able to obtain this information herself – should she wish to proceed."

She looked at Emma with a piercing gaze.

"So you won't tell us anything?"

Emma's mouth drooped in disappointment.

"I cannot. But your friend's aunt would be told – as would her son, should he enquire."

"And has he ever enquired?"

Andy leaned forward, suddenly interested.

"I have no idea. Not to my knowledge, certainly, but he would be able to gain access to that information without coming through me."

Emma stood up, her face tense.

"Well, I am very sorry you don't feel more inclined to be helpful. We've come a long way – Andrew actually cut short his visit to his aunt to try and find out – we thought you'd be glad to help."

"These are matters of great delicacy and confidentiality. Only the birth mother and the child have the right to receive this information. I'm sorry if you feel your journey has been wasted."

They were dismissed. Emma had found her match in Mother Ignatius. The sweet old nun who could be hoodwinked did not exist here. Mother Ignatius was made of more realistic stuff. They trooped out of the building with sagging shoulders.

"I told you it would be a complete waste of bloody time," said Andy as soon as the door closed. "And money! Another twenty quid! That's *it*, Emma. *No more*. I've had enough of it. I've found out what Angie asked me to find out – Roy Cavalieri is happily married in Italy and that's all she wanted to know. I'm not doing any more traipsing around convents and medical centres and old ladies' houses. It's fucking ridiculous."

He stomped up the drive ahead of her and walked very fast, back towards the station. Emma scowled after him. What a defeatist he was. But she hadn't finished yet.

Chapter Fourteen

"Hello, Rita? It's Andy Carter. I said I'd ring but I'm afraid I've nothing much to tell you. Mrs Rose said she didn't know anything and then my girlfriend found out where some of the nuns from the home live and we went belting down there on a wasted journey. They can't tell us anything – but they would tell Angie – so if ever you feel she really wants to find out where he went – I can give you their number – OK?"

Rita felt her shoulders relax in relief.

"Oh I am glad! Thanks ever so much for ringing. I don't think she will want to know – not after all this time – but I'll take the number anyway. Hang on – I'll get a pen."

He waited, staring round the squalid room. He must sort it today; Emma could call round at any time.

"OK?"

He gave her the number and the address.

"It's a Mother Ignatius you need," he said.

"Oh God!" said Rita. "That rings a bell. Only I think it was *Sister* Ignatius back then – not Mother. Oh, I feel sick, I do. It's all coming back to me. She was the one who came and took him away. I was with Angie and it was so terrible. Really terrible. I've never heard a sound like it – she let out this dreadful cry. I thought I'd forgotten all about it. And then she just sobbed and sobbed *for hours*. I thought she'd die of crying. I remember wondering if you could. She shook with it. And then they came and gave her a pill of some sort – Valium or something – and eventually she went to sleep and I went home. And another thing I remember – now you've said that name – God, it's like a key opening the door – she never cried again. No, not ever. We never talked about it. She just had this terrible shut look and Patrick and I went to pick her up the next day – Sister Ignatius was there then too. They'd given her more pills – pills to stop her milk and pills to calm her down – and Sister was saying all this stuff about how she'd made the right decision and what a good life the baby was going to have with people who'd love him, and how they had money and everything and could give him a good life – and I remember thinking 'Well, sod you – we'd have loved him' – cos

142

Angie and me were going to keep him, you know, until Dr Rose and the nuns started on at her. They told her it was selfish and all that – but Patrick and I had agreed she could live with us and keep him and we'd all share the work. But when she didn't cry anymore I thought – well, she's got over it pretty quick so maybe it was the best thing."

Andy intervened.

"But she *hadn't* got over it, had she? She told me all about her breakdown and going into that terrible place."

"Did she? I wonder why she told you all that stuff. Are you *sure* she wasn't drunk? I can't believe she told you all that. We don't ever talk about it. Not ever."

"It's probably easier to tell a complete stranger. And it is quite an intense relationship when you're painting someone – it's unusual – I told her things too."

"When are you going to tell her you've been doing all this Inspector Morse stuff then?"

"I don't think I shall. You know her best, Rita. You'll know if there ever comes a time when she needs to have that number. But she'd better not leave it too long – Mother Ignatius looks pretty ancient; we don't want everyone who knows to peg out, do we?"

"Nuns go on forever! Well. I'll think about it. I ring her most weeks."

"Will you? D'you want to tell her that Roy Cavalieri is still married to Heather and living in Italy? She'd asked me to find out and I haven't the heart to break it to her now. Maybe it would be better coming from you – you've got lots of other things to talk about, haven't you – to take her mind off the disappointment, you know."

"Oh no. She asked you to find out – so you should tell her. It's nothing to do with me. You ring her yourself."

His heart sank.

"When's the best time to get her?"

"About five o'clock, Spanish time. That's when I ring. But she sometimes rings me at midnight – eleven o'clock here – when she's finished."

"I'll probably do that; it'll be cheaper and easier to get through. OK Rita. Cheers. Bye now."

Rita replaced the receiver, biting her lip as she looked at the piece of paper with the nun's address and telephone number on it.

"Now what do I do?" she asked aloud, and after hesitating for a few seconds, she tucked it into her address book by the telephone.

Andy, throwing old paperbacks into a cardboard box, surveyed his room in disgust. It really was filthy; a great deal worse than he had realised. He pulled the sheet and duvet cover off his bed – how long had they been on there? Since long before Majorca, that was for sure. Mould was growing in the remains of coffee in a Rod Stewart mug on the floor and clothes were *everywhere*. A sock had even draped itself across the bedside lamp and he hadn't noticed. How long had that been there?

And there was the cooker. A small Belling two-ring effort his mother had supplied a year ago, which was now inlaid with orange tomato soup crust, gobbets of yellow egg, and an unmistakable black mushroom cap squashed between the electric coils. Where would he begin? Actually, he decided, the effect was artistically interesting, so he thought he'd leave it and concentrate on the sink. As it was the only sink he possessed it contained memories of most facets of his life. Blutack tangled in the plughole with a lettuce stalk, paint smeared across the tap, blobs of toothpaste stuck hard as cement and a piece of potato skin dried onto the side. He admitted to himself that he hadn't eaten a potato in the flat for weeks; a depressing thought. He collected fifteen beer cans and Coke cans from around the room and threw them into a black sack, along with the contents of the back of his fridge. He'd wondered what the smell was. A small but charismatic piece of Gorgonzola had oozed through its clingfilm onto the back shelf and was trying to get out. He also removed a tomato covered in a fascinating mould, which he had put aside to paint later.

The girl upstairs had a Hoover. He had borrowed it last Easter when his father had come round. When he'd realised Carolyn was coming too, he'd wished he hadn't bothered, but that had been the last time he'd cleaned up. His mother never came, 'too depressing' she had said, and preferred him to visit her where she could wait on him and lavish as much care as he was prepared to permit.

Samantha upstairs was more than happy to oblige – she offered to dust and hoover for him – but he declined, thinking not for the first time that she would need little encouragement to be in his room on a regular basis.

After an hour and a half the room looked transformed. He threw out the rubbish and put his laundry in another sack and ran to the launderette while the mood lasted. He could feel it evaporating fast.

"Must be love!" he grinned to himself. "I've never cleaned up for a girl before."

But he couldn't bear her to see how he lived. He was ashamed; she was so beautiful and perfect in everything she did; so precise, no neat, so clean.

"I've been living like a pig in shit," he considered. "It's got to stop. If we're going to stay together I've got to get my act together. She won't stand for this mess."

They were going out for a curry later. Maybe he'd suggest they came back to his room. He'd better do it today while it was clean; he knew it wouldn't last. But he *had* to. He must live as she wanted, even if he was an artist; he wasn't prepared to let her go.

"Well ring her tonight then."

Emma was running the hot tap over two mugs and trying not to feel too critical about Andy's revolting room. He was an artist, she supposed, but in her eyes this was a sordid hovel.

"If Rita won't tell her, you'll have to. But maybe we should try my idea first – as a last thingummy."

He looked up from the bed where he was sprawled with his hands behind his head, feeling the evening had gone pretty well. They had brought chicken tikkas back here at nine and he thought the room didn't look too bad. She hadn't said anything.

"What idea's that then?"

"You know – ringing Mrs Rose and giving her the impression that the nuns told us something – so that she will let slip what she knows."

"Umm." He considered the idea with distaste.

"Don't like the sound of that much – and personally I don't think she knows anything – it's too long ago."

"Well, I do. She was much too jumpy – she *knows*."

"Go ahead then. You ring her."

"Shall I? Now?"

She kissed the end of his nose and rummaged in her bag for her phone. It rang and rang.

"Isn't it a bit late? It's half ten."

"Is it? Oh hell – I suppose it is."

"Hello?"

The anxious voice sounded sleepy.

"Mrs Rose? I hope we're not disturbing you – it's Emma Parker – remember? We called and talked to you about Angie Roberts…"

"But I was asleep. Whatever's the time?"

"Oh sorry. It might be a bit late to ring – sorry. Shall I ring back tomorrow?"

"No. Why have you rung me again? I told you I couldn't help you."

"I know. But we've found the nuns – you know – the nuns where Angie had her baby – we traced Mother Ignatius, who knew all about it! Isn't that great news? I just felt I ought to fill you in – put you in the picture."

"Mother Ignatius? Do you mean Sister Ignatius? Oh no! What did she tell you?"

The voice quavered.

"Whatever did she tell you?"

Emma hesitated, but only for a second.

"She knew *all* about it – where he went and everything. She said she remembered the whole thing really well. So I thought you'd like to know. We hope to be able to contact the family soon."

"No! No – you mustn't upset Meg! It isn't fair!" Her voice had a catch in it. "Why are you interfering? She's had enough worry with that boy! Leave them alone!"

Emma met Andy's gaze and raised her eyebrows.

"So you *did* know! I *knew* you did – why wouldn't you tell us anything, Mrs Rose? Did Meg ask you not to?"

Mrs Rose's voice became more agitated.

"No. No – she doesn't know anything about it – *please* just stop asking questions and leave us all alone!"

"That boy has rights too, you know. Have you ever thought about that? That man – he may want to trace his real mother."

"Meg's his real mother – she's been the most wonderful mother – and all on her own since Derek died. It isn't fair. I'm not going to speak to you anymore. You're making me too upset."

Emma changed tack immediately.

"I don't want to upset anybody, Mrs Rose. Believe me, we're doing this for Angie – and she matters just as much as Meg, doesn't she?"

"Angie Roberts gave him up of her own free will – and she's never asked – never enquired – and he couldn't have had better parents, not anywhere."

"I know. I'm sure you're right. Did they have a lovely home?"

"Beautiful. It couldn't have been nicer. Where could be nicer to bring up a child than Devon? He was only five minutes from the sea."

"How lovely!" said Emma. "And what did Meg call him?"

"I'm not telling you that. I'm not telling you anything. Just go away and leave us all alone."

And Mrs Rose did something she'd never done before in her life; she hung up without saying goodbye.

Emma turned triumphantly to Andy, who was sitting up, fiddling with his sock and looking uncomfortable.

"There you are! I told you she knew! She knows the family really well – in fact, I reckon it was a close friend. Meg – the woman's name is – Meg and Derek – only Derek's dead – and they lived in Devon – come on, Andy, write all this down! Now we're really on our way!"

He swung his legs off the bed slowly.

"I'm not haring off to Devon, Emma. I told you – Rita reckons Angie doesn't want to know. Honestly – it's because you've never met her. She'd have a fit if she knew we were charging around nosing into her affairs. Rita said leave it. I've given her the convent's number so if ever Angie wants to know she can phone them herself. I'm not doing anything more. Finito."

"But what about *him*? Mrs Rose spoke about him being a worry and a trouble – so he didn't settle down to be the perfect Catholic boy, did he? He's a rebel – doesn't that suggest to you that maybe he needs to find his roots – find his real mum?"

"Oh come on, Emma – don't play amateur psychologist, please. You're making far too much out of whatever she said. We know nothing about him. And he's twenty-six for God's sake – if we've been able to get this far in a couple of days, I guess he would have been able to trace Angie years ago if he'd wanted to."

Emma's lips were a straight line.

"You do give up easily, Andy, don't you? I can't stand that in a bloke."

She began to collect her shoes and bag and look around for her scarf which was lying in a crimson heap on the floor.

"I'm going home now," she said, winding it round her neck.

He reached out and held her shoulders.

"Don't be like that, Em. I feel – well, it's wrong. I wouldn't give up if I thought it was what Angie would want, but I don't. I feel she…"

He broke off, angry at the expression on her face.

"You're like a bloody dog with a bone, aren't you?" he said, releasing her roughly.

Without another word she pushed her feet into her sandals and left.

He could hear her feet slapping the pavement and he considered running after her.

"Why the hell should I?" he thought, kicking a cushion into the corner. "Bossy cow. Let her get on with it."

Tomorrow he would paint; not Emma's beautiful brown body, but the interesting mould on a tomato. He was an artist, after all.

Chapter Fifteen

Heather Cavalieri made strawberry jam. Why, she did not know, as the local jam was perfectly good, but such domestic tasks brought comfort to her in her present edgy state. Her mother had always made jam in the late summer, so she would continue to do the same.

In her mind she planned Roy's party; a wonderful buffet with duck pâté, smoked salmon with cream cheese, tiny lamb cutlets, crayfish from Harrods and Italian smoked ham from the special shop in Firenze. She *loved* parties, and liked them to have a theme. She was undecided on this one – perhaps masks from Venice would be more appropriate? A masqued party instead of a masqued ball? The idea grew on her. She had a wonderful white silk gown which would look terrific with a golden mask – perhaps she'd have her hair highlighted in Firenze this weekend as a trial run for the party. She felt happy and occupied for the first time in ages, and telephoned the hairdresser before she changed her mind.

Paolo at Bargello's could do it; it was booked for Saturday at 3.00 p.m. Her spirits rose; she would look at her best for Roy this weekend; she knew how he enjoyed her dressing up and looking pretty – just for him. Now she would do justice to dinner at the Plaza Lucchesi and would perhaps fulfil her role as the lovely Italian wife. She scalded jars and stirred the bubbling strawberries in quiet contentment. Maybe she'd ring Rachel tonight; share the plans with her, and then contact would have been made with all her children today. That was how she liked it; reassurance that all was well in their worlds, and then it would be in hers.

She heard a car hurtling up the hill and her heart lurched. She must stop doing that; cars squealed and screeched around here every day – she should be used to it by now. She stood stock still with the wooden spoon in her hand as she realised the car had turned into their drive. Surely Roy was not home yet? He'd only been gone two hours. Anyway, it had not sounded like the Alfa; she listened intently for a moment and then jumped as someone rapped on the door. For some reason she did not want to move. She did not want to place one foot in front of the other and walk to her front door. But she had to, and she opened it to see a gum-chewing officer of the Carabinieri. She looked at him in horror – knowing – already knowing. It was as if her heart were a lemon, to be squeezed slowly and then discarded.

He stopped chewing for as long as it took him to explain. He spoke no English. Signore Cavalieri had been cornering just out of Pratilino – the S65 – when a lorry coming the other way – he very much regretted – the Hospital of St Luca, Firenze – he would take her now – she should come with him.

That much she understood. A cold casket slipped over her, turning her to stone. She behaved like a robot. She made no sound. She took her jam from the stove and locked the doors. She knew already. He would say nothing more. On the drive down into Florence she did not utter one sound. She knew for certain they would be visiting the hospital morgue.

An English-speaking nurse had been found to take her to see Roy.

"He's dead, isn't he?" she blurted out as they walked along the corridor. "Tell me the truth – I know he's dead."

The nurse put her arm around her shoulder and squeezed in a kindly fashion.

"No, no, Signora. He's not dead. A nasty fracture and some concussion, but he's very much alive."

"Oh dear God, thank you. Oh, I'll never complain about anything ever again. I was *so* sure. When I saw that policeman standing there I just *knew*. Or thought I did. Merciful God – thank you, thank you."

She began to cry. Huge plopping tears welled up and fell onto the corridor as they walked past doctors and patients and visitors, oblivious to them all.

"Up here," the nurse said, ushering her into an elevator. She pushed '2' and smiled at Heather.

"Blow your nose!" she ordered cheerfully, offering a tissue out of her own pocket. "Signore Cavalieri doesn't want you weeping all over him. You must smile to cheer him up; he is in pain, poor man."

"Oh dear – is it very bad? My poor darling – he will be a terrible patient – terrible!"

"We have given him quite strong painkillers but they will wear off soon and we must leave a certain time before we give more – you understand. So no more tears – he is in very good hands. Dr Morcelli is in charge of him – he is a very fine doctor."

She blew her nose hard and dabbed her eyes.

"What has he broken?"

"His pelvis. He has fractured his pelvis but not too badly – how do you say it? Hairline fracture."

"Oh poor, poor love. Can he walk?"

"No, no. He will have to lie flat for three to four weeks. It depends. We will take more X-rays tomorrow."

"Four weeks? Oh no – he was flying to England next week!"

"Well he won't be doing that. He may be in hospital longer than that – it just depends; it varies so much from patient to patient."

The lift stopped smoothly and the doors slid apart. Another corridor and more double doors and then a small room with four beds in it. Roy was lying in the first. His cheeks were sallow and a small plaster lay above his right eyebrow.

"Oh darling!" Heather rushed forward and clutched at his hands and kissed his head tenderly. He opened his heavy-lidded eyes and looked at her briefly.

"Darling," he said, and closed them again.

"He's sedated of course," the nurse explained, and pushed a wooden chair towards her.

"He's cut his head – what's he done to his head?" she asked, but the nurse was disappearing the way she had come.

Heather looked down on his exhausted face in thankfulness. This was bad enough, but how could she have borne him being taken away from her forever? She could not imagine it. She held his hand and stroked it gently. A faint smile crossed his face and relaxed.

"I'm here, my darling," she said. "And I'll stay as long as you need me to."

She would have to telephone the girls and Richard. They must be told as they would need to make arrangements to fly out to see their father. She watched his quiet rhythmic breathing for half an hour and then gently freed her fingers. She must find a doctor and speak to him. Maybe she could stay overnight or if not she could find a bed and breakfast place nearby? Her thoughts were tumbling into some sort of order.

"I'm going to speak to the doctor, Roy, and then I'll be back. I won't be long," she said, but he didn't stir.

Her shoes clipped across the small ward until she found a nurses' station through double doors at the far end. "I'm Signora Cavalieri," she said. "Could I speak to my husband's doctor please? Roy Cavalieri's doctor?"

Her Italian was up to this but she hoped the doctor spoke English.

"Doctor Morcelli is in another part of the hospital at present. He will be back in the morning. Your husband will see him again tomorrow after the X-rays. You can talk with him then."

"Can I stay in the hospital? I need to be near him."

"Only until 9.30. The Station Hotel is only five minutes away – perhaps you could take a room there?"

"Yes. Yes, that sounds a good idea. Could I use the telephone, please?"

"Down the corridor to the elevator and back on the ground floor there are public payphones."

"Thank you. I'll just go and make a few phone calls and then I'll be back. If my husband wakes, will you be sure to tell him I'll be back?"

"Yes. Surely. I will tell him."

She walked slowly back past his bed and kissed his sleeping lips. He hardly stirred at all.

Who should she call first? Richard probably – he would need to make arrangements with Robert to be able to come out here.

She found the phone booth and dialled his office number. His secretary answered and said he was out. Didn't know how long he was likely to be – could she take a message? Heather hesitated – no – this was too serious to convey by a telephone message, so she said she would call him later at home. She rang Carla; Marta answered.

"Hello Marta. It's Mrs Cavalieri. Could I speak to Carla please dear?"

"She's out. She cocktail party with Dominic. Be back ten o'clock please."

"Right. Could you tell her I rang? It is important. I'll ring again just before eleven. All right?"

"Eleven. Yes. I tell. Goodbye."

Rachel would be in. She felt sure Rachel would be in. She looked at her watch – five-thirty in England – Rachel would be giving the baby her tea. She dialled, her head beginning a dull thumping.

"624?"

Rachel's voice caused the tears to start again and Heather blurted out. "It's me sweetheart. Papa's been hurt in a car crash – but he's not dead!"

"God! Mummy! Whatever's happened? Are you all right?"

"Yes. Papa was on his own, driving to the golf club. He was on the S65 and a lorry hit the car and pushed it down the bank apparently. I'm at the hospital now – Saint Luke's in Florence. He's fractured his pelvis but he's going to be all right. I'll see the doctor in the morning. Oh Rachel – when the policeman stood there on the doorstep I was so sure – I thought for certain he was telling me he was dead!"

"Oh mummy – don't cry. We'll come out as soon as we can, darling. I'll see if Laurie's parents can have Poppy for a couple of days. If not, I'll come out on my own as soon as I can get a flight. Have you spoken to Papa?"

"Not really. He's sedated, but he knows I'm here. He sort of smiled at me and then closed his eyes."

"Oh poor thing. I'll go now mama, and fix things as fast as I can. St Luke's Hospital, did you say? Are you going home now?"

"No. I'm going to try to get a room very close by – I want to be here all the time for the first few days. Yes, St Luke's. It's the main big teaching hospital in the centre of the city."

"Right. Well in that case, you'd better ring me again from your hotel tonight, and by then I'll know when we can get out to you. Oh poor Papa – it's so awful."

"I know. But it could be worse. I'll ring you at about half past nine then. Bye-bye sweetheart."

"Bye mama."

She knew Rachel was crying and she mopped her own eyes once more as she returned to the main reception desk and enquired about hotels. The receptionist rang the Station Hotel but it was full, so she tried a small pensione and found Heather a room five minutes' walk away.

"Pensione Ariele," she said, pointing to the map. "And try Ristorante Silvano – here – cucina alla casalinga – home cooking."

"Oh thank you, but I couldn't eat a thing."

"Well maybe tomorrow. It's very good and not far to walk. You must eat Signora! Keep your strength up!"

She smiled weakly and returned to Roy's bedside.

"I'm booked into a pensione, darling," she said, and his eyelids fluttered. "So I'll be here all evening and then back as soon as they'll let me in in the morning! I'll be banging on the door!"

His eyes opened and a grimace of pain crossed his face.

"Is it very bad?" she asked. "Shall I fetch the nurse?"

"No." He spoke very quietly. "I can't have another painkiller until 9.00. What's the time?"

"Half past seven. Someone will come soon. Oh darling – can I get you anything at all? A drink of water?"

He shook his head wearily and closed his fingers around her hand.

"Try to sleep again," she advised. "Rachel will be here tomorrow I expect. I'll ring Carla and Richard again when I get to the pensione – they were both out."

His brow looked clammy, she realised, as she studied his pain-soaked face. She would have to try to sleep in a strange hotel room without him. They hardly ever spent a night apart, she considered, and now it would be weeks. She must be strong for all of them, but especially for Roy. She looked as his face relaxed into sleep once more. Her dearest, darling Roy.

Chapter Sixteen

Mrs Rose awoke at seven, her eyes dry and gritty and her limbs aching. She'd had a restless night, tossing and turning and worrying about poor Meg. Would it be best to warn her? Devon was such a long drive, she wasn't sure she was up to it nowadays. Philip had been the driver; four hours on the motorway would have been no trouble to him at all, but she hated motorways and tried to avoid them.

She pictured Nethway; the pretty whitewashed cottage. Jude had left home long ago, of course. By all accounts, he was a champion surfer – but that was hardly what Meg had expected after the education he'd received from the Brothers. But Jeremy was nearby in Dartmouth, with his sweet wife – a lovely girl. They at least were a comfort to Meg and usually had her over for Sunday lunch. Why was Meg so upset now – all of a sudden? Her sister's last phone call had been so distressed and helpless, she must do something.

She made some toast and a pot of tea. She'd ring Meg later. She wouldn't decide what to say until they were speaking; that was best. Oh, it was such a worry. Who could she talk to, now that Philip was gone? Father Davey was kind, of course, but she couldn't keep bothering him with every anxiety – he'd never get a minute's peace. Who would Philip have turned to if he'd had a problem to chew over? Herself, of course, but also Graham. Yes, she could ring Graham – such a wonderful listener and now he'd retired, he must have plenty of time. Of course he'd lost Izzie after Christmas and she should have asked him over long before this. Where on earth had this year flown to? She would ring him and ask him to lunch on Sunday. She hadn't seen him for nearly two years and he was only an hour away round the M25 the way he drove. She turned the pages of her telephone book, with a slice of toast in her hand.

There is was – under B

BOTT Dr Graham
The Pines
Redlands Road

Ascot   Telephone 01344 516342

Rita dialled the code for Spain and waited. Lines busy. Damn; she wasn't going to stay up much longer. You'd think you'd be able to get through at this time of night.

"Who on earth are you ringing at this time of night?" shouted Patrick from upstairs.

"Angie!" she yelled back, and heard him splashing in the bathroom.

The back door slammed and Stu came in, holding a Giant Mac in one hand and a can of lager in the other.

"Mind where you're going with that!" she shouted. "It's dripping ketchup."

He leaned his head back and took a huge bite. She shuddered.

"Eat that in the kitchen," she said automatically, and dialled again.

She heard the bleeps and then a pause – a hiccup – and then it was ringing. She imagined Angie's hotel, the Majorcan floor tiles, the white walls, the blue sea – always that unbelievably blue sea.

"Hola?"

"Hi Angie – it's me!"

"Hello, sweetheart! How're things?"

"Fine. I heard from Andy today. I don't think he's going to do any more poking around in your affairs, thank God. I told him I was sure you didn't want him to."

"Too bloody right. And you think he accepted that? I can't imagine what set him off in the first place."

"Well I think he's stopped now. Anyway, he said he was going to ring you, so you can ask him for yourself."

"Right. And he and Emma seemed together, did they?"

"Oh, I should say so. 'An item', as Stu would put it."

Angie laughed.

"Haven't heard that one before out here! Ah well – he followed my advice and protested undying love over armfuls of flowers then?"

"Dunno. What about you? Have you seen Eduardo again?"

"No and I shan't. I told you, it's completely over. He

behaved like a pig – I shan't see him again."

"Oh, Angie, I always hoped you'd find someone and settle down – you know – somebody special. You're too old for all these changes, you know."

"Thanks a bunch, kid! No, no – you're right, I agree. No more men! I'm quite content with my lot, Rita, you know I am. I love this place; it's my home and my family. Jose, Conchita, Julio – they're all my family, and I've got you and Patrick and the kids safely tucked away in the background – I can call you whenever I want – I'm so lucky really."

"So you're all right? I worry about you, you know."

"Well, don't! I'm fine. Why should you worry about me, for God's sake? Most women would give their eye teeth for what I've got."

"I know – but I just felt last time we spoke – well – you'd stirred up all those memories you know – I was just worried, that's all."

"You're lovely, Rita, but stop it! I'm absolutely fine, honestly. Tomorrow I'm hosting a dinner for the town dignitaries from Soller – I shall be helping Julio all day – we have planned this fantastic menu – conejo al Ajillo – Solomillo Parrila and for pudding, Tortilla Alaska and Crepes Imperiales – I shall be cooking for hours! So I'd better go to bed now. I'm just sipping a small whisky before I drop into bed. Cheers!"

"You're not drinking too much, are you Angie?"

"No, no. I often have a nightcap. It helps me unwind. I've had a really busy week. What about you?"

"Oh, the usual. The Centre's always busy. We're off to see Sharon with Clare on Sunday. I'm looking forward to that."

"Great. Give them both my love. *And stop worrying.* I'll speak to you soon. Loads of love. Night night."

"Night night, Angie. God bless."

She climbed the stairs wearily. Sometimes she hated having thousands of miles between them; it seemed like tens of thousands.

She just wanted to see her – her little sister. Then she'd know if she was really all right. She was a great actress, was Angie. A great actress.

"Shall I uncork this for you?"

Graham Bott was standing holding a bottle of Chianti Classico and watching Janet Rose in gentle amusement as she basted the lamb in a flustered manner.

"That smells amazing!" he said, as he picked up the cork screw.

"Oh, I do hope it's all right. There's nothing like a really good leg of lamb, is there? And I bought it from the old butchers in Sawbridgeworth; they're very good. They haven't let me down yet. Yes, please dear. 'Let it breathe', as Philip would have said. Gosh, I do still miss him, Graham, you've no idea."

"Of course I have."

She turned quickly, horrified at her own thoughtlessness and nearly knocked the roasting pan onto the floor. Graham saved it and opened the oven door for her, stepping back at the blast of hot air which engulfed them.

"I'm so sorry, Graham. I've become so self-centred lately. I've noticed it in myself – *of course* you know. It's less than a year since poor Izzie… I still can't believe it."

"I know. I sometimes think I can hear her coming up the stairs when I'm in bed. You know, she didn't sleep well, so she often watched television late and I'd be dozing when I'd hear her feet on the stairs at one in the morning. A couple of times I've thought I'd seen her at the bottom of the garden from the kitchen window – odd, the tricks your mind plays, isn't it?"

"Yes. I sometimes thought I saw Philip drive past me in the car just after he'd died. You know – *really* – thought it was him. It was so frightening because it made me feel as if I was in some sort of nightmare and that maybe I'd got it all wrong, but I couldn't wake myself up. That doesn't happen anymore, thank goodness. Not for over a year, but I still miss him just as much as in the beginning."

"When I think of all the facile crap I spouted at patients over the years – clichés about time healing and them making a new life, you know? Complete bollocks."

Janet turned from the cooker and they both sat down at her kitchen table. She poured two dry sherries from a bottle of Tio Pepe Graham had brought.

"Old friends are such a comfort," she said, sipping

appreciatively. "And family, of course, but with my boys being so far away and Meg in Devon, I do feel rather isolated sometimes. At least you've got Jane living near you; you're lucky there."

"Yes, I know. She's a darling, but they have their own lives to lead. I spend a lot of time at the golf club – and I do still see some private patients of course. I'm OK. I thought you were. What's on your mind at the moment? I got the feeling you wanted to talk to me about something."

"Yes, I do. You always know what people are thinking, don't you? It's Meg's boy – Jude. I've had her on the phone nearly out of her mind with worry. She doesn't know where he is."

"Why? Has he gone missing?"

"Yes. She wrote to him after Christmas and he never replied. Both she and Jeremy have been to where he used to live – some kind of squat, I believe – but he isn't there and nobody seemed to know where he'd gone."

He put his glass down carefully and spread his elegant fingers on the smooth yellow tablecloth.

"Has she tried the Salvation Army? I believe they trace missing people."

"She hasn't so far. She's also worried that he may be in trouble – drugs, you know. He's taken drugs for years, and she thinks he may have started selling them to other people."

"God, what a mess. He was such a lovely looking kid, I seem to remember. I think I only saw him once or twice – at your place one New Year's Eve, certainly."

"He is very striking looking. But he's been a terrible worry for years."

Graham looked at her carefully.

"Did he ever…" he hesitated over his words. "Did he ever try to contact his birth mother at all?"

She jumped visibly.

"No. No, I don't think he ever did. But actually – I wasn't going to tell you this – but someone rang here a few days ago asking questions – upsetting me– wanting to know things about him – they said because the – the birth mother needed to know."

"Really? How extraordinary. And who were these people?"

"Well, I'm not sure. They said they'd met the mother in Majorca or something, and that she needed to know where he was. But of course I didn't tell them anything. I said I didn't know. It really upset me, and of course if they find out anything and get to Meg, it will just be one more agony for her – it's just the worst possible time for this to happen to her."

Graham rubbed his finger across the cloth and said nothing for some time. All sorts of extraordinary possibilities were occurring to him and his head was reeling. Eventually he said, "And you know nothing about these people other than that? What were they like?"

"They were a very young couple. They called here when Moira was staying. He said he was an artist and had painted the portrait of this woman who ran a hotel in Majorca..."

He pressed his hand against his mouth and stood up, walking towards her open back door and staring down the garden, with his back to her.

"They said she was feeling pretty low and needed to know what had happened to her son. I'm not sure that I altogether believed their story actually. And it certainly wouldn't do my poor Meg any good if they turned up and went through all this stuff with her. You don't think they'll trace her, do you?"

"It's highly unlikely. These things are confidential – I imagine only the birth mother and the adopted child would be given any official information. But I do wonder about poor old Jude – maybe he needs to know – did you ever feel he wanted to trace his roots at all?"

"No. No, I honestly think he just got in with a bad lot. After all, Jeremy's adopted too and he turned out just fine. They both had everything going for them – everything."

"Derek's death would have been a terrible blow how old were they then?"

"Jude was eleven. But Jeremy was nine – and he's been a rock – never a minute's worry, not ever."

"I should give Meg a call and see how she's sounding this evening. If she sounds OK, don't say anything, but if she's had these people pestering her she'll soon tell you. But I doubt they'd be given any information at all."

Her face, quartered with anxiety, relaxed a little.

"Shall we eat in the garden, dear?" she said, joining him in the doorway. They stood looking out at the honeysuckle and late roses.

"What a marvellous smell everywhere," he said. "Roast lamb in the kitchen and honeysuckle at the back door. I shall have to spend more Sundays in Sheering – Sheer Heaven, I'll call it!"

She pulled off a dead head and then sat on the garden chair by the door. He sat beside her.

"It's extraordinary," he said. "Remember Angelica and Rita Roberts?"

She looked up and frowned.

"Yes of course I do, Well, particularly Rita. She worked at the Centre for years. Still does, as far as I know. I lost touch with the younger one though. I had no idea you still knew them."

"I never completely lost touch. Angie was my patient at St Ebba's when she was a youngster – remember?"

She gazed out into the middle distance and closed her eyes briefly. "Yes. Of course. I used to drive Rita to see her. I had forgotten you were her psychiatrist then."

"Well, after she left the hospital she trained as a cook and we kept in touch. I got her a few contacts. Even in the last few years Izzie and I had a few days' holiday at her hotel – it's a beautiful spot in Majorca – and she runs this very lovely small guest house up in the mountains."

"I see."

The silence between them was becoming awkward and Janet stood up.

"Well, shall we eat out here, Graham, or is it getting too chilly?"

"No, it's fine. Out here would be delightful."

He followed her back into the kitchen to carve the lamb. A cloud passed over the sun and a breeze got up enough to bang the door shut.

"Maybe we'd better eat in here after all," Janet said, looking out of the window. "It seems to be changing and getting colder all of a sudden. We don't want to catch a chill."

Chapter Seventeen

Emma banged into her flat like a crashing train. She threw her bag onto the floor, and went straight to the kitchen to pour herself a beer from the fridge.

"Hi!" shouted Susie from her room, emerging with a towel around her head.

"I didn't think you'd be back tonight; had a good time?"

"No – bloody awful."

She walked with the can of beer into the sitting room and threw herself onto the sofa, legs crossed on the arm.

Susie followed, rubbing her hair and squatting down beside her. She'd known Emma since they were eight – temper tantrums had often been aimed at her in those days and she recognised the signs.

"Won't do as he's told then? God, I thought he'd drop dead if you told him to. What's the problem?"

"The problem is I'm pissed off with blokes who give up at the first spot of inconvenience. I – and let's face it – it's been me all along – I found out that the baby was brought up in Devon by a woman called Meg and a guy called Derek; who's dead. Meg is obviously Mrs Rose's friend because she got all upset about it and wouldn't tell us any more, but she knows something – and pathetic bloody Andy won't do anything about it. Just because it's Devon – he's as mean as hell, honestly he is. He keeps on saying Angie doesn't want to know – but I ask you – it's not psychologically likely, is it? As if you could give up your baby and *not* want to know how he is and where he is and whether he's happy – I mean – imagine – could *you* just live your life without ever wanting to know? Ridiculous."

Susie stayed on the floor rubbing her hair in silence. Emma continued without looking at her.

"I know I couldn't. Ever since he told me about it I knew I had to find him. And I've only got a few days – three days left before I start this new job. Well, I'm not giving up. I'll go on my own."

"Devon's quite a big place," was Susie's only comment as she dried each ear in turn.

"It's likely they go to one of the Catholic churches, isn't it? I'll start by listing them and ringing the priests. I can think of some reason why I don't know the surname – friend of the family – been abroad – I'll think of something. It's no good mentioning adoption – they won't tell me anything. But I might be able to check out Meg and Derek who had a son, now in his mid twenties – and near the coast, she said, so that cuts it down."

"Why are you doing this, Em?" Susie asked, stroking Jasper as he wound his way round her, purring like a tractor. "I know you get stuck into things from time to time, but why this? I just don't see it. You've got this brilliant new job next week – and a new man – why risk them with this stupid obsession – that's what it's becoming."

Emma looked at her sharply for the first time.

"Is it? Well I know I can be a bit obsessive but that's why I'm so *good* at things – I get stuck in and really focus. I don't know why this has got to me but it has – as soon as Andy told me about it I felt – it's hard to describe, Suse – I just felt like – well, connected in some way. Thinking about that girl – she was only twenty – a year younger than us – but not educated; no advantages – no parents to help her – it just seemed so terrible that I really wanted to do something about it. And I know I can."

"But by all accounts she's a successful woman now, running a hotel in Majorca – and he's *twenty-six*! You're talking about him as if he's a child – he's older than us – if he'd wanted to trace his mother he could have – *he's* the one who has rights and would be given all the information you're trying to put together. I guess he really didn't want to know. He's probably had this fantastic life with a wealthy family down there – you know – sailing. Young Farmers, all that. Why should he worry about something that happened when he was a few weeks old?"

"Mrs Rose said he was a worry and a trouble, so he hasn't settled down, has he?"

"Em! God – you know *nothing* about this guy; you're making it all up. You should never have done that Sixth Form Psychology class. You're forever trying to analyse people's motives. Leave it, will you, or you're going to spoil your relationship with Andy. You said that was special, didn't you?"

Emma drained the beer and placed it carefully on a raffia

mat on the table.

"I thought it was, but tonight he made me so *mad* I just had to leave. And his room is *disgusting*. I mean – I couldn't live with that – it's like – filthy. He just really peed me off. I'm going to have a shower now and get to bed. If I'm going to Devon tomorrow I need to make an early start."

She loped out of the room, leaving Susie scratching Jasper's ear thoughtfully.

"You're a spoilt cow, you know that, don't you?" she called at the bathroom door, laughing. "If you leave it till Saturday I'll come with you. I've got nothing planned. I could see if mum'll lend me her car and we could drive down really early. It'll be cheaper than the train."

Emma peered around the bathroom door in bra and pants.

"OK. I can make phone calls and get a map and get really organised tomorrow then. Great! Thank God someone is backing me up."

She disappeared and Susie heard the shower drowning some other remark. She had a pretty good idea what it would have been. Poor Andy – he was about to join the cluttered ranks of other good-looking males who had not quite made the grade. 'Emma's discards' she called them. She wasn't surprised. No one ever dumped Emma; she was always in charge. Susie picked up the cat and walked into her bedroom. She'd always bossed her around too, but she didn't mind. Life was never dull with Emma; she would always provide the unexpected.

Emma put the telephone down for the fourth time; no use. She hadn't enough to go on. She'd developed a good line on her mother asking her to look up an old school friend, Meg, as her mother now lived in Australia, but she'd lost the piece of paper with Meg's name and address on it. It sounded reasonable to her but so far no Catholic priest in Devon had heard of Meg and Derek with an adopted son of twenty-six. It was so little to go on.

'Could you telephone your mother and ask her?' had been the last priest's sensible question, and she had sighed impatiently. She'd got so near and now – nothing. She knew even she could not ask Susie to drive all the way to Devon if they had no definite lead and no destination. Everything depended upon her phone calls this morning. She was working her way along the south Devon coastline – the Diocesan Office had given her all the priests in the district, which was fantastically helpful, but now she was beginning to doubt her detective skills for the first time. Dear old faithful Susie – she'd persuaded her mum to lend them her VW for the whole weekend, so they could take their time to track Meg down – providing they had somewhere to start from. She dialled a North Devon number for the first time – Barnstaple.

"Barnstaple 362," the voice said, and she tried again.

"Could I speak to Father Fenton?" she asked, and the voice said, "Speaking."

"The Diocesan Office gave me your number. I'm trying to trace an old friend of my mother's, whose surname and address I've mislaid. My mother lives in Australia and she'll be furious I've lost the details, so I'm hoping you'll be able to help. She's called Meg and she's a Roman Catholic – do you know her? She used to be married to Derek, but he died."

"And it was Barnstaple, was it?"

"I'm not sure, I'm afraid. It might have been. I lost the address, you see, but I do know it was Devon and near the coast, and that they had an adopted son who's now in his twenties. Does that ring any bells with you?"

"This is quite a large parish, and no, I can't say it does. Do you have anything else to go on at all?"

"Well only that the son has been in some sort of trouble. Meg would be in her sixties I should think."

"It doesn't ring any bells I'm afraid. Do you not know any other friends of your mother who could help you?"

Emma hesitated.

"No. Not really. Can I give you my phone number in case you – well – remember anything."

"Certainly. But I've been here for eleven years and I can't think of a Meg and Derek at all."

"OK. Thanks anyway. It's a London number…"

"Hold on a minute – this pen's not working."

She gave him the number and hung up. This was hopeless. It just wasn't enough to go on. Maybe she should try Mrs Rose again; she could let something else slip.

She rang the number and waited, turning over various possible openings in her mind.

"Hello?"

She assumed a Scottish accent – she had a good ear and enjoyed mimicry.

"Mrs Rose?"

"Yes. Who is that?"

"It's Fiona Cameron from the Diocesan Office in Plymouth. We're doing a quarterly magazine now, and I'm writing a feature on good Catholic ladies in the diocese. Meg's name came up and I wondered if you could fill me in with any helpful tit-bits for my piece. She's a wee bit modest and won't blow her own trumpet, you know what I mean?"

"Oh she is! She always underrates herself – always has! Well now, isn't that lovely? Let me think – well of course Father Sedgewick could tell you all the good work she does in the parish – and then she used to do those summer holidays for deprived children from Bristol – she did that for years."

"Marvellous. Just the sort of thing I need. Father Sedgewick, you said?"

"Yes, her parish priest. And of course, she's been a *wonderful* mother to those two boys and Jeremy's such a credit to her. And she's always run the Christmas Bazaar – oh, for years and years. Fund raising and actually making things. She knitted blankets for Africa too."

"And Jeremy – would he still be at home?"

"Gosh no – he'd be twenty-four or twenty-five by now. He's married, with a lovely wife. They live in Dartmouth. He adores his mother; he would be able to think of things – shall I give you his number?"

"That would be great."

Emma's heart was pounding. It was so *easy*. She should have been an actress. She hoped her accent wasn't slipping in her excitement.

Janet Rose gave her a Dartmouth number and said, "I'm so thrilled you're doing this. Meg's been a wonderful church worker all her life, you know. And it so often goes unappreciated, doesn't it? Will you send me a copy when it's done? I'd love to see it."

Emma felt a pang of conscience for the first time, but said, "Of course. What's your address?"

Janet repeated it slowly and then hung up.

"Well it was the only way," said Emma aloud, breathing out slowly. "God I was brilliant! She had *no idea*! And now I've got his brother's phone number! Fantastic!"

Her fingers were shaking slightly as she prodded the numbers and waited, hearing the repeated ringing and then the answer phone click in.

"They're at work," she thought, looking at her watch. "But I can ring this evening and then I'll know! I'll know all about him!"

She threw herself onto her back on her bed, a smile spreading across her features. She felt like a huntsman seeing the fox slipping through the trees; the prey in sight and the prospect of a good chase immediately ahead.

Graham Bott picked up the mail from his doormat and straightened his stiff back – a little localised pain in the lumbar region from an old rugger injury. He threw the BT bill onto the hall table with two circulars and looked at the blue air letter with curiosity. He slit it open, and read it twice, a half smile spreading across his face.

'Dear Gabby' he read.

'I was so shocked to read your letter with its terrible news that I've only just got around to writing to you. I was going to telephone but I cannot express my sorrow adequately enough – what a loss Izzie's death is to you I can hardly imagine. I only hope that in these intervening months you will be beginning to build some sort of life again, and I wonder if you would enjoy a few days here in Deya as my guest? It would be marvellous to see you again. I've had a strange summer here, with all sorts of old memories resurfacing; just when I thought I'd really put my life in order. It would be wonderful to talk things through with you, if this didn't seem like work – you always understood me so well.

Things quieten down here at the end of September so if you have any free time soon just let me know. Of course you may be retired but somehow I doubt it. I'd be glad to have you here.

*My fondest love,
Angie.'*

It would be great to see her of course. The past nine months had been dreadful; a long, dark tunnel of despair, and while he knew the clinical stages he was going through, and what he would recommend to anyone else, nothing had held out any hope for him until his conversation with Janet Rose had brought thoughts and reminders of Angie. He had also felt that crazy stab of recognition – he could only call it that – when Janet had been talking about her nephew. Could he possibly be Angie's son? The dates fitted, of course, but how could the Roses have kept it from him all those years? And should they have been involved at all, as Angie had been a patient? It was all very unprofessional. He had had no reason to make the connection before but that conversation had been like switching a light on. Everything had come into focus and made sense. Did Angie know? Almost certainly not. He put the letter down by his computer and clicked on to the Internet. He would go. He checked flights and dates. The change of scenery was just what he needed, and if the conversation turned to the subject of her son, so be it. He could only wait and listen.

For two weeks he tried to get fitter. He played tennis and golf and spent more time in the garden. The September sunshine was glorious and his gaunt face improved with a tan. In the past months he had lost a stone in weight; somehow he never fancied food he cooked himself, and Janet's Sunday roast was the best meal he had eaten for ages. He rang her to thank her for it; how she had aged since Philip's death. She was only five years older than he was but she seemed at least ten. Of course she'd never had any dress sense. Izzie had often laughed at the frumpish dresses and cardigans she wore even in her thirties and forties, but it hadn't mattered. The Roses were such a devoted, happy couple that fashion had been irrelevant.

Izzie, of course, had been a woman of great style and colour. He'd admired her more than any other woman he'd ever known; she had been ambitious, clever, a perfectionist and a great mother to their children. And a great lover too – sometimes. Izzie had long stretches of boredom with sex, in between bouts of excited passion. He'd put it down to hormonal swings and exhaustion, as her work was so demanding; and when she'd been cool and distant he had occasionally found other women as diversions. The thought of that disturbed him now far more than it ever had when Izzie had been alive; it felt so treacherous. Angie had been one of those dalliances, of course, for a very short time, but had remained a special friend. Since he'd watched the golden girl emerge from the depressed, deadened twenty-year-old who'd slumped in front of him at St Ebba's he'd felt her strong sexual allure many times, but had kept a guarded distance between them until she was no longer his patient, and he was certain she was on a steady emotional keel. He'd helped her in her career at first, encouraging her to go it alone with her catering business, and putting smart dinner party clients her way as she got started. She hadn't disappointed him in any way, and he was only amazed that she had never married or found a lasting partner in her beautiful lifestyle in Deya. He was sure it wasn't for lack of offers.

He started up the car and purred out of the drive, his black Audi gliding along the Ascot road seductively. He drove well, noting traffic lights and pedestrians and a faltering cyclist with one part of his brain, while another part leapt ahead to Deya and La Casa d'Or. He had been enchanted with Angie's small hotel and even Izzie's exacting standards hadn't been disappointed. Their bedroom had been white and cool with a blue tiled floor and an old Spanish bed in strange dark wood. The sheets had been soft white linen and the shower – amazingly for a mountain village in Spain – had worked perfectly. Angie had cooked for them herself, and he could still remember the bowl of mussels in white wine she had served on their first evening.

"Mejillones al ajillo!" she had announced proudly, but there had only been a hint of garlic with those wonderfully fresh mussels from Andraitx harbour. Casserole of kid had followed; a local delicacy from the black mountain goats which leapt nimbly over the rocks from Deya to the Formentor Point.

Izzie had been very relaxed and sexy the whole weekend.

What a great time they'd had, and how he'd admired her ability to accept or ignore – he wasn't sure which – the relationship he had had in the past with Angie. She too had behaved impeccably, treating them as equally dear friends, although she hardly knew Izzie at all, and being meticulous not to behave in a flirty or intimate manner. What fantastic women they both were; and now there was only one. Just Angie left. He let out a deep sigh as he swept up the sandy drive of the golf course. That was all in the past. He had to go on living – what did he say to patients? 'This is now' – how trite he now felt that to be, but maybe Angie might even be his future. He must wait and see.

Andy tried ringing Emma again. Still engaged. What the hell was she doing? She'd been continuously on the telephone for fifty minutes – maybe there was a fault on the line. He deliberated whether to go round or just wait. He was still smarting under her behaviour yesterday and his male pride needed her to make the first move. He threw his mobile on the bed, determined to wait.

Placing the tomato on a dish, he gazed at the mould in fascination. He moved things around until he was happy with the light, and began to paint, his brow furrowed in concentration. In years to come people would assume the parallel lines on his forehead denoted superciliousness, but they did not – simply hour upon hour of hot concentration. He painted for two hours and then stopped to search for a lager. The room was hot and airless; he threw open the only window and wiped his T-shirt across his face. His concentration refused to return; who the fuck was she making all those calls to? The 'friend' she'd gone clubbing with the night he'd returned perhaps? 'Not important', she'd described him dismissively. Would he, too, be described in that way before long? He wrenched his thoughts back to his work; work was the answer. When he had a decent portfolio, he could make things up with Emma. Until then she must come to him. He painted for another twenty-five minutes before hurling his brush across the room in despair. It was terrible. A still life with as much originality as a fucking tea tray. He picked up his mobile again and stabbed. It rang and rang. No reply. Susie's voice informed him they were not available and would he please leave a message. No way. He sat on his bed depressed and demoralised. What a bloody powerful creature Emma was. How quickly she could wreck his day. He looked at the painting again, deciding that only one tiny patch of mould was of any interest. Maybe he could work on that as an abstract; a metaphor for a disintegrating relationship. Yes – forget the fruit and rework the mould. He picked up his brush, lightening a little. He covered the tomato in broad brush strokes of black, roughly suggesting a skull, and became interested in his idea.

What had Angie said? 'Put your pain into your painting'. Something like that. He must channel his anger and hurt somehow – over his parents, bloody awful Carolyn, his feelings about Emma and now this – the fear that he might have lost her.

'Get back to London and paint what you're really feeling'.

"God, Angie," he said aloud as he painted. "If only I could."

Chapter Eighteen

Angie looked at his letter again in delight.

Gabbie here – and on his own – here for four whole days!

She turned the single paper over in her hand to gaze at it again; to make sure there was no mistake.

'I would love to visit Deya again, and could come out on September 25th until 29th. I can get a flight arriving Palma 17.07, Easijet. Hope these dates are convenient for the hotel. Looking forward to seeing you again enormously. Yours, Gab'.

To his inner circle he had always been Gab; when not listening he was a great raconteur, with a talented and witty way with words. Angie found herself lifting the note to her lips and standing on tiptoe in her excitement. There were no free bedrooms on those dates; she knew that without checking. Ah well; she would give him her own room and sleep in the office. No problem.

Conchita cleared the table, surprised that for once Angie had nothing to say, but secretly delighted by the expression on her face – pure happiness.

"Icuidado," she said to Julio as she banged into the kitchen.

"La Senora encanta! Ivaya, vaya, vaya!"

Julio, peeling prawns, grinned and made a coarse remark, which offended Conchita, and she flounced out of the kitchen.

"Pronto me lo levo yo al infierno," she informed Angie, crossing herself devoutly as she laid the table for the guests' breakfasts.

Angie looked up and grinned.

"If Julio's going to hell you can be sure Jose will be there before him!" she laughed, walking towards the reception desk to see if the flowers were still fresh.

'Your room is ready – can't wait', she wrote on a postcard of the hotel, and drew a small angel where her signature should have been. She wrote his address from memory and stuck on a stamp. She had fifteen minutes before the first guests might emerge. She wandered into the garden; a slight heat haze had formed and the air was still. She stood stroking the trunk of an olive tree as old as a grandfather, and pictured Graham. She had not seen him since he and Izzie had stayed one Easter – when? Three years ago? It must be. He had looked no more than fifty, still slim and virile, with a thick hatch of brown hair and distinguished silver sideburns. A gorgeous looking man. She prayed he had not changed too much. Did he ever think of her? What mattered was that he thought of her now and was coming to Deya in two weeks' time. In two weeks he would be here, breathing the same mountain air and sleeping in her bed. She would lie on the couch in her office knowing he was only a few paces away. Somehow until then she must drag her thoughts away to her niece's wedding in Harlow, and her hurried visit to Rita and Patrick for a quick two days next weekend. The bridal suite must be made quite perfect for Clare and her new husband – she owed it to Rita to ensure that everything was as wonderful as it could be.

It was strange being on a flight with a bride and groom en route to their honeymoon. Angie smiled protectively across the aisle at Clare and Greg. They seemed so sweet and happy, and even the discovery that their original honeymoon choice had not been Deya but the Caribbean did not spoil her pleasure that they were now to be her guests.

"I've always loved it," Clare said. "And Greg's never seen it, has he? He'll be knocked out. Like he wanted Barbados more than I did but the travel company went bust and we lost our deposit. Never mind – I didn't fancy that long flight – not after all the excitement of the wedding and that. Too much really; this is much better. It feels like going home. All those holidays we had with you when we was kids!"

Angie had left Conchita in charge of the arrangements. The best and largest bedroom was to be theirs – with the original marble bathroom and solid brass taps – and best of all – a stunning view of the sea through the pine trees, as her own bedroom had. 'Del Pinar' she called the room. All her guest bedrooms had names; numbers she left for the large hotels. Conchita would make sure all her instructions were carried out to the letter – the bed covered in new white linen from Palma and sprinkled with rose petals, the curtains freshly laundered, vases of flowers everywhere. Angie herself had bought new fluffy towels in Soller before leaving; white with golden suns in a band around the edge. She was satisfied Clare would be thrilled.

"There's no timetable at all at La Casa d'Or," she promised Greg, as they unwrapped the plastic lunch boxes provided by Iberian Airlines. "Your time's your own. I won't get in the way. You can spend as little or as much time as you like in the hotel. Meals are completely flexible and I can arrange picnics. You can borrow my car whenever I don't need it or take the Valeria taxi. Just feel free as birds."

Greg grinned; Clare's auntie seemed great and not at all like her mother. Much younger and sexier somehow. The prospect of a honeymoon in Clare's relation's hotel instead of Barbados had seemed a big let-down, but they couldn't afford another deposit. Now suddenly he was looking forward to it. Clare was unscrewing the tiny bottle of red wine that came with their meal. "Oh I think we ought to have some bubbly, Mrs Peterson!" he laughed, and called over the cabin stewardess.

"God! *Mrs Peterson*! I sound like your mother – it's going to take years to get used to that. But I do feel different – it's like – no, don't laugh – I feel kinda safe. Oh Greg – we must go to Formentor – the beach there has these little straw huts and straw umbrellas all along it – like the Caribbean really. We can take a boat from Pollensa – oh, I'm so excited! We used to do that when I was a kid. It's going to be so great showing you everything. And Pollensa market – that's brilliant – I want to buy a handbag and some shoes. We've got a whole week – isn't that fantastic?"

They toasted one another and giggled. Angie leaned across and said, "I've got pink champagne waiting for you in Deya. The real stuff. Julio is cooking some fantastic dishes for you tonight – it will be very quiet and private; just you two. You don't need to speak to another soul if you don't want to."

Greg grinned.

"Well we won't want to be that unsociable! What's the beach like?"

"Rocky. Long climb back up, but there are others not too far away. Soller's good."

"I love that little rocky beach. Mum would never let us go

down there on our own – we always had to wait for her or dad to go with us. It'll be great to do as we like."

She seemed so young. Well, almost twenty-six was young, but in many ways Clare still seemed a teenager. She had had a pretty sheltered upbringing and her job as a nursery nurse was hardly sophisticated. Greg was a dear and she was sure they'd be happy. As Rita and Patrick had, she guessed. Stable and uncomplicated lives, not like hers at all. She drank her wine. Twenty-six. Clare would be twenty-six in October. He would be twenty-seven in December. Only fourteen months apart. Was he married? Did he look at all like Clare? Probably not. Clare was like her father, and Rita and Angie did not even look alike. Rita's brown hair and ordinary looks had never competed with Angie's green eyes and blonde hair. People had commented on the marked difference all through their childhood; she looked like her father's mother, apparently. She gazed at the thin slices of chicken in gravy and tiny tinned potatoes and knew she could not eat a thing.

Her mind, now freed from the social requirements of today's wedding, was wandering back in the well-worn direction of her son. That old tormentor. Sometimes now when she thought of him, she sensed a crushing in her chest, and worried that she might be going to have a heart attack, but it passed. The pain drifted slowly away like a moon shadow, and she could think calmly of a young man living his life somewhere – if only she knew where. Maybe looking a little like her. Did he know about her at all? Did he wonder about her even half as often as she did about him? And –worst of all – what did he think of her decision to give him up? 'It wasn't a decision', she thought, as she covered up the lunch tray with a napkin. 'No one could say I was in a fit state to make a rational decision. He was taken from me, and I was cheated of my son. That is how I shall always see it. Cheated. It was unforgivable'.

The stewardess passed down the aisle with coffee and tea and Angie handed her cup for coffee with relief. Coffee she could always drink, night or day.

"Can we just go for lunch at the Hotel Formenter?" Clare asked, leaning across Greg with a cake in her hand.

"Course you can, sweetheart. Then you could use their

hotel pool. It's stunning. Their beach is one of the best, Greg – pine trees right down to the beach and this fantastic garden all the way along the width of this *huge* hotel. Bit pricier than La Casa d'Or, of course, but it is your honeymoon. Less character too!"

"Do you remember the time we all went swimming when the hotel was shut for the winter? And the guards drove down the beach in a jeep to check us out? They looked like the mafia – I was so scared!"

"I wasn't with you, sweetheart. I was cooking your Christmas lunch. That was *years* ago – before I got Julio."

She watched the man sitting next to her packing up his lunch and unfolding The Times to do the crossword. She suddenly thought longingly of Gabbie. As soon as these lovebirds had returned home *he* would be coming for four days. How she longed to see him again; she hoped passionately that Deya would help him regain some sense of purpose, as it had done for her all those years ago.

"I don't know why I get up in the mornings, Angie!" he'd told her sadly when she'd rung him to confirm their dates and times. "There just doesn't seem to be any point to any of it now – without her. I care about my children; of course I do, but they have busy lives. And my patients can be quite absorbing – but then I go home to my quiet, empty house, and all I can see is where Izzie should be and isn't."

"Have you thought about moving and starting afresh?" she'd asked.

"No. This was our home together for twenty years. I can't see myself leaving it. At least I can visualize her here. I can't bear the thought of being somewhere she never lived. It will get better eventually, I guess, and then I'll be glad I stuck it out."

She *must* help him as he had helped her all those years ago. Deya would do its part – the soothing sound of the waves on the rocks so far below, the wind in the pine trees and the soporific sun on his face in the garden. If she and her house couldn't do it, nothing could. Together they would heal him. Physician – heal thyself. He clearly couldn't do that. She must do it for him.

Chapter Nineteen

"You are a dear, bothering to drive all this way – thank goodness you got here before it was dark!"

Janet Rose sank onto her sister's chintz sofa with relief. Her hands were still shaking slightly, she noticed, as she accepted the Spode cup of Earl Grey Meg was offering.

"I was beginning to wonder if I would. The motorway was so terrible – and I was afraid I'd miss the right turn off. Anyway – I'm here now! How's Jeremy?"

"Oh fine. They'll pop over tomorrow. Ellie's bringing a raspberry pavlova – you know what a super cook she is. Oh Janet, it's so good to see you!"

Meg held out her hand and squeezed her sister's arm appreciatively. Janet sipped her tea and regarded her sternly.

"Well – you look just as bad as I thought you might. I've hardly had a wink's sleep you know, worrying about you. No news from Jude still, I suppose?"

"No, nothing. Jeremy says we have to accept that he's cut himself off from us and that's how he wants it. That maybe he'll see sense in a year or two and make contact again. But I can't just let him go, Janet, can I? I love him – he's always been a handful but I thought at one time we were quite close. He's got such a lot of good in him, Janet. He has really. I don't know what to do."

Janet sniffed.

"He's an ungrateful, selfish, inconsiderate young man, Meg, who's caused you years and years of worry. I think Jeremy's probably right. He's made his own bed – let him lie on it for a bit. He'll probably be in touch again – he knows where you are for goodness sake."

"I can't just do that. I lie in bed imagining he's been knifed, or ill and no one cares, or drowned by a freak wave when he's surfing – oh at three o'clock in the morning believe me I can come up with all kinds of horrors. I just need to know where he is – I need to hear his voice – just for a minute. To know he's all right."

Janet put her cup down and passed her sister a tissue.

"Oh dear. What are we to do? Jeremy doesn't know any of his friends I suppose?"

"No. They never had the same friends. Not even in school. Then Jeremy went away to college of course, so he hasn't got many friends from way back – mostly his work colleagues and his and Ellie's new friends. Jude's friends were always – well – dubious, weren't they?"

Janet studied her fingernails while she thought. Suddenly she asked, "Have you tried Social Services? What about the dole money? And where he's picking that up?"

"Yes, I've tried that. He's an adult and it's confidential. No go there. I seem to draw a blank everywhere. But why doesn't he *know* how worried I am, Janet? Why doesn't he care? I am his mother."

"I saw Graham Bott last Sunday," Janet said. "We were talking about Jude – I hope you don't mind – but I felt his advice might be useful – especially as Izzie had a lifetime's experience working with youngsters on drugs."

"No, I don't mind. What did he say?"

"He asked if Jude had ever tried to trace his natural mother. He hadn't, had he?"

"No. Never. As far as I know he hardly ever gave her a thought. He knew from a little boy that she couldn't keep him and that he'd come to us at two weeks old. I was the only person he ever thought of as mother."

"He's going to see Angie Roberts. She lives in Majorca."

"Angie Roberts? Who's she?"

Janet folded her hands in her lap and looked at her sister carefully.

"I've decided to tell you everything I know," she said. "Since 1975, Jude could have checked all the details and so could Angie. When you adopted Jude from the Harlow home for mothers and babies, the birth mother was a young girl called Angie Roberts. She was Philip's patient and had been some sort of call girl in London. She didn't know who the father was. She had no job and no home for the baby, so Philip talked to her and she agreed it was best for the baby to let him go. She had a breakdown the following year, and Philip sent her to Graham for psychiatric treatment. She made a full recovery and apparently has lived on Majorca for over ten years – maybe longer. She runs a hotel, and Graham has kept in touch. He's going to stay there next week. I wondered if it might help if you knew all that now. Or maybe if Jude did?"

Meg pushed her fingers into her hair and then her face crumpled.

Janet got up and sat beside her – one arm around her shoulders, patting rhythmically.

"Graham seemed to think Jude might need to know. That perhaps all his problems stem from *not* knowing. It's only a theory, of course. What d'you think?"

"I don't think he's ever wanted to know. I think it's a lot of nonsense. And anyway – if I don't know where he is how can I tell him about her – about this woman in Majorca? And we got Jeremy through the same home – do you know his mother too?"

There was a bitterness in her voice Janet had never heard before and it smote her.

"No darling. I don't. It was irregular the way Jude happened. I accept that. Philip probably shouldn't have fixed it up but you and Derek were so desperate for a child and we knew you'd make such perfect parents – those boys couldn't have asked for better parents anywhere. I know that. But we had nothing at all to do with Jeremy's case. I know no more than you do about his mother."

"Maybe I should try the Salvation Army. They do trace people for relatives, don't they? Oh I feel even more mixed up now. What's she like – this Angie?"

Janet removed her arm and took another sip of her now cold tea.

"I can hardly remember her. She was very gorgeous looking – that I do know. She used to work in a Bunny Club apparently. I imagine if Graham kept in touch she was always an attractive person. He says she's made a great success of things in Majorca and has a beautiful hotel up in the mountains."

"Goodness. I don't know what to think. I suppose she was never a real person to me at all. Just a shadowy figure who had supplied me with my little Jude. He was such a pretty child, wasn't he, Janet? And such a good baby – a joy. Such a joy. It all seemed to go wrong when he went to school. Up until then he was fine. School didn't seem to suit him somehow."

"I expect Derek dying like that was very hard on him – he wasn't very old, was he?"

"Ten – almost eleven. It certainly seemed to make him even wilder. He was smoking at ten, you know. Drinking at twelve. He always seemed attracted to the wrong sort of friends – usually much older than he was. The Brothers used to beat him – but it made no difference. He didn't seem to care."

"What does he care about? Girls? Did he have a special girlfriend when you last saw him?"

"Not really. Girls liked him all right. There were queues of them ringing up and coming round when he lived at home. They never lasted long though. All he seemed to care about was surfing. Surfing and drugs. Jeremy said it's danger he likes – the more dangerous the better. So it's no wonder I lie in bed worrying. He could be doing anything. He might even be dead."

"I think you would have heard if that was the case. No. We need some definite action," said Janet, sounding far more confident than she felt.

"We need to ring the Salvation Army and maybe put an ad in a surfers' magazine. I bet there is one. And what about his photo in a few surfers' shops? He's probably still in Devon or Cornwall – but we need to act before the season's completely over. I don't imagine there's much surfing in the winter and then he'll be even harder to trace."

"Oh Janet! You are a tonic! I feel more hopeful already. What a star! I'll get the phone book and the Yellow Pages! Why didn't I think of that? I've been too tired and depressed to think clearly. I'll find a fairly recent photo of him – won't be that recent, but never mind. I feel we're really getting somewhere after all these months!"

She had sprung across the room and opened a drawer. She pulled out a packet of photographs and riffled through them excitedly.

"Look!" she said. "That's him on Bude beach two summers ago. He'd won some championship or other. I'd bought him that surf board for his birthday – it was the best money could buy. I know where I got it! We could try a photo in that shop, couldn't we?"

"Have you got a photocopying shop in Dartmouth? We could have it blown up and lots of copies made. Let me look."

Janet studied the photo of her nephew with care. He was wearing a black wet suit and laughing into the camera, his spiked blonde hair wet from the foam. His chin had the hard cleft in it she remembered from his childhood, and his pale green eyes looked back at her. She had seen those eyes before. Gazing at her over a mug of tea and a Penguin biscuit in a ward at St Ebba's; eyes troubled but arresting. You could never forget them.

Chapter Twenty

"Let's tip all this stuff onto the bed and start from there," said Carla, upturning one of the deep drawers from her father's study onto the blue duvet on the single bed.

"What is all this anyway?"

"Oh, family paperwork that wasn't financial – things like your baptism certificates, you know, diplomas you won – our wedding licence – things like that. Your father's such a hoarder! When we left England he wouldn't throw a*nything* away – it drove me wild. He insisted on bringing absolutely everything with us!"

"Oh, God, mama! Look, my piano certificates and that picture papa took of me sitting at the piano in that concert hall – you remember – where the school gave that musical evening just after I could actually play a tune!"

They laughed together and Heather said, "He was so proud of you – oh gosh – look at that frock you're wearing – Rachel had it in pink, didn't she? I remember, you were eleven! Look at your curls, Carla – oh, you must have your hair cut like that again, it was so pretty!"

Carla riffled through the odd snapshot which had escaped the volumes of photograph albums which lined the study walls, meticulously catalogued and dated.

"Rachel on a pony! The first and last time I should think. She looks terrified! We must show that to Caroline – she doesn't believe any of us has ever touched an animal, I'm sure."

But Heather was not looking. She had picked up a tiny photograph from the bottom corner of the drawer, its edge caught fast and the face smiling up at her. A beautiful blonde in a bunny-girl outfit.

"What's that?" said Carla, looking at her face.

Heather picked at the corner of the photograph with her nail and lifted it out of the drawer. It was dusty and black and white.

"I think it must be Angie," she said. "The only other woman your father ever loved."

"What do you mean? I didn't know papa ever loved anyone but you."

Carla's eyes were filling with tears as she took the tiny

photograph from her mother and stared at it. She rubbed the back of her hand over her eyes and sniffed.

"When was this then? Papa never had an affair, did he? I can't believe that – not of him."

"No, no. Of course not. This was before I met him. That was his first club – a bunny club where he worked as manager when I first knew him – he took it over a couple of years after we married. That's Angie – papa was in love with her when I first met him, but she'd gone off with a much older man – he was quite heartbroken really, because I think he felt so responsible for her. She was very young – eighteen or nineteen, I think. We met her again after you were born – she was cooking at a dinner party we went to in London. A beautiful girl."

"Weren't you worried? How did papa react? I'd be bloody worried if one of Dominic's old lovers suddenly turned up – particularly if she looked like that."

"Yes, I suppose I was worried. I was pregnant with Richard at the time, so I was easily upset. I got very tearful when we were back home, I remember, but your father was so loving and sweet about it that I knew she meant nothing to him any more; just a happy memory. He was so glad to know she was all right. He had worried about her. She was a *wonderful* cook – I do remember that!"

Carla stared at the photograph carefully, as if expecting it to lay an egg.

"Mustn't it be terrible if you find out all sorts of dark secrets after your husband has died? I mean – I know we shan't – and papa isn't dead but just imagine... I'm sorry, mama, I'm being stupid."

Heather retrieved the photograph with a wry smile and placed it back in the drawer.

"We shan't find anything dramatic, darling. Your father and I have no secrets. I know what you're saying, and yes, it must be very terrible if that happens. But I've been so lucky – he's been the best husband in the world, and I've got you three and darling Charlotte and your boys. I've got such a lot to be grateful for."

Carla put her arms around her mother and rested her head on her shoulder.

"He's certainly been a wonderful father, too. God, when I

think how near he came to being killed... it doesn't bear thinking about."

They stayed in that position for some minutes, kneeling on the floor with Carla's arms around Heather, both silent in their thoughts.

Heather was the first to break away. She returned to the contents of the drawer, patting her daughter's arm and saying quietly, "It's only another ten days and he will be back home. I don't really know why I'm going through all this. Something to keep me occupied, I guess."

"Why don't you and papa come and stay with us for a month while he's recuperating? A really long stay – we'd love it."

"I won't make any decision just yet, darling, but that might be lovely – perhaps later on. He might find your imps a bit tiring just at first."

"Oh God, yes! I never thought of that. Look – there's a photo of us all up the tree at the bottom of the garden at Pantiles. I loved that tree – I always went up it if I was annoyed with you and wanted to sulk! I can remember sitting up there, hearing you calling me and staying as quiet as a mouse. I was a brat, wasn't I? I deserve my two."

Heather smiled happily at the memory.

"Yes, you do, sweetheart! You were wicked sometimes. But your father could always manage you – as soon as he arrived you were down that tree like a snake. You didn't play him up. I just wish your boys were the same with Dominic."

Carla shrugged.

"He's not the same kind of father at all. He wouldn't know where to begin, would he? Children are not the same anyway. They don't seem to be in awe of anything or anybody. I was a tiny bit frightened of papa sometimes – I absolutely adored him but I knew where he would draw the line and that was it. I certainly didn't dare to go over it. My two don't have any lines!"

"You and Dominic must draw them."

Heather stood up and put both hands on the small of her back.

"I think I've had enough. Shall we have coffee? We can carry on later if we feel like it. Just leave it there."

"I'll make the coffee. You go and sit down. What else needs

doing today?"

"Well, I need to speak to the insurance people. That's all really."

"What happened to the lorry driver?" Carla asked suddenly.

"He was released from hospital on the same day. Only minor injuries – nothing serious."

"Will we prosecute him? Was it dangerous driving?"

"I don't know yet. The police were involved. Richard will look into all that with the Carabinieri on Monday. It's finished as far as I'm concerned. I only care about your father being well enough to come home. I'm glad the driver's OK of course."

"Well, I know, but if he was driving dangerously… you said yourself how idiotic Italian drivers are, then it might be right to throw the book at him."

"We mustn't feel hatred, Carla. Just be thankful no one was killed. Come on, let's have a cup of coffee. It's upsetting all this talk of the lorry driver. I don't want to think about it at all."

Carla watched her mother walk into the kitchen, glancing back into the drawer as she dropped a couple more papers in, and the tiny, smiling photograph looked up at her.

Imagine papa having loved a bunny-girl; it seemed so strange. She closed the drawer on it with a determined click.

Chapter Twenty-One

"We had a bit of a thing, you know, on holiday," said Emma. "But I've lost his address. I looked you up in the phone book and thought you were Jude."

"Sorry?"

Jeremy sounded confused, and pushed his glasses back up the bridge of his nose.

"You thought *I* was Jude?"

"Yes, that's it," Emma gripped the telephone in her excitement. "I met Jude on holiday and he gave me his address but I lost it. So I looked you up in the phone book and thought you were Jude."

"But Jude doesn't live in Dartmouth. He lived in Bude – or he used to."

"I didn't know that – I told you, I lost the piece of paper with his address on it. Anyway – have you got his phone number?"

"Maybe he's bought himself a mobile – didn't have one last time I saw him. You know Jude – he changes squat pretty regularly and he's never got any money. Did he give you a phone number, then?"

She changed tack quickly.

"Uum – I'm not sure. Perhaps it was just an address. I gave him my number but he hasn't rung. I'm coming to Devon tomorrow and I wanted to look him up."

"Sorry. I'm not really in touch with him any more. We fell out. He was living in Bude somewhere last winter but he wasn't there a few months ago. He moves on. He could be living on the beach somewhere. He spends most of his time surfing, as you probably know. He's quite good at it."

"So you don't know where he is?" Her voice cracked with disappointment.

"No idea. I haven't seen him for – oh – eighteen months probably."

She thanked him and put down the phone. Jude. That was Angie's son's name. Jude the Obscure indeed. A surfer. A beach bum. And she didn't even know his surname. How could she have told Jeremy she didn't know his surname when she'd said she'd looked him up in the phone book? Still – at least they could drive to Bude. And Jude was such an unusual name – surely some surfers would know him. Her heart pounded. She was so nearly there.

"It's motorway nearly all the way," said Susie. "I'd only do this for you, you know. Have we got everything? Sleeping bags?"

She threw the map onto the sofa and rummaged in her holdall. "Do you think Jasper will eat his food if it's been down all night? You know what a fussy bugger he is!"

"Put some of that dried stuff down and the remains of the milk. That should do him. He'll eat if he's hungry."

Emma was putting on eyeliner in the bathroom, wearing white shorts and a white T-shirt which emphasised her Majorcan tan at its best.

"Come on," she said, emerging and zipping up a bag on the floor. "We ought to go – we said we'd leave at eight – it's half past already."

"Hang on! I must make sure I've got everything. Where is the rest of the milk? There's none in the fridge."

"There was some – it's probably by the kettle."

They slammed out of the front door and clattered down the steps to the Polo outside.

"Your mother is a darling – I love her to bits," said Emma as Susie unlocked it.

"And it's got a tankful – I bet she filled up specially."

"Did you tell her why we were going to Bude?"

"Not really. I just said you were chasing some bloke! She knows you, after all. She thought it was a real laugh – says you won't have time to chase men once you start your new job in the City."

They turned out of their street, heading for the M25. The traffic wasn't too bad on a Saturday morning early, and the sun was shining.

"Anyway," Emma commented, "it's good to be getting out of London at the weekend. I'm not going to think about the job until Monday morning!"

They drove down the hill to the main beach at Bude at 1.40, having had a short mid-morning break.

"God, I'm really knackered," said Susie, throwing her head back and closing her eyes.

Emma looked at her watch.

"It's taken longer than I expected. Now – where do we start? Do you think over there in that café? Shall I go and ask some of those guys if they know Jude?"

"Why not? You've got to start somewhere. Just count me out, Em. I'm going to sit here for a bit. You can get me a coffee if you like."

"OK."

Emma slammed the door and strode across the beach to the café. The crowd of surfers in wet suits eyed her appreciatively as she approached.

"Hi!" she said, dimpling at them. "What's the water like today?"

"Great!" said an Australian, whose tan matched her own. "Gonna try it?"

"Maybe later. I don't surf. I'm looking for somebody actually. Do any of you know a surfer named Jude?"

"Jude O'Neill? Sure. Everyone knows Jude. What about him?"

She tried to conceal the excitement she was feeling.

"Oh, I just wanted to look him up. Will he be coming here today?"

"Not here – Polzeath – along the coast. He hangs out there mostly."

"That's brilliant. Thanks. I'll just get a couple of coffees. My friend and I have just driven from London. It's a long drive."

"Sure is."

She collected two polystyrene mugs of coffee and loped back up the beach to Susie.

"They *know him*, Suse! He's called Jude O'Neill and he hangs out at Polzeath."

"Oh no – not more driving! I can't – you'll have to drive and hang the insurance. Just be careful, that's all. My dad would go mad."

The Australian was now strolling casually along the beach

past their car. He gave them a cheery wave.

"Wow!" said Susie. "He's drop-dead gorgeous. Maybe I'll just stay here and swim!"

Emma looked at him automatically – typical Aussie – tanned, blond crew cut – good looking in a rather plasticky fashion. Not her type at all.

"You're welcome, sweetheart, but we are here on *business* – may I remind you. Not pleasure."

Susie sighed and sipped her coffee. It was too hot to drink. She was used to all eyes turning to Emma and not to her. She learned to cope with that years ago, and occasionally got landed with Em's cast-offs, even if it usually meant hearing a lot about her on the first few dates.

"He is edible, though, isn't he?" she said, watching him splashing into the water.

"And doesn't he just know it."

He came back up the beach and Emma wound down the window and called out, "Not surfing yet then?"

"Nah, I'm giving some kid a lesson in ten minutes. Just hanging about waiting for him to turn up."

"Does Jude teach as well?"

"Jude? Hell no. No self-respecting mother would entrust their little darlings into Jude's wild hands, that's for sure!"

"What do you mean?" Susie looked interested.

"Well – you know Jude – he gets blind drunk some days or stoned – or gets into fights – you just never know what he's gonna be like. Some days I don't know how he stays upright in the water – but he does."

"What does he do?" asked Susie.

"How'dya mean – *do*?"

"Well you know – for work – a job?"

"Oh Jude doesn't go in for work much. He signs on mostly. He had a bar job for a short while but he got stroppy with the bloke who ran the bar, so that didn't last long. And he did get paid for being an extra in a film once."

"Really?" Emma finished her coffee and lobbed the cup accurately into the litter bin.

"Yeah – some bloody costume drama the BBC was doing down here. He's so bloody good-looking they snapped him up straight away. I think he actually turned up on time too."

"Why's he so wild, d'you think?" asked Emma, casually.

"Hell, I dunno. I think he was born wild. He was in trouble as a kid he told me."

"No family around here?"

"No idea. He never mentions them. Wanna smoke?"

"No thanks. We must get going, OK Susie?"

"Uumm, I suppose so." Susie handed her cup to Emma and got out of the driver's seat. She gazed longingly at the surfer as he wandered away and then walked round to the passenger's seat as Em slid across.

"What a waste!" she said, as they reversed up the slope from the beach. "You don't often see one that gorgeous."

"Forget it!" said Emma, turning back onto the main road. "Have a read of the map, will you, and see where Polzeath is?"

The van hit the kerb as Alex braked rather later than he intended and Jude slid back the van door with a crash.

"It's only fucking boarded up," said Alex, looking at the red brick house on a high grass bank above them.

"It's OK. I'll go round the back. Hang on."

He ran up the broken steps and tried the rotting green door at the side of the house. Locked. He ran round the back and saw a small crouched figure, half lying against the wall, with overflowing black bags all around the small Doc Marten's boots.

"Hi," he said. The figure looked up but said nothing.

"Where's Bono?"

She shrugged.

"They threw us out last night," she mumbled. "I'm waiting for Mick. He said he could get us a Dormobile – some guy he knows in Polzeath. I thought that's who you was."

"Nah. I was moving in. Jesus – what am I going to do with all my stuff? I've got Tiki gear in the van."

"You got a van?"

She looked animated for the first time and stood up stiffly.

"I bin here all night," she admitted, as they carried her few belongings to Alex, who was inspecting a front tyre.

"What you doin'?" he asked, as Jude opened the back doors of the van and heaved three black sacks inside.

190

"I thought…"

"Yeah. Bloody bailiffs have been in, haven't they? We'll go down to the beach and look for Stu."

The girl clambered into the back of the van, her long knitted coat catching on the lock and tearing. Her white elfin face was topped with unkempt straw-coloured hair interlaced with cheap, coloured beads. She had a cascade of silver rings down the side of one ear, two in her nostril and a stud like acne in the middle of her chin. Neither man gave her a second glance as they slammed doors and drove off, van bouncing down the hill to the beach. A cold easterly wind was whipping sand along the shore as they skidded down towards the café.

"There's Stu," the girl said suddenly, pointing at a tall sandy-haired lifeguard surrounded by girls. As Jude approached they all turned towards him like a shoal of fishes and mouthed "Hi Jude!" in a chorus of excitement.

"OK if I doss down in the van for a few nights, mate?"

Stu shrugged and glanced at the silent figure beside him.

"She with you?"

"Nah. She was at the squat. Didn't know what to do next, did you, kid?"

"Mick said he could get a Dormobile, but he never came back." She pulled the thin coat around her and began to shiver. "Did he mean yours?"

"You get some tea in Finns." Stu nodded towards the café. "Mick came down last night – I dunno where he went."

She stood, uncertain what to do next, while Alex shouted from the van, "I've gotta go, mate! I'll leave your stuff here, OK? You owe me, right?"

Jude turned back up the beach and began unloading boxes. There seemed nothing else to do.

"I'll see ya around. Cheers."

He handed Alex a small, brown package from his jeans' pocket and clapped him on the shoulder. Alex looked down at it, muttered "It better be good stuff", and climbed back into the van. He reversed in two jerky movements and clattered off into the distance while Jude staggered onto the beach with bulging black sacks and a rucksack. There were a few spots of rain in the wind now and he looked at the girl on the beach.

"Better get your stuff into Finn's," he said. "I'm throwing mine into Stu's dormobile before it chucks it down. D'you wanna smoke?"

She nodded and he handed her Rizla papers and a small tin as they walked back up the beach. Rain was beginning to fall quite hard; he picked up two surf boards and a box and the girl lifted hers, dropping jumpers and boots all over the beach as the bag split.

"Shit," she said quietly as she trudged after him, retrieving odd socks and a dirty bra as she went. "Where the hell is Mick? This is doin' my head in."

In the steamy warmth of Finn's café they sat surrounded by bin bags and ordered tea and toast, the first food since the previous day for either of them.

"I'm Annie," she said, cradling the hot mug in her thin white hands.

"You're Jude, aren't you? I seen you before – surfin'."

He inhaled, looking at her without interest. Girls from the beach had followed him in and were swarming along the counter buying coffees and cokes.

"Mick will probably be along later," she said, the small hope bobbing up like a cork. "He surfs on this beach, dun he? I better wait for him here."

"Yeah," he said, winking at a blonde behind her who had caught his eye.

Annie gulped her tea and relapsed into silence. The blonde came over and sat down.

"Are you going in today, Jude?" she asked him, her eyes meeting his with a challenge in them.

"Reckon so," he replied, grinning with his usual lazy charm.

"Good. I'll join you. I was surfing in Sydney in January. Might go back there at Christmas. Ever been to Oz?"

"Nope. Thought about it though. Might do. You could tempt me."

Their easy banter excluded Annie and she watched them miserably. Where would she stay tonight if Mick didn't turn up? She had no idea. Summer on the beach had seemed a brilliant idea when he had suggested it in May, and she'd left school with him. But now, four months later, cold, wet and with no money, she was not so sure. Maybe she should just pack up and go home. Hitch up the M5 and face it. Dad would probably kill her but she'd risk it. If Mick didn't turn up today that's what she'd do; go home.

A woman was wiping tables with a pink J-cloth.

"Don't smoke that stuff in here matey," she said, poking Jude in the arm. "You wanna get me in trouble and closed down? Smoke it on the beach, OK, but not in here. Right?"

He lifted one eyebrow and continued to smoke. Annie looked from one to the other in anxiety, like a nervous spectator of ping-pong. After a few seconds the woman held an ashtray under his face and stood over him.

"Come on, sweetheart! Stub it out."

He had almost finished anyway. He took a last deep drag and stubbed the rest into his saucer.

"Anything for you, Maureen," he grinned, and the woman turned, a smile of contentment on her hot face.

"I'll make you a sandwich," she called over her shoulder, as she disposed of his saucer and threw the J-cloth into the sink.

"Cheese – masses of pickle! You're a star!"

His mother said that. 'You're a star, darling!' – usually to Jeremy, he had to admit, rarely to him. He felt an unfamiliar pang of guilt and concern. That letter. She had written in February; she'd be out of her mind by now. Maybe he should call her. As soon as he had some change he would call her. Or reverse charge? She'd want that – he knew she would. He'd do it now, before he changed his mind. He stood up, dismay clouding the pretty face opposite.

"Oh, you're not going, are you, Jude?"

"Nah. Just got a call to make. Be back…"

He walked to the payphone in the lobby and pressed 100.

"Nethway 482 – call collect."

The operator rang the number and returned to him.

"Line busy. Please try later."

He hung up, a sudden unexpected loneliness washing over him; a melancholy looming like sea mist over the morning. She was probably talking to Jeremy; she wouldn't need his problems – he was just a nuisance. A millstone round her neck. That's all he ever was. That's how he'd started out life – a millstone round somebody's neck – but she'd had the good sense to get shot of him. She hadn't wanted him at all. He turned back into the café and saw Annie's pinched face and the pretty blonde's expectant smile. Maureen was bearing down on him with a plate of sandwiches as if she'd found him the Crown Jewels, silly cow. Some women wanted him anyway – that was never a problem. He sat astride the wooden chair with his knee pressing the blonde's and bit into his sandwich. She leaned towards him and touched his face. It was so easy. Too easy.

"You're a star, Maureen," he forced himself to say as she passed by.

"No, you are," the blonde said, leaning even closer, tiny droplets of perspiration appearing on her tanned upper lip.

He took another bite of sandwich, his green eyes meeting hers. He felt a stiffening of desire and an urge to lash out at the same moment.

"You can help me sort out Stu's van," he said. "I'm staying there for a bit. D'you want to shelter from the rain?"

"With you I do. Sure. What are we waiting for?"

They stood up, Jude taking another bite and pushing the plate aside. They left the café together, his right hand on her buttocks and his left raking through his spiky hair. Annie stared at his plate and pulled a face. At least she could finish his sandwiches.

Chapter Twenty-Two

Palma Airport was crowded as usual and as Angie passed through the wide glass doors her heart was pounding with excitement. Originally she had decided to send Alfonso Valeria down to meet the plane but her anticipation was so great that she couldn't contain herself.

For days she had scoured the hotel to a sparkling perfection, driven Julio crazy with her nagging; pointed out everything that needed doing in the garden to Arturo and generally driven everyone to distraction. At last the day had come when Gabbie would step onto the tarmac and she would see that handsome face again.

She stared up at the 'arrivals' board and saw that his plane was in. A few yards away he was waiting for his luggage and probably thinking of her. She had starved herself for the past two weeks, drinking nothing but mineral water, and visiting the best hairdresser in Palma twice for almond oil treatments and highlights. She was looking as good as she could make it at forty-seven, and Jose had assured her this morning in very vulgar terms how good he thought she looked! She'd squeezed his arm in grateful appreciation; that had been just what she needed to hear. She and Conchita had filled the bedroom with flowers and put new white embroidered sheets on the bed.

"El medico – duerme aqui esta noche." She had found she was blushing.

Conchita had giggled.

"Si Senora. Y usted?"

She had explained in haughty tones that she would be sleeping in her office on the couch, and would Conchita please lay out linen and a pillow for her, but Conchita had giggled mischievously again.

"Vamos a ver!" she'd said, as she patted the corner of the bed and swished out of the room, leaving Angie angry and amused at the same time. It was ridiculous; so unlike her to feel coy but it added to the unreality of the situation. Conchita had behaved as if she were preparing a bridal suite instead of simply an extra guest bedroom.

People were walking through the barriers carrying cases and bags with the usual stunned look of passengers who are glad to have their feet on the ground but are not sure where to go or what to do next in a strange airport. You could tell the regular commuters by their small bags and confident stride out to the palm tree-lined car park and the queue of taxis.

She scanned faces anxiously, the pit of her stomach sick and hollow.

A woman with two small children, both crying.

Young lovers in identical T-shirts and jeans, arm in arm.

Two businessmen in suits – oh God, it was him! She thought her heart would stop as she saw Graham Bott's silver hair above a pale beige cotton suit – he was a good deal thinner but hardly changed at all. She ran forward in joy with both arms outstretched.

"Oh darling – it's so good to see you!" – and they hugged like bears.

He released her and held her at arm's length.

"You look marvellous, Angie," he said. "It's great to see you."

She hung onto his arm as they walked out into the sunshine.

"Merc! Very impressive – things are going well, then?"

Graham tapped the bonnet of the pale blue Mercedes as she unlocked it.

"It's ages old, but I adore it. You know how I love fast cars, darling. I got a very good deal through a friend in Palma. But yes – the hotel is thriving – we're full even as late in the season as this, and I've lots of repeat bookings for next year. Oh I'm *so* happy you wanted to come and see me in my lovely Deya! I do love it so. And how are you? You've been very sad, I can see. It must have been terrible – poor Izzie – I could hardly believe it when I read your letter."

"Yes. Pretty bloody. In fact, nothing had seemed worth bothering about until I thought of you – and the possibility of seeing you again."

He slid into the passenger seat beside her, throwing his small grip bag onto the back seat. She dared to pat his knee quickly in a friendly fashion as she pulled out of the car park.

"Well now you're here, we're going to have a wonderful

time – no more cares for a few days. We'll be like a couple of kids doing just what we fancy – right?"

"Right." He breathed out and looked through the window at the drab concrete flats on the outskirts of Palma. Even in the last week of September the central reservation of the dual carriageway was full of flowers, although their pink and purple heads were heavy with dust and the blue sky relentless in the afternoon heat.

"It's cooler up in the mountains," said Angie, reading his thoughts and noticing his high colour. "My house is wonderful – cool in the summer and warm in the winter."

"When do you close?" he asked, relaxing as the car's air conditioning became effective.

"November. Everything finishes here then. It has a sleepy feel the winter here but that has its own special charm. Christmas is great – the weather's usually warm and sunny around lunchtime but cold enough for log fires in the evenings. Some years Rita and her family come out and the staff bring their families and we have a big Christmas dinner all together – everybody pitching in and helping because the staff aren't really working – it's terrific fun. When Rita's youngest was fourteen, Julio – that's my cook – dressed up as Father Christmas – it was such fun. He has three sons and two daughters so they were all here – except the youngest who wasn't born! They're all family to me now. I don't know what Rita will do this year – Clare's married now. She had her honeymoon here last week."

Angie overtook a truck and speeded up as they left Palma behind and took the westerly road towards Andraitx. She was a good driver, he remembered, relaxed and confident and well able to chatter and watch the road at the same time. He was glad of that as the road climbed upwards, often with a sheer drop on his side as they rounded Z bends with no room for another car to pass.

"Hairy, isn't it?" she grinned, as she heard air escape from his mouth while he looked down into a wooded ravine below. "Wait till we get nearer Deya – it's breathtaking!"

"I think we came in the bus last time," he remembered. "Izzie loved it – I know she told everyone how entirely false her impression of Majorca had been before our trip."

"Only this bit. If you want to talk about her – please Gabbie – if you need to – just talk away."

"I'll probably mention her quite a lot; she's in my thoughts so much, but I'm coming to terms with it. I'm hoping you'll make me look forward again, Angie, not backwards. I've been living in the past for months now I'm afraid."

"Of course you have. You talk about her as much as you need; that's fine by me. I wish I'd known her better. Look – see – Valdemosa – that's where Chopin stayed with Georges Sand. We must go there one day while you're here."

She slowed the car down and pointed at a road leading off at a fork.

"It's beautiful, and so atmospheric. We could have dinner there one night if you like."

They drove on through heavily wooded hillsides dropping spectacularly into the brilliant azure sea. The road wound up and down and round the cliff – now giving glimpses of the sea sparkling below, now rambling lazily through a tiny hamlet of farms and olive groves – through the grand estate of Son Marroig with its marble temple, and on until the terracotta roofs of Deya village were spread beneath them. She drove downhill, slowly past the café, and turned left up the dirt track which led to la Casa d'Or.

"Here we are," she announced, as they sailed through the black wrought iron gates and past the olive trees. "We're home!"

Dust flew as she pulled up outside and Conchita opened the front door, smiling shyly. She stepped forward to take Graham's bag.

"No, no! I can manage, thank you."

He walked past her approving gaze and Angie ushered him into the dark, cool hall.

"Tea or iced coffee, darling?" she said smiling. "En la habitacion."

"Si Senora."

Conchita disappeared with a bounce in her step. She loved seeing Angie look so happy and pretty again. Her affection for her employer was very like a Labrador's for a good master.

Gabbie carried his bag up the dark red pine staircase and exclaimed in pleasure at the sight of Angie's room.

"This is charming," he said, dumping his bag on the floor in relief. His lower back pain was beginning to nag him. "And what a view!" He stood, looking out of the window that had captivated Angie when she had first visited the house with Liz all those years ago.

She pulled a small cream armchair forward and said, "Sit down, darling, and relax. The tea will be here in a minute. I'm glad you like it because I chose every single thing in here myself. Oh, it's so good to have you here!"

She stood gazing at him in delight as he sat down.

He grinned up at her.

"You're looking smug, Angie – like the cat who's found the cream."

"That's just about how I feel! Now, when we've had that cup of tea I'll leave you alone to shower and unpack and whatever… it's…"

She looked at her watch. "It's six-forty – so feel free to do whatever you like. I've fixed things so that we'll have dinner here at about eight tonight – that suit you? We can explore tomorrow."

"Perfect. You think of everything. I may have a quick lie down after a shower – I have an old rugger injury in my lower back which is hinting trouble. I want to nip it in the bud."

"Oh no! Why didn't you say? I could give you a massage – would you like that? I did a training you know – along with First Aid."

She gazed at him, her green eyes cloudy with concern.

He held out a hand to her.

"If it gets any worse I'll tell you. For now I think I'll just have a shower and unpack and join you in the bar in about forty minutes. Is that all right?"

"Of course it is. I'll see you downstairs. Just ring down if you need anything."

"I will," he smiled, his eyes warm but a little preoccupied. She suspected he was remembering being here with Izzie – thank heavens she had not tried to put him in the same room.

She closed the door behind her and walked thoughtfully downstairs. This was not going to be easy. She must not underestimate his pain.

Graham stared at the darkening garden and wondered if he had been right to come. A familiar melancholy was threatening to engulf him – this time of day was particularly difficult as it was when he would have returned home and joined Izzie with a martini or a gin and tonic before supper. He was watching his drinking – counting the units – as he was only too aware of the pitfalls of a quick lift from alcohol. He'd advised so many patients against it and was surprised to see that his hands were shaking slightly. He turned to his bag and began to unpack. He hung linen trousers in the dark Spanish oak wardrobe and slipped shirts into the deep chest under the window. Angie was a sweet thing – but was he ready for all this socialising? He suspected not; it all seemed so pointless somehow. He threw off his jacket and considered his tired face in the mirror.

God – he looked old. He must lighten up a little and think of Angie. She was so transparently pleased to see him and she'd had a tough time of it, poor dear. He wasn't the only one to know the hell of losing the person you loved most in all the world, was he? And should he pursue the issue of Janet's nephew? Would it do any good to dig all that up again? He really had no idea. He stepped into the shower and turned the cold tap on. He was pleased the temperature had dropped a little and the freezing water startled and invigorated him. His spirits rose as he soaped his body with the deliciously scented lotion Angie had provided. What had Janet said? 'Old friends are the only real comfort'. That was true. And Angie still had a sparkle and a sexual chemistry that was very attractive. He must relax and stop punishing himself. Izzie would want that. She had always wanted him to be happy.

He saw Angie cross the small bar before she saw him. She was standing in a soft pool of light from a cream lamp on the bar smiling up at the distinguished looking guest by her side, her golden hair framing her tanned face, and a black cashmere pashmina tossed casually around her shoulders. She became aware of him standing looking at her, and looked up, her green eyes lightening and her smile deepening.

"Excuse me," she said, touching the guest's sleeve.

"Darling – you look heaps better! What are you drinking?"

"Just a beer, thank you – one of those bottles of Lowenbrau will be fine."

"Are you sure? Right – Cerveza por favour," she indicated to Jose and gave Gabbie a twenty-two carat beam as she squeezed his arm.

"We are going to have *such* a good time!" she promised. "Shall we take a boat to Dragon Island tomorrow?"

"Sounds like Swallows and Amazons," he laughed. "Are you packing the ginger pop? I shall feel about eleven years old."

"Good. That might be a good time to regress to. Where were you at eleven? You know where I was – boring old Harlow with mum and Rita."

"Eleven? Let me think – I was a boarder in the Junior House at Alleynes. I'd been boarding for a year and was beginning to rather enjoy it. In the holidays we went to Climping in Sussex – I'd go off for hours in a dinghy with my chum Paul – our parents always holidayed together in adjoining cottages – all very predictable but rather nice. Very happy days!"

She sipped her Martini Bianca and frowned.

"I don't think you've ever told me anything about your boyhood before," she said. "Not in all the however many years it is that we've known each other. I can imagine you as a perfect little swot."

He smiled and put his beer on the bar, wiping the foam from his lips with the back of his hand.

"I was too into sport for that. Captain of Cricket, that was me – Under 13s swimming team, rugger team – I lived for sport in those days. That's why bits of me are dropping off now!"

"And girls? When did girls come on the scene? I can imagine you were drop-dead gorgeous!"

He smiled and picked up the beer.

"Course I was – oh, not until about fifteen or sixteen. I remember my first girlfriend – a sweet little thing whose father coached us in tennis, and who rode a small white pony every Saturday morning past the tennis court where I was having lessons!"

"The scheming hussy! How long did that last?"

"God! Now you're asking. I've no idea – it seemed quite a long romance but it was over before my A levels because *they* were complicated by a Danish au pair our next door neighbours took on! She made Britt Ekland look plain as a dog biscuit! I'd forgotten her – Birgitta! Wow! Did she brighten up that summer and take my mind off exams!"

"But you presumably still passed them – you got to university?"

"Yes, but not Cambridge. I'd set my heart on Kings but I didn't get in. I went to London instead – which was where I met Izzie, so I owe Birgitta that much. We met in my second year and that was it. No other contest."

He looked down into his beer and then drained it, standing holding the empty glass as if uncertain what to do next. Angie took it from him and placed it on the bar.

"Shall we eat?" she asked softly, and he looked at her in surprise.

"What? Yes, yes – that would be marvellous. I'll follow you."

She led him into the peppermint green dining room, smiling at her other guests and exchanging quick comments with them as they crossed the room. In the far corner Conchita stood guarding a table set for two, with pink candles surrounded by white flowers from the garden, and a view of the floodlit trees beyond.

"It's beautiful, Angie. I don't remember the garden being floodlit before."

"No. Arturo arranged that last winter. Cost far too much money because most of the year it's unnecessary and I don't know why I let him talk me into it, but tonight I'm really pleased I did. This time of year it comes into its own."

An owl hooted outside and Angie put her hand over his on the pink linen tablecloth.

"That's supposed to be very lucky round here," she said. "An owl hooting over your house is a very good omen."

He turned his hand upwards and entwined his fingers with hers.

"We don't need omens to tell us we're lucky," he smiled. "I knew as soon as I saw you at the airport we'd be able to pick up where we left off. That's the marvellous thing about old friendships – years can go by and you can pick up as if it were last week. It's knowing so much about one another. What I *don't* know, and have always wondered, is why you never married – you must have had plenty of offers."

She broke her roll into small pieces and popped one in her mouth. She chewed thoughtfully. He knew her so well; all her hopes and fears and guilt and anger had been poured out to this man, after all.

"Gracias, Conchita," she said, as steaming bowls of fish soup were placed in front of them.

"I never really got over Roy; remember – Roy Cavalieri?"

He sipped his soup and nodded.

"I remember. Your first love. What happened to him?"

"He's a happily married man with three children and he's living in Italy."

"Have you seen him?"

She picked up her soup spoon.

"No. Not for about twenty-five years."

"How do you know he's living in Italy then?"

"I got someone to check him out for me this summer. He lives near Florence."

"It's just a fantasy, Angie. You know that. It bears little relation to real life. You don't know the man at all now – it's a golden memory, that's all. We all have them."

"OK Senor Medico! I know. He's a grandfather and probably fat as butter with a bald head! Why do we hang on to our dreams? That's the good thing about you and me – it's real. You know everything there is to know about me – well, everything that matters – and you feel free to tell me anything you like about yourself. So it works. I was a bit afraid it wouldn't – were you?"

"A little. But I'd felt so bad I hadn't much to lose. I felt I needed to see you again – to get away from all my memories and my lonely house. I've got to work of course – I see about five or six private patients a week – sometimes more."

"Do they still fall in love with you?"

"Occasionally – but not as often as in the old days!"

"Arrogant beast! I shall never forget Sister Whats-her-name's face when she looked at you – sick sheep nothing! You were like a film star in that place."

"You don't still think about St Ebba's do you?"

She sipped her soup for a moment and fiddled with a ball of bread.

"Hardly ever for years. But this summer I found myself going over it all again. There was this young student…"

"How young?"

"No, nothing like that! He was only twenty-one or something – he was an art student and he painted my portrait – I'll show you later – it's flattering but not bad. I more or less told him my life story. God knows why. I wished I hadn't afterwards."

"Why?"

"Well because it was like turning on a tap I haven't been able to turn off since. Memories just hitting the deck and leaving me drenched I suppose. Stuff I thought I'd completely dealt with and forgotten – all pouring back. Does anything ever really go away, Gabbie, or is it just submerged? Waiting to pop up like an iceberg when we least expect it?"

He looked at her over his soup spoon and drank noisily.

"No. I don't believe these things go away. They make room for more pressing events but they're still there – lurking – as you say. Do you mean Roy in particular – or other things?"

"That whole time. St Ebba's – you – everything."

"Everything? Your son? That too?"

She looked at him and said nothing for a while, sipping her soup and considering her words carefully.

"I always believed I had no right to interfere," she said at last. "He had a good life with a wonderful family, so I was told – and I had given him up. So I had no right to mess up that life and disturb him – did I? Of course there never was a time I didn't think about him – almost daily – but I convinced myself all was for the best, you know?"

"And now?"

"Now I keep wondering – where is he and what he's doing. At night I lie for hours wondering if he's happy, and healthy, and what he looks like. My niece had her honeymoon here and she's almost the same age, so I suppose that compounded it. The need to know. He might even be married! I might even be a grandmother! God forbid!"

She picked at an invisible spot on the tablecloth and pulled a face. He rubbed his hand along her arm softly, waiting for her to speak again. She said nothing.

"And you're afraid? Is that it? Afraid to really know?"

He leaned back in his chair and watched her face intently.

"I don't know. I am afraid, of course I am. It's far more comfortable having a vague idea of some lovely person somewhere who belongs to me, rather than meet a complete stranger who may not like me – and that's just my side of it – presumably he feels something similar – if he knows he's adopted, of course. He may not."

"It's pretty unlikely he was not told. That would be most unusual."

"Well he's never tried to trace me, has he? After all, I may have lived here for eleven years but there were fifteen years before that when I was in England, and Rita is still there. I could have been traced through Rita. I know no one's ever tried to, so presumably he's managing very nicely thank you without any interference from me."

Conchita approached tentatively. Angie now looked sad and distant once again; why was this? Why was the lovely Senor not saying sweet things to keep her smiling? She placed their main course in front of them as unobtrusively as possible and almost tiptoed away. Graham stared down at the steaming plates and sniffed appreciatively.

"This smells wonderful!" he said, picking up his fork and stabbing a tiny cube of pepper and diced rabbit together.

"Morteruelo – it's Julio's speciality! It's chopped partridge, rabbit, ham, garlic, tomatoes and raisins – it's absolutely delicious. Why ask for trouble, Gabbie, when my life here is so good? I think it's asking too much. I should be grateful for what I've got and leave well alone. Of course – if *he* wanted to find me that would be different. But I don't think he ever will – not after all this time surely. If he'd been going to look for his mother he would have done it in his teens, wouldn't he?"

"Not necessarily. People have crises at different times in their lives when they feel the need to trace their roots. But you must be sure in your own mind what *you* want to do – if anything."

"I think I am, really. I'm not prepared to risk upsetting his apple cart after all this time – and giving myself the terrible disappointment and heartbreak if he's not at all how I want him to be."

"How do you want him to be?"

He smiled affectionately at her over the top of his wine glass.

"Oh – just about perfect, of course! Good-looking, intelligent, a bit like my father – an individualist – you know – a bit of a 'one-off' – not too much an establishment figure – a sense of humour – as I say, as near perfect as I would expect any son of mine to be!"

He laughed and raised his glass to hers.

"Here's to our dreams, Angie – whatever they are – but also to you and me – because we're not a dream. We're real and we're both here in this fabulous place. Here's to friendship!"

She lifted her glass to meet his and smiled into his crinkling blue eyes – and they both drank. Conchita noticed approvingly from the far side of the room, and removed a soup plate so absent-mindedly that she knocked the guest's elbow.

"Perdon," she said, moving towards the kitchen with one eye still on Angie.

Later, much later, they sat in Angie's side garden watching the moon and clouds performing a slide show behind the pine trees. They were drinking white Rioja and one another's presence in equal measure. He reached out for her hand and kissed it quickly.

"It's your room, isn't it Angie? You've given me your own room."

"How did you work that out? I'd taken all my things out and cleared the bathroom. What gave me away?"

"Oh – just about everything. The room has your personality all over it! And the bathroom smells wonderful – it smells of your perfume – what is it?"

"Givenchy. You must lie in bed tonight with the curtains open and watch the moon slide across the bedroom window – it's wonderful with the black skies you get up here. I'm still thrilled by it after eleven years."

"That's one of the things that's so marvellous about you, Angie. You're still like a kid – everything's fun. Not many of us have managed to stay like that – I know I haven't."

"You've had a hell of a year. And your work is being immersed in other people's misery. Mine is one long holiday!"

"I don't believe that for one minute! It's bloody hard work running a hotel – especially one as perfect as this one."

"Some days life here does seem pretty perfect and then all these questions raise their heads and I have no peace of mind at all."

"I could find out for you, if you really wanted to know," he said quietly, putting down his glass.

She froze, and looked at him.

"You know something – don't you?" she said. "I felt so nervous about this week – I know I was excited about seeing you again after all this time, but it was even more than that. I sensed something – as if I felt something huge was about to happen. Tell me – what is it?"

He reached across to hold her hand; a light breeze ruffled the hairs on his arm and he spoke quietly.

"I think I know where he is. Well – not exactly where – but near enough – and more importantly *who* he is."

Angie pulled the cashmere shawl around her arms and shivered. She stared at Graham with round, frightened eyes in the dark and said nothing. A dog barked in the distance and she jumped.

"I can't believe this is happening," she said at last. "How do you know? Is that why you came out here?"

"No. I've only known for sure for three days. After I'd arranged this trip I had lunch with Janet Rose. Remember – Philip's wife?"

"Dr Rose's wife? God – yes. She was really kind to me when I was in St Ebba's. She used to bring Rita to see me and take me home for the weekend."

"So she said. Well, Philip died the year before Izzie – and I hadn't seen her since the funeral when she rang me up out of the blue and invited me to Sunday lunch. She obviously wanted to talk something over and it turned out to be her sister Meg's child – not a child now, of course. A man of twenty-six. He's been pretty wild I gather, and she's now lost touch with him, and dear old Janet is desperately worried about Meg and wondered if I could help."

"Go on."

"I suddenly made the connection. The timing was right, of course, but that could easily be just a coincidence. So I asked her outright if she knew the circumstances of Meg's son's adoption."

"How did you know he *was* adopted?"

"Oh she'd let on that much."

She clutched at her stomach and closed her eyes.

"So what you're saying is…?"

"Hold on a minute. I felt I'd made a connection but when I asked Janet she wouldn't tell me anything at all. Said she knew nothing. Of course – perfectly correct. She couldn't discuss it with me. But she did ask me to talk to Meg, who by all accounts was getting in a dreadful state. Janet went down to see her and they put ads in local shops and surfing magazines, asking him to get in touch, but no go so far. She'd asked me to speak to Meg, so I rang her three nights ago."

"And what did she say?"

"She told me that Jude was born in the home for mothers and babies in Harlow on December 30th and would be twenty-seven this year. It's not conclusive of course, but it's a hell of a coincidence."

"Jude? He's called Jude?"

"Yes. Jude Kennedy."

The garden tilted a little and Angie clutched at her forehead.

"Why are you telling me all this, Gabbie? I've never thought I had the right…"

She tailed off and he stroked her hand, now cold, with white fingertips.

"You've had the right in law to find all this out for yourself for years. So you can check the facts if you want to know for certain. It seems to me that you both need to."

"He's wild you said. How wild?"

"The usual. Left home with no real idea of what he was going to do apart from surfing – which apparently he is very good at – no qualification – lived in squats and on the beach – bit of drug taking – no real focus to his life by the sound of it. Nothing really criminal as far as I know."

"God. I'd always been so sure he was having this fantastic

establishment upbringing and that he was probably a doctor or a lawyer by now."

"Well his brother's an accountant so you could have been right."

"Was he adopted too?"

"Apparently. No problems at all, Janet said."

Angie took a deep breath in and took her hand away.

"What shall I do?" she asked after a while. "What on earth shall I do, Gabbie?"

"What do you want to do? You can write to the authorities and ask where your baby went. That will confirm if it is Jude. I feel pretty certain it is myself."

"Yes. So do I. It makes sense. Hell – it's like a jigsaw, Gabbie. A big, complicated jigsaw. And you've arrived with all the pieces. I feel so – sort of sick and frightened. As if my whole life is about to be turned inside out – just when it had been feeling so comfortable."

She was beginning to cry he could just make out, and he leaned forwards and crushed her in his arms. She clung with both hands to the sleeves of his shirt, burying her face in his chest.

"We'd better go up to my room, Gabbie. I can't let my staff or guests see me like this. We can go up the back stairs. I need to calm down and think this through in private."

He followed her through the darkened garden, away from the floodlighting and round to the washing line. Dino the collie thumped his tail from his basket in the back porch. For once Angie ignored him. They walked quickly up the stairs and she unlocked her room and fell onto her bed, curled up in a foetal position. Gabbie did not put on a light but stood by the window in the moonlight, watching her, but saying nothing. After a while she uncurled herself and lay on her back, looking up at him.

"Cuddle me, Gabbie," she said, holding her arms out to him like a child. "I feel so alone and frightened."

He lowered himself onto the bed beside her and kissed her forehead tenderly.

"It's all right, Angie," he said, wrapping her in his arms and enjoying the human warmth of another body in his arms after so many months.

"You're not alone, and neither am I. We've got each other. It's going to be all right. It's going to be all right."

Chapter Twenty-Three

"What d'you want? Es, whiz or hash? I can get you anything."

Jude was standing at the back of the beach talking to a group of travellers who had just pitched camp in the car park. They wouldn't be allowed to stay there, he knew, so if he was to make a quick buck he had better act fast. They'd be moved on by the weekend.

They mumbled their preferences and he arranged to meet them later. He wandered off into Finn's and used the pay phone. That's all it took – a call to Big Eddie and he was in business. He didn't do it often, but it was easy money and times were hard. Stu had made it clear that sharing the Dormobile could only be a very temporary arrangement, and the blonde yesterday hadn't helped.

Annie was sitting in the corner of Finn's he noticed; she didn't seem to have moved far in twenty-four hours. Her pasty face looked even more dejected than the day before. She was staring out of the window, chewing at her cheek.

"Hiya kiddo!" he said, happy now that a transaction had been fixed up. "No Mick?"

"No. I was going home yesterday but I waited for him so long it got dark. Bit stupid to hitch on the motorway in the dark. I'll get going in a minute."

He waved to Maureen in her blue overall behind the counter and she waved a J-cloth at him with a wink. Maybe she'd bring him a free sandwich later on. He sat down and said, "Where's home?" – a sudden picture of Nethway flashing into his mind and being quickly discarded.

"Reading. Me dad'll kill me. He never liked Mick and I've only rung a couple of times. Mum cries – you know? I wish she wouldn't do that – I keep telling her I'm OK."

He knew Mick from surfing on the beach in Bude. A no-hoper who was probably miles away by now, not giving Annie a second thought.

"How old are you?" he asked, noticing her bitten fingernails and spotty skin.

"Sixteen. I'm seventeen next week. D'you think I should go

home for that?"

"Yeah. Go home. D'you want some tea?"

Sometimes he thought his education with the Brothers would never leave him. However hard he tried to shake off their shackles the tenets intruded. It was like being taken over by aliens. He was beginning to feel some sort of responsibility for this kid; ridiculous – she was nothing to do with him – he didn't intend to shoulder any responsibilities ever. That was a decision he'd made; a life he had deliberately chosen.

"You're looking good this morning, Maureen!"

He turned a full-strength smile towards Maureen who looked at him knowingly, raising one eyebrow.

"You've got a bloody nerve!" she grinned. "You want tea and yesterday's Chelsea buns, I suppose!"

"You are a star! This kid here's got to eat – she's hitching home later on – you can't have her fainting on the slip road, can you!"

Maureen bustled about bringing two mugs of tea and a plate of sugary buns to their table.

"You be careful – you're not hitching on your own, are you?"

"Yeah. I'll be all right."

"Well you're a silly girl. Look at the size of you – a puff of wind would blow you over! Give your folks a ring, why don't you? Wouldn't your dad come and get you? Or catch the train – I s'pose you haven't got the money for your fare?"

"Nope. I'm not ringing nor nuffink. I'm just gonna turn up. That's the best thing. I'll be careful."

Maureen stood with her hands in the small of her back looking from one to the other.

"Talk some sense into her, Jude," she said at a last. "Get her to ring home – I know if my Susie was going to hitch, I'd move heaven and earth to stop her – and she's twice the size of this one! You're a silly girl – don't you ever read the papers? Use the phone behind the counter if you like – go on – ring your mother!"

She walked back to serve two swimmers who were now standing at the counter, teeth chattering, wet hair glistening and dripping as they selected pieces of pizza and bowls of pea and ham soup from her cabinet.

Jude bit into a bun, a fine spray of sugar cascading onto the plate.

"She's nice in' she?" said Annie, sipping her hot tea gingerly. "She give everyone free buns?"

"No – only me! She fancies me, poor cow! She's been here for years – I remember her when I learnt to surf here as a kid. She was always chatting up the lifeguards then. Keeps a smile on her face though, doesn't it?"

"I saw a picture of you!" she said suddenly, nibbling at her bun like a hamster. "This morning. I was walkin' round the shops for something to do and you know the place that sells all the Tiki gear? Up near the traffic lights?"

"Yeah – I know."

"Well – it's in the doorway. Just as you go in – there's this big picture of you on the beach – in a wet suit – I dunno if it's here – and it's like a cowboy film – you know? WANTED – that sort of thing."

She paused, not having said so much in ages.

"What are you on about? It can't be me! Why should anybody put up a photo of me? You've got it all wrong."

"No, I haven't. I know it's you. Anyway it's got your name on it, JUDE KENNEDY – MISSING – something like that. Only I thought your name was Jude O'Neill."

He stood up, scraping his chair on the floor.

"Yeah. Well, I changed it. Listen, I'm going to have a look. It must be some sort of joke – probably Stu or somebody taking the piss. You watch yourself – right?"

"Yeah. See yah."

She munched steadily, hardly looking up as he walked quickly from the café. Maureen's disappointed eyes followed him as he slammed the door in the wet wind that blew from the shore. He had half an hour before he met Big Eddie behind the bogs – he was running by the time he got to the steep path up to the main road, and crossed, a bus driver hooting at him in irritation as he swerved away.

He saw the photograph before he reached Rod's shop. It dominated the side window in the porch, among the surfing events and cards advertising second-hand gear.

'HAVE YOU SEEN JUDE KENNEDY?'

…was printed above the photograph, and below it was a phone number:
Nethway 482

"Shit!" he said aloud.

What the hell was she playing at? He was twenty-six, for God's sake – not a kid of fourteen! He ran into the shop and tore down the poster from inside the window.

"Hey! What d'you think you're doing?"

The woman behind the counter was red with indignation but did not move. He had never seen her before.

"It's my fucking photo!" he said – holding it up so that she could see it. And no one asked *me* if I wanted to be stuck all over fucking shop windows like some sort of murderer on the loose!"

He banged out of the shop and opened the picture. He looked at it, his heart thumping. He remembered it being taken now – light years ago – that surfboard had been a champion – his mother had bought it and he'd won the county championships on it that summer. Even bloody Jeremy had come to watch. His mother had taken the photograph on the back of the beach at Bude.

'JUDE OF BUDE'

– 'Surf' magazine had captioned it. Why was she doing this? And how many other places had his picture plastered all over their walls? He tore it into small pieces and threw it in the gutter. He'd have to ring her now – if only to stop all this nonsense. She was obviously more than just worried. Hell – why couldn't she just leave him alone – what did she expect from him? Whatever it was he couldn't give it.

He sat on a low wall looking out to sea. Grey breakers were crashing on the beach in meringue explosions, but for once he was not watching the sea. He was wondering why she still cared. She was not his real mother, after all – had not given birth to him

– did not share his genes. Why didn't she wash her hands of him and concentrate on Jeremy? He felt sure that's what he would do in her situation.

"Cut and run, mum. Cut and run," he murmured above the sound of the waves. "Stop giving yourself all this grief."

He sat there for almost half an hour until rain in the wind made him look at the waterproof watch on his wrist. "Shit!" – he was ten minutes late for big Eddie – he didn't like being kept waiting. He ran across the road and noticed the 'Y' registration black BMW with relief. He was still there.

Eddie was tapping gold-ringed fingers on the steering wheel as Jude pressed his face against the window.

"Sorry mate! How'ya doing?" he said.

Big Eddie did not reply but lowered the electric window and handed a brown paper package to him.

"Sixty-five" was all he said, as Jude brought the cash from his back pocket.

Almost before his fingers had fastened on the brown paper the window went up and the BMW shot forwards, throwing Jude off balance and against the wall. He kept hold of the parcel and steadied himself. Should be able to pass it on for a hundred quid, so it was worth it. He walked into the lavatories and stuffed the package down the front of his jeans. From here it was only ten minutes' walk to the car park and the travellers' camp site. The sooner he got rid of it the better.

He walked back up the hill smoking a thin joint. His anger subsided as his mood mellowed. It wasn't paranoid to feel people were getting at you when there were posters up all over the place, was it? Not unreasonable at all. He must chill out – maybe he'd call and maybe he wouldn't – he couldn't make a decision right now.

A skinny brown dog was rooting though a pile of rubbish as he approached the camp site; two small kids were riding little bikes round and round. He noticed the red-haired bloke who had accosted him on the beach poking a stick into a feeble fire.

"Hi!" he said, as he picked his way through beer cans and chip papers.

"Es and hash?" the guy said.

"Hundred quid – best stuff," said Jude. "We'd better get inside."

The camper van smelt of urine, he realised, as he watched a young girl changing a baby's nappy on a grubby bed at the far end. There were discarded filthy clothes strewn all around and a cut loaf on the table.

"Jez! You got Swede's dosh?"

An enormous blond man appeared from behind a magazine and stood up, reaching into his back pocket.

He threw notes onto the table – "There's ninety there, man."

"I did say a hundred!" said Jude. "Hundred quid – right?"

Jez rummaged again and produced a £2 coin.

"That's all we got – £92. Couldn't get it together man – we'll see you alright."

A car was screeching into the car park and before Jude had time to think the doorway of the camper van was filled with uniformed police.

"Don't do anything stupid now," said the copper stepping up towards them. "Just hand that over and come nice and easy. No hassle. Right. In the car – all of you – MOVE."

Jude was handcuffed to a white-faced policewoman who looked more scared than he was, and the two police cars shot off out of the car park, through Polzeath and towards the main road. He stared at Finn's café as they passed the beach, wondering when he would see it again. Two girls were getting out of a white Volkswagon Polo as they screeched past. One was very good looking, he noticed.

At the red brick police station Jude was cautioned and asked if he understood.

"Yeah," he said, cramps forming in the pit of his stomach. "I need to make a phone call. I got a right to that, haven't I?"

"Sure. You want to ring your solicitor?"

"No – I haven't got one – greedy bastards all of them. I'll make a call though."

They pushed the telephone towards him and he stabbed the numbers, willing his fingers to stop shaking.

"Nethway 482."

How many times had he heard her say that?

Chapter Twenty-Four

Gabbie was awake first, the sun slanting through Angie's open window and the sharp scent of pines wafting in on the light breeze.

He shifted slightly and looked at Angie's blonde hair framed by the white pillow beside him. He felt happier than he had for months, and in a rush of tenderness towards her he gently kissed her tanned forehead. She frowned in her sleep and turned away, an arm thrashing across the fine sheet that covered them and a small grunt making him smile.

"Piglet!" he thought. "Well I must be Eeyore! I *have* been Eeyore for months, I guess, but not anymore. Not in this paradise, anyway."

He swung his legs off the bed and disappeared into the bathroom. Angie grunted again and rolled onto her back. She awoke slowly – her eyes opening and shutting several times before the sound of splashing jolted her memory – darling Gabbie was in her bathroom – had been in her bed – what she had often dreamed of had happened and it had been fantastic. She half sat up; propping herself on one elbow. God – he had seen her asleep! She must look terrible! She sat up and regarded her tousled hair and slightly puffy eyes in the mirror. Not good. But maybe his eyesight was going! He did wear glasses to read now, she had noticed yesterday with amusement.

She got up slowly, lifting her arms above her head and regarding her brown naked body with a frown. Not too bad – she'd look better in her kimono but she had taken all her clothes to her office yesterday. She spotted his comb on the dressing table and pulled it through her hair as she heard him soaping himself noisily in her shower. She felt a rush of love for this man who'd cared for her so often over the years. Maybe she should join him? She looked at her watch; 7.20. Plenty of time. Conchita would be in charge downstairs – she slid back the shower door and stepped behind Gabbie, pressing herself gently against his buttocks.

He turned, laughing, and drawing her into his arms, the cold water making her gasp.

Their lips met and she pulled herself onto him in excitement.

"I like starting the day with you, Angie," he said, tightening his grip and gazing into her eyes as if he'd drown there.

It was like a helter-skelter – while he made love to her she didn't have to think – she could only feel. And Angie desperately didn't want to think at the moment – it was enough to swirl in a maelstrom of sensations. How could she come to a decision about something so tremendous – which had momentous implications for someone else? For *him*. How could she risk hurting and upsetting *him*? And yet from what Gabbie had told her – if Jude was her son – and she felt certain he was – he was making a pretty good job of upsetting his own life right now.

"Darling – you make me feel about twenty-five!"

Gabbie was stepping out of the shower and rubbing himself briskly with a fluffy white bath towel.

She smiled at him and turned off the shower.

"You slept well," she commented, knowing how she herself had lain awake for hours, listening to his rhythmic breathing and being comforted by it in her distress.

What should she do? Did this Jude – this Jude Kennedy – *want* to know her? What would he feel about her decision to give him up? How would she measure up to the woman he'd called his mother all these years? To Janet Rose's sister? It was incredible – Janet Rose's sister? No wonder she had felt she needed to keep an eye on Angie – felt guilty even – when she'd seen how ill losing him had made her. She had colluded in the baby's adoption, after all. Her husband had fixed it up – and now he was gone.

Gabbie saw the troubled thoughts crossing her mind as she dried her hair without speaking.

He reached out and stroked her breast tenderly.

"There's no rush to make any sort of a decision my darling," he said. "I shall go and see Meg when I get back and see if we can trace the fella for her. Maybe I can find a colleague to sort him out – we'll see what the problems really are. I'll keep you informed and you can do as much or as little about it as you want to. Don't panic Angie – nothing's got to be decided overnight! This is not a child you've got to relate to – he's a man of twenty-six with his own life to lead – and your life here goes on whatever happens, doesn't it?"

He kissed her and cupped her face in both hands.

"Be happy. You've made me happier than I could ever have imagined possible!"

She smiled a watery smile and wrapped a towel around herself like a sarong.

"You make me happy too, Gabbie. You know that. I've always adored you. Right from the first time I saw you – in your office – remember?"

"Yes – I remember – you were like a frightened rabbit! I wanted to crush you in my arms there and then!"

"I wanted you to too – but Sister Malpat wouldn't have liked it!"

They both laughed and Gabbie stepped into green tartan boxer shorts. "Are you about to scurry down to your office wrapped in a wet towel?" he grinned.

"It would make Conchita's day, but no – I don't think I'll give her that satisfaction! I shall put my dress on and give every appearance of respectability. Only Jose tumbles the guests!"

"Does he now?" Gabbie laughed, as he pulled on navy blue linen trousers and buttoned them quickly.

"Occasionally. I'm afraid girls seem to find him inexplicably sexy – he always looks as if he could do with a shave and a shower to me!"

"Umm. Just as long as he doesn't have eyes for his employer!"

"Aargh! Please! No – Jose's taste is for very young, very leggy girls with long hair and no bosoms!"

"So poor Conchita doesn't get a look in!"

"No. A little too dumpy I'm afraid. Anyway – she thinks he's perfectly disgusting and constantly assures me he will go to hell – along with Julio – the pair of them tease her unmercifully. It's their favourite game – poor Conchita. I must go and make sure she's coping – and that she is convinced I slept in my office! I'll see you in breakfast."

"Just coffee for me, darling. See you later."

They had a lingering kiss before she opened her bedroom door and looked out, feeling like a naughty schoolgirl after a midnight raid. The hotel was silent and she walked downstairs to her office passing no one. A grey cat stretched as it saw her but did not move from the couch.

"Have you been shut in here all night, Gato?"

She threw open the window and waited for him to get up very slowly and – in his own good time – make a dignified exit into the haze of the garden.

She could hear Julio busying himself in the kitchen now, and somewhere upstairs water was flushing. She wouldn't have long to herself before the Casa d'Or's demands took over and then Gabbie's needs became uppermost for the day. Only now, in the quiet of this early morning hour, could she consider Jude and what to do about him.

"What difference can I make to his life now, anyway? It's too late. Maybe everything's too late. I wasn't there when he needed me, was I? When he felt everything went wrong with the bloody perfect, wonderful Catholic family the nuns said could love him more than I did. And *why* did he feel that? Why had he turned his back on his solid middle class home and middle class values and taken off like that? Just like I did – just upped and gone, like I did!"

So many years ago. She'd had a reason. Perhaps *everything* was in our genes and free will a complete misconception. He'd probably been told she'd given him up of her own free will – but she hadn't really, had she? There had been little choice or informed decision about it – they had worn her down when she was at her most vulnerable and weak. Not much free will about that. Maybe Jude was casting himself loose to see where he drifted – yes – she could understand that. To drift where fate decrees. Or your genes. Perhaps *she* would understand him so much better than Meg – that might help, mightn't it? But then, what would follow? A relationship – mother and son – son and mother. That seemed terrifying. She didn't know how to be a mother. She'd watched other people – made judgements – but to be a real mother to a real son? Could she do that? She had no idea.

But the need to see him – to set eyes on her son – was growing with every hour. She knew she must do that at least, and that Gabbie could make it happen. He would go back and see Meg and help her trace Jude, and they would all take things from there. See what *he* wanted too. He sounded unhappy, she realised with a pang. He sounded rootless and restless as she'd been, until she'd found this place. Maybe Deya could help with Jude too. It had a very powerful magic. It could seep into your soul. And if she had loved it instantly, so might he. Perhaps they should meet here – she had always imagined going back to England to see him – but now the thought was growing – bring Jude back here. Bring Jude to Deya.

Chapter Twenty-Five

"Mum – it's me – Jude."

"Jude? Oh Mother of God! Are you all right? Did you see my poster somewhere?"

"Yeah – no – I'm not all right. I'm banged up in Truro nick."

"What? You're mumbling lovey – what did you say?"

"I've been arrested. I'm in Truro nick."

"Arrested? What – in prison? Oh no – whatever for?"

"Drugs. I'm sorry, mum. I didn't want you involved but I couldn't think who else to call."

"Of course you couldn't – I'm your mother, Jude. I'll ring Tim Simson and we'll come over – he'll know what to do. Truro, you said?"

"Yeah. I'm sorry, mum. I shouldn't be involving you in all this."

"Yes you should. I'm just so relieved to hear your voice – to know where you are – even though it's awful. I've imagined worse over the months."

"Have you? Poor old mum."

"We'll be with you as soon as we can. Is there anything you need?"

"No – apart from a packet of Marlboros."

"Well, say a Hail Mary while you're waiting, Jude. I know I shall."

He knew she was trying not to cry, and was surprised to feel his own eyes filling up as he put the phone down. Never any condemnation – always positive – dear old mum – what a complete shit he'd been to her.

He was led down to the cells where Jez and the red-haired traveller were already sitting, heads in their hands.

"Got a smoke?" Jez asked as he came in.

"No."

Jude's stomach lurched at the stale stink in the cell. He couldn't stay here – he was used to being outside most of the day – to the feel of the spray on his face and the wind in his hair. He couldn't sit here for hours with nothing to do. How long would it take his mother to contact Tim Simson, and could he just leave

222

his office and drive to Truro from Dartmouth immediately? It seemed unlikely; he might even be away. He could be here for hours – or days – or weeks.

"Shit!" he said to no one in particular. "Someone must have tipped them off. Why else would they turn up just then like that?"

"Happens all the time, mate. The bastards never leave us alone. Always turning up uninvited. What happens now?"

"Search me. I've got a solicitor coming, but that could take forever. I can't stay here – I've gotta get out of this place – it's doing my head in."

"Yeah. Me an' all."

They relapsed into gloomy silence until Jez spoke.

"Could do with one now, mate! I dunno what all the fuss is about – it's not hurting anybody, is it? Thought it was s'posed to be a free country. Fuckin' free my arse – you can't do nuffink so far as I can see. Whatever we do – don't matter where we go – it's not right."

This long speech seemed to exhaust him and he rolled over on the bench and closed his eyes. His huge frame rolled over the sides and his mud-caked boots dug into Jude's thigh. He moved slightly.

"You could go down for four years for peddling," said the red-head.

"We was only buying the stuff – in our own van – but you could be in deep shit."

"Yeah."

The pit of his stomach was curdling; a bitter bile came up into his mouth and he swallowed it. What had his mother said? 'Say a Hail Mary while you're waiting'! Where the fuck did she think he was?

The school chapel flashed into his mind with its blue and golden painted Virgin and scarlet Sacred Heart, and a chanting Brother at the Angelus:

Hail Mary, full of grace,
The Lord is with thee;
Blessed art thou among women.
Blessed is the fruit of thy womb, Jesus.

*Holy Mary, mother of God, pray for us sinners
Now, and at the hour of our death.*

Amazing.

He could remember every word.

He hadn't given them a thought for years – ten years – when he had refused to go back to school for his A levels and had promised Meg he'd do some sort of college course at the local technical college. He hadn't stuck that for more than a term and had worked in a sandwich bar for a bit. He'd quite enjoyed that – and then he'd tried DJ-ing at a club on the beach in Bude – but they'd only paid him £10 to work all evening and half the night – so he'd given that up too. Nothing had seemed right – nothing had fitted. It had been like trying on the wrong clothes – always made for someone else and hurting in all the wrong places.

He stood up and paced around for a bit. This must be how zoo animals felt. He had never enjoyed watching anything in a cage – even as a small child he'd been aware of their fear and pain and despair – this is for ever; no one will come and release me now. But he was lucky; his mother had told him all his life he was lucky – maybe someone would open his bars and set him free.

Taking drugs felt like that – just for a short while you were free – of pain, anxiety, of fear of rejection – only afterwards of course it could be worse than before. The padding was removed and you were red raw.

Jez had fallen asleep – a deep snoring now filled the cell as he lay on his back, displaying black gaps in his uneven teeth. Jude ran his fingers through his short spiked hair. Come on, mum, get me out of here. I can't stay locked up in here – you know I can't.

His father had sometimes locked him in his room when his juvenile devilment had got too much for him.

"You'll stay there, Jude, and consider your behaviour. Until you conform to our standards you will be punished. When you've thought better of it you can come down. And if I ever see you smoking again I shall take my belt to you. You're ten years of age, Jude – and I will not be answered back by a small boy of ten."

Poor dad. He was the gentlest of men really and could no more have hit me than he would have got drunk or taken out other women! He must have felt completely out of his depth with me – he used to get so angry – and yet nothing else seemed to upset him at all. I guess I was just one huge disappointment.

And then there was the way he went.

Jude was forcing himself to remember – to try to understand how he had got to this stony place from his comfortable home in Nethway. It had been one week before his eleventh birthday – one day before Christmas Eve – and he had been messing around in the car park at the back of the village pub with some older lads on their skateboards. One of them had a bottle of Daniels and had offered him some. After a few scorching slugs he had felt his skateboarding skills soaring – doing amazing wheelies and jumps and generally showing off to the older boys and having a marvellous time. The whole afternoon had been terrific – he had been Skateboard King for the day, and everyone had liked him. He'd had a few more slugs of the stuff and torn home down the hill, arriving to the wonderful smells of his mother's Christmas baking.

He'd flung open the back door with a wide grin and then seen his father's face. It was mulberry coloured and heavy-jowled.

"Where on earth have you been all afternoon, boy? You were supposed to do your mother's shopping at twelve. It's now five fifteen! And where is it? She's gone out looking for you – as if she hadn't got enough to do!"

Hell. He'd forgotten all about the shopping once he'd met up with the skateboarders.

He'd shrugged, and then suddenly vomited.

He hadn't known he would; it had taken him completely by surprise and had sprayed the kitchen table and his mother's pastry board.

"You've been drinking! Why – you – you little…"

His father's colour had deepened to a frightening purple. He had put out an arm as if to strike him, and then fallen sideways onto a chair, clutching his chest.

"Dad?" he had asked, wiping the sick from his mouth with a dishcloth. "What's the matter, daddy? I'm sorry about the shopping – I'll go and get it."

His father was making frantic gestures and Jude ran from the room.

"Jeremy!" he called up the stairs, but no one came. He rushed back into the kitchen to see his father slump forward onto the table.

"Daddy! It's all right –I'll call the doctor."

His head was pounding as he dialled the surgery number, written in his mother's neat handwriting.

"Call an ambulance right away, son," the receptionist advised. "Get him to hospital as soon as you can."

He'd dialled 999 and felt a bit calmer when he knew they were on their way. He'd gone back into the kitchen and stood, frightened and uncertain in the doorway. He didn't want to touch him.

"Daddy?" he had asked, but there was no reply.

There never had been any reply ever again. No one but Jude had known of their last conversation. He had washed the sick off the table and off his jumper before the ambulance men arrived – a few minutes before Meg.

"Oh my poor darling," Meg had said that night, her arms around Jude on the sofa. "For him to die like that – in front of you – my poor little boy. And you were so brave and sensible – ringing the doctors and the ambulance – doing all the right things – oh, whatever would I do without you and Jeremy? My two big boys? You'll have to be the man of the house now, my darling, won't you? Mummy's right hand – oh, my great big boy. I wouldn't have had this happen to you for the world."

But Jude knew better. He had killed him. His father might be alive today if he had not made him so angry and frustrated. No one else had ever known that. But sometimes he could forget that distorted, purple face. Drugs and drink could do it – they could make it go away. But not for long. Now in this grey prison cell he could see him again.

"You've been drinking!"

Of course he had. It made his life fun. Made people like him – accept him. It had brought him to this place. 'His just deserts' the Brothers would have called it.

"That boy will come to no good, Meg – I'm telling you!" he

had overheard his father saying one evening when he should have been in bed. Never for one moment had he considered they might be talking about Jeremy. And here he was – fulfilling his father's prophecy – being the worthless dross he had known he was. Not worth having – not worth keeping.

He sat down in the corner of the cell, his hands shaking.

He could go no lower than this. Where did he go from here?

"Hello Meg. How are things? It's Graham Bott."

"Oh Graham! I'm so glad you're back. I tried to ring you yesterday; we've found him! We've found Jude. But it's not terribly good news, I'm afraid. No – he's been arrested for selling drugs – cannabis mainly, I think, and not a huge amount – but still – terrible, isn't it? He's home here with me now, on bail – Tim Simson was wonderful and fixed it all up there and then. If he hadn't agreed to come home with us he wouldn't have got bail of course, because he's got no fixed address. Isn't that awful, Graham? My son – with no fixed address? He's pretty down; I've not really been able to talk to him properly – we haven't managed to get back to an easy sort of relationship – not yet. Of course, I hadn't seen him for nearly a year."

"Can I help in any way do you think?"

"Oh yes, I think so. Could you possibly spare the time to come down and talk to him? See if *you* can see what his problem is and why he can't seem to settle to normal life at all?"

"I could get down tomorrow evening. Where are you exactly?"

"Very near Dartmouth. Take the Kingswear Road after Paignton – it's signposted and we're down the hill from the church. Dragon House – it's got a slate roof – you can't miss it. If you could stay over until Sunday evening that would be marvellous. Of course he may not open up to you either, but it's worth a try. I'm pretty desperate, as you can imagine. The court case will be at the end of November – so that's looming over us like a great black cloud. I don't know what I'll do if he goes to prison."

"What does your solicitor think?"

"He thinks he'll get off with a fine and maybe we can plead extenuating circumstances. You could help there, Graham –

prison's unthinkable – it would make everything twice as bad. He might never recover from it."

"We've got six or seven weeks then to come up with something. Don't lose heart. I'll get down to you late tomorrow afternoon."

"You're a star, Graham! What would we do without you? How are *you*, anyway? Did you have a good holiday?"

"Terrific. Feeling one hundred per cent better. Deya is fantastic – it really has restored me. And Angie – well, Angie's marvellous."

"Yes, of course – Angie. Well, I'll hear all about your holiday when I see you dear. Thank you so much for making time for all our problems – it is good of you."

"Nonsense – a weekend in Devon sounds delightful. See you between five and six."

"Lovely dear. Bye now, bye."

She replaced the receiver as Jude came in the back door.

"Did you see Jeremy?"

"I didn't try. I've been for a swim."

"Oh. Where?"

"I biked to Sugary Cove – it was good. No one else there at all."

"Wasn't it cold?"

"Not too bad. I was in for about forty minutes I guess. D'you want some tea?"

"I'll make it."

She bustled around the kitchen, delighting in having Jude at home to wait on once again, however briefly.

"I don't suppose you remember Graham Bott, do you?" she said, as she poured water in the pot.

"No – who's he?"

"He's a psychiatrist friend of Janet's – known one another almost all their lives – Philip was at university with him although he was quite a bit older. Anyway – Janet has kept in touch and his wife was very involved in a drugs rehabilitation unit in London. We met them one or twice at Auntie Janet's house years ago."

"Mum! I'm not a drug addict! It was just an occasional joint or hash brew – or the odd E at a nightclub. No different to a few beers – honestly!"

She turned on him – her eyes flashing for the first time.

"Don't be so ridiculous, Jude! Of course it's different – you could go to prison! You wouldn't be in this position if you'd stuck to beers, would you? And please use an ashtray – there's one on the window sill."

He flicked his cigarette in its direction and looked at her heightened colour.

"Cool it, mum! I'm just trying to explain I haven't got a drugs habit – I don't deal regularly either – I was really short of cash, that's all. I was the middle man and someone squealed. God knows who."

"I'm sure *he* does, Jude. Anyway – Graham is coming for the weekend to see if he can help in any way. It's very good of him."

Jude looked irritated.

"Look, mum – I really appreciate the bail – but I don't need a psychiatrist. I don't need some bloke talking to me about my problems – I'll sort them out myself. Right? I know you're trying to help but don't suffocate me. Don't assume... well, don't assume anything."

She poured the tea carefully and passed him his mug with quiet determination.

"You'll like Graham," she said. "He's a wonderful man with great charisma. You could use this as a turning point, Jude. Don't carry on wasting your life – you've got so many talents."

"No I haven't," he replied. "I can surf – what else can I do? Dad thought I was a complete waste of space."

"Oh he didn't! Why ever do you think that? Of course he didn't, he loved you!"

"Well he had a funny way of showing it. My abiding memory is irritation and frustration. He died thinking I was a confounded nuisance and he was almost certainly right."

She looked at him across her kitchen table and shook her head slowly.

"Where do you get all this from?" she asked quietly. "Didn't we show you how much we loved you? Why do you talk like this?"

"Because it's *true*! You may not have felt like that, but dad certainly did. I messed up his nice ordered existence and untidied his grand plan for a nice little Catholic family of two nice little Catholic boys who worked hard for the Brothers and passed their exams, and followed a career and got married. Like Jeremy did! The saints be praised for Jeremy!"

"Well say all this to Graham and maybe he'll make some sort of sense out of it. I can't. He'll be here tomorrow afternoon."

"Well bloody good for him! Jesus! If I'd known you were going to treat me like some sort of druggy I'd have refused to come home. Chill out, mum – everyone does it!"

She dried her hands on a tea towel and pushed a wisp of grey hair back from her tired face.

"No they don't, Jude. You've been mixing with people who do, but thousands of other quite ordinary folk don't. And Tim Simson said if you'd had more than that one tablet as well as the cannabis in that package, you would certainly be looking at prison. You'd had a caution before."

"Yeah – well, I don't want to talk to this bloke, whoever he is. What does he know about me? What's the point?"

"Just wait and see when he gets here. That's all I ask. Oh Jude – why did you stay away so long? Why didn't you ever ring home? There's so much catching up to do and I don't know where to begin."

She looked at him in helpless confusion. He hacked off a piece of cheese from a chunk of cheddar on the table.

"I'm twenty-six, mum. I'm making my own life. This isn't my home anymore – it's yours."

"But you haven't got another one, lovey, have you? You were sleeping in someone else's dormobile who said you couldn't stay there anymore! So you haven't made yourself another home, have you?"

"No."

He scraped back his chair and walked into the next room, kneeling on the floor at his box of CDs and slotting one into the music centre. Its pounding bass beat reverberated through the house.

"I haven't got a home now and I never had," he said quietly, but the crashing of the Red Hot Chilli Peppers prevented her from hearing a single word.

Chapter Twenty-Six

Gabbie and Jude walked up the hill at Nethway side by side, their long strides matching and the silence between them only broken by the occasional monotonous cooing of pigeons in the elms above.

"Where's the beach from here?" Gabbie asked eventually. "I wouldn't mind walking along the shore."

"Scabbacombe – we'll cut through Pratt's field."

He turned off the road suddenly, through a farm gate, plucking a late dark blackberry as he went, and Gabbie followed, glad he'd thought to bring tough hiking boots with him. He didn't need any authenticating records – he only had to take one look at Jude's green eyes and he knew – this was Angie's son without doubt. His sullen, depressed attitude reminded him of the silent girl who had sat in front of him all those years ago. Sadness stretches a long way, he thought, like elastic. And somehow he had to tie a knot and stop it all.

They walked on in silence, the early October sunshine warming their faces and making Gabbie remove his sweater. Jude's muscular arms were nut brown beneath his black T-shirt, and the hairs on his calves blond from a summer's surfing.

"What do you do in the winter?" Graham tried again.

"Not a lot. Listen – I know mum asked you to come down here and talk to me – but I'm not some kid of fifteen who's been sent to the headmaster and I'm not a drug addict needing a quack – OK? Just because I've chosen a life style my mother doesn't understand."

He broke off, kicking nettles aside as he found the path down to the stony beach far below.

"I realise that, Jude. But sometimes an outsider can be helpful – where relations are too emotionally involved – and you are in a spot of trouble right now, aren't you? A psychiatrist's report could be useful – I have had some experience in being an expert witness over the years."

"Yeah. I dunno what all the fuss is about. Bit of grass – so what? I bet you smoked it in the seventies, didn't you?"

He glanced backwards at Gabbie for a second as they

slithered down the stony path in single file.

"Yes – I tried it a couple of times. Couldn't afford to have my memory and concentration mucked about with in my work, of course, but yes, I tried it. The issue is more whether you're satisfied with the life you've chosen and whether you're making the most of what's available to you. I think your mother wants to know why you feel the need to cut yourself off from them all so completely."

"I don't – it just happened."

He jumped the last three feet down onto the beach and wandered off along it, leaving Gabbie making an undignified descent in a rush of stones.

He caught up with Jude as he was bending down selecting flat pebbles to skim into the blue-grey sea.

"I haven't felt I fitted in here ever," he said, after one bounced five times and he straightened in satisfaction. "Well – not since I was a little kid."

Gabbie threw his sweater onto the stones and folded himself onto it, like closing the blades of a Swiss army knife. Jude had his back to him and continued skimming stones. The tide was out and the sea calm – a gentle rhythmic pounding, lulling Graham's eyelids into closing. He had driven for almost five hours yesterday, only a day after returning from Majorca, and he was exhausted. He fought sleep and opened his eye – regarding the pine-straight back of the man in front of him.

"I'm knackered!" he admitted, and Jude turned to look at him properly for the first time.

"Have a swim!" he suggested. "It'll wake you up. I'm going in in a minute."

"Looks bloody cold to me! I was in the Med two days ago – my poor old body can't cope with these seas anymore – no way! Any way – I didn't bring a towel."

Jude turned away with an expressionless face, the wind flattening his cropped hair like a wheat field.

"Is this where you swam as a kid? Is this your childhood beach?"

"Yeah. Here and Sugary Cove. Jeremy and me had dinghies. We swam here from May to November. Brilliant. I could never live far from the sea. I thought I'd go mad in that fucking cell in Truro."

"Exactly. This is why you need to make absolutely sure you don't finish up in one for a considerable period, I would suggest. Sounds a pretty perfect boyhood to me – lucky sod – why do you think you felt you didn't fit in? In what way? Sounds so terrific – boats, swimming – all that on your doorstep."

"Yeah. That was good – it was fitting in at home that made me mintie. My dad was incredibly straight and I didn't fit his mould – you know? I wasn't the kid he wanted. I knew that."

Graham picked up a lolly stick and scratched in the sand.

"You felt he'd put in an order for a child and got you instead? Got the wrong one? Is that how you saw it?"

"Something like that. I was meant to be this perfect little kid they'd dreamed about – my mum had this spiel she told Jeremy and me about how we'd been chosen – how special we were – you know – all the usual crap adoptive parents tell their kids – how they'd wanted a kid for years and years and then fuck me – along I came! Jesus – it was supposed to make me feel good, but it didn't. All I knew was some other woman had given birth to me – not wanted me and got rid of me – and I'd landed up with them. Like the fucking lottery, wasn't it? For Christ's sake – how was I to know what sort of kid I was meant to be?"

The wind was carrying his words away and Gabbie strained to catch them.

"How old were you when your parents told you you were adopted?"

There was a pause. Jude started to peel off his T-shirt and kick off his shoes.

"I was five. Started school – happy little kid – adored my mum – well, this woman I *thought* was my mum – and she suddenly tells us this story at bedtime – like it was an alternative to Goldilocks or something – dad's not my dad, and she's not my real mum. I was gutted. Absolutely gutted."

He unzipped his cut-off jeans and stepped out of them, standing for a moment in black pants which he removed unselfconsciously. His brown naked body revealed a neat whiter bottom as he charged into the sea, spray rising up around him like fireworks.

Gabbie watched him wading out into deeper water and

thought of Angie. She would understand this dreamer – he was so like her – the same hidden hurt and prickly shell – like a couple of conkers, he smiled to himself. Difficult to catch hold of, but smooth and warm underneath. He mustn't mess this up. Their reunion must be right in every way. Angie had decided he ought to come to Deya; and his condition of bail would prevent him from travelling abroad before his court case – so it would have to be December. December in Deya. That gave him two months – two months to prepare him for the most momentous meeting of his life. He watched the arms cutting through the water and arching upwards towards the sky; he was as at home in the sea as a dolphin – and he would certainly meet all Angie's expectations in looks – stunningly handsome. What else had she said? Intelligent – hard to judge as yet but certainly not stupid. A 'one-off' – undoubtedly. 'Funny and warm' – well he probably wasn't feeling terribly funny right now. 'A bit like my dad' – he couldn't answer for that, of course.

He felt sure she would love him, but what would his reaction to Angie be? Disappointment? Or recognition and a sense of homecoming? Impossible to guess. He felt a sudden rush of protective love for Angie – she had worked so hard to sort her life out – to get to her present state of equilibrium – it mustn't be torpedoed by this boy. What had they started? Well, it was set in motion now, and could not be stopped. The train had left the station and would follow the track, wherever it led. He was only the guard waving the flag. He lay back on his sweater and wriggled to try and make a comfortable groove in the stones beneath. Impossible. But the warm sun on his face and the sound of the waves soon carried him into a dreamless sleep where Angie and Jude did not intrude, and only Izzie remained.

He slept for almost an hour and when he woke, a cloud was over the sun and he was alone. He looked up and down the beach but there was only a woman walking with a small dog in sight. The sea was empty until you scanned the horizon and saw a huge ferry crossing towards Plymouth. He stood up stiffly, his back reminding him it would prefer a firm mattress to a bed of stones.

"God! How long have I been asleep?"

He shook his sweater hard. He had left his watch on the

walnut chest in his small bedroom at Nethway. He looked up at the sun and guessed it was around noon. As he started walking back along the beach, aiming for the steep path they had descended by, he noticed two boys on bikes on a slipway farther along.

"I bet he brought me the hardest way down deliberately, the sod!" he grinned, as he made his way along to the easy incline up to the road.

"Which way to Nethway village?" he called to the lads, and they pointed to a left fork. He waved and walked on, the sun now emerging from the cloud bank high in the sky. He hoped Jude would be at home – he was only here a few more hours – maybe he should extend it till Monday morning, in case he opened up a bit more this evening. He could suggest they went down to the pub perhaps. He had a patient coming at 2.00 tomorrow; if he left early he'd be home well before that. Yes, he would suggest it.

Meg was stirring the chicken soup when he walked in the open back door and Jude – he noticed with relief – was sprawled in a relaxed fashion in an arm chair, reading the Mail on Sunday.

"Good swim?" he asked. "I'm afraid I just couldn't keep my eyes open!"

"Yeah."

Meg clucked around them both, laying out pâté and cheeses and popping a French stick into the Rayburn to warm.

"Do you mind if I go back tomorrow morning?" Gabbie asked her, as he put out the cutlery on the kitchen table. "It's a long drive – would it inconvenience you?"

She turned and handed him three soup bowls.

"Of course not – I think it's a much more sensible idea. Poor Janet was so whacked when she drove down, she stayed four nights in the end before she could summon up the courage to drive back!"

"I like driving – it's just that I only returned from Deya on Friday. So that's OK then?"

"Of course it is. We're just very grateful you bothered to come all this way."

She ground the black pepper into the soup with a flourish and added a tablespoon of cream as she gave it a final stir.

"Are you hungry, Jude?" she asked. "I should think that swim will have given you an appetite! Was it freezing?"

"No. It was great."

"Why didn't you take a towel? I can't imagine getting dressed without drying myself properly!"

"I dried on my T-shirt. That soup smells great!"

"Good. Come and sit up then. Shall we open a bottle of something?"

"Just beer for me will be fine. Oh – Black Sheep – yes – rather! Thanks Jude. What's your local like?"

"I dunno. Haven't lived here for years. We could try it out."

"It changed hands last year. I haven't been in there myself but I think it's all right. Mrs Toze said the crab salads are good."

She lifted the French sticks onto the bread board and began hacking off thick slices.

"What time shall we have supper then? About seven?"

"Whatever suits you. I'm easy. Jude and I could wander down and check it out for you afterwards, couldn't we?"

There was no reply. Jude was dunking his bread into his soup and eating as if he hadn't seen food in weeks.

"He loves my home-made soup, don't you dear?" Meg's face shone with pride and the heat from the Rayburn.

"It's pretty good," was all he said the whole meal. Meg and Gabbie exchanged glances and she sighed. What had she expected? Some miracle cure? Janet had told her how marvellous this man was with young people – how he'd had a lifetime in the psychiatric care of troubled youngsters – but he didn't seem to be impressing Jude. She ate daintily, her appetite shrinking.

"What are your plans for this afternoon?" Gabbie asked the room in general.

"I shall potter in the garden," Meg replied, "and then maybe we could have a barbecue – or do you think it will get too cold? I bought steaks."

"I think it will be dark before seven," he answered. "I'll make a salad if you like – I'm quite good at salads!"

"Right. I'll fry steaks then. What about you, Jude?"

His closed face gave nothing away. He pushed his empty bowl away from him and regarded Graham coldly.

"I shall probably lie on my bed all afternoon and get

completely stoned," he said, scraping his chair back and leaving the room.

"There's nothing else to do here, is there?"

"You see what I'm up against?" Meg pushed her half-finished soup to one side. "I just can't get through to him. He resents being here – he's bored silly, isn't he?"

"And frightened. He's doing a good cover-up job I reckon, but he's pretty worried about the court case I guess. It was quite a shock being in that cell you know."

"Of course it was! Ah well – it might jolt some sense into him and make him rethink his life a bit. Jeremy told me ages ago that he'd finish up in prison, but I didn't believe him."

"I think it's much more likely he'll be fined. But he certainly needs some help. He's like a rudderless ship. Maybe he'll talk to me this evening – he's still angry I'm here at all, of course. I'll do my best."

"I know you will, Graham. And I do appreciate it – really I do. Would you like anything else? Tea or coffee?"

"Just a cup of tea, please. Yes – Earl Grey is great."

They carried their cups into the garden and sat on the terrace where, in Jude's childhood, the chicken coop had stood. The sweet, sickly smell of cannabis wafted down from an open window above them.

"Goodness! Is the jasmine still in flower?" Meg said, as she put down her cup and saucer. "I *must* do some dead-heading today! What would you like to do, dear, read?"

"I'll help you dead-head. I like gardening – very relaxing. I've got quite a bit to catch up on in my own garden when I get back."

"Have you got a huge garden in Ascot?"

"Half an acre. I have a fella in once a week, so he keeps the jungle at bay! I couldn't do it all myself."

"Well, I do! I love it. Of course this isn't half an acre, but it's over a quarter. I just love being out here, Always have."

"Did Jude ever take an interest?"

"Funnily enough he did when he was a child. Not lately of course, but he once got quite obsessed with growing vegetables – lettuces, runner beans, cauliflower – but it wore off – he was like that – mad crazes that absorbed him completely – and then losing all interest in them quite suddenly. Since his teens it's been nothing but surfing and seeing his friends – nothing else mattered at all. I could feel him slipping away from me from about thirteen – there was nothing I could do about it. Nothing at all."

She was inspecting her fingernails carefully and did not look up.

"Were Jude and your husband close?"

"No. Not really. Derek was perhaps a bit hard on him I now think. He was always fair, though, and he would have said everything he did was for Jude's own good. Jeremy was more Derek's sort of boy, I suppose. They were quite alike in temperament, funnily enough. Jeremy hasn't got an unorthodox bone in his body and always does everything very precisely – Derek was just like that. Jude – well Jude is Jude, I'm afraid. Restless – dissatisfied – always looking for something else."

"Or someone. Come on, Meg – let's get on with the deadheading. Perhaps he'll join us later. He will when he smells the steak cooking. You can't rush these things you know. They have their own momentum."

Chapter Twenty-Seven

Angie was patting Rita's hand and beaming.

"It's such a wonderful surprise! And so *unlike* you to be so impetuous, darling. Do you mean to tell me you just abandoned Patrick and Stu and caught a plane to Palma? Just like that – I don't believe it!"

"More or less. Stu was showing me how to get teletext on the TV and we flashed through flight availability and there was a flight to Palma this morning for £92 return! It was so cheap – this was yesterday lunchtime – I'd got a few days off work so I said to Patrick 'You know what I'd love to do? Go and catch that plane and surprise Angie! You boys could manage for a week couldn't you?'"

"Course they can – Stu is what? Nineteen? Do them good – make them appreciate how you wait on them, Rita. Oh, it's so lovely to see you!"

"I just kept thinking about you. And £92 was so ridiculous it seemed stupid to miss it. Patrick was pretty surprised I did it, I must admit."

"I bet he was secretly very impressed. Oh – we've got *such* a lot of catching up to do. I've had a pretty startling few weeks actually. I've wanted to talk to you about it all, but not in a letter, and the phone didn't seem right. You are *brilliant* to have done this – just when I needed you to."

"Good! Give me a long drink then, Ange, and we'll sit in the garden. Have you got many guests?"

"No. Only two rooms taken, so it's very quiet. And they've been before so I don't need to mother them too much. I can spend hours with you – and the weather's still very settled. What d'you fancy?"

"Oh – one of your famous Sangrias with loads of ice, I should think. Lovely!"

Angie went to the bar herself, as Jose seemed to be missing. She poured two glasses from a jug in the little fridge behind the bar and emptied a tray of ice into them. She raised one to her sister.

"Salud!"

"Cheers! Right – where shall we sit?"

"Out of the door and turn left. Hang on – I'll get another sun lounger – I usually sit around here on my own. It'll give you some indication of what's been happening if I tell you that the last time I sat here with someone else was two weeks ago, and it was Gabbie."

"Gabbie? Who's Gabbie? Hang on – you mean that psychiatrist?"

"That's the one. You probably didn't know that he and his wife came out here for a holiday three or four years ago – I may have mentioned it – we've never lost touch completely. Well – she died last January."

"Oh no – how awful."

"Yes – complete tragedy. She had flu. You don't expect a medic to die from flu somehow, do you?"

"She was a doctor, too?"

"Uum – a psychiatrist specialising in drug treatment for youngsters. Anyway – Gabbie had been very down and only wrote and told me in the summer – so I suggested he had a few days break out here – and he did. And it was absolutely wonderful and mind-blowing and terrifying all at once."

"What? You mean – you and *Gabbie*? What – after all this time? I mean – you hadn't *before* – had you Ange?"

"Erm… not exactly. We'd had a bit of a flirtatious thing when I first started cooking, but nothing serious. He was a bit of a ladies' man in those days, you know. I fell madly in love with him in the hospital, but then so did everyone else. He looked like a film star! He still looks pretty good to me."

"How the hell old is he? He must be eons older than you are, Angie."

"He's sixty-one. But you'd never take him for more than fifty-five. He's gorgeous – you could eat him with a pastry fork! I've always gone for older men, Rita, you know that. But the *wonderful* thing about this is it's built on years and years of real friendship. We never expected it to happen – it was just such a natural, comforting, lovely – *happy* thing, and we are both determined not to lose each other – or to rush into anything. But the mind-blowing part of it and the terrifying bit is what he came to tell me."

"To tell you? How d'you mean?"

Angie lay back on her lounger and closed her eyes. Rita looked at her in concern. For someone who had just told her she'd fallen in love with an old friend she didn't look altogether relaxed and contented. In fact, her first impression when she'd stepped out of the taxi and caught sight of Angie through the window was how tense she looked. She'd been pacing up and down, and Rita had known something was worrying her. She leant across to her sister and touched her bare arm – it was covered in goose bumps.

"What's the matter, Angie?"

Her eyes flashed open like a doll's.

"He knows who my son is," she uttered carefully.

"Your son? You mean – but how could he possibly know?"

Angie sat up and took a gulp of Sangria.

"You're never going to believe this, it's so extraordinary. Remember Dr Rose's wife?"

"Of course I do; I've worked at the practice for years, haven't I?"

"But remember her *before* that? When I was ill."

"Yes. She ran me to Epsom a couple of times. Nice lady – very kind."

"Exactly. Very kind. But even kinder to her sister who was infertile and desperate for a baby."

"What? Angie – you've lost me completely, I'm afraid. Is this all to do with that bloke Andy nosing around?"

"No. Well, it may have a connection but that's not important. Dr Rose convinced me – with the nuns – that I should give up my baby – didn't he?"

"Well – yes – I suppose they all thought you didn't have many options at the time."

"But *we* were going to keep him, weren't we? Until they all started interfering and going on about this bloody wonderful Catholic family who could give him such a bloody perfect Catholic home. You want to know who that family was? Only – Dr Rose's wife's sister – that's who."

"No – surely that wasn't right – surely the people aren't supposed to know who the birth mother is? It's all done by the adoption agency isn't it?"

"That's what they told us. Anyway, I don't think her sister did know anything much about me, and Dr Rose *and* his wife were both on the Board and they put such a strong case for these – these Kennedys – that it all went ahead. Bloody quick too."

"So your baby went to live with Dr Rose's wife's sister? Where?"

"In Devon. This perfect, wonderful house by the sea. *But* – and this is where the lovely happy story gets unstuck a bit – my son didn't apparently like it quite as much as everybody thought he would. He was a very wild boy and has now cut himself off from the family and was living rough on the beach somewhere – taking drugs – the whole bit. Oh Rita – he'd have been better off living with us, wouldn't he? Your kids are all OK – they don't take drugs, do they? And Clare's just the loveliest thing I've ever met."

Rita smiled in quiet pride.

"Yes – she's such a dear. It's lovely to see them so happy together. But how on earth did this Gabbie find all this out? Did he know when you were his patient?"

"Hell, no. He and Philip Rose were at med school together, but they never told him anything. It was all utterly hush-hush. Philip Rose was a lot older than Gabbie – went into medicine late or something – and he's dead now…"

"Yes, I know. Heart attack last year. Very sad."

"And Janet Rose asked Gabbie to Sunday lunch – partly because he's an old friend and partly for his professional advice because she was so worried about her sister and Jude."

"Jude? He's called Jude?"

"Yes. A favourite saint's name, apparently."

"And what did Gabbie do?"

"He went down to Devon to see him – oh Rita! I can't believe he's actually *seen* my son!"

"I thought you said he was living rough and all that. How did he know where he was?"

"It gets worse. They'd been contacted but only because he'd been arrested for selling drugs – only cannabis – but he needed bail. So he's back home with Janet Rose's sister as a condition of bail until his case is heard in a few weeks' time."

"Oh Angie – this is awful! I didn't know you still thought

about him much. It's all so long ago. Poor you."

"Would you have ever forgotten one of yours? I've thought about him almost every day, but I'd convinced myself he was fine and having a good life which I had no right to muck up. Until this summer when I couldn't get him out of my head. All sorts of reasons – Clare's wedding being one of them, I suspect."

"So what happens now? Do you want to see him?"

"*Of course I do*! But I think he needs to get this case over with. Gabbie is keeping an eye on him for me, and when he thinks the time is right he'll introduce the subject. We both feel it would be best if we met up here – not in England. Deya is such a special place."

"Yes, it is. But Angie – a drug dealer! Are you *sure* you want to do this? He might claim your money – anything!"

"Only when I'm dead, darling, and then he's welcome to it! It was only cannabis – we're not talking heroin here. Julio and Jose smoke it all the time."

"Do they? Is it legal?"

"No one cares up here in the mountains. You can buy it easily enough. Jude was only selling two hundred quid's worth or something – it's not a big deal, really."

"If you say so. But do be careful, Angie. Please. He could be a real con artist. He may be nothing like you're hoping, you know. He's not a child – God – he's nearly twenty-seven surely?"

"Yes. Twenty-seven on December 30th."

"And you're quite, quite sure this is what you want?"

"Rita – all my life I've had this feeling of – how can I put it – incompleteness. For years I told myself it was Roy – I was pining for Roy Cavalieri. But I couldn't have been, could I? Because when I found out this summer that he was still happily married to Heather and living in Italy, I wasn't heartbroken at all. Merely sort of sad and interested at the same time. Gabbie has made me see it was pure fantasy – as he said – I don't know the man at all now. He would be a complete stranger to me!"

"Yes, but so is this Jude what's-his-name!"

"Kennedy. No – of course he isn't. He's my *son* – with my genes – I gave birth to him, Rita – when I see him again I *know* I shall recognise him – I just know it. Gabbie is so wise – he has made me see that all these years I have buried my yearning for my son – not allowed myself to even think too much about him – because I felt I didn't have the right. I'd given up all rights to him, you see, and he'd got this wonderful life without me. But now – now I know his life isn't like that at all – that he's been lonely and isolated and restless – well, a bit like me really! I ran away from home too, remember."

"Yes."

Rita sipped the Sangria and struggled to find the right words.

"You think you've felt like that all your life because you let your baby go? Is that why you never settled with anybody? Never got married?"

"Yes. I'm certain of it. I have this fantastic feeling now – a tremendous sense of – well, destiny, really. Sounds over the top, but no other word fits!"

"You've always been over the top, Angie! Sounds as if he might be as well. Oh God! What a thing to have to cope with. And this Gabbie thing too – where do you think that's going?"

"I've no idea, and it doesn't matter. We have a very precious, special friendship and the sex was brilliant, but he's still mourning his wife. He loved her very much – they'd been married thirty-seven years or something horrific! I don't want to cause him a minute's anxiety – we just take it as a wonderful gift really. He'll come out here as often as his commitments in Surrey allow – I certainly wouldn't ever contemplate leaving Deya – so there you go!"

"Wow, gosh, Angie – no wonder I felt I needed to come and see you! I feel pole-axed by the whole thing! I was feeling a bit 'empty nest' I suppose, now that Clare's married and Chris is away at college – only Stu left, so I thought it was for me I was flying out here! But then you throw all this lot at me – it's unbelievable. Just when I thought you'd really got your life sorted – that vile agent in Soller sent packing – the hotel really successful – and suddenly, all this!"

"Yes. Suddenly all this."

"You wrote and told me about the picture that student did of you – can I see it? Is it really good?"

"Yes, I think it is. It's flattering, of course, but not *too* flattering. You can't see it, though, as Gabbie has taken it back with him! He says he has to have it to look at while he's away from me! Isn't that sweet?"

"Oh I'm so pleased for you!"

Rita leaned forwards and squeezed Angie's cool arm.

"I always wanted you to meet some lovely bloke who'd make you happy and be there for you. You've picked some real nightmares over the years, haven't you?"

"'Fraid so! But don't start planning bridesmaids, Rita! This is not going to be rushed into or anything – we need to let it flow in its own time. I'm just longing for his next visit – he's coming out for a week in a month's time and the hotel will be closed, so we can spend every minute together. I can't wait! We talk on the phone every night, you know."

Rita threw her arms about her head and gazed at the cloudless sky above her.

"Your life has been so different from mine, hasn't it, Ange? And yet I've never wanted your life – lovely as it is out here – and I know you never wanted mine. There's never been any jealousy between us, has there?"

"No – never. Not since that night when you told me you were expecting Clare. That was the only time. And after that I realised I didn't really want domestic bliss. I would have got bored probably. My life here has suited me almost perfectly. Just that one missing link – that needing to know."

"Gosh! I've suddenly thought – I'm an Auntie! I'm Jude's Auntie Rita and he's my kids' cousin! We never thought they had any cousins – it's so weird. I wonder if he looks like any of them!"

"Gabbie wouldn't describe him at all. Said I must wait a little bit longer. After twenty-six years, a few more weeks is nothing. I feel sick with fear every time I actually imagine him being here. I'm terrified of that, Rita. Suppose he doesn't like me?"

"He *will* like you. Everyone does. You're a lovely person, Angie. Of course he'll like you. Clare thinks you're the best thing since sliced bread – in fact, she went on and on about how fabulous you are when she got back. I nearly did feel a bit jealous!"

Angie sprang up suddenly.

"I need a walk! Come on – let me show you my favourite

spot in Deya – up by the church where you can look down on the coastline and the whole village dotted below you – it's a wonderful place to sit and think things over. I've never shown you before."

"Am I all right in these shoes?"

"It's a bit stony and uneven. I should change into something more comfortable. I'm going to put my walking shoes on. I'll see you back in the entrance hall in a couple of minutes."

They separated and Rita walked up the stairs and into her pink wallpapered bedroom, 'Santa Magdalena', her eyes suddenly filling with unexpected tears. Poor old Angie – she was such a trooper – what a lot to have to cope with now. And yet she couldn't help being caught up in the infectious excitement of her longing to see her son. Unbelievable. She could still see Sister Ignatius wheeling the plastic cot out of Angie's bedroom door and hearing her anguished cries. She had never heard such pain and longing in sobbing since, and hoped she never would again. Her arms had held her sister's sparrow-thin shoulders and felt them racked with the anguish of separation – it had been like witnessing limbs being ripped apart – hideous and unforgettable. A nurse had come in eventually and given Angie a sleeping tablet, but until it took effect her sobs had been audible the length of the corridor. Rita hadn't known what to do. And yet the next day she hadn't cried at all. Her strange, closed face had shut them all out and the subject had not been raised again. Like shutting a coffin lid. And now – it was to be lifted up. Unbelievable. She kicked off her smart coffee and cream high heels and dug into her case for comfortable flat sandals.

"But drugs!" she said aloud. "What if he messes up her life as well as his own? I can't bear it. Not again."

But it was all out of her control. The door shut crisply and her sandals slapped along the brown tiled floor. Angie was waiting for her at the bottom of the staircase, looking up with a smile of happy anticipation.

"I guess she'll cope," Rita thought, as she put out her arm and encircled her sister's waist.

They ran through the open doorway and down the drive arm in arm, as if they were girls again, with the old brown collie lumbering along behind, determined to keep up with them.

Chapter Twenty-Eight

"So you'll come up to London, Jude? Ten o'clock on Tuesday? Good – I'll see you then."

Gabbie replaced the receiver and wrote in his diary:

Tuesday October 12 – 10.00 am Jude Kennedy

He shared the Harley Street office now with two other psychiatrists – only using it himself once a week and seeing other patients at home in Ascot. He had decided against using his house for Jude. He wanted the formal grandeur of his consulting room in Harley Street to impress him – to convince him of the point of having an expert witness when his case came up at the end of the month.

"It would help too if you'd get yourself some sort of job," he'd told him. "Anything – a garage – a shop – just to make it look as if you've started taking some sort of part in society. You're bored in Nethway anyway. Why not try it?"

"The West Country's got a mega unemployment problem, Graham," Jude had answered. "Specially now the season's ended and all the emmets have gone. Petrol station attendant's a possibility – but I'd never stick it."

"You haven't got to stick it for longer than two weeks, fella!" Graham had run his fingers through his hair in exasperation. "Just find something for God's sake! Tesco's – shelf packing – *anything*! Just don't be on the dole by the 22nd – that's all I ask!"

He had scant hopes of Jude fixing anything up in such a short time, but maybe Jeremy or Meg could ring some contacts. They knew everyone in Dartmouth by all accounts.

He dialled Deya that night and felt his mood lift as he pictured Angie in her lovely room staring out of the black window at the stars in the dark Mediterranean sky.

"He's coming up on Tuesday," he told her. "And I've suggested he gets a job."

"Oh Gabbie – will it be all right?"

"Yes, I think so. His solicitor is pretty sure it will only

mean a fine; and Meg will pay that of course. I really hope he finds something, as boredom seems a huge problem for him in Nethway. He needs occupying. He's a great reader, mind you. The Brothers did their stuff – he's had excellent education although he tries hard to hide it!"

"What does he like reading? I'm just hungry for every detail now, Gabbie. It's like doing a jigsaw and everything you tell me fills another space."

"He was reading Primo Levi when I last saw him. He's very interested in ideas – he should have gone to university. I'm hoping to persuade him to make an application for next year."

"Are you? Oh darling – you're such a magician! Do you think he will?"

"I've no idea. He's very moody and unpredictable. He's got lots of half-baked ideas – maybe he should do PPE."

"What's that, for heaven's sake?"

"Politics, philosophy and economics. He'll have to take a couple of A levels this year of course. He seems to me to have quite deliberately failed everything just to spite everybody – including himself."

"Poor love. Ah well – I never passed an exam until I did my catering diploma, so who am I to comment? What makes you think he might be tempted?"

"I just get the feeling he'd had enough of his beach bum existence and was bored out of his skull when he wasn't actually surfing or taking drugs. Typical of an underachiever who is actually quite bright. What the Brothers clearly failed to do was to give him any confidence in his own abilities, or sense of his own worth. That's very low."

"Well you are marvellous at that, sweetheart. I can remember saying to you 'What can *I* do?' and you just made me feel the possibilities were almost endless. No one had done that for me before. How are you going to introduce me into your discussions?"

"I'm not sure yet. I'm going to wait and see how Tuesday's meeting goes. He seems less hostile when we talk now. He's a lot more relaxed and often chats quite naturally off his guard for a bit. I gather he's still difficult with Meg though and quite impossibly vile to Jeremy!"

"I haven't warmed to the sound of Jeremy myself. He sounds a complete prig to me! Have you met him?"

"No. This is all via Meg or Jude. Enough of them – how are *you* my furry rabbit? I'm counting the days you know – it's like being an adolescent again – I never expected this. I actually thought that improving my golf handicap would be the most exciting thing likely to happen to me in the future – and now you! It's wonderful, sweetheart."

"I know. I feel the same. It's twenty-four days until you come – I'm crossing them off the calendar in my office every morning. Conchita saw me yesterday, and gave me such a look – pure delight! She can't wait for you to be here again either! She's such a Mills & Boon!"

"Won't she be on holiday? I thought the hotel closed on the 31st?"

"It does. But she has insisted on working so that I can concentrate entirely on you! I'll probably do some cooking – Julio won't be here. But we can eat up whatever he leaves in the freezer of course."

"I told Jane about us this morning. I thought she ought to know what's going on in her father's life, and why I keep flying out to Majorca!"

"What did she say? Did it hurt her, do you think?"

"No. I think she was relieved. I was a bit of a burden to her all those months when I didn't want to do anything. She felt she needed to keep popping in or asking me round. She and Clive are very busy people – long working hours and hectic social life – I think relief was definitely predominant."

"What about the others? When will you tell them?"

"Oh, when the time's right. When it crops up. Jane's the one who's been so marvellously supportive and of course she lives in Ascot so she's on the doorstep as it were."

"Rita's here. We've had such a lovely day. I'm so lucky, Gabbie – I feel surrounded by love. It's fantastic. And I want to make you happy so much, darling – I can't bear it when you look sad."

"I'm not looking sad, Angie, believe me. You do make me very happy, sweetheart. I'll ring you tomorrow – sweet dreams."

"Goodnight, darling. I'm looking at the moon and thinking of you! I lie in bed thinking that you looked out of this same window at these same stars! It's very comforting."

"Good. Keep looking. The stars aren't quite as clear in Ascot as they are in Deya unfortunately!"

He replaced the receiver, still smiling. What a dreamer she was. What a sweet, innocent dreamer.

Jude was hurrying out of Bond Street Station at twenty past ten. Shit. He was always late. The train had been on time but somehow he'd messed up the connections – he hated London, and had only been there twice before. He crossed the road and walked past John Lewis', being jostled and pushed until he turned down a side street and cut across Wimpole Street. Graham would understand; in fact he would almost certainly expect him to be late. At least he had a bit of good news – if you could call washing up in a pub restaurant three nights a week good news – but it was a bit of cash in his pocket.

He found Harley Street and located Gabbie's building. A wire-caged lift carried him upwards and he recognised Gabbie's highly polished black brogues as they appeared at his eye level as the lift ascended. Their bodies were aligned with a noisy clanking and Graham pulled open the heavy door.

"There you are!" he commented wryly.

"Yeah. Sorry. It took longer than I thought from Paddington and I got on the wrong tube. I told you I was a complete idiot."

Graham led him into his panelled consulting room and indicated a green leather armchair. Jude flopped down onto it, his black denim legs splayed out and scuffed black boots turned uppermost. His T-shirt had 'Surfers do it standing up' emblazoned across his chest.

"How's it going?" Gabbie asked, sitting not behind his desk but in an armchair alongside him.

"I've got a job in the Queen's Head – start Saturday night."

"Oh – excellent! Bar work?"

"Maybe. Just washing up first – I probably won't be able to stick it."

"Try to for a couple of weeks. It's preferable to watching TV all day, surely?"

"I don't do that. I never do that."

Jude's eyes were wandering around the room; over to the

mahogany leather-topped desk, over the oak bookcases and oak panelling, past the sash windows, until they alighted on the picture above the stone fireplace.

He stared at it and then looked away.

"Can I smoke?" he asked suddenly, fumbling in his jeans pocket.

"Sure."

Gabbie said nothing more and watched him lighting up a Marlboro with grubby fingers ending in badly bitten nails. Jude closed his eyes as he inhaled deeply. When he opened them again they returned to the portrait above Gabbie's head.

"Is that a famous picture?" he said at last.

"No. An amateur painter – a student actually – did it last summer. I like it very much. Do you?"

"I dunno. I thought – well, I thought p'raps I'd seen it before you know? Like the Mona Lisa or something."

"No. It's not famous. Now Jude – I'm preparing a report to be handed to the magistrate, which will suggest that your drug dealing had a direct connection with various personality problems you experienced all through your adolescence and boyhood after your father died and after you discovered you were in fact adopted. Do you want to tell me anything which could be helpful to me in compiling that report?"

"I think it's a load of crap, Graham. I know dozens of guys who smoke dope and take drugs whose fathers aren't dead and who weren't adopted – but if you think it'll get me off then go ahead. I don't know what to tell you. You already know my mum told us when I was five, and that my dad died of a heart attack in the kitchen when I was ten. He was getting wound up with me at the time – I'd forgotten to get mum's shopping and I'd been drinking. No one else knows that."

"So are you saying you blame yourself for his death, Jude? He must have had a heart condition – it would have happened at some time anyway – even if you hadn't been an annoying ten year old. And ten year old boys annoy their fathers all the time – I know mine certainly did!"

Jude was staring at his cigarette and was silent for a few moments.

"So you reckon it would have happened anyway?"

"Almost certainly. Don't be so hard on yourself, Jude. Your dad was angry – OK. Dad's do get angry; it doesn't make ten year old kids responsible for their deaths if they have heart attacks. He may have had heart disease for years. It wasn't your fault."

Jude looked up at him and smiled for the first time.

"God! That sounds good. No one's ever said that to me before – it wasn't my fault."

He dragged on his cigarette again and Graham waited. After a few moments Jude looked up at the picture and frowned. Gabbie shifted in his chair.

"Do you want to talk about how you felt when you were told you were adopted? I remember you said you were gutted. Did you tell Meg that?"

"How could I? She kept saying it didn't matter because *she* was our real mother and she loved us and that was all that counted, when of course I knew it wasn't. All through my childhood I had this fantasy – that my real mother would come and get me – this fairy princess would arrive like some sort of golden film star and drive me away to her palace! Kids are so stupid, aren't they? When of course all she'd wanted to do was to get rid of me as soon as she could!"

Graham waited while Jude smoked and glanced up at the picture again. At last he spoke, very quietly.

"I've seen many women as patients, Jude, who have never recovered from the trauma of parting from their babies – even twenty or thirty years on, the day is as fresh in their memory as yesterday – and their overriding motive was to give the baby a better chance in life than they felt they could offer. Can you understand such unselfishness? It marks them for life."

Jude stubbed out his Marlboro in a green Wedgewood ashtray on the desk.

"No. I guess I can't. I'm not a woman and I've never had a kid."

"And you never tried to trace your natural mother? Never wanted to know where she was or what she was doing?"

Jude hung his head and wiped the back of his hand across his nose.

"Nah. I reckoned she didn't want me. If she never came looking then she didn't want me. If people don't want me then I don't want them. My dad thought I was a waste of space and I guess she did too."

"But you could be wrong on both counts. And now you're an adult – how do you feel about possibly meeting her now? The law gives you every assistance in tracing your birth mother now you know."

Jude looked up suddenly and met Gabbie's eyes.

"If I thought... but she wouldn't. She wouldn't want to know about me now, would she? Up on a drugs charge? Oh terrific! Every mother's idea of a perfect son! I've fucked up mum's life, haven't I? Why would I want to do that to some other poor cow? I don't think so!"

The silence grew between them until Gabbie spoke softly.

"If you ever wanted to know, Jude, I could help you."

"Well I don't want to know. There's no fucking point, is there?"

He clenched his hands to stop them shaking and stood up to go.

"That's it then? You got enough to write this report?"

"Sit down, Jude. No, I haven't got enough. You must help me. I need to be able to convince the court that what you went through in your childhood is still affecting your actions today. And I believe that to be true. This is unfinished business, fella. Unfinished business."

Jude ran his fingers through his short stubble and looked down at his boots. He said nothing for a very long time and then he looked at Gabbie again. He sat down.

"What do you think I should do then?"

"I believe it would be beneficial to you to make some enquiries about your roots. I believe you feel rootless and that your life will be that much richer for filling in some gaps. And when you've done that – then it may be time for you to plan the next few years in a way that you will find fulfilling – maybe apply to university for instance."

"You gotta be joking! I didn't do A levels for a start!"

"I know. You told me. That's not insuperable; you could do a couple at your local college of further education – but sometimes mature students aren't required to have the same number of A levels to start courses as eighteen year olds."

Jude closed his eyes and with his eyes shut said to Gabbie, "And all that other stuff – you know – roots – her – what good will it do?"

"It needs to be looked at, Jude. It needs to be resolved. You haven't any peace of mind have you? You don't feel that you are a real part of Meg and Jeremy's family – you don't know where you belong, do you?"

Jude kept his eyes shut and replied, "Sometimes I thought about killing myself, you know. I walked around with pills once. It seemed the only way out."

"It's never the only way out, fella. There's always another option."

"Yeah. I must have known that, cos I never did it, did I? I don't know about all this roots stuff – I guess I'm shit scared, that's the truth. I don't want to know. I want her to be the perfect princess – I need those dreams. Have you ever heard anything so bloody ridiculous?"

"It's not ridiculous, Jude. We all need our dreams, but we also need reality – and there is a reality for you. Somewhere – a woman needs to know where her son is and what has happened to him nearly twenty-seven years after she let him go to another woman. Only a woman would understand how that must feel. We can't begin to. She's had her dreams too. But now perhaps you both need to shed those fantasies and meet and put real life in their place. Make a connection, you know?"

Jude shivered, despite the heat of the room.

"Where would I start?" he said very quietly.

"The records are kept in the City Council. You could find out who your mother was – her name, her age at the time, and where you were born. We could take it from there."

"Mum told me she was a young kid; she had no job and no money and so she couldn't keep me. That's what she always told me."

"Then I expect that was near enough the truth; certainly as Meg saw it."

"I used to feel this terrible *anger* with her – it was like the floor giving way beneath me or an earthquake or something when she told me she wasn't my real mother. It was unbelievable – I'd adored her when I was a little kid. And she wouldn't take on board how much it mattered to me – she tried to make out it was *nothing*. That she loved us and so somehow that wiped out everything else! And then when dad died – and I felt it was my fault too – that just about finished me off. I was always in trouble – got a name for it – you know – drinking, glue sniffing, nicking stuff from the local shops, dope – you name it, I tried it! Trying to get her to notice that something was wrong – but she was always so bloody calm and understanding about it – can you imagine? Always the fucking martyr she was. And yet I still love her in a way – she's been a bloody brilliant mother really. I've been a complete arse hole."

He paused; full of childhood memories. Gabbie pressed his fingertips together and looked at his perfectly manicured nails with careful attention.

"But then what? If I get given a name – oh God! The name of some real woman somewhere – what the hell am I going to do then? And what makes you so sure she'd want to get a phone call from *me*? You're off your trolley, Graham. You are really. Look at me – what is some…?"

He broke off, his voice tremulous.

Gabbie hesitated and then changed tack.

"Look at the portrait here, Jude. Does that look like a happy woman? Make up a story about her – what sort of person do you think she might be?"

"What?"

Jude looked up, his eyes blurred and red from rubbing.

"It's a helpful psychological game we sometimes use. Role playing. Putting yourself into someone else's shoes. Try it. Trust me, Jude."

"You're bonkers, all you psychiatrists are. Everybody knows that. Bloody bonkers."

He looked up at the picture again and stared at it hard.

"No. She doesn't look happy. I'd say she's trying bloody hard to look happy and to kid somebody else that she is, but she isn't. Does that make sense?"

"It certainly does. Most perspicacious – maybe you should consider a psychology degree. You might enjoy it. Keep looking. What else do you see?"

Jude's leg was beginning to twitch. He looked down a

couple of times and then back at the portrait.

"It's weird," he said at last. "I'm sure I've seen that picture somewhere before. It makes me feel – I dunno."

He bit his lip.

Gabbie stood up and walked behind his desk and rummaged in a drawer. He passed a mirror to Jude and said, "Now what do you see?"

Jude let out a puff of irritation and looked in the mirror.

"What am I supposed to say now? I see me of course. What the fuck is this?"

Graham scratched his neck and waited. Jude threw the mirror onto the desk and looked back at the portrait. Tears began to course down his face as he stared at the face in the portrait.

"You bastard, you've known all along, haven't you? It's her. What the hell is going on?"

Graham leant towards Jude and put a hand on his shoulder and left it there.

"Yes. It is her. I've known for some short time – only a matter of weeks, not longer. But I have known your mother for the whole of your lifetime, Jude, and she is a very wonderful woman. Quite worthy of your dreams of a princess. Quite worthy."

Jude stared up at Angie's picture and took a deep sobbing breath.

"Shit," he said. "I can't believe it. I can't take in that you know her and that that's her. I look like her, don't I?"

"Yes, you do. Fortunately for you, you have your mother's good looks. And quite a few of her other qualities too, it seems to me. She's a dreamer too."

"Where – where is she?"

His voice was so quiet that Graham only just caught the words.

"She's living on Majorca – in a beautiful house which she runs as a guest house in Deya – up in the mountains in western Majorca. She's lived there for about eleven years."

"Right. And has she – has she got other kids?"

"No. No other children. She has never forgiven herself for losing you. Like you, she shoulders blame. Like you, she thought you would not want her."

256

"And you know she wants to meet me, do you? Has she said so?"

"Yes. She's said so. She said that hardly a day has gone by in the twenty-seven years that she has not thought about you – wondered who you are – what you're doing. She's never really let you go."

"Then why – why didn't she ever check me out when I was a kid?"

"Because she had convinced herself that you wouldn't want her. That it would have been interfering with a happy home life that the adoptive family had given you. She was so sure you were having this wonderfully secure, cherished, middle class family life and she didn't want to interrupt that or upset things for you in any way."

"Mum wanted to give me that sort of life; she tried hard enough. I just never felt it was right for me somehow. I can't explain."

"You explain very well, Jude. You are far more articulate than you make out. I'm certain you could get on a degree course if you wanted to in a year or so."

"I dunno. I dunno anything any more. A few weeks ago, I was just surfing and bumming around and life seemed normal – and then suddenly – all this lot blows up in my face. I need to chill out and get my head round all this, I do, Graham. I don't know what I'm going to do at all."

"There's no pressure on you to do something immediately. In fact, all you can do before the court case is apply to the City Council for the records and be given the facts. I can help you do that. You wouldn't be allowed to leave the country while you're on bail."

"No. I guess I wouldn't. Well, that's something. I can just go back to Nethway and think the whole thing through. It's mind-blowing."

"Why don't we meet for a pub lunch, Jude? I've got another guy to see at 11.45, which is shortly, and then I'm free until 3.00 – why don't you walk around the gardens and I'll meet you at the pub down the road for a bite of lunch at say, one o'clock? We don't need to talk about this then if you'd rather not. Whatever you want. There's a garden out the back here you could wait in."

"No – I need to go to HMVs while I'm here. I'm OK. I'll meet you at the pub. What's it called?"

"The Chequers. Turn left out of here and left again at the crossroads. One o'clock?"

"Yeah. OK. One o'clock."

Chapter Twenty-Nine

"It's a good pint, Jude, isn't it? It's going down very well indeed."

Jude did not reply, but swallowed his bitter with thirsty gusto and replaced his empty glass on the wooden counter.

They were alone at their end of their small Georgian bar; two businesswomen and a man were huddled at the other end and the barman looked bored.

"Are you worried about the case? I know I would be."

"Well, put it this way, I'll be glad when it's all over and I can get on with my life. But now – suddenly it doesn't seem so important – not after what you told me in there. That's so mind-blowing I don't know where I am."

"I feel sure you can handle it. I wouldn't have told you so much if I hadn't been convinced you could take it. You're like her – a survivor."

"Maybe. I dunno. I'd like to feel I was."

"You *can* feel you are. She ran away from home when she was fifteen you know – she came to London, just a kid – all on her own in London."

"Is that when you met her?"

"Not quite. She was twenty by then. But I'll leave her to tell you her story – I was just illustrating the similarities between you. It's not just physical, the resemblance. D'you want another pint?"

"Ta. I just don't know how I feel about it all. And what about mum? What's she going to make of it?"

Graham put a ten pound note on the bar and said, "Same again, please" to the sandy-haired barman. He did not look at Jude but studied the beer mat in front of him as he said quietly, "I believe Meg to be a truly unselfish person who would give anything to see you happier in your own skin and more at peace with yourself. If that means you getting to know your natural mother, however painful that may be for her, she'll go along with it. I had indicated to her that I felt you needed to trace your roots. She finds that difficult, I'm sure, but her relief in being back in touch with you is greater. I'm very glad to hear you're concerned about her feelings too."

He picked up his glass and took a small gulp. Jude slid his along the bar without speaking. They stood in quiet companionship, drinking contemplatively, while other drinkers came into the pub and the room filled with noise and smoke and laughter.

"You don't have to go back to Devon tonight if you don't want to," Graham said at last. "I'm catching the 4.50 from Waterloo so I can give you supper and a bed for the night if you'd like to talk things over this evening. I've got two patients this afternoon, but I'll be free just after 4.00. Meet me at the Oxford Circus end of Wimpole Street if you like."

"Right. I don't feel ready for Nethway somehow. I couldn't talk to mum about it and it's all kind of whizzing around my head, you know? I need to kinda sort it. Is that all right?"

"Of course it is. Ring Meg from my place. I'm going to have a ham sandwich – what will you have?"

"Um – cheese – yeah – cheese and pickle'll be good. Cheers."

They ordered and moved to a corner table, carrying their beers carefully between the jostling arms. Jude's head was aching and he longed for some hash and the sea air at Scabbacombe. He hated London, he decided, and hoped it would be a very long time before he had to visit it again. He fished in his jeans pocket for his packet of Marlboros and offered one to Graham.

"No thanks – I don't. Did you get what you wanted in HMV's?"

"Yeah – it's brilliant – they must have just about everything! It's the latest Red Hot Chilli Peppers."

"Is that a group? Sounds more like lunch."

Jude ignored this and inhaled with his eyes shut. Graham regarded him with a mixture of professional perception and genuine concern. He had been horrified to learn that this young man had been carrying the burden of belief that he had killed his father for fifteen years, and was watching for signs that what he had learned today might be too much for him. He did not believe that to be so, but was well aware that he could be wrong.

"What will you do until four?" was all he asked. Jude shrugged.

"Dunno. Stay in here and get ratted probably."

"Not a terribly useful plan. You'll throw up on the train – I'd rather you didn't. Why not come back with me and read in the garden? I can lend you something interesting I feel sure."

"What – one of your psychology manuals? I don't think so."

"No – there's a reasonable library in the waiting room on the ground floor. May not be any Primo Levi but we could find something to interest you, I'm sure. Thank you." He smiled briefly at the waitress who brought their sandwiches and placed a white paper napkin carefully across his chalk-striped trousers.

Jude had already bitten into his sandwich.

"All right then," he said, with a mouthful of cheese and brown bread.

Graham relaxed and picked up his sandwich.

The train pulled into Ascot Station and Jude looked up from his book.

"We here?" he said, as Graham stood up.

"Yes. Only five minutes in the car and we'll be home. Food from the freezer, I'm afraid. I don't cook much; do you?"

"I can. When I bother I cook quite decent stuff. Mostly I don't bother of course but I do a wicked pancake. Fill it with peppers and mushrooms – really great."

They stepped down onto the platform and walked side by side into the car park.

"Nice," Jude commented as they reached the Audi, and Graham smiled.

"The advantages of private patients," he said, and he threw his briefcase onto the back seat and eased himself into the driving seat.

"Do you drive?"

"I had lessons and passed my test, but I've never had the dosh for wheels, so I'd need a few more lessons by now, I guess. I liked it."

"Your mother drives a blue Mercedes. It's old but in very good condition. No rust on Majorca, I suppose."

"Does she? Hell! I never imagined her in a car at all – funny that. I suppose because all I was told was she was this poor kid who had a baby – I never really saw her as a middle-aged woman doing ordinary things like driving. And certainly not a Merc!"

"Women who've made a success of things against all the odds enjoy showing off a nice expensive car just as much as men do, I can assure you! And she really has earned every penny by extremely hard work. When she bought her hotel it was a complete ruin and I believe she did most of the decorating herself and a lot of the gardening, as well as all the cooking. She's a terrific cook – believe me – I know – I've eaten a great many meals cooked by your mother over the years."

They pulled out of the station car park in a queue of slow moving vehicles as Jude muttered, "It all seems weird. It's unreal. You calling her my mother and telling me you've eaten her cooking – it's just unreal."

Graham turned his head briefly and smiled at Jude.

"It will get better. You'll get used to the idea that she's a real woman living a normal life – but in a fantastic place. It's so beautiful – and since you love the sea – it will knock you out – you can see the coastline and the Med for miles. Just brilliant."

They drove on in silence for a few minutes until Jude said, "Have you got any pictures? Pictures of her, and her place?"

"Yes. I've got photos from my holiday there with my wife four years ago, and I've got a few from last month when I was out there for a week. You can look at them tonight if you want to. There's no pressure to do anything, Jude. No pressure at all."

They drove the remaining half mile in silence. As they turned through the open gates and round the sandy drive to the electronically operated garage doors, Jude drew out an appreciative whistle.

"Man! This is all right, isn't it?"

"Yes, I'm very lucky. I know that. My wife worked hard too, of course, so this was all earned by her as much as by me."

"Where is she? I never asked. You divorced?"

Pain flittered briefly across Graham's face, Jude noted in astonishment. He had rather grown to feel that Graham did not have private emotions, but saw that he had been wrong.

"No. Not divorced. Never that. We had a very happy marriage. My wife died from complications following flu last winter."

"Sorry. I didn't know that," Jude mumbled, climbing out of the car awkwardly, and banging his head.

Gabbie got out and zapped the garage doors shut. They walked through a side door and into a lobby where he unlocked another door. He stepped inside and waved Jude in.

"Here we are, fella!" he said, tousling the stubby stalks of Jude's hair roughly and then pointing to a door ahead.

"Let's go into the kitchen and sort ourselves out a drink. Then we'll ransack the freezer and see what we fancy."

They found a huge salami-topped pizza and a tub of Rosti and Graham uncorked a bottle of red Bordeaux, while Jude sat on a kitchen stool sipping lager out of a can. He was relaxing, Gabbie noticed with relief, and even wandered off into the sitting room in an easy fashion, exclaiming in tones of approval at the beauty of the garden in the twilight beyond.

"It's far too much work. I may sell up and buy a flat," Graham said suddenly, and sat down in surprise. "I had no idea I was going to say that!" he admitted to Jude. "I didn't even know I was considering it – but now I've said it to you, I realise that it's actually what I want to do; how extraordinary!"

"Sure is. I wouldn't ever want to get rid of this place if it was mine."

"Yes. I always felt like that. But now I can see that is in the past, and that actually it's ridiculous living on my own in a huge place with five bedrooms. Too absurd."

"And you've only just realised? Really? When you said it to me just then?"

"Yes. Absolutely. As I said, it became obvious. This was my family house – where my children grew up and I lived happily with my wife – but that's all in the past. I have to make a new life now; my children all have very nice homes of their own, and what I need is freedom to come and go – a nice flat overlooking the golf course. That's what I need. I'm so glad you came here, Jude! You've made me see sense."

Jude grinned and flopped onto a huge cream brocade sofa.

"Glad to be of service, doc! Should think this'll fetch a fortune."

"Yes. Probably. Right – I'm going to put the pizza and stuff in the microwave – if you want to wash, your room's at the top of the stairs on the left – there's soap, towels, and a new toothbrush in the bathroom cabinet. Izzie was terribly good about organising guest bathrooms and things like that."

Jude loped up the stairs two at a time and gazed at the green and white bedroom with matching bathroom in astonishment. It was like a film set. In the last three weeks he had slept on the beach, on a damp mattress in a seedy room, in a Dormobile, narrowly missed a night in a prison cell, his own room in Nethway, and now this! He could no longer call his life monotonous.

His spirits lifted suddenly – maybe this really was a beginning; maybe with this guy's help, meeting his mother might be good – even terrific.

He turned the gold tap on and rinsed his bristly face and his hands in cold water. He lifted his head and gazed at his dripping face in the mirror above the basin. There was hope in his green eyes. Hope. He recognised it although he had never seen it there before.

He dried his face on the soft green towel and ran down the stairs, following the aroma of hot cheese and toasted salami. He was smiling by the time he entered the kitchen and Gabbie looked up.

"Hungry?" he asked.

"Ravenous!" Jude replied, holding his hands out for the mouth-watering plateful he was offering to him.

Chapter Thirty

Angie watched Alfonso Escales pushing his bike slowly up the drive and leaning it against an ancient olive tree before dropping a pile of letters and packages through the open doorway onto the mat. Gato, the Siamese, had been lying there in a shaft of sunlight, and sprang up in disgust at such crass, insensitive behaviour. He wound his way through her legs as she walked to pick up the post, calling, "Gracias Alfonso," at his vanishing back.

By late November all the guests were gone and the house was quiet. Conchita was visiting a pregnant sister in Pollensa and the winter re-decoration plans had been shelved until the New Year. She sat at her desk and sorted bills from bookings and personal letters from business mail. A blue airmail letter caught her eye as she so rarely received them. She didn't recognise the attractive looping handwriting and tore it open immediately.

'Dear Angie', he had written

It's too early for a Christmas card – and I don't send them anyway – but I thought you'd like to know that I took your advice and got down to some serious painting this term. I actually spent a weekend with dad and Carolyn, which was difficult, but I sketched her when she was sitting reading in the garden, and worked on it afterwards, and it's been shortlisted at the Slade for the Life Drawing Prize – I won't know until next term whether I've won it but it's cool to have got this far. My Life Class tutor seems pretty impressed with it – I wish he could see my portrait of you. Any chance of bringing it to the UK if you ever come over? I could collect it if you go to visit your sister or something, and let you have it back. I may specialise in portraits. I did one of Emma too, but I'm not satisfied with it yet – it needs more work – that's oil on canvas. We didn't make it through October as a couple – too bossy for me. As you can see I'm working hard and feeling I'm getting somewhere at last. Your romantic heart will also be gratified to know there's a new woman in my life.

She's a first year doing sculpture and she's great. Her name's Nina and if we're still together in the spring maybe we'll come out to Deya and see you. I hope you're over the disappointment of Roy by now. Is the hotel closed? If so – what do you do all winter? If you're planning a trip to England get in touch and we'll get together to rake over old times.

Cheers

Andy

She smiled, and read it again. She was so happy for him. She would ask Gabbie to lend him the portrait for long enough to show his tutor. She had no idea when she would visit England again. It all depended on him. Everything depended on him now. On his visit. How it went. Her Jude. No longer Paul, but Jude. Surprising how quickly she'd got used to it. Her own Jude.

Her stomach churned with the familiar anxiety. How would she cope with meeting him? Would Gabbie be able to persuade him to come out here after the court case was over? And that was assuming Jude was free to go anywhere. The possibility of a prison sentence just wasn't real at all. Only three days now until the case was heard. She prayed for a sympathetic magistrate; a liberal woman, perhaps, who had sons of her own and understood how difficult young manhood could be. Gabbie sounded confident and had prepared his report, but anything could go wrong. In the long quiet nights she lay awake for hours, rehearsing all the awful possibilities, and then going over and over what little she knew about her son. Her excitement and longing to meet him versus her fears that she would disappoint. Would she appear unattractive – not his idea of a mother at all? What did he imagine she was like? What did he expect from her? Wouldn't it have been easier to do all this years ago when he was a little boy to be cuddled and given toys? What could she possibly say to him now? Her mounting panic drove her into the garden to chop and prune and sweep. Only physical labour would enable sleep to come; otherwise hours of exhausted questioning lay ahead, and she feared looking haggard and bug-eyed when they arrived. If he'd agree to come at all.

Tonight she would drive to Soller to meet her friend, Liz, for dinner. They could talk of other things, as Liz knew nothing about Jude or Angie's life in England all those years ago. Nothing of the anguish swirling in her soul right now.

"You're always such fun, Angie," she would say. "Such great company. You buck me up no end."

They would talk of local gossip, Majorcan friends, Liz's children and the bliss of having the island to themselves in winter.

"Not that we do in Palma," Liz had said on the telephone yesterday morning. "That's why we're buying the apartment in Soller. It's so different on the west coast. It's ten minutes from Ramon's office. I'd like to sell the house in Palma – get rid of it altogether. Maybe I'll persuade him now the children are both away. Did I tell you Sabina's moving to Barcelona?"

Such harmless nonsense. She had listened and responded but none of it meant anything to her at all. She had wanted to shout, 'Liz! My own son may go to prison – I've not seen him for almost twenty-seven years and if he doesn't go to prison he will come here – soon – in a few weeks – I can't get interested in anything else. I don't care if Sabina moves to Barcelona.'

But all she had said was, "You'll miss her. But it's only a ferry ride away."

They would look at the new apartment and then have dinner at La Colobra. Ramon would not join them; he was a workaholic and rarely went out socially midweek. Liz was a dear friend and yet Angie felt unable to confide in her about the momentous changes in her life. She needed to be able to retreat to this uncomplicated relationship – to have some short respite from her tumultuous emotions for now. And yet it all seemed shallow and pointless. Perhaps she should share it with Liz. It was a temptation, but she knew she would resist it. Gabbie was all the confidant she needed, and he was perfect. She would telephone him as soon as she got back from Soller. Lying in her bed she would dial his number slowly, staring at the stars through her open window.

'Staring at the stars' – that's what she'd always done. Maybe Jude had too. Soon she would be able to ask him.

Chapter Thirty-One

"They used to trap birds here – caca a col, they called it, but it's been stopped for years. Tourists didn't like it."

"I'm not surprised – how horrible! At least with an English shoot the bird is flying about one minute and gone the next – they don't know much about it. You've got a marvellous place up here – I am so sorry you're closed. Do you have a brochure or anything? Maybe we could come and stay next year. When do you open?"

"March 1st. You'd love the island then – it's just *covered* in the palest pink almond blossom everywhere. Wonderful sight. Yes – hang on – I'll get you a brochure. They're here somewhere."

The woman was looking around the bougainvillaea-filled garden in delight, her faint red hair falling across her freckled face.

"It's unusual just chancing on somewhere so special – we were driving through the village on our way to the monastery at Lulch – and I spotted your sign at the end of the lane."

"Here you go – take two – give one to a friend! Yes, it is a heavenly spot – I'm so lucky to live here – I know that."

"Thank you very much. I'll write and book something early next year."

"Good. Easter is already fully booked, so don't leave it too long, will you?"

"No, I won't. Thanks a lot. Bye."

I watch them drive away – their white BMW gliding down the track and hiccuping over the stones in the road. They seem nice enough people but I can't concentrate on anyone. Today he will be here. Today Gabbie will bring my son. My heart keeps skipping a beat or leaping in a most disconcerting fashion, and I hope I don't drop at his feet in a female faint. Too undignified. Darling Gabbie – he has prepared me so well. Our nightly conversations for the past two weeks have contained nothing else. The relief that the case is over and that he was only fined was tremendous. I was shaking uncontrollably when I put the phone down, and have taken to giving Dino long walks at midnight so that I have some hope of sleep. Poor old dog – he waddles along in the pitch dark faithfully but clearly thinks I'm off my trolley and that I should have more consideration for his advanced age. He's a comfort, too – his smelly old coat beneath my hands calms me and I can tell him things even Gabbie hasn't heard. Dino knows a thing or two about loyalty – I know he'd never abandon me whatever anyone else suggested. I should have listened to my instincts and not my head. What have we missed, Jude and I? A whole childhood and adolescence together – thrown away and out of reach – never to be recovered. Never. What can we do with our lives to reconnect it? Is it really possible? Gabbie says it is.

I'm shivering although the sun at eleven-thirty in the morning is warm even in December, and I'm going back indoors to hunt for that essence of sartorial Englishness – a beige cardigan. The cardigan found, I walk to the church and sit on a gravestone looking down at the sea. Somewhere my son is preparing to board a plane and to fly out to meet me. I can hardly take it in. Gabbie says Jude is even more terrified than I am. I have caused him so much pain; both of us so much pain. But maybe we can end it now. We can get to know one another and 'put the past in the ground' as Gabbie puts it. Is it really possible? I honestly don't know. I used to love the John Lennon song 'Imagine' but suddenly it seems empty and rather heartless. You can't imagine a world where peace and harmony come because people don't care enough about anything – human nature isn't like that. Love hurts – that's from a song too, and I know it's true. But now I welcome the pain because it means I'm alive and I love someone enough to be hurt. That's fine. As long as *he* isn't hurt anymore. He's suffered enough. Does he really want to find his mother at twenty-six? It's his birthday in three weeks and I have bought the first present I have given my son since I bought three sleeping suits before giving birth. It's a brass birdcage – no bird in it of course – just a birdcage. Julio was selling them outside his studio a few weeks ago and it seemed appropriate. Some people hang plants in them outside their doors – I have no idea what Jude will make of it as a present – I don't know him yet. How do you buy a birthday present for a man you don't know? And yet I feel sure he'll understand. The door of the cage is swinging open. That's very important.

I hug my knees and wonder how I will get through this day. Conchita has insisted on staying and is defrosting delicious meals from the freezer. I shall not be able to eat a thing and of course Jude may feel exactly the same. It's still a little strange calling my Paul 'Jude'; but I'm gradually getting used to it. Almost liking it – as it's so unusual.

Jose and Julio have been sweet in their concern for me. I think the three of them assume my odd behaviour is all to do with Gabbie and our love affair. I certainly don't intend telling Conchita about my son until I know how this first meeting goes. And yet –despite all my fear – I feel an underlying certainty that it *will* be all right.

Gabbie seems so sure we'll get on, and he knows both of us after all. Where would I be without that darling man?

My legs are going numb now so I stand up and walk round the stone church to the front door. I try the handle and the heavy door creaks open. I haven't been in here for years – the old familiar church smells of mustiness and incense overwhelm me and tears are pouring down my face. I stumble into a pew and sit there but can think of nothing to say as I stare at the wooden crucifix on the golden altar. The light slants across the white linen table cloth and the thick waxen candles. A pale blue and gold statue of the Virgin is all the decoration I see; a spangle of stars encircling her head.

"Hail, Mary, full of grace..." I start to say, but can go no further.

They're just words and don't seem to help at all. I look at the alabaster calm of her face and can well imagine how people think they see her smile or cry in moments of personal anguish. I could easily imagine a tear dropping down her pale cheek, and look away at such fancifulness. There seems to be nothing for me here. For too many years I have abandoned the habit of prayer so it hides from me now when I need it most. I light a candle and watch it flicker indecisively. All those birthday candles I never saw on his cakes; Meg lit them, not me. Twenty-six birthdays and I missed them all.

"Let it be all right," I mumble as I stand up and stumble out into the bright sunshine. What did I expect? I have no idea.

Dino is pottering about in the lane and he wags his whole bottom as he sees me – peering up with rheumy eyes and total devotion. I tussle his head and say firmly, "We're going to have to comb those ears, Dino! They're looking horribly knotted again! Come on, chap – I think we can find you a marrow bone somewhere – good dog – you are a good dog!"

I try to eat the sandwich Conchita has made me, but two bites are as much as I can manage and the rest goes down the garbage chute, which is Dino's throat. Chicken and mayonnaise is absolutely his favourite filling.

I'm going to lie in a warm bath now and try to relax and then drive down to Palma for a hair appointment. By the time I get back there will only be a couple of hours before he comes. My heart does one of those mad blip-things again and I try to breathe deeply. I run the bath and tip in an Arden essence Gabbie brought out last month – he always arrives laden with presents – it give him so much pleasure.

The warm water calms me a little and I close my eyes. I never even bathed him. The nuns had done that for me.

"Don't worry your head now at all," they'd said. "You're not going to need to learn, so we'll do it for you. You sleep."

I must have been half asleep to let them take him from me. Half asleep or half dead. Animals kick if their young are taken from them; why didn't I have the same instinct? Such mealy-mouthed meekness makes me sick. I had just lain there and let them. Unbelievable.

I close my eyes and see his face. That tiny, red, wrinkled face I have never forgotten. Tears squeeze out of the corners of my eyes and I cover them with a cold flannel. I must not cry. If I start I may never stop. He does not want the first sight of his mother to be puffy red eyes and a blotchy skin. I sniff – determined to pull myself together – and stand up – water cascading everywhere. I dry myself and dress with care – white underwear – pale cream slacks and a very fine chocolate coloured cashmere sweater. I brush on a little beige lipstick and climb into the car.

I know I am driving very badly. I jump a red light at Puerto Andraitx and narrowly miss hitting an old man on a bike. I pull over by the harbour and try to gather my wits. The silver sea glitters in front of the yacht club and a young woman walks out with a small boy hanging onto her hand and chattering non-stop. The woman looks down at him and smiles; an easy smile of love and joy, and he looks up at her returning it. They are a complete world. Mother and son. No one else matters. No one else exists at all. I feel the tears returning and lay my head on the cold steering wheel.

"Lord – please – I know I don't deserve it – but let it be all right. Forgive me – and let it be all right." What else could I ask for? "Let it be all right."

I take a deep breath and restart the car. In a more controlled fashion we purr along the coast road and into Palma. The sight of the hairdressers is somehow very reassuring. I have been coming here for seven years; its ordinariness and familiarity are wonderfully steadying. Margarita greets me as if it were a normal day. She does not know it is not, of course. It is the beginning of my life.

At ten to five I am standing in my immaculate white kitchen, fiddling with the rings on my fingers. The oven is already on and Conchita has left little dishes defrosting all along the huge stainless steel table in the centre of the room. Her love and care for me are like a mother's.

"Pero non tranquila," she had said quite crossly as she looked at me, before going to light the fires in the dining room and the lounge bar. It is such a delight here in the winter – roaring pine log fires in the evenings as the sun disappears into the sea, doing its nightly conjuring trick.

I am trying to cut lemons and limes into neat quarters when I hear the swish of the Valeria taxi spluttering to a halt outside the front door. My heart thuds and a sickening lurch weighs down the pit of my stomach. I must not be sick. I must not be sick. I run to the tiny side window where I had peered in all those years before, but the car is too far round, and I open the kitchen door a tiny crack, hand shaking. The moment seems encased in ice, like an insect in an ice cube.

Conchita is opening the heavy front door with a laugh and for an eternity I listen and wait. My life is in aspic. I hear Gabbie joking, "Tienen alguna habitacion libre?" followed by another laugh from Conchita. "Que desea?"

I crane my neck and peer fearfully into the hallway.

A small black leather grip appears around the door, followed by a tall blond man with short cropped hair, wearing jeans and a leather jacket. His face is tanned and his chin has the strong cleft in it I remember in my father's; my childish finger touching the groove as I sat on his lap. I draw in a sharp breath of shock and pain as I recognise the expression on his face; well hidden anxiety under a veneer of self confidence; a trick I have perfected over the years. He is striking-looking, with the wariness of a fox. There could be no doubt about it – my son – my longed-for son – walking into my home and into my life. I step back from the door, breathing fast. After all those empty years, at last I am looking on the face of my son. I steady myself on the door frame against a sudden dizziness. Gabbie is greeting Conchita.

"Que tal, Conchita?"

Taking two deep breaths, I hang on to the cold steel table behind me. It feels solid and dependable. For once I am not looking at Gabbie. What had he said?

"He has your genes – he's bound to love you."

I must make myself go out and meet him.

I am closing my eyes and holding my breath like a diver.

"Dear God, let him love me – don't let me be another terrible disappointment. Please. Please. Let Jude love me."

I open my mouth and let my breath escape in a long sigh. Such a long sigh. I open my eyes, hold my breath and step forward to pull open the door.

He is looking straight at me. His green eyes meet mine and I open my longing arms to reach out to him.

They used to trap birds in La Avenida San Juan. Small birds, like thrushes and finches, who struggled frantically in the nets until they gave up. But I have not given up, have I? He is walking towards me with outstretched arms through a curtain of tears. I step forward. And now the door of the birdcage has swung open, and we are both free.